PR

'Just brillia

well

'Heart-in-mouth stuff, with a twist I didn't see coming. Edwards is at the top of his game.'

—Erin Kelly, for *Keep Her Secret*

'I was hooked by this clever, fast-paced and addictive thriller . . . I loved it.'

—Claire Douglas, for *Keep Her Secret*

'Like a Reacher, but with a hero like the rest of us.'

—Linwood Barclay, for *No Place to Run*

'*No Place to Run* is another cracker from Mark Edwards.'

—Elly Griffiths

'The perfect thriller to pack in your suitcase this summer . . . A high-tension, exhilarating read.'

—*Heat* Book of the Week, for *Keep Her Secret*

'My head is spinning from all the twists!'

—Katherine Faulkner, for *Keep Her Secret*

'An almost unbearably suspenseful thrill ride . . . Edwards never lets up on the throttle . . .'

—Lisa Unger, for *Keep Her Secret*

'The King of Thrillers does it again with *Keep Her Secret* – dark, twisty and full of OMFG moments.'

—Susi Holliday

THE PSYCHOPATH NEXT DOOR

ALSO BY MARK EDWARDS

The Magpies

Kissing Games

What You Wish For

Because She Loves Me

Follow You Home

The Devil's Work

The Lucky Ones

The Retreat

A Murder of Magpies

In Her Shadow

Here to Stay

Last of the Magpies

The House Guest

The Hollows

No Place to Run

Keep Her Secret

The Darkest Water

With Louise Voss

Forward Slash

Killing Cupid

Catch Your Death

All Fall Down

From the Cradle

The Blissfully Dead

THE PSYCHOPATH NEXT DOOR

MARK EDWARDS

This is a work of fiction. Names, characters, organizations, places, events, and incidents are either products of the author's imagination or are used fictitiously. Any resemblance to actual persons, living or dead, or actual events is purely coincidental.

Published by Thomas & Mercer, Seattle

www.apub.com

EU Product Safety contact:
Amazon Publishing, Amazon Media EU S.à r.l.
38, avenue John F. Kennedy, L-1855 Luxembourg
amazonpublishing-gpsr@amazon.com

ISBN-13: 9781662508974
eISBN: 9781662508967

Cover design by Dan Mogford
Cover images: © Alexey_M © OSTILL is Franck Camhi © Aleksandrs Muiznieks / Shutterstock; © Anh Nguyen © Kike Algarra / Unsplash; © Miguel Sobreira / Arcangel

Printed in the United States of America

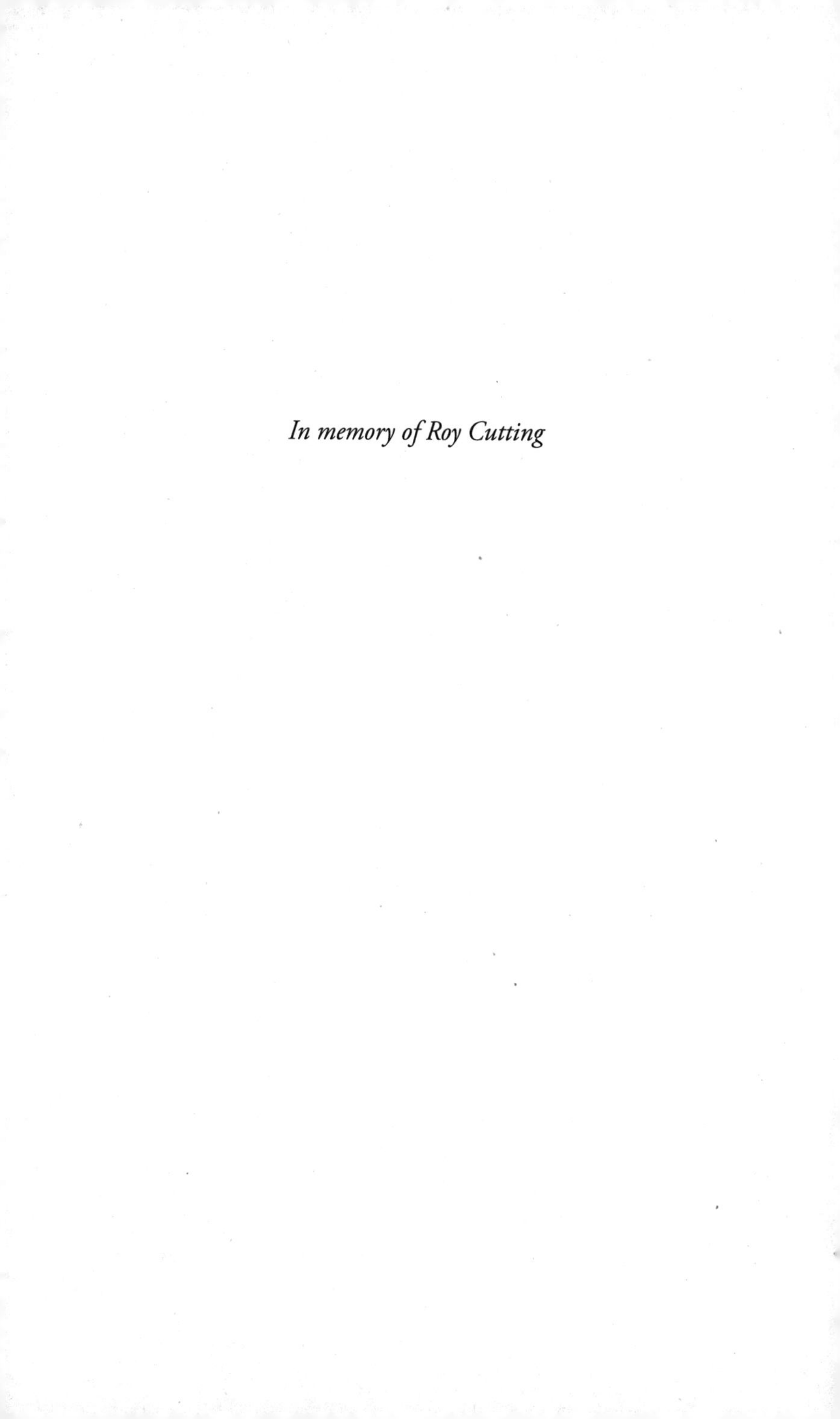

In memory of Roy Cutting

PROLOGUE

September 2021

There was no one to meet her outside the prison gates. She had left her only friend, if that term could be used for her relationship with Lucy, behind her on the inside, and she hadn't seen her family in a very long time. Standing outside Franklin Grange, breathing in air that tasted of freedom and promise and something else – was that coppery tang the anticipation of vengeance? – Fiona realised that, for the first time in years, she was completely on her own.

'Me against the world,' she whispered beneath her breath, remembering how Maisie had always said the same thing, except it had been *us against the world*, hadn't it? *Us.* The dark alliance that had started back in Australia when Fiona was young, still learning about her nature. It had been Maisie who taught her who she was. What she was.

Different.

Special.

Better.

She walked away from the prison without looking back. They had given her directions to the local train station, a twenty-minute walk along a wide, quiet road, and a ticket that would take her south, back to London and temporary accommodation, where a bank card awaited. She wasn't one of those unfortunate women who emerged from prison penniless, needing to seek help from the state. She had the money Maisie had left her, an amount that had been sitting in the bank for two years now, gaining interest.

The money was going to make everything so much easier, and she would have been grateful to Maisie, if gratitude were something she was capable of – if she didn't believe that everything that came to her was hers by right. She was pleased, though. Happy that Maisie had bought that flat when it was cheap, back before London property prices went crazy. Someone else was living there now, a young couple with a baby, and Fiona wondered if they knew the history of the people who had lived there and whether they would care if they did. She liked to think that she and Maisie had imprinted their energy on the place. Liked to believe the place felt haunted. Liked to imagine the couple's baby waking up screaming in terror, standing in its cot, rattling the bars and wailing as a cold dread it couldn't understand crept beneath its soft, plump skin.

It was the kind of image that could keep Fiona going for an hour or two.

She left the main street and walked along the approach road to the station. There was a little shop here with a dog tied up outside it, a Staffy, eyes fixed on the door. Fiona was tempted to untie the lead, to take the dog with her. Teach its neglectful owner a lesson. Instead she crouched beside the dog and petted it, whispering secrets in its ears.

'There are three of them,' she told it.

The dog cocked its head, trying to understand.

'What do you do when someone hurts you, wrongs you? Do you bare your teeth? Do you bark? I'm not going to do that, little one.'

She stroked its soft head. Through the shop door she could see a tall man with a double chin paying for an energy drink, the assistant putting a pack of cigarettes on the counter.

'I'm not going to bark, little one. I'm not going to let them know I'm coming. Do you know what I'm going to do?'

The dog's tail wagged back and forth, but it looked unsure. She imagined the thoughts in its boxy little head. Who was this human? Why did she seem different to the other people it knew? Why was she special, better? She leaned closer, feeling its warm and meaty breath on her face.

'I'm going to get really close, little doggy. So close. And then do you know what I'm going to do?'

The Staffy's owner was coming now, lumbering towards the door with his sugary drink and his Marlboros. He saw her and his brow furrowed, though he didn't look too annoyed because, well, she was cute.

The man reached the door and came outside. Fiona just had time to whisper her last words.

'I'm going to bite,' she said.

The dog's owner was here but it hadn't even noticed him. It stared at her like it understood. Like it wanted to join her pack, make her its leader.

'I'm going to rip their throats out.'

PART ONE

1

July 2023

The first thing I thought when the doorbell rang was that Rose, my twelve-year-old daughter, must have lost her keys, just as I'd lost track of time. We'd only given her the keys last month, when we moved into this house. Keys and a phone, encouraging her to be more independent, which involved getting the bus home from her new school rather than being picked up in the car.

Could it really be four o'clock already? I'd taken the day off to sort out my home office, and if Emma got home and found it in this state she would know I'd allowed myself to get distracted. *So predictable*, she would say. But it was just too easy to get sidetracked when sorting out my vinyl collection. So many treasures I hadn't listened to in years. Records I'd forgotten I had, like the one spinning on the turntable now, a surprisingly rare copy of The Cure's *Bloodflowers*, which was much better than I remembered.

The doorbell rang again and I hurried downstairs. Through the frosted glass, I could see that the caller was not Rose. It was a woman. My heart skipped. Rose should be home around now. Had something happened to her? An entire scenario played out in fast motion: Rose running through the school gates, excited about it being the last day of term, not looking where she was going; a car taking a corner too fast . . .

I yanked open the door, a little breathless suddenly, and found myself face to face with a woman. She was tall, about five-ten. Blonde hair. Late thirties, I guessed, six or seven years younger than me. Undeniably attractive, with a smattering of freckles across her nose, and large hazel eyes. The only other thing I noticed about her was that, despite being slim, she had impressive arm muscles, like a tennis player's.

Beside her stood my daughter. I couldn't read Rose's expression, which was something that was happening more frequently these days. When she was little I had always known exactly how she felt. Joy and anger shone out of her face. I put her recent inscrutability down to the upheaval of the move, like a shield she'd put up to protect herself from her own emotions.

'Hi, sweetheart. Is everything okay?'

The woman answered for her. 'I saw her being hassled by these bigger kids when she got off the school bus?' Her voice went up at the end of the sentence, and it took me a moment to recognise that she had a faint Australian accent. 'Teenage boys. I told them to clear off and then thought I'd better walk her home in case they came back.'

My attention snapped back to my daughter. 'Oh. Are you okay? What did they do?'

I put my hands on her shoulders. She had the same light brown hair as Emma, the same hazel eyes, shot through with green. A 'lucky' gap between her front teeth, which she got from me. My little girl.

'I'm fine,' she said. 'It was those two brothers.' She waved a hand vaguely in the direction of the houses across the road. 'They were just being idiots.'

'Looked like typical teenage dickheads to me,' said the woman. Yes, she was definitely Australian, the accent more prominent when she spat the insult.

I looked across to the house Rose had pointed at. Number 36. We were number 27, Snowdon Close, one of several streets – all named after mountains – on this recently completed estate in South Croydon. All the houses were semi-detached, arranged in pairs, with small front lawns and rectangular back gardens. I hadn't met the family who lived at 36 but I'd seen them. The dad was a big guy and the mother looked fierce. Their two sons, who must have been around the same age as Dylan, our fifteen-year-old, had a dirt bike which they'd ride around the fields behind the estate, the buzz cutting through the summer air like a hornet.

'Can I go inside?' Rose asked.

She pushed past me without waiting for an answer, dumping her school bag by the coat rack and heading for the kitchen. I heard her greet our dog, Lola.

The Australian woman met my eye. 'She'll be all right. The boys were just teasing her, you know? Nothing major.'

'I'll talk to their parents,' I said. 'Thank you for bringing Rose home.'

'No worries. Just trying to be a good neighbour.' She tilted her head to indicate the house attached to ours. The empty one. 'I'm moving in this weekend.'

'Oh! Welcome to the neighbourhood.' I realised I hadn't yet introduced myself. 'I'm Ethan. Ethan Dove. And that was Rose.'

She put her hand out. 'Nice to meet you, Ethan Dove. I'm Fiona Smith.'

She stood there, looking at me, and I found myself saying, 'Do you want to come in for a cup of tea? Or a cold drink?'

Fiona grinned. 'Yeah, actually, tea would be lovely. Thank you.'

I led her to the kitchen. Rose had already vanished up to her room. Lola, our cockapoo, came over from her bed in the corner and sniffed the newcomer, tail wagging.

'She likes you.'

'She's cute.' She dropped her voice to a stage whisper. 'Better not tell her I'm more of a cat person.'

I put the kettle on and Fiona looked around the kitchen. It was still a little like a kitchen in a show home, all shiny tiles and clean chrome. We hadn't made our mark on it yet.

'So you're moving in?' I asked.

'Yeah. Tomorrow.'

'We haven't been here that long. We were living in south London before and decided it was time to get out of the city.'

'But not too far out, eh?'

'Exactly. I wouldn't want to live too far from a Starbucks.'

She laughed harder than the joke merited. Being polite. I asked if she wanted milk and sugar – yes and no – then gave it to her in the mug with the Rolling Stones lips logo.

'What do you do?' she asked.

'I run a record shop.'

'Oh, really? You mean vinyl?'

When I told people I owned a record shop they either started listing all the vinyl they owned, asking me if it was worth anything, or told me they had assumed records were a thing of the past. I'd seen a lot of eyes glaze over. But Fiona seemed genuinely interested.

'I must admit I haven't got a clue when it comes to recent stuff,' she said. 'I used to date a guy who was the singer in a band but I haven't listened to anything new for around ten years, and even that would have been a download. I still have some old records in crates back in Australia, though.'

So I was right about her origins. 'How long have you lived over here?'

'I came here straight after uni.' If she was late thirties, that would have been, what? Fifteen years ago?

She told me that she originally came from a little seaside town called Fremantle, close to Perth in Western Australia.

'Is your wife into vinyl too?' she asked, then quickly added, 'Sorry, I'm assuming you have a wife. Rose said something about her mum but . . .' She trailed off.

'It's fine. I do have a wife. Emma. I also have a fifteen-year-old son called Dylan. And no, Emma doesn't really share my enthusiasm for vinyl, but she does love music. We all do.'

'That's cool.'

There was a sudden awkward silence.

Fiona broke it: 'So, what are you going to do? About those boys?'

'I don't know. I'll follow Rose's lead. She might not want me to make a fuss.'

Fiona raised her eyebrows, apparently surprised that I wasn't planning to steam over there with my sleeves rolled up and my fists clenched. Did she think I was a chicken? The truth was that, yeah, the family across the road were a little intimidating, but I wasn't scared of them. I just didn't want to fall out with our new neighbours and ensure years of awkwardness ahead of us.

But I could feel Fiona judging me as all this went through my head, and I found myself saying, 'Yeah, I'll talk to the parents, let them know it's not the kind of behaviour we'll put up with.'

Had I really just made my voice deeper?

'I think Rose would appreciate that.' She put her mug down on the side. I noticed she'd only drunk half of it. 'I should go. I came here to do some measuring up and I'd better get on.'

She looked out through the kitchen window at the back garden. It had been a rainy July so far and the grass needed cutting. Her garden would be on the other side of the fence.

'If there's anything we can do to help, just let us know,' I said.

'I sure will.'

We passed the bottom of the stairs on our way back to the front door and something occurred to me. I asked Fiona to hold on a moment and called Rose, who came to the top of the stairs.

'Come down and thank Fiona,' I said.

I expected at least a tiny eye roll, but she trotted down the stairs and, rather shyly, said, 'Thank you.'

'You're very welcome.'

'Fiona is going to be our new next-door neighbour,' I told her.

Rose, who had been looking at the carpet, lifted her head to regard Fiona. 'Really?'

'That's right. If those boys ever give you any bother again, I'll be right there.' She put her fists up, like a boxer, and jabbed the air.

'Cool.' Rose seemed genuinely pleased.

'I'll be here too,' I said. 'I'm going to speak to their parents later. Put a stop to it.'

Rose groaned. 'Please don't. It'll make it worse.'

I'd known that would be her reaction. Not returning Fiona's gaze, I said, 'Let's talk about it later.'

I opened the front door to see Fiona out. 'Like I said, if you need any help with the move or anything else, just give us a shout. And thanks again for helping Rose.'

'It's absolutely no problem.' She looked at Rose. 'We girls have to stick together, don't we?'

They locked eyes. It was a strange moment, like they were communicating, saying something I couldn't understand. Female bonding. Something I would never truly understand.

'Great to meet you, Ethan,' Fiona said. 'I think we're going to get along and be great friends.'

She didn't look at me as she said this. She looked directly at Rose, holding eye contact.

Then she walked away, calling, 'See you later,' as she went.

2

Emma got home an hour later. I was making dinner, efforts to organise my office abandoned. I'd spent way too long on my Cure records, and had only just made it to the Ds and my collection of Depeche Mode twelve-inches.

'Smells good,' she said, coming in. 'What are we having?'

I subscribed to a food box service which delivered several recipes each week along with the ingredients. Tonight's dish was a chickpea and tomato curry, one of my favourites.

'How was work?' I asked.

Until recently, Emma had worked as the marketing manager for a little company that sold yoga products, mostly online. She had loved it, but in order to afford the house move, she had taken a job with a bigger, more corporate firm, marketing a product she was far less passionate about: pet food. There were some perks – for Lola anyway, because she got sent tons of samples of dog treats – but I knew Emma wasn't happy.

'Same old bullshit,' she said, launching into a typical tale of how her boss, the dog-food-empire equivalent of a nepo baby – his grandfather had founded the company – had asked her to prepare a presentation for a new product, about which he'd now changed his mind.

She took a bottle of wine out of the fridge and poured herself a glass. I watched her gulp it down and reminded myself what our relationship counsellor had said: it was important for our marriage that I not keep reminding her of the chain of events that had led to her working there.

Emma refilled her glass, then went upstairs to get changed, taking her wine with her. Moments later, Dylan appeared.

'What are we having?' he asked, sniffing the air. 'Curry? Can I have a whole naan to myself?'

At fifteen, Dylan was going through his ravenous teenage-boy phase, when there was never enough food in the fridge and ordinary portions simply didn't suffice. He sat down at the table next to Rose, who was already there, phone in hand.

'Good last day of term?' I asked Dylan.

'It was all right.'

Everybody told us that, while Rose was the spit of her mum, Dylan looked just like me: dark brown hair that was almost black, a little cleft in his chin, tall and skinny, and usually clad in a band T-shirt, a few of which he'd stolen from me. Right now he was still in his school uniform, collar undone, shirt untucked, hair ruffled and sticking up at the back just like mine used to before it started falling out. Was it narcissistic of me to think he was a good-looking kid?

Emma came in, smelling of soap, having changed into jeans and a baggy T-shirt. Sometimes, the sight of her still made me catch my breath. Her hair was loosely piled up on the top of her head, and the neck of the T-shirt was so stretched it hung loose to expose a clavicle and most of one shoulder. I abandoned the curry, which I was halfway through serving, and pulled her into a hug, kissing her cheek. Behind me, I heard Dylan groan, and Emma pulled away gently, going over to the table. Lola followed her, taking up position by her feet, where she would spend the mealtime gazing up, begging for scraps with her soft brown eyes.

'Phone away please, Rose,' Emma said, as I put the plates in front of them.

Rose huffed a little but did it without any real protest.

'I met our new neighbour today,' I said as I sat down beside Emma and poured myself a glass of wine.

'Oh?'

'Her name's Fiona. Australian, though she said she's lived in the UK since she graduated. Late thirties, I'd guess. Seems nice.'

'Is it just her?' Dylan asked.

'Why, are you hoping she might have a teenage daughter?'

'Urgh, Dad.' His face had gone pink. 'You're so lame.'

'It's part of my job as your father to be lame. The most important part of this story is that she rescued Rose from a pair of kids who were teasing her on the bus.'

'What?' Emma put her fork down. 'Rose? Are you okay?'

She nodded. 'Yeah, it was no big deal.'

'Who was it?' Emma asked. 'What did they say? What did they do? Are you *sure* you're okay?'

'Mum, I'm fine. They were just going on at me, calling me Tay-Tay because one of them decided I look a bit like Taylor Swift.'

'As if,' said Dylan.

Rose narrowed her eyes at him.

'See?' I said. 'It was just teenage boys being typical teenage boys.'

'Do you know them?' Emma asked Rose. 'Do they go to your school?'

'It was those boys across the road,' I said. 'The ones with the dirt bike.'

Dylan spoke between mouthfuls of naan bread. 'Oh God. Albie and Eric. They're the worst. Albie was suspended last year after telling a teacher to eff off. And Eric nearly got expelled for selling vapes in the playground to year sevens.'

'How old are they?' Emma asked. Her fork lay abandoned beside her plate.

'Thirteen and fifteen, I think.'

'And they're bullying a twelve-year-old girl.'

'They weren't bullying me, Mum. And anyway, Fiona frightened them off.'

Emma looked at me. 'Where were *you*?'

'Me? I was here, trying to get organised. We agreed we don't need to meet Rose from the bus stop every day, didn't we?'

'Yes, but maybe we should.'

'Oh my God, Mum, that would be so embarrassing,' Rose said.

'And it's the holidays now,' I pointed out. 'We don't have to worry about it for six weeks. And then maybe Dylan can keep an eye on them on the bus.'

'I don't need Dylan to look after me. I'm not a baby.' She looked to me for support.

'And I'm not her babysitter,' said Dylan.

'For goodness' sake,' I said. 'I'm going to sort it. I'll talk to their parents.'

Emma groaned. 'I hate this. Why do we . . . ?'

She trailed off, but I knew what she had been going to say: *Why do we have to live opposite a family like that?* In our old neighbourhood, even though the house had been smaller and cheaper, there had been no dirt bikes on the lawn. No vape-dealing teens. Again, I reminded myself not to allude to the reason we'd left there.

'I really don't want you wandering around the estate on your own,' Emma said.

'What, are you going to lock me up in my room? Keep me prisoner?'

'Rose!' Emma said, eyes widening.

'Don't talk to your mum like that,' I said. Then, to Emma: 'I really don't think it's a big deal. A bit of teasing. It's not like they threatened her.'

'Hmm. I don't like it. I think—'

Rose interrupted her. 'Can I get down from the table?'

'Don't you want dessert?' I asked her. 'We've got that chocolate pudding you like. With ice cream.'

She hesitated, and I felt something that had hit me often recently – especially during the last year, since her move to secondary school. Rose was still a child, only just twelve, but she was changing. *I'm not a baby* was a phrase we heard a lot these days, and with it, this new tension between her and Emma, who took the brunt of Rose's occasional moody outbursts.

But Rose was still a kid, really.

'Chocolate pudding?' She thought about it. 'Okay.'

She might not be a baby, but she was still very much my little girl.

3

Fiona got out of the shower and wrapped a towel around herself. She had been living here for a few days now, and free for nearly two years, but she was still able to appreciate the luxury of being on her own, of having her own stuff. Not having to look at or be looked at by anyone else. That had been one of the worst things about prison: the lack of privacy. The guards, the other women. Inside, there was always someone eyeing you up.

At least until you taught them better. Like that woman in the first place they'd sent her, the one who'd given Fiona loads of shit her first day, calling her a skinny bitch, trying to act tough. She hadn't been so tough afterwards, screaming that Fiona had blinded her, stupid bloody drama queen.

Wrapping the towel tighter, Fiona turned towards the mirrored cabinet above the sink. It was coated with condensation so her reflection was nothing but a blur, a ghost formed of water droplets.

She reached out with a finger and, in the condensation, wrote three names.

First.

Second.

Last.

Her list.

She concentrated on the names for half a minute, then rubbed them out with her palm, knowing she would do the same tomorrow, until she was satisfied that all three of them had paid for what they'd done.

She left the steamy bathroom and went into her bedroom. As she dressed, she stood behind the curtain, looking down at next door's back garden. It had been raining all morning, just as it had rained every day since she'd moved in. Almost twenty years on, she still couldn't believe the British had the audacity to call this season summer.

Now, as she watched, the teenage boy – Dylan, that was his name – entered the garden with the dog. He threw a ball, the cockapoo ran after it and brought it back. Both boy and dog seemed bored by this game, as was Fiona. But as she finished dressing, the rain stopped and the clouds parted to reveal a patch of blue sky.

And Rose appeared in the garden.

It was the first time Fiona had seen the girl since she'd escorted her home last Friday. Her mother, Emma, had been round to introduce herself and to thank her. Fiona had also exchanged pleasantries with Ethan when they'd passed on the street. But she'd been so busy – moving in, unpacking, familiarising herself with the area and, most importantly, plotting – that she'd hardly had time to think about Rose and that little tingle she'd felt when she'd first seen her.

That peculiar sense of familiarity.

The girl and her brother were talking. They were too far away for Fiona to read their lips, but Dylan went inside and came out with a dog lead, which he clipped to the dog's collar. As Fiona watched, they went out through the back gate and began to walk towards the recreation ground, a large grassy area that was mostly used for dog walking and ball games, which everyone here called 'the fields'.

Fiona made a quick decision.

She went downstairs and slipped her trainers on, then left the house. Not wanting it to be obvious she was following them, she took the longer route towards the fields, out through the gap in the high wooden fence that formed the estate's northern border, then along the footpath.

It was wet underfoot, squelchy and muddy. The alternating rain and sunshine had supercharged nature, turning the country lush and verdant – the country that Maisie had described to her all those years ago, so different to the desert expanses of Western Australia. Her dad's parents had been ten-pound poms, part of that wave of British emigrants who took cheap passage down under, arriving on a ship in Fremantle in the fifties. 'Why don't you come home?' Maisie had said, and eventually, Fiona had thought, *Why not, indeed?* In England, she would make her fortune, and she and Maisie would live like queens.

It hadn't quite worked out like that, had it?

She stopped because she could hear voices up ahead. Kids' voices, Dylan and Rose, and a dog yapping. She peered through the trees and there they were, throwing a ball, using one of those long plastic sticks to propel it a great distance. Lola went charging off through the overgrown grass, tongue lolling, and Fiona was about to climb over the stile so she could say hello when she heard a loud buzz coming from across the other side of the field.

It was a small motorbike. A dirt bike, Fiona believed it was called. Stripes of lime green and black. Fiona recognised the teenage boy riding it as one of the brothers who'd been hassling Rose last week. What were their names? Rose had told her when Fiona escorted her home. Albie and Eric, that was it. Albie, who was on the bike, was the older one. His younger brother hurried along beside him, with two huge German shepherds on leads.

Through the trees, Fiona saw Rose and Dylan stiffen. Dylan immediately called Lola to them, urgency in his voice, but she was too busy searching for the ball in the grass.

Fiona watched as Eric unleashed both his dogs, and the two shaggy beasts charged towards Lola like greyhounds let out of the traps. Lola, who was about fifty feet away from her owners, looked up, saw the bigger dogs coming and belatedly obeyed Dylan's command to 'Come'. But she was too slow. The German shepherds reached Lola and charged at her, teeth bared, barking and growling.

They're going to kill her, Fiona thought, and she climbed the gate hurriedly. Dylan was sprinting towards Lola, who was running in circles, the bigger dogs surrounding her.

'Call them off!' Dylan yelled. 'Call your stupid dogs off now.'

Lola let out a yelp as one of the German shepherds went for her. Dylan shouted her name; Rose was frozen in place, staring helplessly. Fiona increased her pace, running past Rose and towards the boys with their dirt bike.

'Get control of your dogs *now*,' she shouted.

They both turned towards her, and the older one, Albie, who was sitting astride the stationary bike wearing a baseball cap and a baggy North Face T-shirt, sneered and said, 'Why should I? It's a free country.'

Eric, the younger one, sniggered.

Fiona was aware of Albie staring at her chest and the urge to slap him was intense. Unfortunately, society didn't allow adults to go around hitting children, even obnoxious teenagers like this. At least the German shepherds had stopped trying to attack Lola, both of them running over to see who was talking to their humans. They sniffed at her, one of them attempting to shove its nose into her crotch, which made the boys laugh.

'Mario,' said Eric. 'Get away from that bitch.'

'What did you say?' Fiona strode over and squared up to him. He was almost as tall as her, long and stringy – the kind of boy her dad would have described as a beanpole.

Albie called over, 'Hey. Leave him alone.' He was still staring at her chest, even as he tried to defend his brother.

Out of the corner of her eye, Fiona saw Dylan scoop Lola up, cradling her in his arms. Rose stood beside them, glaring at Albie and Eric. The two German shepherds had now lost interest in both Fiona and Lola. One of them had found some fox poo to roll in and the other had run off in pursuit of a bee.

Then Rose said, 'I hope you crash that bike and die.'

Albie's expression was classic. His mouth formed an O, but then he grinned, and Fiona tried to intervene but her words were drowned out by the bike's engine as Albie started it up again. He rode it straight at Rose, who broke into a run towards Fiona, and the bike buzzed past her, just a metre away, making her stumble. Albie roared with laughter as he sped by, turning the bike in a circle and coming back in their direction.

Fiona shouted, 'What the hell are you playing at?'

Fiona, Rose and Dylan stood together as Albie circled them on the bike. His brother stood where he was, watching Albie go round and round. Albie didn't say anything, just kept grinning that shit-eating grin as he sped through the long grass, the engine loud like a prodded wasps' nest.

Fiona felt it build inside her. Red and hot and strong, spreading through her veins, her stomach, her chest. These little squirts, these nothings . . . How dare they? She watched Dylan: he was scared, a sensitive boy, but trying to appear brave for the sake of his younger sister. Rose, though, didn't seem afraid. She continued to look angry. Ablaze with contempt.

I hope you crash that bike and die.

'Don't look at him,' Fiona said, over the noise of the engine. 'He'll soon get bored.'

She was right. Less than a minute later, Albie pulled the bike to a halt, skidding on the damp grass, almost losing control of it. Fiona walked straight up to him. At the same time, Eric came over, with his dogs back on their leashes, which made Dylan, who was still holding the trembling Lola, back away.

It was time to take charge of this situation.

'You're going to leave Rose and Dylan alone,' Fiona said. She kept her voice calm and even.

'Oh yeah?' said Albie. His voice was high. He was just a boy, pimply and half-formed. She could picture him in his bedroom, playing video games and sending abusive messages to female celebrities. His younger brother, even less formed, pale and mottled, like he was made of putty that hadn't set yet, stood there snickering.

'*Yeah*, you are. You're going to stay the hell away from them and their dog.'

Albie and Eric exchanged amused smiles. 'Or what?'

They'll find your bodies hanging from these trees.

'I'll talk to your parents.'

They both scoffed at that. 'They won't care.'

Fiona took half a step closer to them. She lowered her voice and spoke quietly so Dylan and Rose couldn't hear.

'Why don't you go back to your little house and do what you do best. Wank yourselves into a stupor.'

That shocked them. Their mouths opened in tandem and they looked at each other.

'You're sick,' said Eric.

'I think she's a paedo,' said Albie. 'Fantasising about boys wanking.'

Eric guffawed and Fiona was about to do it, she was going to bang their heads together, when Albie said to Eric, 'Come on, let's go. I'm bored. Let's get away from this paedo.'

He started up the dirt bike and Eric ambled away, taking his dogs with him. But before Albie set off on the bike, he nodded towards the staring Dylan and Rose and said to them, 'Next time you might not have your bodyguard with you.'

He drew a finger across his throat, then sped away across the fields, letting out a whoop as he went.

Fiona turned to Rose and Dylan. 'Are you okay?'

Dylan was shaking like the dog he was holding. He'd gone so pale that Fiona thought he might vomit. 'We're fine.' He kissed the dog's head. 'Aren't we, Lola?'

Fiona turned to Rose. 'How about you?'

She didn't reply straight away. She was watching the two boys retreat across the fields. The contempt was still there on her face but Fiona could see something beneath it. A familiar look. The same one she was sure she'd seen the other day.

'I'm good,' Rose said. She sounded surprised with herself, as if she didn't understand her own reaction. The anger that burned instead of fear.

Fiona understood it very well – and, understanding what it might mean, she had to fight hard not to let her excitement show.

4

Friday afternoon, after work, I found Emma in the garden. The sun was out and she was pulling up weeds from the flower beds and depositing them in the garden bin.

'Look what I've got,' I said, holding up my phone. 'Two tickets to see Pulp.'

I had driven home in a state of excitement, eager to see the look on her face. Pulp was her favourite band, and she'd had a thing for Jarvis Cocker back in the day. When we were first dating she'd said I reminded her of him, a southern version, and I wasn't sure whether that was a compliment or not. Jarvis was skinny with pasty skin and terrible eyesight. But he *was* a kind of sex symbol – albeit the type you'd only find in England – so I was happy to be compared to him.

'How much did you pay for those?' Emma asked.

'Nothing. One of the regulars gave them to me as a thank you for finding him this record he's been after for years. He was meant to be going but his wife is sick so they can't make it. Said he'd rather transfer them to me than tout them.'

'So there *are* perks to running a record shop.'

I had always dreamed of opening my own record shop, even though vinyl was already on its way to being phased out and replaced by CDs when I was a teenager in the early nineties. I was the only person I knew who kept his turntable when everyone else replaced theirs with a CD-only system. I kept buying vinyl when Napster and LimeWire almost killed the music industry. And I watched the revival, even as everyone adopted streaming, as middle-aged men tried to rediscover their youth, buying all those albums they'd grown up with, and teenagers discovered the joys of owning something tangible, something you could collect and display.

Rebel Records, based in a quiet street not too far from the centre of Croydon, had opened when Rose was a toddler and Dylan was only six, and we were living in a tiny house in West Wickham. Emma had taken a career break and we had very little money coming in – and then I got made redundant from my job in the sales department of a publishing house. The payout was generous, and Emma and I had long discussions about what to do with it. She encouraged me to pursue my dream. I was certain that it was the perfect time to open a record shop. I could see the vinyl revival on the horizon. This would be a shop that catered to both serious collectors and kids looking for limited-edition new releases. There would be none of the snobbery that many people associated with shops like this. Jack Black's character in *High Fidelity* would never get a job at my place.

I was worried about taking such a big gamble when we had small children, but Emma reminded me she'd be going back to her marketing job soon. We'd be putting Rose into nursery, although that didn't end up going well, which was another story.

So in 2014, Rebel Records had been born, and it was still going strong today. We'd had a few wobbles. Okay, a lot of wobbles. I'd had to go cap in hand to my bank manager several times. But we had made it through, and thanks to our friendly policies, regular gig nights where we hosted artists in-store, and the service we provided that set us apart from online retailers and the big high street chains, we had a loyal clientele – plus our own popular website.

Emma took another look at my phone screen. 'Hang on. It's tonight.'

'I know.'

'So who are you going to go with? You could take Dylan, I suppose.'

'No, I thought we could go. Me and you. When was the last time we had a night out?'

She thought about it. Thought about it some more. 'You know, I can't remember.'

'It was our wedding anniversary. The one before last.'

We hadn't been to a single gig together since Rose was born, even though it had once been our favourite thing to do.

Emma sighed. 'Ethan, I'm knackered. I was looking forward to eating a takeaway in front of *Gogglebox*. Plus, look at the state of me. My hair needs a wash, I've got dirt under my fingernails and – most importantly – we don't have a babysitter.'

Rose had appeared in the garden during this exchange.

'What's going on?' she asked. 'Why are you talking about babysitters?'

'Your mum and I have tickets to a gig in town. I was about to say that Dylan can babysit. He's fifteen. I used to do it for next door's toddlers when I was his age.'

'I don't need looking after,' Rose said.

Emma was shaking her head. 'I'm not leaving you and Dylan on your own in the evening.'

We'd had this argument several times and it was one I always lost, as Emma conjured images of burning houses, choking children, home invasions and electrocutions. I thought she was overprotective, and she said I didn't worry enough.

'I'm the only kid in my class whose parents treat her like this,' Rose said. 'I'm amazed you even let me out the house.'

Oh God, here it was again. The mother-daughter argument. I was preparing to step in when someone said, 'I could watch them for you.'

The voice came from next door's garden, and all three of us turned to see Fiona peering over her fence at us, only her head visible. She must have been on tiptoe.

'Sorry, I didn't mean to eavesdrop,' she said. 'But I don't have any plans tonight. If you want me to come round and sit with them, I'd be very happy to do it.'

I turned to my wife. 'Emma? What do you think?'

She looked unsure. She had only met Fiona briefly, although I think her main issue with the gig was the sheer effort involved in getting ready, and travelling across London and back – more than her fear about leaving the kids with a relative stranger.

'I'm not sure,' Emma said. 'It's very kind of you to offer, Fiona, but I don't know if I've got the energy.'

'Come on,' I said. 'It's Pulp. It'll be amazing.'

I expected Rose to shoot daggers at us, silently trying to tell us she didn't want or need to be left with a babysitter. But instead, she said, 'Go on, Mum. You should go.'

She smiled at our new neighbour and I raised my eyebrows at Emma, trying to communicate that this was a positive that we should take advantage of.

'All right,' Emma said. 'But I need to start getting ready now.'

She hurried towards the house.

'Thanks, Rose,' I said.

She seemed excited, as if we'd invited one of the TikTok influencers she idolised to babysit. Was Fiona that cool in the eyes of a twelve-year-old?

Then I thanked Fiona.

'Oh, don't mention it,' she said, her eyes falling on Rose. 'What else are neighbours for?'

5

As soon as Ethan and Emma had gone, Fiona followed Rose into the kitchen. This house was the same as hers, but mirrored, everything in reverse. It was also cluttered, every surface piled high with the stuff of family life. Seeing unopened mail and loose pens and scattered crumbs on the counter made Fiona twitch.

'Are you okay?'

'Huh?' She realised Rose was watching her carefully. She pulled out a smile. Enthusiastic. Happy to be here. She clapped her hands together. 'What do you want to do?'

Rose shrugged. 'My dad left money so we can order pizza.'

'Food. Yes.' She took the menu Rose was holding out. 'It's been a very long time since I had a pizza.'

'Really? Why? Have you been on a diet?'

Fiona smirked. 'Something like that. What does your brother like? A meat feast, I'm guessing. Or pepperoni?'

'We're vegetarian.'

'Of course you are.'

'And he'll just want cheese and tomato. He's boring like that.'

'Is he? How about you?'

Rose scanned the menu quickly. 'I'll have the hot one. Extra chilis.' She waited, as if daring Fiona to protest.

'A good choice, madam.' She called to place the order, then said, 'Want to show me your room?'

Rose hesitated. 'Why?'

'I'm interested to see it, that's all. But if you don't want to . . .'

'No. It's cool.'

Fiona followed Rose up the stairs. They reached the landing and Fiona could hear music thumping inside Dylan's room, like rap music but not quite. Was it called grime? Fiona was completely out of touch, and had never been a big fan of music anyway. To her, music was nothing more than noise. She was the last person who would ever visit Ethan's record shop, though she would never tell him that. In the past, she had tried to force herself to like music, to understand its appeal, until she realised that a lot of normal people weren't into it either.

They went into Rose's room and Fiona was almost floored by an unfamiliar sensation. What was it? Nostalgia? Homesickness? More likely it was simply a form of disorientation caused by familiarity. Because this room was so similar to Fiona's own room when she was twelve years old, it was almost as if she'd stepped through a hole in time.

Yes, of course, this was a modern version. The computer on the desk was infinitely superior to the one Fiona had once owned, the curtains and bedding were modern, and it all had that twenty-first-century sheen. But Fiona recognised it instantly. The walls were painted white and the carpet was a neutral biscuit colour. Everything was neat and shelved in an orderly fashion. There were a couple of trophies on the bookshelves: a spelling bee and a maths cup, but nothing sporty. A few posters on the wall of an attractive young woman who Fiona guessed must be a pop star.

And there was one more thing that made Fiona feel like she was visiting her childhood bedroom. There in the corner, on the floor, was an old steamer trunk with several Barbie dolls on top.

'You like Barbie?'

'They're old,' Rose said quickly. Her cheeks had gone pink. 'I'm going to get rid of them soon.'

'Oh, that would be a shame.' Fiona dropped her voice to a whisper. 'Don't tell anyone, but I played with my Barbies far longer than everyone said I should.'

'Really?'

'Would I lie to you?' She crossed the room. 'Can I have a look?'

Tentatively, as if she thought Fiona might be taking the piss, Rose opened the trunk to reveal her collection of dolls and cars and ponies and all the accessories that came along with them.

The memories came rushing back. It was an unfamiliar sensation. Fiona lived in the present and the future. It was something Maisie had taught her: to have no regrets, but not to bathe in warm nostalgia either. Both were a waste of time.

Her Barbies, though. She had so enjoyed playing with them. Chopping off their hair, sometimes pulling off a limb. Holding them over a candle until her mum would shout and ask what was burning. Using them to act out her cruellest fantasies.

'Wow, this is quite a collection,' she said.

Rose had lifted out a Barbie with vivid auburn hair, dressed in a ballgown, all lace and frills. 'This is my favourite,' she said, her voice hushed. 'She's the ruler. She tells the others what to do.'

'Oh, really? What kinds of things?'

Rose didn't reply with words. Instead, she took out a blonde Barbie who was dressed in little shorts and a pink tank top. The hair had obviously been hacked at with scissors and the doll looked like she'd been to the world's worst make-up artist. There were also dark circles on her arms and legs. Burn marks.

'Oh my God,' Fiona whispered.

Rose immediately said, 'It was an accident. I didn't mean—'

Fiona laid a hand on her arm. 'No. It's cool. You don't need to explain.' She wasn't gasping because she was horrified. It was because it was, again, like staring into the past.

But Rose clearly felt uncomfortable. She scooped the toys up and dropped them back in the trunk.

'I don't want to play this. Not now.'

'Of course.' Fiona adopted her understanding smile. 'What would you like to do instead?'

Rose had crossed the room to the window, drawn by noises from outside. Fiona went over to stand beside her. The window gave a view of the street, and the house where Albie and Eric lived.

They were out the front now, with their dad, a big bloke with a shiny head and inflated muscles that were on the verge of turning to fat. The three of them were standing around the dirt bike, and although she couldn't hear him through the double glazing, he looked angry, like he was admonishing his sons. The younger one, Eric, hung his head, while Albie waved his arms like he was arguing back, which made the dad go even redder in the face.

Fiona glanced sideways at Rose, trying to read her reaction. Two days had passed since the incident in the fields, and Fiona wondered if Rose's anger had dissipated. It didn't appear to have. Her gaze was still intense, and there was something else. Anticipation – the hope that Albie and Eric were about to get torn a new one by their dad. But then the dad laughed, and he ruffled Eric's hair.

The anticipation on Rose's face turned to disappointment. Fiona could see the tension in her body, her desire for the boys to be punished unfulfilled, like a sneeze that wouldn't come. Fiona watched as Rose walked over to one of her Barbies – a dark-haired variant who had been left out of the trunk – and stepped on it, slowly and deliberately, pressing down with all her strength and scrunching up her face as she did so. Then she exhaled, apparently feeling better.

Fiona knew exactly how Rose felt. Understood the release Rose would have experienced as she stomped on her doll. It filled Fiona with exhilaration.

They went downstairs and, not long after, the doorbell rang. The pizzas were here. Fiona opened the door. From across the street, the teenage morons and their dad looked over at her while the driver handed over the pizzas. He stood there for a moment, clearly waiting for a tip. Fiona closed the door in his face.

'Bitch,' he said, the word muffled but unmistakable.

Immediately, anger surged through her and she grabbed the handle, ready to pull it open, to go after him, make him apologise. At the very least, she could get him fired.

Or, better yet, she could hurt him.

She stopped herself, exhaling and closing her eyes, counting to five. *Let it go*, she told herself. *Let this one go. Use your imagination instead.*

She pictured him shrunken, crushed beneath her foot like a doll, and the pressure in her slowly ebbed away, though the euphoria she would have felt if she really had hurt him was absent.

Still, she felt calmer.

In the kitchen, where Rose was waiting, she set the boxes out and watched Rose help herself to several slices of the spicy pizza. Dylan came down and piled his plate high.

'It's fine for you to take it to your room if you want,' Fiona said.

'Are you sure?'

'Absolutely.' She exhibited what she thought was a conspiratorial smile and he grunted and exited. She was pleased. She wanted to spend more time alone with Rose.

'Mum would never let me have this,' Rose said after eating a slice that was smothered with red chilis. 'She hates hot food and assumes everyone's like her.'

'But you're not?'

'I don't know. Everyone says we *look* like each other.'

That was true. Emma and Rose had the same hair and eye colour, and their lips were an identical shape. Rose was less expressive, though. On the two occasions Fiona had met Emma, both brief, it had been easy to see the emotions right there on the surface of her face. She was an easy study, an open book, as was Dylan. Ethan was a little harder. He came across as placid and mild, but Fiona got the sense there was more going on underneath. Duck feet paddling furiously beneath a calm surface.

'Do you want to watch a movie?' Fiona asked, slipping Lola the dog a piece of crust as she spoke.

'Sure. What, though?'

They went into the living room, Lola trotting after them, and Rose showed Fiona how to work the telly. Fiona flicked through the list of recently released films.

'How about this one?'

It was a movie called *M3GAN*. The poster showed what appeared to be a life-size, realistic doll, gazing at a little girl around Rose's age.

Rose's eyes widened. 'But that's a horror movie.'

'Is it?' Horror was the only genre of film she really enjoyed. She particularly liked slasher movies, the old-school type in which a group of attractive teens were hunted down and butchered, one by one.

'I've seen clips of it on TikTok,' Rose said. 'She does this dance . . .'

'Well, that sounds like fun. We can rent it through my account, and I won't tell if you don't.'

Rose's eyes were even wider now. Shining with glee. It was the most kid-like Fiona had seen her. 'My mum doesn't let me watch scary movies. She says they'll give me nightmares.'

'And what do you think?'

'I think I'll be fine. I can handle it.'

'Then let's do it,' Fiona said in a whisper.

The movie started pleasantly enough, with the tweenage protagonist's parents dying in a car accident. The girl was then taken in by her aunt, who worked with AI toys. She brought home M3GAN, an experimental doll, who quickly formed a bond with the girl – and became homicidally protective of her. Fiona's favourite part was when the doll killed a bully at some sort of outdoor activity centre, ripping off his ear and causing him to be hit by a truck. The neighbour's dog was killed – Fiona's least favourite part – and at one point M3GAN got hold of a nail gun. Mayhem ensued.

Fiona kept one eye on Rose throughout, gauging her reaction. The girl was fascinated – as hooked as she had been when watching the neighbours through her bedroom window. She winced when the dog died, but was clearly thrilled when the bully was killed. Her attention only appeared to flag towards the end, but the film was short, thankfully. Fiona found it impossible to concentrate for longer than ninety minutes, and Rose appeared to be the same.

At one point, Fiona sensed a presence in the doorway and turned to see lanky Dylan, hovering, clearly surprised to see what they were watching. She opened her mouth, intending to invite him to join them, to involve him in the conspiracy, but he was already gone.

'What did you think?' Fiona asked after the credits began to roll.

Rose blinked several times. 'I was sad when M3GAN got ripped in half.'

'Me too. But I think they'll rebuild her for a second film, don't you?'

A nod. 'I didn't like it when the dog died either.' Lola the cockapoo was asleep on the carpet in front of the telly.

'I agree. I hate seeing pets killed.'

'Although . . .'

Fiona looked at Rose. 'What?'

Rose hesitated, looked away.

'Those German shepherds?' Fiona began. 'When they tried to attack Lola. Do you wish you had a doll like M3GAN to protect you?'

Rose looked back to her, thought about it. 'That would be cool. Or actually . . .'

'Yes?'

'I'd like to *be* M3GAN. Not a robot, but . . .' She trailed off.

'I know what you mean. No one messes with her, do they?' Fiona had that tingle beneath her skin. 'It would have been great if we'd had a killer robot with us in the fields, wouldn't it?'

Rose stared at the blank TV screen. 'She could have blown up their stupid bike.'

'Yes. Wouldn't that have been awesome?'

'Lola would have liked that.'

At the sound of her name, the dog lifted her head and hauled herself to her feet. Rose lifted her on to her lap.

'Lola hates those dogs,' Rose went on. 'And those boys.'

This was interesting. Rose had switched over so she was ascribing her emotions to her pet, perhaps because she had started to find it too uncomfortable or intense to talk about her own feelings.

'What about me?' Fiona asked. 'Does Lola like me?'

The dog was resting on Rose's lap, snoozing again, her throat pressed against the girl's thigh.

'She does like you, yes.' She said this while concentrating on the dog. Stroking her head. 'And not only because you gave her a piece of pizza.'

'That's good. I like her too. And you can tell her that she doesn't need a robot doll – or even a robot dog – to look out for her.' She dropped her voice to a whisper. 'Not when I'm around.'

ϖ

Ten o'clock came and Fiona said, 'I think it must be bedtime.'

Rose didn't protest. She went upstairs and changed into her pyjamas, then came out of her bedroom to clean her teeth.

'I hope we can spend more time together over the summer,' Fiona said, standing outside the open bathroom door.

Rose spat the toothpaste into the basin. 'Me too. Lola would definitely like that.'

Their eyes met and held for a moment, and once more Fiona felt that frisson. The thrill of recognition. Rose felt it too, she was sure.

But it was too early to talk about it.

Rose went into her room and shut the door. Fiona hesitated outside Dylan's room for a moment, listening. It was quiet inside, but surely he wouldn't be asleep yet?

She looked down and saw lights flickering beneath the door, knocked gently, then went in without waiting for a response.

He was at a computer desk, playing some fast-moving game that appeared to be set on a spaceship. He had a headset on so the room was silent, but the light spilling in from the hallway made him spin round in his chair. He pulled his headset off.

'Just wanted to check you're okay,' Fiona said.

He stared at her. 'I'm fine.'

The room was dark, lit only by the computer monitor. He had a double bed with a black bedspread and there were posters of bands and more pop stars Fiona didn't recognise on the walls. Some framed record covers and a turntable sitting on a chest of drawers. Like father, like son. The room smelled of teenage boy, the musty stink of hormones and cheap deodorant mixed with the lingering odour of the pizza she'd allowed him to bring up here.

She went closer to Dylan, peering at the screen. 'What are you playing?'

'Just a game.' In the glow from the computer, she could have sworn he'd gone pink, and she could feel waves of awkwardness coming off him as she got closer.

There was a black box in the corner of the screen, messages scrolling upwards rapidly. One of them was asking him what was going on, why he wasn't responding. Lots of question marks and confused emojis.

Dylan saw her looking and whirled back around to minimise the chat window, but it was too late. Fiona saw the message appear:

> *Hey, don't tell me you hooked up with the hot babysitter LOLOLOLOL*

He spluttered something unintelligible, and Fiona suppressed a genuine smile. So he thought she was hot, huh? That was very interesting.

'Dylan,' she said, enjoying the way he tensed, 'I know you saw Rose and me watching that movie. I just wanted to reassure you that I didn't know what it was about. And if I'd thought Rose was scared or disturbed I would have turned it off.'

He blinked at her. 'Okay.'

'I wouldn't want your parents to be upset.'

She was standing very close to him, so close she could feel the heat coming off him. Could almost hear the blood pumping inside his body. She flicked her gaze towards the part of the screen where the chat box had been, hoping he would get the message. *You tell your parents about the movie, I'll tell them you called me the hot babysitter.*

'I'm not going to say anything,' he said.

She nodded. 'Well, I'll leave you to your game. And your chat.'

'Hold on,' he said as she reached the door.

It took him several attempts to get the words out. 'You've met Albie and Eric. Do you think they'll actually come after us like they said they would?'

'What do you think?' she asked.

'I don't know. I mean, they are psychos.'

'No they're not.'

He blinked at her, confused. She probably shouldn't have said that.

'You don't need to worry,' she said. 'I have a feeling it's all going to be fine.'

With Dylan's door closed behind her, she hesitated in the hall, then – feeling confident neither of the kids would come out – she opened the door beside Rose's room. It was Ethan and Emma's bedroom.

She went in and had a quick look around. Ran her hand over the bedspread. Opened one of the bedside drawers and peeked inside, hoping to find something interesting like handcuffs or a dildo, but there was just some hand cream, a box of condoms still in its shrink-wrap, and a bottle full of loose change.

She went over to the dresser, where Emma kept her make-up. She picked up a lipstick, an expensive one, and slipped it into her pocket.

After that, she went back downstairs and sat on the sofa with the TV on, staring into space, like a robot in standby mode, until Ethan and Emma came home.

6

I used to think that Lionel Richie must have written 'Easy' before he had kids – Sunday mornings were far from relaxing for a long time! – but now Rose and Dylan were at secondary school they didn't get up until mid-morning and even made their own breakfast, allowing Emma and me to have a lie-in most Sundays.

This morning, though, two days after the Pulp gig, we were woken by a commotion coming from across the street. Dogs barking and a woman yelling. Screeching, really. Panicking. She was shouting a name: Tommy. The man at number 36. The father of the boys who had harassed Rose on the last day of school.

'What's going on?' Emma asked, her eyes still closed.

I got up and went to the window, standing there in my boxer shorts, pulling aside the curtains just in time to see Tommy come running out of his house. He was dressed only in his underwear too, and I got a full view of his impressive pecs and the tattoos that covered half his torso. He was twice as broad as me, clearly very strong and unexpectedly fast.

'It's Albie,' his wife screamed, standing there on the lawn with her hands in her hair. What was her name? Nicola, that was it. The younger boy, Eric, was there as well, hopping from foot to foot, agitated and in tears. 'On the footpath.'

Tommy ran back into the house at the same time that Emma came to join me beside the window, smelling of sleep and looking so beautiful in her little pyjama set that it caused a stab of pain in my stomach. I summarised for her what I'd seen so far, then Tommy came running out having hurriedly pulled on some clothes. He legged it up the road towards the path that led to the fields, Eric following him.

Emma put on a pair of joggers and a T-shirt. 'I'm going to go and see if we can help.'

'Are you sure you want to get involved?'

'We're their neighbours, Ethan. That's what good neighbours do.'

I almost said, *You know all about being a good neighbour.* But I swallowed the words down and said, 'Yes. Of course.'

I put some clothes on too and went downstairs. As I stepped into our front garden, Fiona came out of her house. She was wearing sports gear and her hair looked damp at the roots, like she'd just got back from a run. No make-up. The thought went through my head that she didn't need it. Meanwhile, Emma had crossed the road and was standing at the edge of number 36's property, waiting for Nicola to get off the phone.

'Any idea what's happening?' Fiona asked me.

'Something to do with Albie.'

Fiona took a sip from the water bottle she was holding, then wiped her lips. 'That's the older one, right? This is why I'm glad I never had kids. The fear that something awful might happen to them. That's a thing, right?'

'Yeah. It's a thing all right. Thank you for watching mine the other night.' We hadn't chatted with Fiona when we'd got back from the gig because she'd told us she was tired and wanted to get straight to bed. That had been fine by me.

'It was my pleasure. I didn't see much of Dylan.' She paused for a micro-second, as if waiting for me to comment. When I didn't she went straight on. 'Rose is a delight. Such a sweet girl.'

'She is.'

'How were the band?'

'They were amazing. Honestly, it was such a great night.' I swallowed. 'Best I've had in ages.'

She studied me like she could tell something was awry. 'I'm glad to hear it. It must be hard, trying to find time for your marriage when you have children and demanding jobs.'

I had a moment of paranoia. Our bedroom wall adjoined her house. Had she been listening to us? No, surely she wouldn't be able to hear our hushed conversations through the walls. Or note the lack of any other noises coming from our bedroom.

'Must be hard to find time for yourself too,' she said. 'To be a man, and not just a dad and husband.'

Taken aback, I said, 'I like being a dad and husband.'

'Oh, I'm sure. But sometimes you have to think about yourself, don't you? As an individual.' As she said this, her eyes flicked up and down my body, sizing me up. I could hardly believe it. No woman had looked at me like that in years.

Flustered, and temporarily forgetting what was going on over the road, I lost the ability to speak.

'If you ever want me to babysit again, just ask. Anytime. I honestly really enjoyed doing it. Not that they're babies.'

I recovered the power of speech. 'As Rose keeps reminding me.'

'Another difficult thing for a dad, I bet. Seeing his little girl grow up.'

'Yeah. I always thought I'd be cool about it. When they were little, keeping us up all night, drawing on the walls, having tantrums, I used to long for the days when they were older. It's hard – though, actually, it's harder for Emma than it is for me.'

'Oh?'

'Yeah, there's . . . tension. Rose thinks Emma babies her, doesn't give her the freedom she craves. And Emma is a little bit . . .'

Fiona waited, and I started to feel like I was being disloyal. I didn't want to say any more.

But Fiona didn't let it go. 'Overprotective? Tries to keep her wrapped up in cotton wool?'

'Something like that.'

It wasn't only that. Rose constantly complained that Emma bossed her around too much, and I had to confess I had allowed Emma to take on that 'bad cop' role. She was the one who told Rose to tidy her bedroom, brush her hair, do her homework. I had the easier role: the fun parent. The one who played video games with them and took them to gigs and bought unhealthy takeaways.

'Dylan seems easy enough.'

'Yeah, he is. Girls are harder, though, right? That's what everyone says. Or is it sexist to say that?'

She smiled. 'Girls are definitely more of a challenge, especially to their mothers. That's what mine said, anyway.'

While we were having this conversation, Emma had been talking to Nicola. Now she made her way back over the street, frowning. She nodded at Fiona but addressed me.

'She's in a terrible state.'

'What happened?'

'The boys were out on their bike this morning, riding up and down the footpath.' She meant the path that ran alongside the fields. 'According to Eric, when Albie was taking his turn, the front tyre burst and he was thrown off the bike into a tree. Hit his head pretty hard.'

'Oh dear,' said Fiona.

'Eric said he wasn't talking or responding.'

I could picture it. Hear the crack. 'God, how awful.'

'Terrible,' said Fiona.

We heard movement and turned to see Tommy approaching with Albie in his arms. Tommy was attempting to jog but the boy was a dead weight. Seeing them, Nicola sprinted towards them, making a distressed keening noise, arms outstretched. Eric was there too, loping along behind his dad, looking pale and sick.

At the same moment we heard an ambulance, just before it came around the corner, blue lights flashing. Albie's mum waved at it and it sped across to where they stood, two paramedics emerging, a man and a woman. Almost everyone in the neighbourhood was out on their front lawns, watching. The paramedics helped Tommy get Albie into the back of the ambulance, then Tommy came back out and Nicola took his place. Tommy and Eric stood outside the vehicle, the big man rubbing the back of his neck with one of his huge hands, his son small and scared beside him.

A minute later, the ambulance doors closed and it sped away, leaving father and son behind. Eric began to cry and Tommy put an arm around his son's shoulders before leading him to their car. He almost stalled it in his haste to pursue the ambulance, black smoke emerging from the exhaust pipe as they turned off the estate.

Emma looked sick. 'God, I hope he's okay. He wasn't moving, was he? And did you see the blood?'

'Poor kid,' Fiona said, before abruptly announcing, 'But I can't stand around gossiping all day.'

She went into her house, and as we turned to do the same I sensed movement above me. I looked up to see Rose at her bedroom window. She was gazing across the street towards Albie and Eric's house.

There was a smile on her lips. Faint, barely visible, as enigmatic as the Mona Lisa's, but absolutely there – until she saw me looking up at her and quickly rearranged her face, frowning with worry.

A smile? I made myself believe I had imagined it.

ϖ

Back inside, I made coffee and thought about what to have for breakfast. Emma came into the kitchen, clearly disturbed by what had happened. 'I'm going to have a bath,' she said.

'You don't want a coffee?'

'I'll have one afterwards.'

As she passed me to leave the kitchen I said, 'Do you want a hug?' – spreading my arms, hoping she would step into my embrace, but she evaded me.

'I stink.'

'No you don't. Besides, I like it when you're a bit smelly.'

She wrinkled her nose. 'Don't be gross. And if you really think I'm going to be in the mood now, after what we just witnessed . . .'

'What? I was just trying to give you a hug. To comfort you.'

'Okay. Whatever. If that's true, I'm sorry.'

It was true. I really had been offering her comfort, nothing more, but I could tell she didn't believe me. More miscommunication, more tension caused by sex. It was the elephant in our bedroom, and had been since The Incident.

'Go and have your bath,' I said.

I finished making coffee, then sat at the kitchen table, not hungry enough to want breakfast, thinking about how I'd lied to Fiona about my and Emma's night out. It hadn't gone how I'd hoped, and I knew it was because I'd had this perfect image of what the evening would be like – relaxed and fun and like the old days – and when it wasn't I had driven Emma crazy by repeatedly asking her if she was all right, which had eventually led her to snap at me, telling me to chill out or she'd go home.

We had stood and watched the band with this terrible atmosphere between us, the volume making it impossible to talk until, six or seven songs in, Emma told me she was going to the loo and didn't come back. I went looking for her and eventually found her waiting outside the venue, saying it was too loud and crowded and someone had spilled beer on her. I accused her of deliberately spoiling our night out and the young bouncers watched us with smirks, this middle-aged couple bickering as the middle-aged band played inside. Finally, I persuaded her to come into the nearest pub so we could talk.

'What do you want to do?' I asked.

'Go home. Go to bed.'

'I mean about us. Do you want a divorce?' I had to speak quietly so the couple at the table next to ours couldn't hear. Meanwhile, I was almost shaking with stress.

'Please. Not this again. I can't have this conversation again tonight.'

'But . . .'

'I don't want a divorce, Ethan. I'm just exhausted and on my period and not in the mood to see a band, and I'm sorry I've ruined our night out, okay? I'm really sorry.'

When we arrived home, thank God, Fiona didn't want to hang around to chat. Emma went straight upstairs to check on the kids. Rose was asleep but Dylan was still awake, playing games with his friends, headphones on. We pretended to him that the gig had been amazing and then Emma went to bed.

Earlier, before the argument, I had hoped the evening might end with sex, which would have been the first time in months, but I knew there was no hope of that happening now. I sat downstairs and watched something on Netflix, Lola snoozing beside me on the sofa, until I knew Emma would be asleep, then went up.

Sitting at the kitchen table now, I finished my coffee. Told myself to be more positive, to stop being so bloody self-pitying. At least our children were healthy and happy. Unlike that poor boy across the road.

I got up and looked across the street at their empty house. It was a sunny morning, vapour trails looking pretty against a blue sky. From upstairs I could hear footsteps, Rose walking around her room. I knew I ought to have a word with her when she came down. That smile. *Yes, those boys were horrible to you,* I would say. *But one should never take pleasure in others' misfortune.*

I was saved from having to make a decision by the dog. Lola came into the room, wagging her tail expectantly.

'Is it that time, eh?'

She trotted over and sat at my feet, then gave me her paw.

'Come on then.'

I put her lead on and we went up the footpath towards the fields. It always tickled me how Lola could do the same walk daily but seem just as excited every time. The footpath was smooth, tarmacked at the same time they built the estate. In autumn it would be crunchy or soggy with leaves, but now it was relatively clear, slightly warm from the sun that made its way through the branches.

Halfway up the path, I stopped. The boys' dirt bike was still here, lying on its side between two trees, the front tyre visibly flat. I crouched for a closer look and saw the rubber was shredded, like it had gone over something viciously sharp. I squinted at the path, looking for glass or a nail, but couldn't see anything. Could it have just burst on its own? Maybe, I supposed, though I couldn't imagine why it would. Being careful, in case there was glass hidden on the path, I steered Lola around the tree closest to the bike's front wheel. There was a dark mark on the trunk and I realised, with a lurch in my gut, that it was blood.

I shivered in the sunshine, glad it hadn't been one of my children. But also thinking again about how Rose had smiled, before my thoughts lurched on to the memory of what Fiona had said about me being not just a dad and husband. The way she'd looked me up and down.

Jesus, what a morning.

'Let's go, Lola,' I said. Dogs were easy, uncomplicated. We walked on.

7

'I'm bored.'

It was Monday so the shop was closed – we opened Tuesday to Saturday – and Emma was at work. Rose had come into the garden, where I had been mowing the lawn and was now weeding, my least favourite job in the world, especially when it was this hot, nudging into the thirties. Lola sat on the decking in the shade and watched me.

'Why don't you give me a hand?' I said to Rose, going over to join her. She looked at me like I'd asked her to climb on to the roof to fix a leaky gutter.

'*Gardening?*'

I resisted the urge to tell her how her great-grandad had worked in the hop fields of Kent from the age of nine. I hadn't exactly done much gardening when I was her age. 'Have you done your holiday homework?'

'Dad, that doesn't have to be done for five weeks.'

'Um, have you completed *Tears of the Kingdom*?' That was the new game we'd bought her for her Switch a few weeks ago. I reeled through a list of things she could do, from watching Netflix to tidying her bedroom.

'Everything's boring.' She approached Lola and petted her. 'I could take Lola out.'

'Not on your own.' Dylan was out with his mates. 'And don't say you're not a baby. Twelve is too young to take a dog out on your own.'

'But it's fine now. Safe.'

I turned to look at her. 'When was it not safe?'

'I mean . . . I'm old enough.'

'No, Rose. What if she, I don't know, slipped her leash?'

She tutted. 'That's such a lame reason.'

Then, for the second time in a week, a voice came from over the fence. 'I've got something that might entertain you.' Both Rose and I looked to see Fiona peering over from her garden. 'Maybe Rose would like to come and meet my new friend.'

'New friend?' Rose said.

'Wait there.'

From my position on the decking, which gave a view over the fence, I watched as Fiona went back into her house. She was wearing cut-off denim shorts and had bare feet, and I could see the dirt on her soles as she walked away, and a little heart-shaped mark on her ankle. As she reached her house she surprised me by looking back over her shoulder. She must have thought I was staring at her body and I quickly looked away.

She didn't appear annoyed, though. In fact, she smiled. And a minute later she came back holding something black and white and almost unbearably cute.

'Oh! A kitten!' Rose rushed over to the fence where Fiona stood, holding the cat out so Rose could stroke it.

'She's a little girl, and I need to think of a name for her. Maybe you could come over and help me – if that's all right with your dad.'

They both looked at me. The kitten looked at me too. 'That's absolutely fine by me. Just as long as you don't outstay your welcome, Rose.'

'I'll kick her out as soon as we've come up with a good name,' Fiona said. She winked at Rose, then let her in through the back gate. She paused and said to me, 'Oh, do you want to come over too? I have cold lemonade in the fridge.'

It was tempting. Rose wasn't the only one who liked kittens. And there was Fiona, standing there in her little shorts, a hand on her hip, skin glowing with perspiration. Then I noticed Rose staring at me like she didn't recognise me. Shit, I didn't recognise myself.

'I need to finish this weeding.'

'Suit yourself.'

They disappeared into the house with the kitten and I consciously didn't look at Fiona's legs, or her bum in her little shorts, as she walked away. I blamed the heat. I needed a cold shower.

Instead, I finished the gardening, then took the bin that contained the mown grass and weeds out to the front of the house. As I placed it in position I saw Iris, the woman who lived next door to Tommy and Nicola. I'd met her a few times. She was in her early seventies; grey hair, slim and fit. She could often be seen out running in her lime-green Nike gear and baseball cap, and she drove an electric hybrid, proud of her eco credentials. She had its hood open now and was refilling the windscreen reservoir.

'Oh, hello Ethan,' she said as I approached.

We exchanged small talk about her car and the weather.

'Business good?' she enquired. 'I still need to get Alan's old records out of storage, let you take a look at them. He kept them pristine, you know.'

'Definitely. Just let me know when.'

I was a little sceptical. Over the years, a lot of people had asked me to look at their record collections. Since the vinyl boom, everyone thought there was treasure lurking among their old LPs and 45s, and they would always insist their records were in great condition, lots of gems among them. Then I would turn up and find a load of scratched copies of *Brothers in Arms*, yet another *Best of Blondie* with a torn sleeve and coffee rings on the cover, and tatty seven-inch singles that looked like they'd been rescued from a skip. Every now and then I'd find something decent – an original *Exile on Main St.* or someone's cherished Northern Soul collection. But I wasn't in a rush for Iris to dig her late husband's vinyl out of wherever it was stored.

I turned towards her neighbours' house. I hadn't seen them return to their home since yesterday morning, which obviously didn't bode well.

'Any news about Albie?'

'No. That poor family. A chap came yesterday afternoon – Tommy's brother, I think – to collect the dogs, and I asked him what was happening, but he was extremely vague. I'm not . . .' She trailed off, grimacing.

'What is it?'

'Well, I feel bad saying this, but they're not the easiest family to live next door to, with the dogs barking and the sound of that bike and, well, I'm sure you've heard Tommy and Nicola fighting from across the street. But seeing that poor boy yesterday, it made me sick. Do you have any idea what happened?'

'It seems like the front tyre blew out. I saw a police car parked over there this morning, a couple of cops taking a look. I was asking Dylan about it and he pointed out that there's a little ridge on the ground where it happened, right between two trees. He said he's seen them racing up to that ridge so it becomes a kind of ramp, and they jump the bike between the trees. I guess the front tyre burst as Albie was doing this and it sent him flying off course, straight into the tree.'

Iris winced, picturing it.

'I would never let my kids on something like that,' I said.

'I never would have either.' I could see her force herself to brighten. 'How are your two?'

'Oh, they're fine. Dylan's out with friends. Rose has gone round to Fiona's to help her choose a name for her new kitten.'

'How lovely.' She looked across at Fiona's house. 'So that's her name? I haven't met her yet. What's her surname?'

I thought about it. 'Smith.' I only remembered that because, when she'd said it, I'd thought *like Robert Smith*, the singer with my favourite band. 'I don't know much about her, though, except that she seems nice. Is that bad, that I'm letting someone I hardly know look after my daughter?'

Iris waved a hand. 'In the old days we all used to look after each other's kids. It takes a village and all that.'

'That was in the East End, right?' Iris had told me before that she was a proper Cockney, raised in some part of east London that had since been gentrified. She had moved out to the suburbs after she retired.

'That's right. And I think it's nice to see that happening here. Neighbours helping neighbours. We actually have a decent little community here. Quite rare nowadays. But that Fiona . . . I'm sure I recognise her from somewhere.'

'Oh?'

'Yes, I haven't actually spoken to her, but she looks familiar. Do you know where she's from?'

'Somewhere in Australia.'

'I wasn't expecting you to say that. Maybe I *don't* know her. To be honest, a lot of young women look the same to me these days. She's not as attractive as your Emma, though, I'll say that.' She winked at me. 'You're a lucky man.'

'I . . . Thanks.'

I could see her trying to read my expression, perhaps surprised by my muted reaction. I was gripped by an urge to ask her if she and her late husband had ever been through rocky patches, if she had ever felt hurt and betrayed by Alan. But I already knew the answer. Of course their marriage would have had difficult spells. Every marriage did. My own parents hadn't weathered their marital storm; they'd run aground and gone their separate ways. I was still determined that Emma and I would – at the risk of stretching this metaphor too far – get back in the boat and sail on together.

'I'd better get home,' I said. 'Let's hope for good news about Albie.'

'I'll mention him in my prayers tonight.'

I went back over the road and into the house. Ten minutes later, there was a knock on the door. It was Rose, with Fiona. Rose insisted that Fiona come in and I didn't argue. Fiona was still barefoot, her toenails painted turquoise. I noticed she was wearing make-up now too. Lipstick, the same peach shade that Emma wore.

'Did you come up with a name?' I asked, once we were in the kitchen.

'We did. Rose had loads of great suggestions but we went with Karma.'

'I like it. After the Taylor Swift song?'

Fiona looked at me blankly. 'Taylor . . . ?'

'You've never heard of Taylor Swift? She's the biggest pop star on the planet.'

'Oh, yes, of course I've heard of her. I just don't know that song.' She seemed flustered – and I could feel Rose looking at me disapprovingly.

'My dad always does this. Shames people for their music knowledge.'

'No I don't!'

'It's fine,' Fiona said. 'We can't all be hip and cool in our middle age.'

Was there an edge to her voice? A trace of sarcasm? Also – middle age? I was only forty-three and Fiona certainly wasn't middle-aged.

'Are you going to ask him?' Rose said.

'Ask me what?'

Fiona smiled, any trace of annoyance vanishing. 'I was going to make a suggestion. You and Emma are both at work Tuesday to Friday, aren't you? Rose told me that Dylan usually has to stay home to watch her, and that you were thinking of signing her up for a holiday club.'

'Which I really don't want to go to,' said Rose. 'It's so lame.'

'It's really not lame,' I said, irritated that this word had popped up again. The club was a local scheme, run by the council, that put on activities for tweens: sports, team-building, video games, volunteering in the community. I had thought it sounded ideal for Rose. It would stop her moping around the house complaining of being bored, and it meant Dylan wouldn't be stuck at home looking after her. 'The alternative is having to come and hang out at the shop with me.'

Rose groaned.

'There is another alternative,' said Fiona. 'I could watch her for you. I don't start my new job until September so I'm at a loose end, and I'd be very happy to take Rose under my wing for a few weeks. And, before you ask, I wouldn't want any money.'

I couldn't believe what I was hearing. 'You're offering free babysitting?'

Rose folded her arms. 'I am *not* a baby.'

'Sorry. Childminding.'

Rose narrowed her eyes. Did she disapprove of 'child' now too?

'It's just a word, Rose.'

'Whatever you want to call it,' Fiona said, jumping in, 'I'm offering my services. It would be my pleasure, and I'd make it educational and healthy. We can go on trips, go for walks in the park, look round museums.'

'Play with Karma,' said Rose.

'Absolutely. Karma is going to be a big part of it.' Fiona smiled.

'*Please*, Dad,' said Rose. 'I really don't want to go to the holiday club. I want to do stuff with Fiona. It will save you money too. You won't have to pay for the stupid club.'

That was true. It was relatively cheap for what it was, but it was still a substantial chunk of our income. Any savings would be welcome.

'I know you can't give a decision now,' Fiona said. 'You'll have to ask Emma.'

'I bet she'll say no.' Rose stuck out her bottom lip, just as she'd done when she was three. She might not be a baby anymore but she could act like one when she thought it would help her. 'She never wants me to do anything I want to do.'

'I'm sure that's not true,' Fiona said.

'It isn't,' I said. 'It's just that Rose knows I'm a softer touch – don't you, Rose?'

'Can you call her now, at work?' Rose asked, not smiling. 'Please?'

'She might be busy.'

'She's always busy.'

I took a deep breath. 'Rose, I'll talk to your mum when she gets home. Okay?'

'But *you* think it's all right?' Before I had a chance to reply she said, 'Thanks, Dad. Please try to make her see sense.'

I found myself saying, 'I'll try.'

She ran up the stairs, shouting, 'Bye, Fiona,' as she went.

I met Fiona's eye. 'Why do I feel like I've just been twisted around someone's finger?'

She laughed. 'Dads and daughters. But, listen, if it makes either you or Emma feel uncomfortable, I won't be offended. I just want you to know the offer's there. It would be my pleasure.'

'Thank you. What is your new job, by the way? The one you start in September?'

'If I told you the details you'd die of boredom, but I'll be working for a bank. Right, I'd better get back to Karma.' She paused. 'Taylor Swift. I must remember that. Maybe listen to some of her music?'

I had to bite my tongue to stop myself from offering to make her a playlist. Instead, I said, 'I'm sure Rose will insist on it.'

Fiona ran one hand along her bare arm. I could see all the fine little hairs standing on end, as if she were cold. Maybe she didn't feel the heat, having grown up in Western Australia. Perhaps she didn't think this scorching weather was actually hot.

'Rose is so lucky, having a cool dad who knows about music and stuff.'

'That's what I keep telling her.'

'I might not be as cool as you, but I promise if you let me look after her we'll have fun.' She looked me in the eye, biting her lower lip. 'It will be the best summer of her life.'

8

Fiona stood in her steamy bathroom, the fan whirring and attempting to suck the moisture from the room. She reached out to the mirror and wrote the three names.

She circled the top one before rubbing them out with her palm, and she smiled.

All the plans she'd made in prison.

Finally, it was happening.

ϖ

'Where are we going?'

Fiona and Rose sat opposite each other in the packed train carriage, which had filled up after they'd boarded at Sanderstead: a noisy group of teenagers, parents taking their kids into London to seek school holiday entertainment, businesspeople heading to meetings. Fiona breathed in through her nose and out through pursed lips, practising the exercises she'd learned years ago, the ones that helped her maintain control when surrounded by too many people. Their noise, their inane conversations, worst of all their *stink*. It was hard to focus on her excitement – the beginning of her summer project – when she was surrounded by so many bleating sheep. Rose had to repeat her question several times before Fiona realised the girl was talking.

'Sorry, Rose. Where are we *going*? Well, I promised your dad this would be an educational summer and today is going to be about history. And architecture.'

'*Architecture?*'

Fiona smiled. 'It'll be fun. Trust me.' She found that, by concentrating on Rose's face, her freckles, the gap between her teeth, she was able to block out the noise and smell of the herd, including the sweaty man beside her, who kept scratching his beard, flakes of skin – illuminated by the sunlight that streamed through the train's windows – falling into his lap like pathetic snow.

'We'll go to the park too,' she said as a sweetener. 'Get an ice cream.'

Rose frowned with confusion, and Fiona sensed it was because she didn't know how open to be with her. Fiona wanted to tell her it was fine for her to be completely herself. That she could reveal her inner thoughts and that Fiona wouldn't judge her. But there were too many people around. That conversation would have to wait.

Scratch scratch, went the man beside her. He was in his thirties, staring at his phone, fingernails too long.

'It's great that your mum agreed to this,' Fiona said.

Emma had been round to see her last night, after she got home from work. Apparently Rose had been texting her mum all afternoon, making the case for why hanging out with Fiona for the next few weeks would be better for her than going to the holiday club.

'My issue is that I don't really know you,' Emma had said to Fiona. 'It's not that I want to appear like I don't trust you, but . . .'

Fiona, who had wiped off the lipstick and changed into a long skirt, put her hands up. 'I totally get it. What do you want to know? Actually, before we start, do you want a cup of tea? Or a glass of wine? You look like you could do with one.'

'Am I that transparent? I'm tempted, but I'd better stick with tea.'

Fiona knew that Emma worked selling pet food. A booming industry, apparently, though Fiona could hardly imagine doing something that tedious. Had the young Emma foreseen her future as one in which she flogged dog meat? Something must have gone wrong along the way.

Fiona made tea and said, 'Come and meet Karma the kitten.'

They went into the living room, where Karma was asleep in her bed on the floor.

'I'm getting cute rage,' Emma said. 'You know, where something is so adorable that you can hardly bear it and you just want to squeeze it?'

'Oh, I do. So what do you want to know about me?'

The next hour played out like an interview; one in which Fiona got to practise telling her story. Her name was Fiona Smith – 'I know, so boring' – and she had lived in the UK for sixteen years. *First part a half-lie, the second part true.* Both her parents were dead and she had no reason to go back to Australia. *Not true.* Before coming to live here in South Croydon she'd worked in the City, going to an office in Canary Wharf every day, but she'd been made redundant during the pandemic. *Absolute horseshit.* Her new job, doing something in banking that she said was too dull to go into, was due to start in September. *Also a lie. There was no job lined up. She had other plans to make money.*

'I know you're not supposed to ask this question,' Emma said, 'but it feels relevant: have you never wanted kids of your own? I mean, I know you're not too old, but . . .'

She winced and Fiona arranged her face to show mild wistfulness. 'I did once. But my partner never wanted them.'

'He didn't want to be a dad?'

'She. And no, she said she never had that maternal urge.'

'I'm so sorry.' Emma's face flushed pink. 'I shouldn't have assumed.'

'Don't worry about it.' But she let it linger for a few moments. People like Emma had many fears, but one of the biggest was the horror that they might appear prejudiced in any way.

'I always thought I might be able to persuade her, but then . . . well, it was too late.' Fiona squeezed her eyes shut, so they appeared moist when she reopened them. 'She died.'

'Oh my goodness. How awful.'

'It's okay. It was a few years ago. But yeah, I never got to be a mother – though I promise I'm not trying to fill some kind of weird hole in my life with Rose.'

'No, of course not.'

'To be honest, I don't even like *little* kids that much. But eleven, twelve, it's such an interesting age. Between childhood and growing up. I suppose I have this picture of myself as a kind of cool aunt, which I also never got to be because I'm an only child.' She grimaced. 'Listen to me. A full-on self-pity party. Emma, I would totally understand if you didn't want your daughter hanging out with this sad Aussie who you hardly even know. I'm sure this holiday club will be fun. Rose thinks she's going to hate it, but I'm sure it will be good for her.'

It was such a mix of lies and truths that Fiona herself was beginning to lose track, to believe it all herself.

Emma sighed. 'If I make her go to that club she'll hate me forever.'

Fiona didn't say anything.

'Sod it. If you're absolutely sure you don't mind, you would be doing us a massive favour. But I insist that we pay all your expenses, and if you get fed up or she's difficult in any way, you need to let us know straight away.'

They shook hands and then Emma went back to tell Rose the good news.

Fiona sat there with Karma in her lap until it grew dark, making plans. Having a little helper was going to make things so much easier.

ϖ

But it was only when they were out and about that Fiona realised there was a surprising advantage to being accompanied by a child. When she bought the tickets, the woman behind the desk asked, 'Is your daughter under sixteen?' It hadn't even entered her head that people would think she was Rose's mother, but on the train a man nudged his teenager and said, 'Move over, make room for this woman and her daughter.' He proceeded to smile at her as his son huffed. The man rolled his eyes at her, saying, 'Kids, eh?'

'Yes,' Fiona responded. 'Kids.'

'The days are long and the years are short, am I right?'

That man had got off a few stops back, saying, 'I hope you have a nice day out.'

Fiona also noticed a couple of older people smile at her, and something else too. Often, when she went out, she would catch young men giving her the eye. A blonde woman with a nice figure and a pretty face. Of course they did. But when she was with Rose she became invisible to these men. Some of them might be into MILFs in their fantasies, but in real life they just saw a mum. No longer a sexual object. She realised that, in the eyes of society, she appeared to have a new identity. A mother. A harmless mum out with her child.

Half the world wouldn't even notice her. And the other half certainly wouldn't suspect her of anything bad.

That included the grotesque man beside her now, who was still scratching when they pulled into Victoria. The moment the train juddered to a halt, Fiona stood up and trod on the scrofulous dick-head's foot, stamping her Doc Marten down on his soft trainers.

He cried out.

'Oh, I'm *so* sorry,' she said. 'Are you okay?'

She wanted to tell him he was lucky they weren't alone in the carriage – or on a dark platform, late at night, nobody around, a train heading into the station. All it would take was a nudge, followed by flailing limbs, a cry of alarm drowned out by the rush of the train. She could see it. Feel the heat in her bones as she pictured it; pulse accelerating, blood thickening, the hairs on the back of her neck standing on end.

'Come on, Rose,' she said, studying the girl's face for signs, but Rose's face remained neutral. Watchful. 'This is us.'

ϖ

They changed on to a train to Herne Hill and turned right out of the station. Fiona took a baseball cap out of her bag and slipped it on, tucking her ponytail through the gap at the back and pulling the peak low. It might have been four years but there would still be people around here who knew her. Who remembered what she had done.

They passed the pub where she and Maisie had spent many hours at the pool table, beating anyone foolish enough to take them on, then turned on to a side street which was lined with tall trees. Beneath one of these trees was a bench. They sat down.

'What are we doing?' Rose asked, looking all around.

'Before I tell you, let me ask you something. When you heard that Albie had been hurt in that accident, how did it make you feel?'

Rose blinked at her. 'I don't know.'

'Come on. You can be honest with me. Do you want to know how *I* felt?' Fiona glanced around, then put her face close to Rose's. Conspiratorial. 'I thought *serves him right.*' Rose's eyes widened. 'Serves him right for being so mean to you, and for getting his dogs to scare poor Lola. He was rude to me too. Insulting. So no, I don't feel sorry for him.'

She waited for Rose's response. She appeared to be thinking hard. Eventually she said, 'My dad says we shouldn't wish harm on anyone. He says that kids who are bullies or mean probably have bad home lives and that we should feel sorry for them. Try to understand them.'

'Hmm.' The very definition of a bleeding-heart liberal. 'And what do you think, Rose? I promise this isn't a trap. I'm not going to snitch. I just want to understand how you feel. Does Rose Dove agree with her dad?'

'It's wrong to be glad that someone else is suffering.'

'Is that another quote from your dad? It's okay. I'm not going to argue with you. You probably think I'm a bad person for saying I think it served him right. But do you know what else I think, Rose? Something that's even more important. I think you shouldn't fight your feelings.' She laid a hand on her own belly. 'Right here, in your gut, that's where the truth lies. I let that guide me. Put your hand on your belly, Rose.'

Rose obeyed.

'What's *your* gut telling you right now?'

'That I'm hungry.'

Fiona laughed. 'Okay. I promised you an ice cream, didn't I? We can—'

She fell quiet because the front door of the house they were sitting diagonally opposite was opening. It was him. Max. Fiona immediately put her hand in front of her face to shield it, but he was too busy staring at his phone to look over. He began to shuffle up the street away from them, thumbing his phone as he went.

Hurriedly, Fiona said, 'We can go to the café in the park in a little bit. But first, I'm going to tell you a little secret.'

Rose's eyebrows went up. 'A secret?'

'We're not really here to study architecture. That's boring. Houses are houses, right? I'm actually going to teach you something far more useful. We're going to study spycraft. Does *that* sound exciting?'

'Spycraft? Like, what, pretend we're spies?' Rose was looking at her like her bullshit detector was flashing red and beeping. 'Are you for real?'

'One hundred per cent. And we're going to start now. We're going to follow that man.'

Max was already heading away from them down the street, still ambling along, not watching where he was going. Fiona noted that he was wearing a smart shirt and suit jacket on top, but scruffy jeans and trainers on his bottom half. What was that all about? And why was he at home on a Tuesday morning?

She got up from the bench and gestured for Rose to do likewise.

'It's important that he doesn't see us,' Fiona said. 'But I don't want to lose track of him. Okay? So we follow, but keep back. If he sees us, we fail. Got it?'

'I guess.'

'Don't *guess*. This is important.' She took hold of Rose's forearm, momentarily forgetting herself and her own strength.

'Ow! That hurts.'

Rose's voice was shrill and Fiona glanced up quickly, afraid their quarry would turn and see her. But he was oblivious – and almost out of sight.

'I'm sorry. I want you to take this seriously, though, okay? It's part of your education. If this is going to work, if you don't want to go to the holiday club, you need to do what I say.'

Still Rose didn't move, and Fiona realised she'd upset her and that Rose wasn't going to snap out of it immediately. Rose might be special, but she was still a child. Fiona thought back, quickly, to try to remember what she'd been like when she was twelve and upset, and what would have worked to bring her back quickly without too much drama.

'Do this for me and I'll answer any question you have. Anything at all. I promise to tell the truth.'

It worked almost straight away. 'Anything?'

'Yes. And I'm sorry if I hurt you. But we need to get moving before we lose him.'

Rose appeared to forgive her immediately, the promise soothing the pain where Fiona had grabbed her. They crossed the street. 'I can see him,' said Rose. 'He just went round the corner.'

He was heading back towards the centre of Herne Hill. With Fiona keeping her head down, while also trying to look casual and relaxed – not easy – they followed Max past the pub and the entrance to the station, then round another corner. Finally, on Dulwich Road, he went into a café that Fiona had never seen before, one that appeared to specialise in waffles.

Catching sight of his paunch as he pushed through the door, and the way the staff greeted him, it looked like he came here a lot.

That was good. Routine would make everything easier.

Standing outside, diagonal to the window so he wouldn't see her if he turned around, Fiona watched as he waited at the counter with his back to the window. How stupid and arrogant. If she were him, knowing what he'd done, and knowing the woman he'd wronged was out there, she would never stand with her back to anything.

Beside her, Rose was growing restless, shifting from foot to foot. 'Can we go in?'

'No. I told you, we're practising spycraft. Tailing him. I don't want him to see us.'

'But I'm starving.'

'Rose, we can get something after . . . Hold on.'

Max was exiting the café. Fiona hurriedly stepped into a doorway, gesturing for Rose to stay back until he'd crossed the road and gone through the gates into Brockwell Park. Only then did they follow. She hung back as they entered the park, scanning the area then spotting him easily. They tailed him as he went past the lido and into a quiet, shady area, stopping at a bench where he sat to unwrap his lunch. As he ate, he took out his phone and held it to his ear, then produced a slim notebook and pen from his jacket's inside pocket. He rested the notebook on his lap and wrote in it as he talked, his lunch beside him on the bench.

'What are we doing now?' Rose said, her voice very close to a whine. Fiona took a deep breath.

'We're done. For now. You still hungry?'

She led Rose deeper into the park. It was abuzz with life. Kids playing ball games on the grass. Amorous couples lazing on the lawn. Dog walkers, and parents pushing buggies. Someone whizzed past them on a scooter, too close for Fiona's comfort, and she had to fight the urge to push them off. They passed a woman sleeping under a tree, her handbag beside her, unattended, unwatched. Her wallet would probably be in there, and maybe her phone too. People were moronic, always assuming they would be okay, that bad shit would happen to someone else. It was remarkable how many people kept their PIN numbers in their wallets too, or stored their passwords in the Notes app on their phone. People who carried around their house keys as well as something containing their address, like their driving licence. Asking for trouble. Asking to get robbed.

Like rabbits lying on the ground telling the foxes to come and get them.

The Brockwell Park café was in a converted house in the middle of the park. Rose wanted chips and a slushie. Fiona had a salad and a bottle of water. They took the food outside on to the benches. There were too many people, buzzing around like wasps, and Fiona's shoulders knotted with tension.

'Who was that man?' Rose asked after she'd demolished half her chips.

'Is that your one question?'

'No! That's not it. Is he an ex-boyfriend?'

'Urgh, no. You think *he* would be my type?'

'I don't know. I'm twelve. I don't know anything about that stuff. But I know you were lying about that spycraft stuff. I'm not stupid.'

'I know you're not. You're a very clever girl.' She stole a chip from Rose's plate. 'He's an old friend. Someone I'm planning a surprise for.'

'A nice surprise?'

'Oh, it's going to be very nice.'

'Like a party?'

She stole another chip. 'Oh no. Much better than a party.'

9

'So, how was your first day with Fiona?' I asked Rose as the four of us sat down to dinner.

'It was good.'

'Just good?'

Rose shrugged. 'Yeah.'

Dylan laughed. 'Aargh, too much detail. We don't need to know *everything*.'

The look she gave him was so dirty I was taken aback.

'You were the same when you were twelve,' Emma said to Dylan. 'We'd ask you how school was and all you ever said was "normal".'

Before I could ask Rose anything else about her first day with Fiona, the doorbell rang.

'Are we expecting a delivery?' I asked, getting up and going into the hallway to the front door, with Lola following me. I opened the door – and found myself face to face with Tommy, Albie and Eric's dad. Lola had been good up to this point, but now began barking, possibly because she could smell his German shepherds on him. He looked at her like he wanted to kill her, and it struck me what a deeply unpleasant bloke he was. The kind who kept dogs as a macho status symbol. He probably found it pathetic that I owned a cute little cockapoo.

'One second,' I said, scooping Lola up and taking her back to the dining room.

'Who is it?' Emma asked as I handed her the dog.

'Tommy,' I whispered. 'I don't know what he wants.'

I went back, closing the dining room door behind me.

'Hi,' I said. 'How's Albie?'

To my horror, a tear ran down his cheek and his eyelids fluttered, his Adam's apple bobbing as he swallowed, clearly trying to stop himself from breaking into sobs. I was filled with dread. Had Albie *died*? Was he going round telling the neighbours the bad news?

He managed to get hold of himself and said, with his voice trembling, 'The docs are running all sorts of tests. But they don't know if he's ever going to fully recover.'

'Oh, thank God.'

He stared at me, eyes bulging, grief flipping to rage. 'What?'

'I mean . . . I thought you were going to say . . .' I cleared my throat. 'Thank God for the NHS. For looking after him.'

'Yeah. Those nurses. They're angels.' He held on to the door frame with one meaty paw and pressed his face into the crook of his bare arm, breathing rapidly and wetly. What was I supposed to do? Should I . . . hug him? Pat him on the shoulder? I had a lot of experience dealing with crying children – a crying wife too, I was sorry to say – but a six-foot-two man weeping on my doorstep? I was not equipped to deal with *this*. Luckily, a prop came to the rescue: a box of tissues on the hall table. I handed it to him and he plucked two out, blowing his nose loudly before giving the wet tissues back to me. I treated them like they were hot potatoes, dropping them on the table as quickly as I could.

As soon as the tears stopped, the anger returned.

'Someone punctured that tyre deliberately,' he said, fixing me with a death-ray glare.

If I'd been guilty, I probably would have confessed right there and then. But as an innocent man I was able to say, in a surprised tone, 'What makes you say that?'

'Something sharp burst the tyre. Something like a nail or a big shard of glass, right at the spot where they always jump the bike between the trees.'

I was shocked. 'I took Lola for a walk shortly after it happened.' I explained how I'd seen the bike still lying there but no sharp objects.

He narrowed his eyes at me. 'How long after?'

'I don't know. An hour? Maybe a bit less?'

'Plenty of time for whoever did it to go back and remove the evidence. It wasn't an accident. Someone wanted to hurt my boy.'

'But he's a kid. Why would anyone want to hurt him?'

'That's what I came here to find out.'

I took a step back. 'What are you talking about? You think *I* had something to do with Albie's accident?'

'Not you. Your son. Eric told me about the fight they had last week.'

This was news to me. 'What fight?'

'I don't know exactly, but your kids were in the fields with your dog and apparently they were pissed off with my lads for riding their bike.' He paused. 'And I think my dogs might have scared yours, trying to play with it.'

'What, one of your giant German shepherds went for Lola?'

'Did I say that? I said they were playing.'

My hackles were up now. 'Like your sons were playing when they bullied Rose? The last day of school, Eric and Albie were teasing Rose when she got off the bus. I was going to talk to you about it, but Rose didn't want to cause a big fuss.'

'What are they supposed to have done?'

'They called her names. Said she looked like Taylor Swift.'

He blew air out through his lips. 'You class that as bullying?' He muttered something about snowflakes. 'Sounds like a bit of harmless mucking about to me.'

'Our next-door neighbour witnessed it and brought Rose home.'

'Oh yeah?' He jabbed a thumb in the direction of Fiona's house. 'Her? The Aussie?'

'That's right.'

'She was there too. In the fields.'

That was news to me, but I didn't want this bloke thinking I didn't know what my kids got up to.

'Listen, I'm in the middle of dinner. You're wasting your time coming here. There is no way Dylan had anything to do with Albie's accident. It's just not the kind of thing he would do. I really hope your son fully recovers but I don't appreciate you coming here flinging accusations around. Someone placing a nail in exactly the right spot? Then going to remove it before anyone found it? If you ask me, the most likely thing is that the tyre blew out. Maybe there was a sharp rock or something. An accident, that's it.'

Tommy's eyes narrowed and, for a moment, I thought he was going to try to push past me and demand to talk to Dylan. Instead, he said, 'This ain't over.'

He left and I shut the door behind me. As I re-entered the dining room I heard the buzz of Fiona's doorbell from the other side of the wall.

'What was all that about?' Emma asked.

'That guy's an absolute . . .' I didn't complete the sentence, aware of my children staring at me. 'Dylan, you didn't tell me you'd had a run-in with Albie and Eric.'

'What?' said Emma.

I repeated what Tommy had told me.

'That's not what happened!' Dylan said. 'They were riding that stupid bike around and around us and getting their dogs to terrorise Lola.'

'They were horrible,' said Rose.

Emma got to her feet. 'Why didn't you tell us?'

Rose answered first. 'We were worried you might not let us walk Lola in the fields anymore.'

'Is that right, Dylan?' I asked.

'Yeah. I guess. Also, I didn't want to cause you any more stress or worry.'

Emma and I exchanged a glance. Dylan was a sensitive boy. He knew stuff had happened between us in our old house and he must have had some inkling that we were making this fresh start to try to save our marriage. It broke my heart to think he couldn't come to us for help because we were too stressed.

'Plus it was dealt with,' he said.

'By who?'

'By Fiona. She talked to them, told them to leave us alone. She was great, wasn't she, Rose?'

'Yeah, she was amazing.'

Emma looked towards the door, and I thought she was about to march outside to give Tommy a piece of her mind. 'This is a lot to process. Tommy really thinks Dylan might have had something to do with his son's accident? That's unbelievable.'

'That's what I said. It's ridiculous.'

'He probably feels guilty about letting them ride around on that dangerous thing and is trying to find someone else to blame.'

Here we were, agreeing. United. It felt good.

'I don't want you going near that house, okay?' Emma said to Dylan and Rose.

'What about taking Lola to the fields?'

'I don't know.'

'It's fine, isn't it?' Rose said. 'I mean, isn't Albie in a coma? He's not going to be able to bother us now, is he?'

'You sound like you're actually glad he's in a coma,' Dylan said.

Rose shrugged. 'I can't deny my feelings.'

We all looked at her – surprised, I thought, more by the phrasing than the sentiment.

'I don't know if he's actually in a coma,' I said. 'But we shouldn't be glad he's got a brain injury.'

Rose muttered something.

'What was that?'

Without looking up, she said, 'I'm amazed he had much of a brain to injure.'

'Rose!' Emma and I said together, and Dylan rolled his eyes.

'Can I go to my room now?' he asked. 'I've arranged to play FIFA with Sam and Milo, and they're going to be waiting for me.'

I sighed. 'Sure. Go.'

He left, and Rose stayed at the table for a minute.

'Rose,' Emma said, 'you should have told us about those boys the moment you got home.'

Rose pouted. 'Why should I? I don't have to tell you everything.'

I'm not sure if Emma was tired or stressed or feeling that most terrible of things, parental guilt, but she snapped, 'Actually, you do. You're twelve.'

'I didn't think you'd care.'

'What? Of course I care.'

'Only about Lola getting attacked. You don't care about me. You just want to control me.'

Emma stood up. 'If this is how you're going to talk to me after spending one day with Fiona, I'm not going to let it happen again.'

'I'm not going to that club! I like Fiona!' Then, when Emma didn't back down, Rose immediately changed tactics. It was kind of fascinating to watch. 'I'm sorry I didn't tell you. I was scared you wouldn't let me walk Lola anymore or that you'd make me stay indoors. Next time, I promise I'll tell you.'

'Hopefully, there won't be a next time.'

'There won't,' Rose said. 'Can I go to my room?'

'Fine.' I spoke before Emma could argue. I wanted this quarrel to end.

As soon as we were alone, Emma let out a great sigh.

'What is it?' I asked.

'What do you think? Not only is this woman next door minding our daughter for us while we go to work, but she's fighting our kids' battles for them. Battles we didn't even know about. It should be me spending the summer with Rose, not this *stranger*. It makes me feel like . . .'

'What?'

'A bad mother.'

I reached for her hand. 'Emma, you've got a career. We're both here for our kids every morning, every evening. You're a great role model for Rose. You're a brilliant mother.'

'Am I? Do you really think that? It wasn't long ago you accused me of being a selfish bitch.'

I stared at her. 'That was in the heat of an argument.' I had been so angry that night; a fury like I'd never experienced before. Later, I had apologised for using the B-word, but she hadn't forgotten. It was still there, festering.

'I don't even like my job anymore,' she said. 'I'm sick of it. I'd rather be here, with my kids, but we can't afford for me to give up work now, can we? Not since you made us move here.'

I couldn't believe what I was hearing. 'You know why we had to leave the old place. That was not my fault.'

'Maybe you—' She stopped herself.

'Maybe I what? Overreacted? Is that what you were going to say?'

'No, actually, I was going to say we didn't have to buy somewhere so expensive. There was that other place . . .'

'It was a shithole, Emma.'

'It was fine. And it might have allowed me to go part-time at least. But no, you insisted. You said this estate would be perfect for our fresh start, for our family. And now you don't even like it here.'

'What? Yes I do.'

'You think the neighbours are morons. Oh, apart from Little Miss Perfect next door.'

'So, what? You want to sell up? Move somewhere worse so you can quit your job, just because you're weirdly jealous of someone who's doing us a favour?'

I hated this. Hated that we were arguing again. I had to get out of there before my emotions completely took over and threw petrol on to the flames.

'I'm going to take the dog out,' I said. 'I need to calm down. Where is she?'

I left the room to look for Lola – and bumped straight into Rose. She was standing in the hallway outside the dining room. She'd clearly heard every word we'd said.

'Rose,' I began, but before I could say any more she flung her arms around me.

'*I'm* glad we moved here,' she said.

'Even with those boys?'

'Yes.' She pulled out of the hug. 'Please don't let Mum stop me from seeing Fiona. I really like spending time with her. If Mum makes me go to that club, I'll kill myself.'

'Rose! Never say things like that!'

But now she was crying, and then Emma appeared in the doorway. 'Rose? What is it? What's going on?'

'She's worried we're going to stop her from spending her days with Fiona.'

Emma came over to try to give Rose a hug, but Rose stepped behind me. Emma looked shocked. Wounded.

'Dad, don't let her send me to that club.'

I made eye contact with Emma, silently imploring her to go easy on Rose. I could see this going either way. But – to my relief, because I wanted Rose's tears to stop – Emma said, 'Okay, fine. But if anything else happens like this, you have to tell us straight away. All right?'

Rose wiped her tears away and smiled.

'I promise.'

10

Over the rest of the week, Fiona and Rose didn't venture far from the estate. It rained nearly every day, so they stayed indoors, playing with Karma the kitten, watching movies, or venturing out between rain showers to take Lola for walks. The fields were peaceful without those little shits riding around on their dirt bike, and Fiona was sure it wasn't just her who felt it. Every other dog walker they came across seemed happier and more relaxed. They were able to let their pets off their leads without worrying they would get mauled by a pair of badly trained German shepherds.

Every neighbourhood needs someone like me, Fiona mused. *A spider to keep the fly population under control.*

That day in the fields, when that boy had been riding around them on the dirt bike, she'd decided something needed to be done. She had pictured the bike skidding, crashing, exploding. In the fantasy, the boys' clothes had gone up like firelighters, and they had flapped and screamed as the flames engulfed them. In her head, she could smell their flesh cooking; could hear their final screams before they fell silent forever.

Well, she had thought, perhaps she couldn't arrange something as aesthetically pleasing as that, but an accident – something that would scare them and damage the bike – should be quite easy to make happen. There were a few people who went up that footpath on bicycles, but Albie and Eric were the only ones who traversed it on a motorbike. She had watched them a couple of times, speeding up and down the path, jumping between two trees that were only a couple of metres apart. Later, she went along the path when no one was around, to take a better look, and realised that the ridge they used as a ramp would be the perfect spot for a little accident. There was a crack in the ground across the ridge, a couple of inches deep. If she hammered a few sturdy, sharp nails into a strip of wood and wedged it into the crack, with the nails sticking up, it would only take a little luck for the wheel to hit them, which would surely send them flying and put the bike out of action. Maybe whoever was riding it would break an arm.

That morning, at the crack of the dawn, she went up the path and set the trap.

And it worked even better than she'd hoped. Albie had flown straight into one of the trees. Not a broken arm, but brain damage. He wouldn't be bothering anyone around here for a long time.

While the morons across the street had been riding in an ambulance, she'd sneaked along the path and removed the strip of wood before anyone could investigate the cause of the accident. Easy.

And if the kid never recovered? She didn't care either way.

ɷ

Among the movies she and Rose watched, there were several that she personally found boring, but she had to choose them because she wanted to see Rose's reaction to them. *My Girl. Home Alone. Bambi. ET.* Films that were specifically designed to make you cry. They watched them with the curtains drawn, and Fiona hoped Rose didn't notice how her attention was mostly on the girl's face instead of the screen.

Rose never shed a tear. Not when ET said 'Be good' to Elliott. Not when Bambi's mother was shot by a hunter. Not even when Macaulay Culkin was stung by a load of bees and died. In fact, Rose had smiled at that bit.

They played board games too. Cluedo, Risk and chess, which Rose was surprisingly good at. Fiona, who had been taught to play by Maisie, was hard to beat for most casual players, with an Elo of 1300, and she expected playing Rose to be unchallenging, but she had to use all her experience and knowledge of gambits and endgames to beat her.

She set about coaching Rose, teaching her all the most common openings and how to respond to them, and working on tactics and strategy. It passed the hours while the summer rain beat against the window.

When they got bored of the games and movies, or of playing with Karma, Fiona would ask Rose to tell her stories from her childhood. Stories about her mum, dad and brother. It was all useful information-gathering. She found out that Rose's earliest memory was seeing her brother almost choking on a piece of LEGO.

'What about when you started school?' Fiona asked. 'Did you enjoy it?'

'Not really.'

'Why not?'

Rose needed coaxing, eventually saying, 'There were all these groups of girls that seemed to make friends on day one and I ended up sitting on my own in the playground.'

'They didn't invite you to join?'

'I think maybe they did. At first.'

'And then?'

Rose shrugged. 'For some reason, once they got to know me, they didn't want me to play with them anymore. I ended up making friends with this girl called Jasmine who everyone said was weird and smelly. She was my best friend for ages.'

'And what happened to her?'

Rose said, 'Can we have another game of chess?'

It was a subject she clearly didn't want to talk about.

'Why did you move to this estate?' Fiona asked a little later.

She had learned that sometimes you had to wait a long time for Rose to answer. She knew that most people would give up and start talking about something else, or suggest the answer because they couldn't bear the silence. But Fiona was patient.

'Mum and Dad were fighting a lot.'

'Oh, really? That must have been horrible for you and Dylan.'

'Yeah. I guess.' Another long silence. 'Dad was so angry. I never saw him get mad before. Mum's always been the strict one. The one who yells at us if we do something naughty.' She frowned like she was remembering something that pissed her off. 'Dad's pretty chill.'

'Sounds like he was stressed out about something,' Fiona said. She was intrigued but not surprised. She also knew the tension between Ethan and Emma was still there. She'd felt it last week when they'd got home from the Pulp gig. It was obvious they'd had an argument.

She was sure it was something she could use.

A week on from their first trip to Herne Hill, she and Rose were baking cookies in Fiona's kitchen. Chocolate chip, using a recipe Fiona had found online. She wasn't a great baker; cooking, in general, bored her. But shop-bought cookies wouldn't do for the next stage of her plan.

When the cookies had almost cooled, Rose went over to grab a couple.

'Just one,' Fiona said.

'What? Why?'

'They're not for us.'

'Then who?'

'Remember my friend? The one in Herne Hill?'

'Uh-huh.' Rose immediately sounded bored.

'Did I tell you that he and I have this thing where we play pranks on each other? No? Well, it's something we've been doing for years, and I owe him one.'

'A prank?'

'Yeah. It's a good one. But I don't want to spoil it for you, so you're just going to have to trust me. Tomorrow, we're going back to see him. That will be fun, won't it?'

'I suppose.'

Fiona smiled. 'Do your part properly and you can have two cookies.'

Rose thought about this for a moment and said, 'Can I have four?'

ω

Now, here they were, back on the street where Max lived. Fiona was holding the tin of cookies, and had promised Rose she could eat however many were left.

'For the prank to work, I'm going to need to get inside his house,' Fiona said. 'When he's not there.'

'Okay.'

Fiona patted her shoulder. 'Good girl. Now, we're going to be practising your acting skills. Here's what I need you to do.'

Fiona had been here two days ago – Monday, when Ethan's record store was shut, so she didn't have Rose – to double-check Max's routine. She had figured out from calling his law firm – using a made-up name, putting on an English accent and pretending to be a prospective client – that he worked from home. Both days she'd watched him, he'd gone out to get lunch at the same time, eating it in the park, on the same bench. Looking very much like a man with a clear conscience; one who slept very well, thank you.

Did he ever think about her? Did Maisie's face loom from the darkness of his subconscious? How about Fiona's face? She didn't know what guilt felt like, but was aware most people suffered from it. Did Max? Did he feel any responsibility at all?

'Ready?' she asked Rose. She knew he would be going out for lunch in five minutes. This was the perfect time.

The girl nodded.

'Don't be nervous. You'll be fine.'

'I'm not nervous.'

Fiona had undergone a trial once, wearing a heart rate monitor and taking a series of tests, both physical and mental. It had showed that, although her heart rate increased during exercise, like any normal person's, it never increased or decreased due to stress, no matter how much she was put under. It increased a little when she was shown the right porn or particular images that were appealing to her. But she didn't feel trepidation like regular people, and when she experienced fear it was practical, sensible – her body making her react to danger because it benefited her, kept her safe from harm.

She wished she had a heart rate monitor to measure Rose's pulse now, to see if she was right about her.

Fiona went a little way along the road, standing behind a tree and peering around it. She watched Rose ring the doorbell then stand straight, shoulders back, the tin of cookies in her hand.

He came to the door and Fiona heard him speak, the drawl of his Essex accent, but couldn't make out the words. She heard Rose's voice next, and knew she would be telling him she was selling cookies to raise money to pay for an operation for her dog. She had a photo of Lola ready if he asked. Fiona knew that Max was a dog lover – it was possibly his only good feature – and that he would be a sucker for a pet-related sob story.

He pointed into the cookie tin, and Fiona knew what question he would be asking. This was another reason why she'd got Rose to bake the cookies with her. Rose shook her head and, satisfied, Max went back inside, presumably to look for some coins. She gave Rose a thumbs up. Rose didn't respond, just stood there primly, arms wrapped around the cookie tin.

God, she was good.

Max reappeared and reached out a hand, passing Rose what looked like a five-pound note. He put his hand in the tin and took a couple of cookies.

Then Rose did what Fiona had instructed her to do. She asked Max if she could pop into his house and use his loo.

Fiona watched his face. He looked taken aback, then alarmed. She knew that, for all his faults, he wasn't interested in little girls. But he would be very aware that the world was quick to be suspicious of men who had any interaction with kids who weren't their own. What would the neighbours say if they saw a twelve-year-old girl going into or coming out of his house?

Fiona thought there was a very good chance he would say no and tell Rose to use the toilets in the park. But, after glancing around, he nodded, then pointed into the house. As Fiona had suspected, he was cautious. He stayed outside, holding the tin of cookies Rose had handed him, while she hurried inside.

Fiona crossed her fingers. Would Rose do her job properly now? While she waited, Fiona watched as Max peered into the cookie tin, glanced at the front door, then sneaked another one out and put it in his pocket.

The greedy sod.

Then he lifted his head. Rose must have called him from inside, just as Fiona had instructed her to do. He hesitated, then went through his front door.

Two minutes later, they both came out. Max shut the front door behind him, and Rose waved at him then walked towards Fiona, going straight past her as instructed. At the same time, Max strode off in the opposite direction, off to get his lunch.

When she was sure he wouldn't look back, Fiona hurried after Rose and caught up with her on the corner.

'How did it go?' she asked immediately. 'Did you get it?'

'Three nine four four.'

His burglar alarm code, which his old-fashioned system required to be entered before leaving the house. Fiona had instructed Rose to watch closely as he punched the code in.

'You've done brilliantly,' Fiona said. 'Now, all we need to do is get his keys, then I'll be able to carry out this prank. Oh, it's going to be—'

She stopped dead. Rose was holding out her hand, palm open. In it sat a pair of keys and, attached to them, a key fob with a label.

'They were hanging on a nail on the wall outside the bathroom.'

Fiona took the keys and read the label. *Front door spare.*

'He just leaves them hanging there?' she said.

'Yeah. Some people are just . . . stupid.'

Fiona grinned and patted Rose's shoulder. 'Oh, you got that right. They're asking to be pranked, aren't they? They're just begging for it.'

11

Thursday was a rare hot day. I stopped off at the supermarket on the way home, deciding it was the perfect day for a barbecue. Along with the veggie sausages and burgers, I picked up a bottle of Pimm's and some lemonade, along with the wine Emma had asked me to get.

The sun was still high in the sky when I set up the barbecue. While it was warming up, I poured Pimm's and lemonade into a jug and fixed myself a glass. Emma had some work to finish off so she sat at the kitchen table on her laptop, the kids still in their rooms, while I prepared the food, cooking the first batch of burgers and sausages.

'It's like being back home,' came a voice from the next garden.

I went over to the fence. Fiona was lying on a sun lounger wearing a bikini. A very small bikini that showed off her lean body. Her skin shone with sunscreen and she was wearing big retro sunglasses. She had, I noticed, a tattoo on her left thigh. An ornate 'M', encircled with barbed wire and flowers. I looked away quickly in case she thought I was staring at her long legs, though I realised I'd already been looking long enough for my glance to be described as lingering.

'Want me to chuck a few prawns on it?' I asked.

'That would be ripper, mate.'

I laughed and she laid a hand on her bare belly, fingers slightly spread. 'The smell is making my stomach rumble.'

I said it without thinking: 'Why don't you join us? I have to warn you, it's all veggie stuff, but there's plenty if you want to come over.'

I told myself this was the neighbourly thing to do, and that, also, I had asked her because I wanted to see how she and Rose interacted. The depressing truth, which I wouldn't admit to myself until later, was that I knew if there was a fifth person there Emma and I wouldn't be able to argue. There was still tension between us following the row the other night.

'You sure?'

'Absolutely. I know Rose will love it if you join us.'

She wriggled into a sitting position. Now I had a full view of her cleavage. I made myself look away.

'I think she might have seen enough of me today,' Fiona said.

So have I.

'I don't know, I think she'd move in with you if she could.'

'That's sweet. But she talks about you loads. "My dad this, my dad that." She's definitely a daddy's girl.'

'Yeah. That's because I'm the one who never says no to her. Emma is— Shit!' Something was burning. I rushed back over to the barbecue. Luckily it was just a charred sausage.

'I'm going to have a shower and put some clothes on,' Fiona called from over the fence. 'If you still want to have me.'

'I do. I mean, you'd be very welcome.'

I was sure I was flushing again. I poured myself another glass of Pimm's, spilling it down my T-shirt, soaking myself.

'Wet T-shirt competition later?' Fiona said. Then she walked away, laughing.

ϖ

Two hours later, the table was piled high with empty plates and leftover food. Before coming over Fiona had changed into a simple summer dress, pale blue and white, and her bare legs were hidden beneath the table. Dylan sat to my left, clutching his belly. Emma sat on my other side. She hadn't eaten or drunk much but had been on good form, not showing any sign that she was worried about Fiona taking over her role as Rose's companion and protector. In fact, she was chatting happily with Fiona, and telling her about some of her more eccentric colleagues, like the guy who insisted on sampling all the dog kibble they sold.

'He always says, "It's just meat and biscuit. You'd eat it if there was an apocalypse."'

'What did you two do today?' I asked Rose, looking from her to Fiona then back again.

'Stayed in and played chess,' she replied.

I had been delighted when Rose had first told me that Fiona was coaching her at chess. I had taught both the kids when they were younger, but neither of them wanted to play these days.

'Did Rose tell you that I won my school's chess tournament when I was eleven?' I said.

'Fiona doesn't care about ancient history,' Rose said.

'Hey!'

But it made everyone laugh, except Dylan, who was still clutching his belly. I'd noticed him sneaking a few looks at Fiona, who was almost glowing after her sunbathing session. Every now and then something would remind me that he was far from a child – that he was a young man who'd been on dates and who no doubt watched all sorts of horrible stuff on his phone. Emma had made me talk to him about how porn was not a realistic depiction of sex, the importance of consent, etc. It had been a painful conversation for both of us, and I'd been relieved when he'd asked me to stop. *They drill all this stuff into us at school.*

So yeah, he was a teenager, fizzing with hormones, but it was still uncomfortable to see the way he looked at Fiona, who was old enough to be his mother.

'Can I go to my room?' he asked.

'Good idea,' I said.

'Are you not feeling well?' Emma asked. She leaned over to lay her palm on his forehead. 'Were you out in the sun today? I hope you put plenty of sunscreen on. And drank enough water.'

'I just ate too much. Or maybe the burgers were undercooked.'

'I thought they were perfect,' Fiona said, and I was surprised to see Dylan's lip curl. He muttered something under his breath.

'You're not too invalided to help carry some plates in,' I said, standing up. 'Come on.'

I handed him a couple of plates and grabbed some myself, then followed him through the patio doors into the kitchen.

'Are you sure you're all right?' I asked him.

'Yeah, I'm fine.'

'You were muttering under your breath at Fiona. You shouldn't be rude to her.' *And you shouldn't stare at her either*, I wanted to say.

'Why, because she gives you free babysitting?'

It was rare for Dylan to be grumpy like this. Recently, anyway. There'd been times at our old house when his moods had been black, but I had always believed that was because of the atmosphere in the house at that time. Since coming here, he'd seemed a lot happier.

'Do you have an issue with Fiona?' I asked.

'Huh? No, of course not. I just . . .'

'Just what?'

'I dunno.'

I sighed. I wasn't going to get anything out of him. 'All right, I'll talk to you later,' I said. I grabbed the dessert, a shop-bought lemon tart, from the fridge and carried it out with me.

On my way back to the garden I swayed a little and realised I was tipsy. I'd lost track of how many times I'd refilled my glass from the jug of Pimm's, although I was the only one drinking it. When I got back to the table I saw that my glass was full again and the jug was more than half empty.

I set the dessert down and addressed Fiona. 'Want some?'

'I'm not sure. Does it have any nuts in it?'

'Oh. Let me check the box.' I went back and fetched the box from the kitchen. 'Sorry. *Not suitable for persons with an allergy to nuts because of manufacturing methods.*'

'Damn. Oh well.'

'You're allergic too?' Rose said to her.

'Uh-huh. I shouldn't have any more anyway. I'm watching my weight. I want to still look good in my bikini.'

She met my eye. I had been going to ask what Rose had meant when she'd said 'too' – who else was allergic to nuts? – but I'm ashamed to admit the bikini comment distracted me.

'Emma told me you got made redundant during the pandemic,' I said, hurriedly changing the subject. 'That must have been hard.'

'It was a relief, actually. My boss was a massive dick.'

'Seems to be a common trait among bosses.'

'Not you, though, I bet.'

'He's way too soft on his staff,' Emma said. 'He hires them according to their taste in music rather than how reliable they are.'

'It's a record shop. They need to have some kind of good taste in music – don't you agree, Fiona?'

She put her hands up. 'Don't get me involved. You know I'm completely ignorant about music.'

'I'll make you a playlist,' I found myself saying. 'If you like.'

'Educate me, you mean?'

'Please don't do that, Dad,' said Rose. 'It's so cringe.'

I turned to see Emma both rolling her eyes and shaking her head at me. The double whammy of marital disgust. 'I'm going inside to check on Dylan and then I have some work to finish off. Rose, I don't want you staying out after dark. I know it's the school holidays, but you still have a bedtime.' She turned to me. 'Can I leave you to clear up?'

'Yeah, of course.'

'Sorry to be unsociable, Fiona. I just need to get this work done.'

Fiona raised her glass. 'Totally understood.'

Emma went inside and I turned to Rose. 'I've got an idea. Shall the three of us have a little chess tournament?'

I went in to find the chess set, which was somewhere in my study. As I reached the top of the stairs, Emma came out of Dylan's room. 'How is he?' I asked.

'He'll be fine. He ate too much, like he said. I think he might have caught the sun too. What are you doing?'

I explained that I was looking for the chess set.

'Don't go all "competitive dad" with Rose,' she said. 'You know how she gets when she loses games.'

Ever since she was a little girl, Rose had hated not winning. She had been known to throw snakes and ladders boards across the room, and had even broken a Switch controller after a frustrating game of Mario Kart.

'I'm sure she's better than me now anyway.'

I headed for my study and Emma said to my back, 'Just try not to embarrass yourself with Fiona.'

'What?'

'Flirting with her in front of Rose.'

Heat entered my cheeks. 'I wasn't flirting.'

'Come off it. You even offered to make her a flipping mixtape.'

'A playlist.'

'Oh yeah, that's completely different.' She folded her arms. 'Don't get me wrong – I'm pretty sure she's not going to want to have an affair with you. I just think it's embarrassing, and hypocritical.'

There were so many things I could have said. Ugly things about how I wouldn't feel tempted to flirt if my own wife showed any interest in me. I could tell her she was being the hypocrite. But perhaps I knew there would be no coming back from either of those statements, so I managed to bite my tongue. After taking a deep breath, I said, 'I have no interest in Fiona.'

'All right. Whatever. I need to get this work done.' She turned to go, then stopped. 'Did you know her former partner died? A woman.'

'Really?'

'Yeah. So I don't think you stand much of a chance with her anyway.'

'Actually . . .'

'What?'

I shook my head. The first time I'd met Fiona she'd told me she used to date a singer in a band. A man. So she'd had some interest in men, in the past at least. I decided to keep this information to myself.

'I'm going to say it again: I wasn't flirting with her. I just want to play chess with her.'

Emma shook her head. 'Don't let Rose stay up too late, okay?'

ϖ

They both beat me: first Fiona, then Rose. They were close games, and I was rusty, but I was amazed how good Rose was.

'Have you secretly been playing online for the last few years?' I asked.

'She's a natural,' Fiona said.

'I think we need to get you into a club,' I said to Rose. 'Maybe enter some tournaments.' I was starting to get visions of Beth in *The Queen's Gambit*. Fame and fortune in the chess world. Rose dedicating her world championship victory to 'my dad, for introducing me to the game'.

'No.'

'What do you mean, *no*?'

'I don't want to join a club. It'll be full of sad nerds.'

'Chess is cool these days, Rose. And I think you've got talent. You could—'

'I'm not interested!'

I sat back, surprised by her outburst. 'Whoa. Okay. I'm sorry, I'm not trying to be a pushy parent. If you just want to play for fun, that's cool.'

I tried not to look too disappointed.

'Can I go to bed?' she asked. 'I'm tired.'

'Of course.' I kissed her cheek and hugged her, which made her wrinkle her nose.

'You smell of that stuff you've been drinking.'

She made her way inside, waving goodnight to Fiona, who said, 'I should go too, but I'll help you clear up first.'

I protested, but half-heartedly. I didn't want to be on my own just yet. I was enjoying Fiona's company, even though I was a little tense, trying to make sure I didn't say or do anything that could be classed as flirting. And while Rose was around, Fiona didn't flirt with me either, unless you counted the light teasing as Rose kicked my arse across the chessboard.

We finished clearing up and I checked the time. Just gone ten. Emma was in bed but I still wasn't tired enough to sleep.

'Will you join me for a final drink?'

'I ought to get back.'

'Go on. Just one.'

She cupped her chin in her hand and leaned across the table, looking right into my eyes. 'All right, all right. But I hope you're not trying to get me drunk.'

I swallowed. 'I . . . Of course not.'

She laughed and I went into the kitchen, my face burning. The Pimm's was all gone so I fetched a chilled bottle of white wine from the fridge. It was dark now but still warm, a soft breeze drifting across the patio where we sat. I could hear grasshoppers on the lawn. The solar-powered fairy lights that Emma had strung up across the decking at the bottom of the garden had flickered on, making the space twinkle like a summer grotto.

'Where did you learn to play?' I asked Fiona. Lola, who had been asleep inside, had come out as if to keep an eye on me, and I reached down to scratch her ear as I spoke.

She shrugged. 'I learned at school, then didn't play for ages until a few years ago.'

'Another person who was influenced by *The Queen's Gambit*?'

She gave me a blank look. Another thing she'd never heard of? 'This is nice wine.'

'It is. It's Australian.'

'All the best things are.' She met my eye again, holding my gaze until I was forced to look away, prickling with desire and shame. An image of Fiona and me kissing had popped into my head. An image that quickly progressed past first base.

I mentally doused myself with cold water. My wife and children were asleep indoors, for God's sake. I forced myself not to look back at Fiona and, instead, watched the lights shining at the bottom of the garden, trying to think of a subject that would pop the tension I was feeling.

It didn't take long to think of one.

'I've been meaning to ask you. Did Tommy from across the road come round to talk to you the other day?'

She frowned. 'The guy whose son had the accident? Yeah. But I didn't answer the door.'

'Oh. Why not?'

'Because I'm a woman on her own and he's a huge bloke who looked severely pissed off. I assume the kids told you about what happened with that kid and his brother when we were walking Lola?'

'Yeah. But only when Tommy turned up looking for someone to blame.'

She sighed. 'I'm sorry about that. I would have spoken to you about it but I assumed they would tell you straight away. I guess they didn't want you to stop them taking Lola out.' A pause. 'Did Tommy mention *me*?'

'He did. But he was trying to point the blame at Dylan.'

'What a dickhead. It was obviously an accident. The tyre blew out, right?'

'That's exactly what I said, but he reckons someone must have put something down that caused the crash. A nail or something. I understand him looking for someone else to blame. It's his way of avoiding the guilt. Unless he's one of those people who never think they're responsible for anything that goes wrong.'

'You think we should all be prepared to face the consequences of our actions?'

'Of course. Don't you?'

Again, she held my gaze. 'Oh, absolutely.' She said it so seriously that I laughed, but she didn't join in. The serious expression remained on her face and she raised her glass. 'To facing the consequences.'

A little confused, I clinked my glass against hers.

'So what made you move here?' she asked.

'Oh, it was just . . . we wanted somewhere bigger. Closer to the countryside. The schools are better out here too.'

She nodded like she understood. 'And the kids were okay about moving?'

'Yeah. Well, they wouldn't have liked the alternative.'

I only realised what I'd said after it was out of my mouth.

'And what was that?' Fiona asked, cocking her head.

It came out before I could stop it. 'If we hadn't moved, we probably wouldn't all be together as a family right now. The kids would only see one of us at weekends – and let's face it, that would probably be me, because children nearly always stay with the mum, don't they? It's usually the dad who moves out, even if he's not the one who did anything wrong.'

I had never spoken to anyone about any of this, apart from the marriage counsellor. And, whether or not I was saying it because of how much I'd drunk, it felt immensely satisfying to get it out there.

Fiona sat there with her eyebrows raised. 'You really don't have to tell me any more.'

But I was on a roll, needing to get the words out, to tell someone.

'Emma got involved with someone else,' I said.

'No way.'

'Yeah. A neighbour, in fact. The guy who lived a few doors down. Michael. *Mike*.' I realised that I wasn't telling this story properly. 'She didn't sleep with him – she swears she didn't, anyway. It was an emotional affair. God, I hate that term. Lots of intense feelings, anyway.'

Fiona waited patiently for me to go on.

'I think that was even worse. Maybe. I mean, at least I don't have images of her naked with him to haunt me, of the two of them in bed. But they had a "special connection".' I made air quotes with my fingers.

Fiona shook her head. 'How did you find out?'

'There was a party on our street and I saw them talking to each other. I could just tell from the way they were looking at each other. The way they kept touching each other's arms. At one point he reached over and pushed a lock of hair out of her eyes. A really intimate gesture, you know? Later, when she was in the bath, I checked her phone. She had her WhatsApp locked with an extra layer of security, and I confronted her. Asked to see her messages. That's when she told me what had been going on.'

'Shit. How did it feel?'

'Like someone had put my guts in a spin dryer. Like my world had cracked apart. All those awful, overwhelming emotions . . . I'm sure you've been through similar yourself. We've all had our hearts beaten up a few times, haven't we?'

Her eyes went far away for a few moments before she nodded.

'Then we had all the long conversations. The tears and the arguments. She said it was because I was distant, that I put all my energy into the shop and my "stupid records", that we had become co-parents rather than friends or lovers. I was almost embarrassed when we started seeing the therapist, because it was all so unoriginal.

'We decided it was something we could get over, but only if she broke all contact with Mike, and to do that we needed to move. So here we are.'

Fiona swirled the wine in her glass. 'I bet you're tempted to check her messages every now and then, aren't you? Just to make sure she's not still in touch with him.'

I must have looked alarmed because she said, 'Oh, sorry. I was just thinking about what *I* would do. Ignore me. I guess I'm not as trusting as you.'

It hadn't even occurred to me that Emma might still be in touch with Mike. She wouldn't be. Would she?

'I need to go home. My bed is calling.' She stood up, and I stood too. The conversations about first Tommy and then Mike had well and truly killed the mood from earlier. Now I felt flat and depressed.

'Need a hug?'

She pulled me into an embrace before I could respond. Her body was surprisingly cool to the touch but it still felt nice. I closed my eyes, and the image of Fiona and me kissing entered my head again.

I pulled away quickly, flustered, hot with self-loathing. I looked at Fiona, wondering if she'd noticed, if she could tell what I'd been picturing, half expecting to see amusement, or maybe even horror. But she looked serious.

'You deserve better,' she said before walking away. 'Let's hope Emma has learned to appreciate what she's got.'

12

Rose was drawn to the taxidermied animals, just as Fiona had known she would be – especially the dogs. There was a collie, a bulldog, a greyhound – just their heads – attached to the wall, like hunting trophies in a country house. They stared out from the display cabinet, eyes glazed, impervious to all the little kids who ran around shrieking and leaving finger marks on the glass.

'What do you think?' Fiona asked.

'It's kind of . . . beautiful?' Rose replied.

Dog heads on a wall. Not gross. Or weird, or scary. *Beautiful.*

That's my girl, Fiona thought.

'*She's* my favourite,' Fiona said, gesturing to the wolf at the centre of the display. The head was so much larger than the surrounding dogs'. 'What big teeth she has.'

'She looks a bit like Albie and Eric's dogs.'

Fiona scoffed. 'Those German shepherds? They're pussycats compared to this lady. Top of the food chain, the wolf. Well, almost.'

'Apart from humans, you mean?'

'Exactly.'

They wandered away from the canine display and browsed the other cabinets. Birds and rodents and lizards. Skeletons and skulls. Herbivores and carnivores. Then they found themselves standing beside the enormous walrus who took pride of place at the centre of the room.

'Look at him,' Fiona said. 'The power, the strength. The apex predator. And do you know what makes him even more powerful? No conscience. No guilt. Do you think he feels bad after tearing a penguin apart? Does he hell. And that's what makes animals superior to most humans. We—'

'Excuse me.'

The voice came out of nowhere, and Fiona looked around before realising she was being spoken to by a small boy. A skinny little thing in glasses, about six years old.

'The walrus isn't an apex predator. Polar bears will attack them. Sometimes they even throw rocks and ice at them.'

Fiona's smile was thin. 'Is that right?'

'Yes, it is. A walrus can weigh seventeen hundred kilos, so its size makes it daunting, but polar bears are more agile.'

Where had this child come from? Rose was staring at him with her nose wrinkled. There was no sign of a parent watching him.

'Where's your mum?' Fiona asked.

'She's over there somewhere.' He waved an arm in the vague direction of the door.

'She's left you unattended? What do you think, Rose? Do you think a mother animal would do that in the wild? Let her cubs wander off on their own to bother other animals?'

Rose laughed, and the boy blinked in confusion.

Fiona bent towards him, dropping her voice to a whisper. 'Your mummy should be more careful. There might be predators *here*.'

There was so much ice in her voice that the boy immediately began to cry. Moments later, a woman came rushing over, her phone in her hand. As Fiona had suspected, she had been too busy staring at her screen to keep an eye on her offspring, although she'd tuned in to the sound of his distress impressively quickly.

'What's the matter, darling?' she asked, crouching and pulling the boy against her chest.

He was sobbing too hard to answer.

'He thought he'd lost you,' Fiona said. 'You know, you shouldn't let your kids go off on their own. Something terrible could happen. There are dangerous people around. How would you feel if your little professor here disappeared?'

The mother stared at her, mouth hanging open, while the boy continued to snivel.

'Come on, Rose,' said Fiona, and she led her away before the woman recovered.

Out in the garden, beneath an overcast sky, Fiona and Rose sat at a trestle table eating a mid-morning snack from the café. Fiona was still a little hungover from last night. It was going to take her a while to get used to alcohol again; she'd only drunk it to keep Ethan company.

It had been an illuminating evening. Emma and her 'emotional affair'. Useful information. And Ethan was so desperate, so beaten down, that it was all going to be even easier than she'd anticipated. She knew it would take very little to get him exactly where she wanted him.

Oh, how he was going to regret opening up to her. By the time she was finished, he was going to regret everything.

'Hello? Fiona?'

She realised Rose was talking to her. 'Sorry. I was miles away. What were you saying?'

'Just that I saw that boy and his mum leaving. He was still crying.' She dropped her voice. 'You were so mean to him.'

'Was I?'

'Yeah. Like . . . a baddie from a film.'

'Really? Which one? Cruella? Miss Trunchbull?'

'Like one of *The Witches*.'

'From the Roald Dahl book? He should be grateful I didn't turn him into a mouse.'

Rose giggled. Her eyes were wide. 'You don't hate children, though, do you?'

'Only annoying, swotty ones.' Fiona glanced towards the exit. 'He'll be okay. Maybe he'll think twice about approaching strangers now. I've done him a favour. Not to mention all those strangers.'

Rose was staring at her.

'Why do you think I brought you here, Rose?' Fiona asked.

'I don't know. To look at the dog heads?'

'Ha, yes. But why?'

Rose shook her head.

'Okay, well, think about it. You're a very clever girl, and I know you'll figure it out.' She leaned forward. 'You're not just clever, Rose, you're special. Special like me.'

Fiona got up from the table and gathered up their rubbish, carrying it over to the bin. When she came back, she said, 'Have you thought of the question you want to ask me yet?'

'I'm saving it,' Rose replied.

ϖ

They left the museum grounds and Fiona consulted the Transport for London app on her phone. The bus stop they needed was down the hill, near the train station.

'Where are we going now?' Rose asked.

'Back to Herne Hill.'

'You mean, it's prank time?'

'It sure is.'

They got on the bus and went up to the top deck. She was finding it hard not to let her excitement show, which was probably why she'd allowed herself to get carried away with the little professor.

After all this time, all the planning in prison, the groundwork she'd laid.

'Let's run through it again,' Fiona said, keeping her voice low so the other people on the bus couldn't hear her. She took the sandwich bag containing the cookies out of her bag, gave it to Rose, then went over what she wanted her to do. This time Fiona had baked the cookies on her own, though she'd only kept a couple and had put all the others straight in the dustbin outside. She'd scrubbed all the surfaces and thrown out the bowl and spatula she'd used.

'I don't understand why you needed his keys,' Rose said.

It was still too soon to tell Rose everything, so she was sticking with the story about this being a prank.

'Oh, I didn't need them in the end,' she lied. 'I decided that prank was too complicated and unfunny. This one is better.'

'So . . . after he tastes the cookie and realises it's full of chilies, you're going to jump out from behind the tree and yell "Got you!"?'

'Something like that.'

'It's not the best prank in the world ever, is it? You could have, I don't know, put farting powder in them.'

Fiona laughed. 'I'm not sure farting powder exists, Rose.'

She tingled with anticipation, like a woman who was about to be reunited with her lover after a long absence; a kid who'd been waiting for Christmas since December 26th.

The bus stopped by the park and she hurried down the steep stairs, with Rose following, striding towards the bench in the quiet corner of the park where Max always sat and ate his lunch. If he wasn't there, if for some reason his routine had changed, she would just have to come back another day – but she needn't have worried, because there he was. On the bench beneath the cloudy sky, smart top, scruffy bottoms, finishing his lunch while looking at his phone. His backpack sat beside him.

'Okay,' Fiona said. 'You know what to do. Right?'

Rose nodded.

'Oh, this is going to be so good.' Taking a look around to ensure no one was coming, Fiona slipped behind a broad-trunked tree and watched Rose trot over to the bench. Max looked up, recognition dawning. Recognition but no suspicion, which was just what she'd expected. He was the kind of man who breezed through life believing everything was going to work out for him. He'd never known any different.

She couldn't hear what they were saying, but, just as she had outside Max's house, she watched his lips move as Rose spoke to him, holding up the sandwich bag containing the two new cookies.

Rose would be following the script Fiona had drilled into her. For the prank.

Did you like the cookies? I made some more and have a couple left over.

He nodded, and Rose handed the bag to him.

I think these ones are better. I used more chocolate. What do you think?

Encouraging him to try them right there, right then. That was important, because Fiona needed to know it had worked. He had just eaten lunch, but he was a man who always had room for dessert – and here was this sweet, familiar girl, smiling at him.

He examined the bag and plucked out a cookie, which he lifted to his lips. Fiona felt a cord tighten in her belly. This was it. She didn't believe in ghosts or the afterlife, thought both Heaven and Hell were stupid concepts, but she liked to imagine that Maisie was beside her to witness this. Revenge. *Just deserts.*

Rose was unaware what would happen when he took a bite, expecting him to do nothing more than spit it out and start begging for water, his mouth burning from the chilies Fiona had told her were inside the cookie. At that point, Rose believed, Fiona would spring out, laughing and shouting, 'Surprise!'

He took a bite. Chewed. Swallowed.

Took another bite.

He hadn't detected the taste of nuts, which she had disguised with a lot of sugar and cinnamon.

Rose turned her head to look back at Fiona, frowning with confusion. Why hadn't he reacted to the chilies? Fiona shook her head, silently telling her to turn around, but it was too late. Max had followed Rose's gaze.

He saw Fiona.

The expression on his face was one she wished she could frame. The shock. The horror. She stepped out from behind the tree, Rose looking from her to Max then back again, thoroughly confused. But, right now, Fiona didn't care about the girl's reaction. She was too busy watching Max.

One hand went to his throat. He put the other hand in his pocket and took out the remaining cookie in the transparent plastic bag. He held it up and stared at it, then threw it to the ground. Almost in the same motion, he grabbed his backpack and tore open the front compartment.

Rose came over to Fiona, asking what was going on, but Fiona ignored her. She couldn't take her eyes off Max. He was frantically digging through the rucksack, pulling out envelopes and biros and notebooks, chucking everything on to the grass as he searched for the device he needed so desperately.

His EpiPen.

He held the backpack up, tipping it upside down, shaking out the remaining contents.

Then he looked around, seeking help. His face was pink. He clutched at his throat, his mouth opening and closing, trying to speak, making a horrible gasping, choking noise.

He fell on to his knees and suddenly there were two people running towards him, a man and woman who had seen him collapse. Fiona quickly joined them, ordering Rose to stay back.

Max was lying on the path now, holding his throat, unable to speak. The woman crouched beside him, talking to him, while her male companion called 999. Max tried to suck in air, his eyes bulging, and he tried to speak, to answer the woman's questions, but no air could go in or out.

He pointed a finger at Fiona, and for a second she thought he was going to manage to form a word or two, but then his hand flopped and he gave up. She hoped that among his panic and fear there was some room for regret. For the realisation that he should never have been arrogant. Should never have relaxed.

When the man and woman weren't looking – the man was shouting into his phone, demanding to know where the ambulance was – Fiona scooped up the bag with the cookie he had dropped and slipped it into her pocket. Then she went back to Rose, pulling her into an embrace.

'Don't look, sweetheart,' she said in a loud voice, for the benefit of the couple who were trying to help Max, and for others who had started to gather around. The rubberneckers, arriving on the scene when it was too late to do anything.

She wanted to say something else. She wanted to tell her, *Some people are predators, Rosie, and some people are prey.* But the girl wasn't ready. Not quite yet.

So instead she urged Rose not to say anything, whispered to her that she needed to keep quiet. And she pressed Rose's face against her own damp torso as she watched the show.

As the first person on her list stopped breathing.

PART TWO

13

Fiona sat with the other visitors, waiting to be called. It was strange to be back at HMP Franklin Grange, the women's prison in Shropshire where she had spent the final part of her sentence. Weird to be on this side of the heavy doors that separated inmates from those who had come to see them. Not that she'd received any visits the whole time she'd been inside, because Maisie had been her only friend. There was no one else.

Until Lucy, that was. But Lucy was inside too, serving a whole life sentence. On top of that, Fiona wasn't sure if 'friendship' was the right term for what she and Lucy Newton had. It was a connection. A likeness. A recognition that they were both different from other people.

Different. Special. *Better.*

They were the apex. And they had recognised that in each other as soon as they met.

An officer opened the door and the visitors filed through, Fiona among them. There were a few husbands and boyfriends. Some mums. Girlfriends and sisters. Lots of hugs, which were allowed here, in this open prison.

Fiona and Lucy didn't hug. In fact, Lucy wore a murderous scowl, and when Fiona sat opposite her, Lucy's first words were:

'You took your time.'

Lucy had often been described as Amazonian. Six foot tall, broad shoulders, powerful-looking. Her blonde hair was tied back in a ponytail, her face free of make-up and, because she so rarely smiled or showed much in the way of expression, remarkably free of lines. Who needed Botox when you were a psychopath?

'Hi Lucy. Lovely to see you too.'

'It's been nearly two years since you got out.'

'I know. That's how long it took for them to give me permission to visit. Apparently it's unusual for ex-cons to want to go back and see their old cellmates, if you can believe that.' She chuckled. 'I only got the letter giving me the go-ahead last week.' Lucy barely seemed appeased by this. 'Anyway, I think the time has flown by.'

'Not for me.'

'I guess time moves faster on the outside. But you look well. And at least you-know-who isn't around anymore, annoying you.'

Lucy's frown lessened a tiny bit at the memory of what they'd done, removing an annoying woman who had seen herself as the prison's queen bee. On the eve of Fiona's release, Lucy had decided to ruin the party. She and Fiona had lured her outside that night, to a spot where the women had been working during the day. They'd killed her, Lucy smashing her skull in with a brick, and then framed one of the less intelligent inmates. It had been delicious fun, and more proof, to Fiona, that what Maisie had taught her was true: that it was easier to live the life you wanted if you paired up with someone else, their own twist on the old maxim that 'the world is built for two'. Built for two to wreak havoc. To prey on the weak. To get the things you wanted.

Lucy looked around, speaking softly so none of the officers could hear her. 'There were *some* repercussions. They brought in a new governor, fired a few people, and half the old staff got transferred elsewhere. Security's been tightened up.'

'But no one suspects you of anything?'

'I'm sure some of the other women have a good idea what happened, but they all know what a mistake it would be if they allowed their tongues to wag.'

'They'd get cut out.'

'Exactly.'

Even among apex predators there were hierarchies. One polar bear would always be bigger and fiercer than the others, and – among all the women Fiona had met who were like them – Lucy Newton was that bear. After getting out of Franklin Grange, Fiona had read up on Lucy's history. She and her former husband, Chris, had once lived the life of a pair of spiders, crouched beneath a web into which they would lure and trap flies, getting their kicks from tormenting their prey. At the same time, Lucy was working her way through the elderly residents of the nursing home where she worked, Orchard House, murdering them according to her whims. A dark angel, as the press had called her.

It had been a good life for Lucy and her partner-in-evil, until it all went wrong. Now Chris was dead and Lucy was in prison serving a whole life sentence. Fiona had learned in prison that Lucy had got out on appeal – a technicality – only to wind up back in jail after a revenge scheme that went wrong. Remembering this biographical detail gave Fiona pause. Might her own revenge schemes backfire? But she quickly dismissed her fears. She was cleverer than that.

And besides, the desire for vengeance burned so hot that nothing could divert her from that path. It was a craving that needed to be fed.

'Let's not talk about this place,' Lucy said, leaning forward. 'It's boring. Tell me what's happening out there. You look completely different. I'm not sure about the blonde. It looks better on me.'

'I think it suits me. Don't you think I look hot? My new neighbour does.'

Lucy grunted. 'How's it all going?'

Fiona smiled. 'It's going great. You know I had three names on my list? The first one was dealt with last week.'

Lucy's eyes glinted. 'Which one?'

They were talking very quietly now, faces close, their words further cloaked by the babble of conversation around them. 'The lawyer.'

'Perfect. How did you do it?'

'Did I tell you about his peanut allergy?'

Lucy rubbed her hands together. 'Love it. Rule number one: use their weakness against them – although, don't you have a nut allergy too?'

'That's how I knew about his. When I was arrested, the police offered me lunch and I told them about my allergy, and I guess he wanted me to think we had something in common. Told me he'd almost died when he was kid after eating a tiny morsel of peanut butter. But yes, I had to be ultra-careful baking the cookies. I don't even like having nuts in my house.'

Lucy's eyes sparkled 'Did you watch him die? Tell me.' She was clearly in need of vicarious thrills.

'First, I need to tell you about Rose. My neighbour's twelve-year-old daughter.' She dropped her voice even further. 'I'm pretty sure she's like us, Lucy.'

Lucy's eyebrows lifted with surprise. 'How sure?'

Fiona glanced around before she spoke. She was, in a way, reluctant to share this information with Lucy. Rose was a rare, precious discovery. But she couldn't resist showing off.

'I've been testing her. Playing games, describing hypothetical situations. She reminds me so much of myself at her age. I remember you telling me that your great-aunt recognised it in you, and was able to offer advice and warnings.'

'She was my mentor.'

'Yep, and I'm hers – and she's, well, my little helper. My apprentice. We both get something out of it.'

'So you've told her? Explained everything to her?'

'No, not yet. I want to see how much she figures out on her own.'

Lucy stroked her chin. 'Be careful, Fiona. If she freaks out and starts telling tales . . .'

'She won't.'

'Children are not reliable. Not fully formed. It sounds to me like you'll be taking unnecessary risks if you reveal yourself to this girl.'

Fiona was irritated. She wanted Lucy to tell her how clever she was – finding Rose – not to start issuing warnings. Lucy thought she was so superior, but who was the one who was going to die in prison? Fiona found she didn't want to talk about Rose anymore, except to explain the role she had played so far. Lucy would surely be impressed by that story. Would get the vicarious thrill she sought.

'Let me tell you about Max.'

She explained how she had set everything up. She had decided a long time ago how she was going to kill him, but she knew that Max carried an EpiPen with him everywhere he went, just as she did. Both times she had seen him leave his house he had been carrying a little backpack. The EpiPen was almost certainly in there, she'd deduced.

To remove the pen from the backpack, she'd known she needed to get into his house, but that he had a burglar alarm. Keys would be extremely helpful too. This was where Rose had proven to be so useful, and the cookie idea had been a stroke of genius, even if Fiona did say so herself. Rose using her initiative and getting hold of the keys before she'd even had to ask had made everything even easier.

Fiona had gone back to Herne Hill, to Max's street, in the dead of night and used the keys to open his front door, quickly disabling the alarm before it woke him up. Of course, there had been a few moments of tension when she feared he might have heard the front door or detected the shift in atmosphere as she let herself in. But she had seen the empties in the recycling bin outside and knew he enjoyed a drink before bed. He didn't wake up, and she was easily able to remove his EpiPen.

'Did anyone see the girl give him the cookies?' Lucy asked.

'No. Some people came along when he was dying, but no one saw us before that, I'm quite sure. I really don't think the police are going to be searching for the source of the cookies. A guy with a nut allergy gets complacent, buys some cookies thinking there are no nuts in them . . . I'm certain the coroner will rule it an accident.'

'Won't they wonder why his EpiPen wasn't in his rucksack?'

Fiona shrugged. 'It's very common for people with allergies to forget to take their pen with them. You only have to google it to see how often it happens.'

'How's the girl?' Lucy asked. 'I mean, I assume she doesn't know you intended to kill him?'

'No. She thinks it was an accident.'

She was going to tell Lucy her plan for the remaining two people on her list, but visiting time was almost up and Lucy was beginning to look restless and bored. Fiona braced herself, because she knew there was another topic Lucy would want to discuss.

She didn't disappoint.

'What have you done for me since you got out? I've been waiting all this time for news.'

She was talking about Jamie and Kirsty, Lucy's nemeses. The flies who had fought back against the spiders. The way Lucy described them, they were a sappy pair of weaklings, but somehow they were responsible for Lucy being in prison. She was obsessed with them, and when Fiona was in prison she had promised Lucy she would target them on Lucy's behalf – make their lives miserable, maybe even do something to their daughter.

It was easy to make promises inside prison, though. As soon as she'd got out, her enthusiasm for the project had waned. She didn't know these people. They'd never done anything to her. She had her own revenge scheme to think about. Huge amounts of admin and planning. All the work to get her own life back on track. Change her name, buy a house, do all the things she needed to do to keep her probation officer happy for the first year and a half she was out.

'I haven't had time to do anything about them yet.'

'What?' Lucy's eyes flashed with anger.

Fiona didn't want to enrage Lucy so she said, 'I went by their place, took a look at them. Saw them go out for a walk with their daughter. They don't look like they're going anywhere, so there's plenty of time. Once I've finished with—'

'No! That could take forever. And what if you get caught when you're feeding people poisonous cookies or whatever you're planning next? Then there'll be nobody to get them back for me.'

'I'm not going to get caught.'

'Fiona, I can't wait. You know how hard it is being stuck in here for the rest of my life, knowing those two are walking around enjoying their lives? I need you to destroy them. The daughter. If she went missing, her body never found . . . That would be perfect.'

Fiona sighed, irritated. 'All right, all right, I'll think about it. I'll figure something out.'

'You do that. Now, tell me your address. I'm going to have someone drop something off.'

'What?'

'Something that allows us to communicate.'

Reluctantly, Fiona told her. Then it was time to leave. Everyone was getting up, saying their goodbyes. Fiona stood and Lucy stood too.

'Make sure you report back to me,' Lucy said. 'Oh, and Fiona? This child. The neighbour. Be careful.'

14

Monday morning, I found Rose in her bedroom, playing with her Barbies on the floor. It surprised me that she still played with dolls and I had been expecting her to lose interest for ages, especially as she was constantly reminding me that she was no longer a baby. When we'd moved into this house she'd insisted on having neutral, 'grown-up' colours in her bedroom: white and cream rather than the pink and purple she'd preferred in our old place. Most of her cuddly toys and her My Little Pony collection had gone straight to a charity shop. She had stopped watching Nickelodeon and TV shows about mermaids, and now preferred old sitcoms like *Friends*, though I noticed she watched it with a serious face, like it was a documentary about the past rather than a comedy.

Her Barbie dolls were the only accessories she had kept from her childhood, and she didn't want me to read her bedtime stories anymore. As Emma always reminded me, you had to let them grow up. Rose would be entering puberty soon. She'd be a teenager before long. If popular wisdom was to be believed, that was when the true nightmare would begin.

The Ken doll was lying on his back, Rose making him writhe around, choking noises coming from his throat. One of her Barbies was standing over him, watching.

In her Barbie voice – which had taken on a bizarre Cockney twang – Rose said, 'What's wrong? Ken?'

In return, the Ken made more choking sounds, then lay still.

Her Barbie doll sobbed and threw herself on to the carpet. 'Oh Ken, Ken.'

'Rose?'

She whirled around. 'Don't do that! You made me jump!'

'Sorry, sweetheart. Are you okay? It looks like poor old Ken here just kicked the bucket.'

I picked him up and she snatched him from me, but didn't say anything.

'What was wrong with him?' I asked.

She turned him over in her hands for a little while before saying, 'He had an allergy. An aphyl . . . apyhlantic . . . anaflac . . .'

'Anaphylactic shock?'

She nodded.

'Was he stung by a bee or something?'

'He ate a peanut. And he couldn't find his special pen.'

'His EpiPen.' I paused. 'Do you know someone who's allergic to peanuts? Oh wait, Fiona is, isn't she?' She had mentioned it at the barbecue. 'Are you worried about her?'

'Why would I be? Fiona is careful, and she always carries an EpiPen.'

'That's good.'

'But the man in the park didn't.'

I looked at her. 'What man?'

She was still turning Ken over in her hands. 'On Friday, me and Fiona went to Brockwell Park and we saw a man eat a cookie then fall over, and then he died.'

I was too shocked to speak for a moment. 'You . . . saw this happen?'

She nodded, her expression deadly serious.

'Oh, Rose. How much . . . I mean, you actually saw him . . . die?'

'Yeah. His face went totally red and he held his neck like this and then he couldn't breathe anymore.' As she spoke she put her hands around her own windpipe.

Horrified, I thought back to Friday evening. When I'd got home from work Rose had already been back for a couple of hours and she had seemed completely fine. Maybe a little quiet, but I had assumed that was because it was the end of the week and she was tired.

'Did you tell Mum about this?'

'No. I was going to tell her, but when I got home she was on the phone for ages, and then I forgot.'

'You *forgot*?'

She shrugged.

'Really? It doesn't seem like the kind of thing that would slip your mind. Rose, you promised us, if anything happened while you were out with Fiona . . .'

'I forgot, okay?!'

She had form for this. When she was eight, her pet goldfish had died, and when Emma noticed, finding Nemo floating in his tank, Rose had said, 'Oh yes, he died a few days ago and I forgot to tell you.'

There had been other incidents too, like when she was in the last year of primary school and her best friend, Jasmine, had decided she didn't want to be Rose's friend anymore. For months, Rose had acted as if everything was normal until a teacher told us he was concerned, as he'd seen Rose standing on her own in the playground every day, while her old friendship group ignored her. Rose said she had forgotten to tell us she and Jasmine had fallen out. When Emma phoned Jasmine's mum to see if we could engineer a reconciliation, Jasmine's mum said that Jasmine had started crying when she asked her about it but wouldn't give any details. It was so close to the end of primary school that we'd let it go, aware that kids fell out all the time and thinking Rose would make a new set of friends at secondary school. But it was another example of Rose forgetting to tell us important stuff.

What was more shocking to me now was that *Fiona* hadn't told us. Or had she told Emma, who was at work now? Things had been tense between Emma and me since the Pulp gig and especially the barbecue. There was a thick atmosphere that hung inside the house like fog, and I had been avoiding her, spending the evenings in my 'man cave', listening to music, continuing to catalogue my collection. Emma, meanwhile, would sit downstairs with a bottle of wine watching true crime documentaries. Lola would wander back and forth between us, as if trying to broker peace. But after the last year of trying to save my marriage, I was tired of hearing myself say, 'Can we talk?' I wanted Emma to come to me. So poor Lola's efforts went unrewarded.

There was another thing, something I was ashamed to admit even to myself. I kept thinking about Fiona. Picturing her leaning towards me over the table. Imagining her kissing me.

Wondering what it would be like to be with her instead of Emma.

I said to Rose, 'Come down for breakfast and we can talk about this afterwards. I'll make you scrambled eggs.'

She promised to come down when it was ready. Downstairs, I found Dylan in the kitchen, his head inside the fridge, complaining there was nothing to eat, and pulled him aside while the pan was warming up. 'Did you know anything about Rose seeing a guy die the other day?'

'She saw someone *die*? Whoa. You mean, when she was with Fiona?'

'Yes.' I explained what Rose had told me.

'Is she upset?'

'I can't really tell.'

'I bet she isn't.' He exhaled sharply through his nose. 'Rose is such a weirdo.'

I was shocked to hear this from him. 'What makes you say that?'

'Dunno. Just . . . Yesterday she was telling me about this museum Fiona took her to, and all these decapitated dog heads she saw.'

'The Horniman? I took you there when you were little. You had nightmares afterwards.'

'Yeah? Well, Rose loved it. She was going on about wolves and apex predators. She loves horror movies too. Fiona lets her watch them. She probably enjoyed seeing a dead body.'

'Dylan! That's a terrible thing to say.'

He shrugged and left the room.

I made the scrambled eggs on toast and called Rose down, then texted Emma.

> *Did you know about Rose seeing some guy go into anaphylactic shock in the park on Friday?*

The reply came back immediately. *WTF? No! What happened?!*

> *The guy died and Rose saw it. She said she forgot to mention it!*

Three dots appeared, disappeared, then reappeared again. *Sorry, I have to go into a meeting but we can talk to her later.*

I went over to the kitchen table, where Rose was sitting. She had put her headphones on and was watching videos on her phone while she ate.

I pointed at my head, gesturing for her to take the headphones off. 'I'm popping next door to see Fiona.'

I wanted to know why she hadn't told us about the dead man.

'She's not in. She's gone to see an old friend. Going to be out all day, she said.'

I sat down beside her. 'Dylan said something about you watching horror movies.'

Her brows furrowed. 'He's such a snitch.' A pause. 'It was only one.'

'Rose, you're too young to watch scary films. Which one was it?'

'It was . . .' She hesitated. '*M3GAN*. It's not even a proper horror. It's for kids.'

'The one about the robot doll?'

'Yeah, all my friends have watched it. It's all over TikTok.'

I looked it up on my phone. 'Rose, it's a fifteen. You're not allowed to watch that.'

'You told me you watched loads of horror films when you were a kid. You said you saw *Nightmare on Elm Street* when you were twelve.'

'Yes, and it scared the crap out of me! I didn't sleep for two weeks. Did Fiona let you watch this movie?'

She pressed her lips together.

'I don't want you watching any more horror films, okay? If there's a movie you want to watch, come and talk to me or Mum and we'll make a decision.'

She exhaled loudly. 'Can I go now?'

'Sure. But Rose – what you saw on Friday in the park. Are you okay? How are you feeling about it?'

She looked me straight in the eye. 'It was horrible to see and shocking, and I hope I never have to see anything like that again. But I'm fine. You don't need to worry about me, Dad.'

She got up and left the room, leaving me wondering whether I'd just listened to a prepared speech.

15

Fiona was about to step into the shower, keen to wash the day from her skin – the prison, the train, all the people she'd been around; dust and dead skin – when the doorbell rang.

She checked the Ring app on her phone and, seeing that her caller was Ethan, experienced something rare: a flutter of fear in her belly. What if Rose had told tales? Spilled the beans about the cookies and the visits to Max's house?

No – then it would be the police calling.

If she believed Rose was going to betray her, she would have already run.

Killed her and then run.

She put her robe on, leaving it loose around the neck, ensuring a little flesh was on display, and headed down to the front door, flashing back to Friday and the immediate aftermath of Max's death.

ϖ

'I don't understand,' Rose said. 'You told me it was a prank.'

Fiona had brought her home, the two of them hardly speaking on the way back, Fiona telling the girl to save it until they were somewhere private. She had always known this would be the first big test. How would Rose react?

Now she would find out.

'Are you upset?' Fiona asked. 'I mean, do you feel sad about what you saw? About Max dying? Look inside yourself and be honest.'

Rose, who was sitting cross-legged on the rug in Fiona's living room, shifted around, clearly made uncomfortable by this question.

'I don't know,' Rose said after one of her customary pauses. 'I don't know how I feel.'

Fiona had expected that. She needed to give Rose permission to tell her truth. 'Let me tell you a story,' she said. 'Don't roll your eyes.'

'Sorry.'

'It's not a boring story, I promise. When I was your age, I lived near a beach and used to go there all the time with my mother, some of her friends and their children. I liked swimming and was really good at it. People used to joke that I'd been a dolphin in a previous life, though I preferred to think I'd been a shark.'

She could see she was losing Rose already, so hurried the story on. 'One day, when I was almost twelve, I went swimming with this girl called Sienna. She was a little bit younger than me, but a real show-off. Always bragging about how great she was at sport, how rich her dad was, blah blah. She drove me nuts.'

'She sounds a bit like Jasmine,' Rose said. 'My old best friend.'

'Yeah. An annoying little cow, huh?'

Rose laughed.

'Sienna was *the* most annoying girl, and this day at the beach she was going on and on about how she had won all the medals at her swimming gala and could swim further and faster than anyone else. So I challenged her. When our mums were busy chatting, I told Sienna I was going to swim out to this buoy that was, like, two hundred metres out, maybe more. I could see she was sceptical, but she couldn't bear the idea that I was better than her, so she followed me.'

Rose was hooked now, waiting to see what would happen.

'I'm sure she thought I would stop and turn back before we reached the buoy, but we kept going. I just wanted to prove I was better than her. I didn't know she'd get a cramp. That she'd go under. I didn't even notice at first. She was behind me and I was exhilarated, knowing I was going to beat her to the buoy and shut her up. When I turned back and couldn't see her I was confused. Then I saw her, thrashing in the water. Going under. By the time I got to her, it was too late.'

'She drowned?'

Fiona nodded. 'There was a terrible hoo-ha about it. Sienna's mum was screaming. My mum was totally freaking out. The lifeguards hadn't spotted us until it was too late. They hauled me out and wrapped me in a silver blanket even though I was totally fine. Then one of the lifeguards carried Sienna out, limp in his arms, and her mother howled. I can still hear it. And do you want to know how I felt, Rose?'

Rose's voice was hushed. 'Yes.'

'Confused. I didn't understand why everyone was so upset. Sienna was so freaking annoying. Surely the world was a better place without her in it? Watching the reactions of all the other people, seeing their distress, was fascinating to me. All the tears, the hysteria. I was like, get a grip. The only part that worried me was that I might get the blame, but I had already figured out I should tell them that swimming to the buoy had been Sienna's idea, not mine. I got treated like I was strong and precious, and like my parents were so lucky. The only person who didn't seem thrilled by my survival was Sienna's mum. She resented me. But no one ever blamed me. See, it wasn't a boring story, was it?'

'No.'

'Now, back to my question: how did you feel watching Max die?'

Fiona could see Rose's brain working as she struggled to articulate it. 'I was . . . surprised, because I thought he was going to spit the cookie out and complain it was hot. Confused too, that he didn't have his EpiPen. And I was worried he would tell people I had given him the cookie.'

'I knew you'd be worried. But did you feel upset?'

'I . . .'

'Come on, Rose. You can be honest with me like I was just honest with you. I'm not going to judge you. I promise.'

Rose fidgeted and shifted her position on the rug. Then, finally, she admitted it: 'I guess I felt . . . curious? Wondering why it had happened? Once I realised it was because of his allergy, I didn't understand it. You told me there weren't any nuts in our cookies.'

Fiona had expected all this. Numbness. A lack of empathy. Cold, scientific curiosity overwhelming emotion. But it was still too early to tell Rose everything.

'I know. I didn't understand it at first either. But here's the thing: I told you a little lie.'

'A lie?'

'Yes. Those cookies. I didn't make them. I bought them from a bakery. I was feeling too lazy to bake and, well, I didn't want you to know that. I brought them home from the bakery and rubbed chilies on them, for the prank, thinking it would be enough, but I guess it must have come off in the bag or I didn't put enough on . . . I don't know.'

Fiona glanced up at Rose. Was she buying this? She didn't want her to believe it entirely. She wanted her to figure it out herself – with Fiona still having plausible deniability, just in case Rose didn't react the way Fiona thought she would.

'So . . . there were nuts in the cookies you bought?'

'There must have been. Or maybe they'd just been baked in a kitchen where there were nuts around. It only takes a tiny amount. Thank God I didn't eat any myself, eh?'

Rose furrowed her brow. Fiona could see her struggling, trying to figure out whether to believe this. She would be asking herself, *Why would Fiona lie?* Because if Fiona was lying, didn't that mean she had intended to kill Max?

Fiona needed that to remain a question in Rose's mind.

'The problem,' Fiona said, 'is that if anyone knows that we gave Max that cookie, we're going to get asked a lot of questions. Difficult questions.'

'Like . . . they might think we did it on purpose?'

'Exactly. The police might not believe it was supposed to be a harmless prank. I'll get into a lot of trouble.' She flicked her eyes towards Rose. 'We'll both get into a lot of trouble.'

'Me?'

'I'm afraid so. I mean, it was you who actually gave him the cookie that killed him.'

Now Rose looked scared. She didn't seem to care that Max was dead. But she clearly did care about getting the blame for it.

'It's okay, though,' Fiona said. 'Nobody saw us with the cookies. You just need to be careful not to tell your mum and dad. Because even if they say it was all my fault . . . well, even in the best-case scenario – where I don't get charged with murder or manslaughter – they won't let us see each other again.'

Rose had gone pale. 'That would be the worst thing ever.'

'I agree.'

They sat in silence, listening to Karma purring from her bed in the corner.

'So whatever you do, don't tell anyone we gave Max those cookies, okay? Promise?'

Rose nodded, then spoke very softly. 'I promise.'

ꙍ

She opened the door to Ethan. It was still bright outside, pink-tinged clouds stretching languorously towards the horizon. It was the first time she had seen him since the barbecue, forcing herself to flirt with him that evening when she would rather have pushed his face on to the hot grill.

She conjured a smile from her repertoire.

'Hi Ethan.'

He cleared his throat. 'Can I have a word?'

'I was about to get in the shower,' she said, letting the words linger, noticing how his eyes strayed to the open neck of her robe. Her clavicle. A hint of cleavage. So predictable and easy. 'Is it urgent?'

He tore his eyes from her flesh. 'It's kind of urgent, if you don't mind.'

'Of course.'

She gestured for him to follow her inside, taking him into the kitchen.

'What's the problem?'

'Rose told me she saw a man die in the park on Friday. Anaphylactic shock.'

Fiona let that sink in. So Rose hadn't kept the whole secret. But was that *all* she'd said? Should she expect the flash of blue lights next, the wail of sirens? Was she going to have to make a quick getaway? Would Ethan try to stop her? Her eyes flicked towards the block of knives on the counter.

'Is it true?' Ethan was asking.

She cleared her throat. 'Ah. Yes. In Brockwell Park.' Time to bring out the actress. Act concerned. Use the soft voice. Be maternal, not sexy. She pulled the robe tighter around her upper half. 'How is she doing?'

'She seems fine. But the thing is, I only know about it because I found her re-enacting it with her Barbies. Why didn't you tell me or Emma?'

'I was going to talk to you tomorrow when I picked Rose up.'

'You didn't think it was important enough to inform us straight away?'

This was interesting. He wasn't flirting with her now. His only concern seemed to be his daughter's well-being. 'I had to visit an old friend in Shropshire. Anyway, I assumed Rose would tell you, and that if you had any questions you'd come round, like you are now, or phone me. What exactly did Rose say?'

He spelled it out and Fiona inwardly breathed a sigh of relief. There was no hint that she'd revealed where the cookies had come from.

'I looked it up online,' Ethan said. 'It was in the south London papers. It says police are looking for witnesses. Did you speak to them already?'

She considered saying yes but wasn't sure what follow-up questions he might have. But what if he contacted the police himself, volunteering his daughter as a witness? She really didn't want that to happen.

'No. I didn't realise they needed witnesses because it was obviously an unfortunate accident. I'll call them tomorrow. Do you . . . want me to mention Rose? It might be quite distressing for her, having to talk to the police about it.'

Now he seemed unsure. 'I don't know. Can you tell me what happened from your point of view?'

She parroted what he'd said back to him. Rose's version of the story. No mention of Rose giving Max the cookies. Being careful not to use Max's name or give away that she knew him.

'How did you know he died of anaphylactic shock? How did you recognise it?'

'I told you I'm allergic myself, didn't I? I've imagined it happening, watched loads of videos about it. I recognise it when I see it.'

'And you couldn't have helped him? With your own EpiPen, I mean?'

'I left it at home. I know, I know: stupid. I'm terrible at remembering it. But I won't forget it again, that's for sure.'

'Hmm.' Ethan rubbed his face, a little confused. 'Okay. Well, thankfully, Rose seems fine. At the moment, anyway. But if anything upsetting or serious happens again, will you please tell us right away?'

'Of course. But I'm sure there won't be a next time. Tomorrow we'll just stay here and play chess. Zero drama guaranteed.'

She smiled at him, turning on her full beams, and she saw all the annoyance drop away. Once again, he was a rabbit caught in her headlights, blinking at her, confused and guilty.

'Is everything all right otherwise?' she asked, moving a little closer. 'With you, I mean? You and Emma?'

'I . . .' He was flustered. 'Fiona, you won't tell Emma I mentioned why we moved house, will you?'

'Her affair?'

'Emotional affair.'

'Sorry, that's what I meant. Of course not. My lips are sealed.' She reached out and laid her hand on his arm. 'But if you ever need to talk, you know where I am.'

'Yes. Thank you.'

When she closed the front door behind him, the fake smile slipped from her lips. She headed back up to the bathroom for her shower.

Thank goodness Rose hadn't told her parents the full story. Fiona hoped she hadn't told her brother either.

She would really rather not have to kill that *entire* family.

16

'The records are all in the spare room upstairs,' Iris said, inviting me in to her house. 'Lovely that you've brought Rose with you. Teaching her the trade, are you?'

'Something like that.'

Rose hadn't wanted to come with me to Iris's house, but Emma had taken Dylan to a football match and I didn't want Rose to stay in the house on her own, even on a bright summer evening like this. After the revelation earlier in the week about her witnessing the death of that lawyer, I wanted to spend more time with her. Keep an eye on her, to make sure she wasn't showing any signs of trauma. So far, she seemed absolutely fine. Quiet and thoughtful – I kept catching her staring into space, miles away – but apparently okay.

'I'll put the kettle on,' Iris said. 'Rose, would you like a cold drink? Lemonade?'

'Yes please.'

Iris said she'd bring the drinks up and that the records were in the first room on the right at the top of the stairs.

Iris's late husband, Alan, had been born in 1946, which meant he was the perfect age to have been into the Beatles and the Stones and all the other great bands of the sixties, but experience had taught me to be sceptical, so I wasn't excited as I knelt on the carpet beside the bed in Iris's spare room and started digging through the crates of old albums and 45s.

'It smells of dust in here,' Rose complained, sitting on the bed, where I had placed one of the crates for her to look through.

I wasn't really listening. I was too busy pulling out records from the crate I was kneeling in front of and turning them over in my hands, slowly getting that most wonderful sensation in my belly, the one that told me my scepticism might have been misplaced. This crate was full of Bob Dylan records, all in excellent condition. There were also albums by Marvin Gaye, the Small Faces, Nina Simone, Etta James . . .

'Bloody hell, Alan had good taste.'

I found a copy of *The Velvet Underground & Nico* and held my breath. If this was an original American pressing, with the peelable banana, it could be worth thousands. I exhaled; it wasn't that edition, but it was still highly collectable and could fetch a few hundred pounds. I set it aside carefully as Iris appeared in the doorway holding a mug of tea and a glass of lemonade.

'Hold on,' I said quickly. 'I wouldn't bring those in here. You don't want to risk spilling anything on these records.'

I held up one of the albums, *The Freewheelin' Bob Dylan*. 'This is a first pressing. It's worth about two hundred pounds in this condition. And this Velvet Underground LP, there are dozens of different editions, and I could bore you about the differences between the photos on the back and the bananas on the front, but I think this is a pretty rare one. There's lots of other good stuff in here too, and I'm only on the first crate.'

'Goodness.' Iris left the drinks on a side table outside the door and came into the room.

'Whoa, look at this,' said Rose from the bed. 'So gross and so cool.'

The album Rose was holding showed the Beatles in white lab coats, holding decapitated baby dolls and joints of meat. *Yesterday and Today*. It was still shrink-wrapped. I gasped, springing to my feet and carefully taking the album from Rose.

I examined it, my heart pounding. My mouth had gone dry.

'Holy shit,' I said. 'Excuse my French.'

'I hate that record,' Iris said. 'The cover is so ghastly that I would never allow Alan to take it out and play it.'

'I ought to be wearing gloves, really,' I said, laying the album gently on the bed. 'I'm going to go home and get a protective sleeve for it.' I grinned at Iris. 'This is the original butcher cover that was withdrawn from sale almost immediately then re-released with a new cover pasted over the original. It was only on sale for one day. It's the stereo version too, which makes it even rarer. And it's unplayed.'

'How rare?' Iris asked.

Rose, sensing my excitement, ears pricking up at the word 'rare', suddenly seemed fascinated too.

'I think if we find the right collector you could get thirty thousand pounds for this. Maybe even more.'

'Thirty *thousand*?' Iris put her hand to her forehead. 'I need to sit down.'

'That's *sick*,' said Rose, reaching out a hand towards the record. Instinctively, worried she was going to damage it even though it was shrink-wrapped, I pushed her hand away – gently but firmly – and she reeled, an expression of absolute fury transforming her face. I was taken aback. I hadn't seen her look at me like that in a long time, and I was suddenly, forcefully, thrown back in time to when she was a toddler, screaming outside the newsagent's because I wouldn't buy her the green drink she wanted, bucking her body and looking not unlike the girl in *The Exorcist*. Iris looked shocked too, though she might simply have been reeling from the news about the record.

'Why don't you go downstairs, Rose,' I said. 'I'm going to pop home to get some gloves and some protective sleeves before I look through the rest. Who knows what else is in here?'

'I can't believe this,' Iris said. 'Alan always said some of these would be worth money one day, but he had his heart attack before he ever had the chance to get them valued. Oh, I've gone all peculiar.'

'Come downstairs,' I said. We all went down and I left her with Rose while I went back to my house to collect the gloves and protectors. I was trembling with excitement, but not because of the money, which would be Iris's, not mine. It was the thrill of being close to history like that. It struck me how lucky Iris was to have asked me to look at them, rather than some unscrupulous dealer who would tell her they were worthless before buying them for peanuts and making his fortune.

As I was about to cross the road back towards Iris's house, Tommy and Nicola sailed past me in their car. I did a double take: *both* their sons were in the back seat. Eric and Albie. I watched from the opposite pavement as Nicola got out and opened the back door of the car. Eric scrambled out, and then Nicola reached in and took the hand of her older son, helping him. He could walk, but looked dazed, holding up a hand against the evening sunlight. He'd lost a lot of weight too.

'What are you gawping at?'

That was Tommy, who had also got out of the car.

'I'm happy to see he's home,' I said, watching Nicola lead Albie towards the front door of their house. 'How is he?'

A tear leaked from the corner of Tommy's eye. 'He's home. That's all that matters, right?'

Then he hurried up the path, after his wife and son, before I could reply.

Before I could move away, Eric glared past me at Fiona's house. He saw me looking.

'My dad's gonna get her,' he said.

'What are you talking about?'

'Eric, come here!' Tommy yelled, and the boy scuttled up the path, disappearing into the house. I was about to go into Iris's when Tommy called, 'Oi.'

I waited, feeling irritated. When he reached me, he said, 'You're friends with her, aren't you? The Aussie. Tell her I want a word with her.'

'Can't you tell her yourself?'

He scowled. 'She's avoiding me. Every time I go over there she pretends she's not in.'

I really didn't have time for this. To get him off my back I said, 'Sure, I'll tell her.'

He pointed a threatening finger at me. 'Don't forget.'

Back at Iris's, I went upstairs to slip the most valuable records into sleeves, then spent the next hour going through the rest of the collection to see if anything else stood out. There were a few others that were rare and in near mint condition, including some more Beatles albums and singles, but nothing anywhere near as valuable as *Yesterday and Today*.

Back in the living room, Iris had opened a bottle of sherry to calm her nerves. I explained that, if she wanted me to, I would come round to catalogue everything and estimate each piece's value.

'Most will only be twenty or thirty pounds, or less, and I can definitely find you buyers for the mid-range stuff, like that Velvets album. I know a guy who's a keen collector of anything to do with Lou Reed. I know loads of Beatles and Dylan collectors too. There's one big Beatles collector near here. I'll call him. Assuming you actually want to sell?'

Iris nodded, still dazed.

'What are you going to spend the money on?' Rose asked. She seemed very excited that something as stupid as a record – these ancient artefacts her dad was so obsessed with – could be worth so much money.

Iris took a sip of sherry. 'I don't want to spend it before I've even got it, but I've got a son in Canada who I haven't seen since before the pandemic. It would be lovely to visit him. I've always wanted to go on a cruise too.'

Rose's eyes glazed over. How quickly she grew bored. 'When are we going home?' she asked me.

I exchanged a laugh with Iris. 'Kids. So restless. We'll go back soon, Rose.'

Iris said to her, 'I've seen you coming and going with Fiona. I hope you've been having fun together.'

'We have.'

Iris put her sherry glass down on the side table and leaned forward, cupping her chin with her hand. 'Has she always lived in Croydon? The more I see her, the more I'm sure I know her from somewhere.'

Rose shook her head like she'd been asked a difficult question by a teacher. 'She's from Australia.'

'Yes, I know, but . . . What does she do again? For a job, I mean.'

'Something in banking,' I replied. 'She has a new job starting in September, apparently. That's right, isn't it, Rose?'

'I don't know. We don't talk about stuff like that.'

'Hmm.' Iris frowned. 'I don't know anyone who works in banking. I've never even met my own bank manager. Things are very different to how they used to be. You know, years ago—'

Rose sprang up from her chair. 'Mum and Dylan are home. Can we go?'

'I . . . Okay, fine.' I shot Iris an apologetic look, which she waved away.

I told her I'd arrange a time to come back and catalogue the records and that I'd talk to that Beatles collector.

As we left the house, I was surprised to see Fiona standing on her doorstep across the street. Rose waved at her and she waved back. If I believed in that sort of thing, I might have thought she and Rose were communicating telepathically – that Rose had beamed some sort of mental distress signal to her.

As soon as we reached her, Rose started to tell Fiona about the valuable record. 'It's really awesome, with these dead babies on it, and it's worth thirty thousand pounds!'

'Wow.' Fiona looked across the road. 'Lucky Iris. Lucky to know someone honest like your dad too. I bet a lot of people would tell her it was worth twenty quid, then make a massive profit themselves.'

'That's what I'd do,' said Rose.

Fiona and I both laughed like she was joking, then Rose said she'd see Fiona in the morning and went into the house. Fiona was about to go indoors too when I remembered what Tommy had said.

'Tommy wants to have a word with you. I think he thinks you had something to do with Albie's accident.'

'What?'

'I know, it's ridiculous.'

She looked a little bit scared. 'What do you think I should do, Ethan? Maybe I should go and talk to him . . . I'm just worried he might not be reasonable. What if he gets violent?'

'I really don't think he would. Not with a woman.'

'I don't know. I've seen him arguing with his wife and I've known men like him before. If he really believes I hurt his son . . .'

She was right. I had no idea what Tommy was capable of. And I hated seeing Fiona frightened like this.

'Maybe I could have a word with him,' I said. 'Tell him I've spoken to you and that I'm certain you had nothing to do with it.'

Her eyes widened. 'You're not scared of him?'

I swallowed. 'Of course not.'

'Thanks, Ethan. That would be amazing.'

To my surprise, she went up on tiptoe and kissed my cheek. Before I could react, she disappeared indoors, leaving me on the garden path, my hand covering the spot where she'd kissed me. When I looked up, I saw Tommy standing in his window across the street, holding the curtain back. He must have seen.

He glared at me, shaking his head, then let the curtain drop.

17

Fiona stood in front of the bathroom mirror, steam from her shower hanging in the air, condensation coating the mirror's surface.

She had written three names with the tip of her finger.

The top name, Max Gallup, had a line through it.

The third name was the most important one. The person whose death she was going to savour. The one she was really going to make suffer.

But before she got to that, there was the name in the middle. And she was going to enjoy that one too.

ϖ

'Patrick Grant.'

She spoke the name softly, as if worried that by speaking it aloud she would invoke a demon. She was definitely going to need Rose for this one, to take full advantage of the world's assumption that the two of them, when they were out together, were mother and daughter. It was something she noticed more and more with each excursion: the mask of motherhood; the costume Rose unknowingly clothed her in. It was fascinating, and it made her wonder if she ought to have a baby of her own, though that thought only breathed for a second before she smothered it. A baby! How revolting. And anyway, why would she need one when everything with Rose was going to plan.

But back to Patrick. He was a much trickier adversary than pathetic old Max, even though Patrick was actually thirty years Max's senior. She had been concerned he might die while she was in prison, which would have robbed her of her opportunity to make him pay for wronging her, but thankfully he was still going, the tough old bastard.

'How would you feel about an outing today?' Fiona asked Rose. 'Don't worry. We're not going to play any pranks on anyone.'

'Oh.'

'You're disappointed?' Fiona smiled. 'Well, maybe we can fit a prank in. We're going to visit someone else I used to know. Someone who's got something of mine. Something I want back.'

'Cool,' said Rose.

ϖ

Patrick had recently moved to a small village in Sussex called Wadhurst, an hour on the train from London. When she picked Rose up, Fiona had asked Ethan and Emma if it would be okay to take her on a day trip into the countryside, and they'd thought it was a great idea. 'It'll be good for her to get out of London after what happened,' Ethan had said. Emma had even suggested that they take Dylan with them, but to Fiona's relief he'd moaned and said he already had plans to meet up with some mates in town.

'Dad's still really excited about that Beatles record,' Rose said with a frown. 'I don't get it. It's not like it's going to be his money.'

'Some people are like that, Rose. They applaud other people's good fortune. I don't understand it either.'

'Yeah. Why should I be happy when other people do better than me?' Rose seemed genuinely puzzled, and Fiona patted her knee. She was about to ask how her parents were getting along at the moment, hoping to hear about tension between them, when Rose said, 'Iris mentioned you.'

'Me?'

'Yes. Last night. She said she's sure she knows you from somewhere, and started asking me and my dad questions, like what kind of job do you do.'

Fiona's internal alarm system blinked to life. She certainly didn't recognise Iris, although most old women looked the same to her, just as babies did.

'She asked if you've always lived in Croydon.'

'I see. And what did your dad say?'

'He just said something about you being Australian. *Do* you know her?'

'No.' Fiona stroked her chin. If Iris did actually recognise her and was able to place her, it would be a disaster. Fiona might have changed her surname and appearance, but anyone studying photos of the old and new Fionas would easily see she was the same person. And although she'd paid that geek a lot of money to push news stories about her way down the search results, they were still out there.

Wadhurst train station was situated some way out of the main village. Leaving the station with several other passengers, a middle-aged woman smiled at Rose, then Fiona, and said, 'After you.' The kind of thing that didn't happen when Fiona was on her own.

'Are we going to his house?' Rose asked, as they stood outside the station, Fiona consulting the map on her phone. In her other hand, she held a carrier bag, into which she had managed to squeeze a box.

'No. We're going to the pub.'

'The *pub*? Is that where this guy hangs out?'

'Kind of.'

She filled Rose in as they walked up the main road, not in the direction of the village itself but the opposite way, towards the outskirts. They passed pretty cottages, a petrol station, a sign that advertised free-range eggs. Fiona had always fantasised about living in a big house in the country, a place with a long drive and large grounds and a swimming pool, surrounded by woods. The kind of place where screams would go unheard. If everything hadn't gone wrong a few years ago, she'd be living somewhere like that now . . .

The thought stoked the flames in her belly. Made her hatred for Patrick burn extra-hot.

The pub she was looking for was called the Half Moon. It proved to be a small, ramshackle place halfway down a wide lane that was surrounded by farms. A pub for locals, not one of these country pubs that was part of a chain, with an area for kids and a carvery with half-price deals for pensioners. She suspected the only food you could buy at the Half Moon was a packet of pork scratchings, and a pickled egg if you were lucky.

They went inside.

'They should change their name to the Slaughtered Lamb,' Fiona said under her breath. '*Don't stray from the path, Rose.*'

'Huh?'

'Never mind.'

Fiona ordered two lemonades. The barman, a middle-aged man with a wispy moustache, regarded her with complete disinterest. There was a caravan park a short distance from here, and Fiona guessed he was accustomed to confused tourists wandering in and then wandering off again when they realised this place didn't sell food.

They took their glasses of lemonade out the side door into the pub's garden, a grassy area with a few trestle tables. It was an overcast day, but warm, and Fiona had been worried the garden might be busy when she wanted as few people to see and remember her as possible. But the beer garden was empty.

They sat down, Fiona putting the carrier bag containing the box at her feet.

'Why did you put on a British accent when you ordered the drinks?' Rose asked.

'You noticed? I don't want anyone to remember encountering an Aussie woman here.'

Rose looked a little confused but didn't push it. She looked around the garden. 'He's not here.'

'No. It's probably too early.' It had just gone twelve. 'We'll wait an hour, and if he doesn't turn up, we'll try plan B. Now, drink your lemonade.'

Rose took a sip and winced. 'It's flat. Can I ask a question?'

'*The* question?'

'No. Just . . . What did he take from you? What are we trying to get back?'

'It was something that belonged to an old friend of mine. A woman called Maisie. My best friend.'

Rose waited.

'Have I not mentioned her before? She died four years ago. Killed herself.'

That part was true. The next part was one of her little white lies, though it was based on a truth – a story she would tell Rose in due course.

'Maisie owned an artwork by a really famous artist, but she wasn't one hundred per cent sure it was genuine. Patrick knows a lot about art, so she took it to him to appraise. Then, after she died, he denied ever having it, even though I know for certain she lent it to him. All this stuff with that valuable Beatles record brought it back to me. Not because I want the money, but because it's so unfair. Maisie wouldn't have wanted him to have it.'

Rose appeared to absorb all of this, giving the distinct impression she didn't really care.

'Patrick knows Maisie had a friend called Fiona, which is why I need you to call me something else.'

One potential problem was that he knew what Fiona looked like – or what she used to look like, back when she'd been a brunette and considerably curvier. Now she was skinny with blonde hair, so she was sure he wouldn't recognise her, especially with the fake accent. Also, he'd never seen her in the flesh, just photographs.

'What do you want me to call you?' Rose asked.

Fiona looked her in the eye. 'I want you to call me Mum. Can you do that?'

'Sure.' Rose hadn't hesitated. 'What makes you think he's going to come here anyway?' she asked, sipping the flat lemonade.

'Did I not tell you? I read his book.'

Patrick had made everything easier for Fiona by self-publishing a memoir a few years ago: *A Man of Many Words: The Autobiography of a Newspaperman*, currently sitting at number 1,364,744 in Amazon's sales rankings.

Patrick had, as detailed in his book, worked as a journalist his whole working life, starting out as a local crime reporter in his native Southend-on-Sea before moving to London and getting a job first with the *Evening Standard* and then with one of the broadsheets. His byline would be familiar to anyone who had read the paper he worked for, but he wasn't famous. He didn't write columns or opinion pieces or appear on TV discussing the issues of the day. *I'm an old-fashioned newsman*, he'd written in his memoir. *I worked the Fleet Street crime beat.*

But although Patrick Grant had focused on crime for most of his career, he had also covered something else.

Chess.

According to his book, he was a keen and capable player himself. *I could have been a professional, perhaps, but getting* really *good at chess requires dedicating one's life to it. I decided to master journalism instead.* The book was full of such boasts about how wonderful its author was. *I am certainly enjoying having more time to practise in my retirement, and if anyone wants to see if they can beat this old duffer I can often be found in front of a board in my local drinking establishment.* And there had been a photo of him standing in front of this pub.

Fiona picked up the carrier bag and slid the box out. The box that contained her chess set.

Half an hour passed. It was almost one now and there was no sign of him. Fiona sighed. If he didn't show, she was going to have to go to his house and try plan B, which was similar to what she had done with Max – using Rose to get into his house. But just as she was thinking it through and wondering how long to give it, Rose tugged at her sleeve.

A bald man, slim and fit-looking even though he was in his eighties, had entered the pub garden, carrying a pint glass full of a dark brown liquid.

It was him.

18

'Of course I'm interested. But I need to see it.'

Rodney Clough was the biggest collector of Beatles records and memorabilia in the Greater London area. His house, Octopus Gardens – a huge, heavily guarded place in Dulwich Village – was stuffed full of it. Every record they'd ever released, in multiple formats. Shelves full of plastic models and dolls and bric-a-brac. Posters and ticket stubs and signed photographs covered the walls. A beautiful Yellow Submarine jukebox sat in the corner of the living room.

I had visited his house once and marvelled at all this stuff, though I hadn't been allowed to touch any of it. I also hadn't been permitted into the vault, an airtight basement room where all the really good stuff was kept. Rodney, who had made his fortune developing and operating car parks, had acquired several of George Harrison's guitars and a bass that Paul had played onstage in Hamburg, along with handwritten lyrics, rare acetates of early singles, various items of clothing that Ringo Starr had worn on album covers, and, reportedly, the actual copy of *The Catcher in the Rye* that Mark Chapman had been carrying when he shot John Lennon.

Rodney and I were sitting in the back office of the shop. Now in his late sixties, Rodney was out of shape and found it hard to walk more than ten metres without breathing heavily and having to mop his brow with a handkerchief.

'Do you not already have a first-issue copy of *Yesterday and Today*?' I asked.

'Oh yes. But mine isn't sealed. Also, I don't want that bastard Takahoshi getting hold of it, do I?' Yukio Takahoshi, a Kent-based, Japan-born shipping tycoon, was Rodney's biggest rival. I knew that their bitter enmity towards each other had forced up the price of many unique pieces of memorabilia as they fought to outbid each other. 'You haven't contacted him, have you?'

'No.' I paused. 'Not yet.'

In the tiny office, surrounded by boxes of records and piles of paperwork, I could smell his perspiration. 'I'll give you thirty grand for it, cash, if it's genuine and I can take it away today.'

'Hmm. I think she was looking for forty.'

Rodney hated Yukio so much that I knew I could force him up at least a little.

'You wanker.' He wiped his brow. 'Thirty-five, final offer. If we can go and look at it now.'

We took his car. He had a driver who was waiting around the corner in a black Bentley. I had half expected him to have a Beatles-themed car – a customised Rolls-Royce like the one Lennon had owned, perhaps – but it was quite exciting enough getting into the Bentley, which had tinted windows and attracted stares as it glided through Croydon towards my house.

'Nice place to raise a family,' Rodney commented when we entered the estate. 'I bet your kids appreciate what you do for them, don't they? I sent my lot to Dulwich College, one of the most expensive schools in the bloody world, and are they grateful? Are they hell. Between you, me and Tyler here, I'm going to leave all my stuff to a museum. Wish I could be there to see their faces when the will is read out.'

He chuckled to himself, and I told Tyler to take a left.

'Iris's house is just on the right, there. We're . . .'

I stopped.

'What is it?' Rodney asked as we pulled over to the kerb.

But I wasn't looking at Iris's house. My attention had been grabbed by my own, across the road.

Why was Emma's car parked outside? She ought to be at work now. Was she sick? Was something wrong with the kids? No, Dylan was at a friend's house and Rose was out with Fiona. Perhaps Emma had popped back to get something.

But whose was the car parked in front of hers? It was a dark grey Land Rover, not a rare sight around these parts, but I'd never seen it outside my house before.

'So where does this old dear live?' Rodney was asking. 'I'm very keen to get a proper look at this treasure.'

I wasn't listening closely enough to respond. I was too busy watching as the front door of my house opened and a man emerged, followed by Emma. They stood on the front path for a minute, not noticing the Bentley, though they wouldn't have been able to see through its tinted windows anyway. Emma had no idea that I was there, watching her stand there with our former neighbour, Mike. The man with whom Emma had formed an emotional bond that had come very close to an affair.

They put their arms around each other and hugged, then Mike – with a smile on his face that made me want to punch him – walked to his car, got in and started the engine. Emma watched him drive away, lifting a hand to wave before her own smile was replaced by a look of utter sadness as he vanished from sight. Her shoulders drooped and she looked like she was going to cry as she walked to her car and got behind the wheel. Almost immediately, she drove away, presumably back to work.

'Ethan?' Rodney demanded. 'What's going on? Who was that? Oh my word, was that your wife? With another man?' He shook his head. 'My ex-missus cheated on me too – with the guy who installed our third bathroom, if you can believe that. A bloody plumber. He even had the cheek to invoice me afterwards.'

He kept rambling on but I had stopped listening. I needed air. In a daze, I opened the door and got out. Rodney appeared beside me, still chuntering on, and then Iris appeared, shaking me out of my stupor and forcing me to engage. We headed over to Iris's house, even though rare records were the last thing on my mind now. I was on autopilot as I watched Rodney don a pair of gloves and inspect the album, turning it over in his hands, squinting at the price sticker that was still on it.

All I could think about was Emma with Mike. Mike coming out of my house after a lunchtime rendezvous. Had they had sex in our house? What else could they have been doing? I suddenly felt horribly sick, excusing myself to go to the bathroom, where I stood hunched over the toilet bowl. Nothing came out.

When I went back, Rodney and Iris were shaking hands.

'Thirty-eight thousand pounds,' Rodney said. 'Done.'

Iris was clearly a better negotiator than I was.

Rodney said, 'Wait here,' then went back to his car. I was still finding it impossible to concentrate.

'Earth to Ethan,' Iris said. 'Are you all right?'

I realised she'd been talking to me for a while. I was struck dumb by the stress of what I'd witnessed. I still didn't speak when Rodney came back with several rolls of banknotes, which he handed to Iris before gently taking the Beatles album.

'Good luck with your missus,' he said to me before he left. 'My advice – bin her and find someone who looks at you like you're made of chocolate.'

'What was all that about?' Iris asked as we watched his Bentley pull away.

I shook my head.

'None of my business, I suppose. Here, this is for you.'

She handed me one of the rolls of twenty-pound notes.

'What's this?'

'What does it look like? That's five thousand pounds. Your commission.'

'But I didn't ask for one.'

'Ethan, don't insult me by turning it down. You've earned it. Use it to go on a nice holiday. Treat the kids and Emma.'

I went to her front door, holding the money, still in a daze.

'By the way,' she said as I stepped outside, 'I had a dream about Fiona last night. Her and a friend of mine who died a few years ago. The three of us were going on a foreign trip together. We were in an airport and my friend couldn't find her passport and Fiona kept saying it didn't matter, that she'd help her. Very strange.'

I wasn't sure what to say.

'The point is, I woke up sure I remembered where I knew her from, but by the time I got downstairs and put the kettle on it had gone. Like a bubble. Pop.' She smiled, a little giddy from making all that money. 'It will come back to me, though. I have no doubt about that.'

19

Patrick walked straight past their table to the far side of the garden, barely glancing at them as he went by. He settled at a trestle table in the corner, in the shade of a large oak tree. A wasp must have made a beeline for his Guinness – *a wasp making a beeline*, Fiona would have to remember that one – because he made a swatting motion before settling down to drink his pint and read a book.

Trying to sound like Maisie, Fiona said, 'We'll give it a few minutes before we start, okay? My English accent? Is it convincing?'

'Yeah. I think so. You sound a bit posh, though.'

'Do I?' That wasn't good. It wouldn't fit with her cover story.

'How about this?' She toned it down, thinking about a woman from Essex she'd shared a cell with for a few months, before she was moved to Franklin Grange.

'Much better. You sound normal now.'

'Normal is good. Now listen, let me quickly run through the plan again.'

She spoke quietly, confident her words wouldn't drift through the still air to Patrick, who appeared to be engrossed in the book he was reading.

'Okay,' Fiona said when she'd finished. 'Let's play.'

She opened the box and took out the chess set, laying out the pieces. Out of the corner of her eye Fiona saw Patrick look up, his attention snagged immediately, like he had some kind of radar for his favourite game.

Without looking over at him, Fiona and Rose started playing. Fiona had instructed Rose to pretend Patrick wasn't there and play as she would at home. If she had been worried the girl might be distracted, those worries were quickly laid to rest. Rose, with the black pieces, played her favourite response to Fiona's e4 opening: the Sicilian Defence. The two of them quickly followed the classic sequence of moves, exchanging pawns in the centre, before the game began to get interesting. Like Rose, Fiona found herself getting drawn into it, especially when Rose surprised her by bringing out her queen early, exposing the piece and allowing Fiona to capture it.

'Oh dear,' said a voice from behind Rose.

She looked up. It was Patrick. She hadn't noticed him cross the pub garden to watch them.

'I blundered,' said Rose.

'Want to quit and start again?' Fiona said, using her English accent.

'Uh-uh. Let me play on.'

'Do you mind if I watch?' Patrick asked with a smile, which Fiona returned.

'Yeah, no problem.'

He stood at the side of the table.

'You can take a pew if you want,' Fiona said. That was an English expression she'd never used in her life. She admonished herself: *Take it easy, Fiona. Don't overdo it.*

'I'm fine standing here,' Patrick said. 'Gives me a better view.'

Rose gave Patrick a little smile then focused her attention on the board. Over the next fifteen minutes she fought hard but, without her queen, she stood little chance, and soon Fiona said, 'Checkmate. Rematch?'

They played again. This time Rose had the white pieces and it was a long, gruelling battle, trading the most valuable pieces until both players were racing to get their final pawns across the board. Rose won, punching the air as she trapped Fiona's king in the corner.

'You're quite good,' said Patrick. 'Although I have to tell you that you missed several chances to win a while ago. May I?'

He leaned over and, from memory, set a number of pieces back on the board, just as they'd been ten minutes before. He showed Rose a couple of moves she could have made that would have led to a swifter victory.

'I only know that because of experience, though,' he said. 'I certainly wasn't as good as you when I was your age.' He stuck out his hand to Fiona. 'I'm Patrick.'

She met his handshake. 'Nice to meet you, Patrick. I'm Bianca and this is Florence.' They had agreed these names before he arrived.

'That's a good old-fashioned name,' he said. 'My mother was called Florence.'

'No way!' As if she hadn't read it in his book.

He chuckled. 'Yes way. Isn't that what you young people say these days?'

'Something like that, Patrick. Fancy giving Florence a game? She's just going to keep beating me now, and it gets depressing.'

He hesitated, but only for a second. 'I can never resist a game. But go easy on me, Florence.'

Fiona shuffled along and Patrick sat down. They began to play, Rose white, him black. Fiona was impressed to see Rose use the Ponziani Opening, creating tension with the pawns in the centre of the board. Patrick looked impressed too, and in the early stages Fiona thought that all his boasting in his memoir had merely been that: boasting. But then his experience began to show as he lured

Rose into a trap and quickly took control, winning the game as if he had a computer in his head telling him the best moves.

'Again,' Rose said. 'Is that okay, Mum?'

She met Fiona's eye and Fiona felt a little thrill run through her. *Mum.* It felt strange but rather wonderful. Not because she had any maternal instincts, but because it meant Rose was going along with her plan and, Fiona was sure, would continue to do so. In that moment, Fiona could see the future unfolding before her: a future that went beyond her modest three-part revenge scheme. A future where she and Rose were together – unstoppable, unbeatable. Because who would ever believe this lovely mother and daughter could be responsible for all the things Fiona's black heart craved?

As they started their second game, Patrick said to Fiona, 'Did you teach her to play? It's wonderful to see so many young people getting into the game these days. Are you a member of a club, Florence?'

Fiona was worried Rose might temporarily forget her fake name, but she was too good. She said, 'I was in my school club, but they're all rubbish.'

The game continued and Fiona chatted with Patrick, spinning him a story about how she was a single mother and how hard it was with childcare in the school holidays, especially as Florence's dad was so useless. He seemed to be taking it in, even if he also didn't appear particularly interested. She told him how she wished she could afford to hire a chess coach for 'Florence' or even afford to buy some good books.

He defeated Rose again, then went back through the game pointing out what she should have done differently. He had a superior tone, quite patronising, which Fiona knew Rose would find annoying.

'Well, it was lovely to meet you, Pat, but me and Flo had better make a move. I want to actually see the village before we go home.

But before we do, could you recommend some books? I could maybe have a look for them in the library.'

'You know, I have a couple of books I could let you have. A little gift as a thank you for entertaining me for an hour.'

'Oh, we couldn't.'

'Honestly, I'd be very happy to give them to you. I'm never going to need them again, and I'd like them to go to a good home. I only live down the road. If you don't mind accompanying me, I can fetch them for you.'

'What do you think, Florence?'

'That would be awesome,' Rose replied.

'Marvellous.' Patrick rubbed his hands together – big, meaty hands that had spent many years pounding away at a typewriter. He was so sure of himself, so confident of his own brilliance. Not at all concerned about inviting strangers back to his house.

Fiona and Rose followed him across the garden to the pub's side gate. On the way, Fiona checked over her shoulder to see if there were any witnesses. But there was still no one else around. The pub's few customers would be huddled inside the bar.

They walked a little way down the road and then Patrick led them down a small lane, just wide enough for a single car. There was horse shit on the road and tall hedgerows on either side.

This was perfect. The almost-deserted pub. The quiet lane. Patrick's interest in their game and his suggestion that they take his books. It was as if fate were smiling on her. And she didn't believe in God or anything supernatural, but she could imagine Maisie walking beside her, whispering in her ear: *The world belongs to us, Fi. It bends to our will.*

Every now and then, it actually felt like that. Soon, it would be her and Rose, and it would be even better than it had been with Maisie. In that relationship, Maisie had always been the top dog, the more experienced one. This time Fiona would be the boss.

It started today. After this, if all went as she expected it to, Fiona would confess to Rose that Max hadn't been an accident. She would tell Rose everything.

And if it didn't go as expected? If Rose didn't react how Fiona thought she would?

Well, that would be unfortunate for everyone.

'I've written a book myself,' Patrick said as they continued to walk down the lane. 'Perhaps you'd like a copy of that too, Florence?'

'No thank you.'

He guffawed, then said, 'Down this way.'

The lane forked and he led them to the right, down an even narrower path which suddenly opened up to reveal a large stone house, set back behind a wrought-iron gate. They followed him through the gate into a front garden that was almost too cute to bear: the scent of apple trees and roses, a neat little lawn, chocolate-box perfection.

'Come in,' he said, opening the front door and gesturing for them to follow.

Fiona shut the door behind her.

'Would you like a tea or coffee?' Patrick asked when they were standing in the hallway. Despite the season and the warm weather, it was cold in here. It was the kind of space the sunshine never touched.

'Tea would be lovely, if it's not too much trouble.'

'No trouble at all.'

They all went into the kitchen and he filled the kettle, flicking it on.

'Now, my chess books are stored in the cellar. If you don't mind waiting here, I'll go and find a couple. A copy of my book too, just in case you think it might be interesting.'

He was panting a little from the effort of walking home, the first physical sign he'd shown of his age. He left the kitchen.

Rose immediately whispered, 'What are we going to do? How are we going to get the artwork?'

Fiona went to the kitchen doorway and peeked out. 'Wait here.'

She wanted to take a quick look around, double-check Patrick lived on his own and didn't have a lodger or a live-in housekeeper. Then she would find Patrick and reveal her true identity. She couldn't wait to see the terror in his eyes as he realised he was all alone with someone who wanted to kill him. And it was going to be so easy to make it look like a domestic accident. This poor vulnerable old man, falling down the stairs. Such a shame.

Tingling with anticipation, she went into the hallway and tiptoed past the open cellar door, glancing down into the dark.

Hold on. Why was it dark if he was down there?

'Looking for someone, Bianca?'

She whirled around.

Patrick was standing at the bottom of the stairs that led up to the first floor. He was holding a gun.

'Except it's not Bianca, is it? It's Fiona.'

The gun – a black revolver, quite old-looking – was pointed straight at her chest. Fiona stood with her back to the cellar steps, hands held aloft. Patrick moved left so he was directly in front of her in the hall, with his back to the kitchen door. He must have lied about going into the cellar. Instead, he had crept upstairs, which was presumably where he kept his gun.

'Did you really think I wouldn't recognise you? Even with the new hair colour, the fake accent, I'd know those eyes anywhere. I've watched all the news reports, Fiona. Looked into those eyes of yours a hundred times. And do you know why?'

He was breathing heavily now. But the hand that held the gun was stable. Not shaking.

'I was trying to see if there was any humanity in there. After what you tried to do to Dinah. I wanted to know if you felt any remorse.'

She didn't know what to say. Theoretically, she knew what remorse meant. But the closest she'd ever got was self-pity. Regret for ways the world had screwed her over.

'I knew you were out of prison,' he went on. 'Though I'm not sure if you can even call that place a prison. Franklin Grange.' He spat the words. 'More like a holiday camp. I bet you had a grand old time, didn't you?'

'Patrick,' Fiona said, dropping the accent. 'I came to apologise.'

'What rot! You've come here for revenge. You know, I saw the report about your lawyer dying.'

Shit. He really had followed the case in detail.

'I bet that was you too. Are you working your way down a list, eh?' His lip curled. 'I hope I'm only number two and that you didn't manage to bump anyone else off before you came up against a proper adversary.' He moved away from the main staircase, the gun still aimed at her heart. The kitchen was to her right, the front door to her left. 'Because that's what you and that other little bitch specialised in, isn't it? Picking on people weaker than you.'

Most people would be going into flight, fight or freeze mode now. Heart rate soaring, cortisol and adrenaline pumping. But Fiona barely felt anything. Annoyance at herself for being arrogant. Surprised respect for Patrick – well, a little, anyway. And, of course, she didn't want to be caught or punished. But she was calm. Calculating. *Cool.*

'Why don't you put the gun down, Patrick?'

'Shut up! Who's the girl, eh? She's not really your daughter, is she?'

He took another step closer. She was trapped in the doorway to the cellar.

'I want you to go down those steps,' he said.

'Into the cellar? What are you going to do?' Fiona asked. 'Keep me prisoner? Use me as a sex slave?'

He made a disgusted noise. 'I'm going to call the police, you bloody sicko.'

So he hadn't called them yet. That was encouraging. All she had to do was get the gun – but the moment she moved towards him he would probably pull the trigger.

'Come on, Patrick. Can't we talk? I could make you happy.'

'You're revolting. You're not even properly human.'

He took another couple of steps towards her. They were only a metre apart now. She could almost hear his heart thudding in his chest.

Where was Rose? Was she completely unaware of what was going on out here?

'This is your last warning,' he said. 'I will take great pleasure in shooting you. Get down those steps now. I'm counting to three. One—'

'Fine.'

Her mind raced, trying to figure out how she was going to get out of this. She couldn't accept that a man like Patrick could beat her. This was a temporary glitch, that was all. But right now she had no choice but to obey him. She began to walk very slowly down the steps, looking back over her shoulder at him, at his silhouette as it appeared in the cellar doorway, preparing to shut the door, to lock it.

And then a blur of noise and motion behind him.

A little later she would realise that Rose – who had been listening to everything – had come charging out of the kitchen at full speed. And as Patrick stood at the top of the steep cellar steps, his back to Rose, looking down towards Fiona, she charged into him, arms outstretched. Shoving him with as much force as her small body could muster.

But it was enough. He flew down the stairs, arms windmilling. He reached out in desperation, trying to grab on to Fiona on his way down, but she flattened herself against the wall, his fingers brushing her chest, and he was past her in a second. He cried out once as he fell, and then there was a crack as he hit the concrete floor below.

The sound of his neck breaking.

20

I couldn't go back to work after what I'd seen. Emma with Mike. The misery on her face as she'd got into her car, as if she couldn't bear to be parted from him. Or maybe she was thinking ahead, with dread, to coming home and telling me the news. I could hear it, imagine it all. She'd tried to make it work with me. She'd wanted it to. For the sake of the kids, she didn't want to break up with me. But she couldn't stop thinking about him. She loved him. Our marriage was over.

I let myself back into the house and almost keeled over in the hallway – found myself bent over, hands on my knees, gulping down lungfuls of air. Could I smell it in the air? The stink of adultery, of animal sex? Had they tried to resist but been unable to keep their hands off each other? Had she screwed him in our bed, or on the sofa where we watched TV together? Had he bent her over the kitchen counter where I cooked our family meals? My entire body palpitated; my vision went black. I was going to vomit, going to faint.

It was only the sensation of something wet on the back of my hand that stirred me, brought me out of the state I was in. Lola, licking me. Trying to comfort me.

'Good girl,' I said in a ravaged voice, crouching to pet her and rub her ears. She licked at my face and I realised there were tears on my cheeks. There was part of me that wanted to phone Emma and tell her what I'd seen. To demand the truth, a confession or, better yet, a convincing denial, though I didn't know if I'd believe her. Despite being almost completely crazed, I retained enough self-knowledge and sense to know I was not going to be receptive to anything she had to say in that moment.

So I didn't call her or text her. Instead, for the next couple of hours, I staggered around the house, not knowing what to do with myself. Trying to make myself a coffee, then finding that so long had passed since the kettle had boiled that I had to start again. Halfway through my final failed attempt to fix myself a hot drink I found myself moving around the house, looking for evidence of sex. Crumpled bedsheets. Tissues in the bin. Alien hairs on the pillow. I even opened her underwear drawer to see if the sexy lingerie I'd bought her several Valentines ago – which I hadn't seen her wear since – was lying on top of her more utilitarian knickers and bras, showing signs of having just been worn.

I was still sitting on our bed when I heard the front door open, then footsteps coming up the stairs.

It was Dylan.

'Why are you home?' he asked.

I couldn't think of an explanation. 'I wasn't feeling well.'

'Please don't give it to me, Dad.' He went into his room, and soon I heard him chatting to one of his mates through his Xbox headset.

What would happen if Emma and I split up? She'd want to keep the kids and they'd no doubt want to stay with her. I'd end up living in the cold, empty flat above the shop, surviving on microwave meals and being rejected on Tinder or whatever middle-aged people used. I had been out of the game so long that I had no clue how I would survive being single.

I went back downstairs, to make another attempt at brewing coffee, but as I reached the hallway the front door opened and Rose came in.

I said hi, and she blinked up at me like she was shocked to see me.

'I wasn't feeling well,' I said, repeating the lie I'd told Dylan, although it was hardly an untruth now. I didn't feel at all well.

'Right,' she said.

She seemed to be in an even bigger daze than me, blinking at me but giving the impression she wasn't really seeing me.

'Is everything okay?'

'Huh? Oh. Yeah. I'm tired, that's all, after that train journey.' Oh yes. I had forgotten Fiona had taken Rose out to visit the countryside. 'I'm going to go for a lie-down.'

She ran up the stairs like she couldn't wait to get away from me, leaving me standing by the front door, having forgotten what I'd come down for. My head was a mess and I had the sudden, overwhelming urge to talk to someone. And who was the only person who knew about Emma's relationship with Mike?

Fiona.

'I'm popping out for ten minutes,' I called to the kids, unsure if they had heard, but going out our front door and taking the few steps to Fiona's anyway.

She answered straight away. She looked a little dishevelled, not her usual groomed, calm self. God, was there something in the air today?

'Ethan?'

'Can I come in? I need to talk . . .' I trailed off.

She hesitated, studying my face, no doubt seeing the pain etched there, then said, 'Okay.'

She led me into the kitchen, just as she had the last time I'd visited. The blinds were open, giving a view of the garden and the fields beyond. I could hear birds singing, music thumping from someone's back garden, the noise of children playing. It all felt unreal. Normal life carrying on while my world had tipped off its axis.

Fiona stood by the counter. 'What's the matter?' she asked. Was I imagining it or did she seem nervous? I'm sure at one point her eyes flicked towards the block of kitchen knives, as if she thought I was going to grab one and hurt myself. Or stab someone else. Did I look suicidal, or murderous? It wouldn't have surprised me if I looked completely mad. She was certainly eyeing me as if I was about to say something monumental.

'It's Emma,' I said. 'I think . . . I think she's seeing Mike again.'

She exhaled. 'Oh, thank God.'

'Yes, I . . . What?'

'Sorry. I thought you were going to say something had happened to Rose or Dylan. But that's . . .' She groped for the word, gave up. 'What makes you think that?'

I told her about seeing them outside this afternoon. The embrace. The expression on Emma's face afterwards.

'Oh God. Poor you. What are you going to do?'

I was speechless. I had wanted her to reassure me, to tell me it was probably completely harmless. Not to say *Poor you*!

'Do you think she's seeing him again?' I blurted.

'I don't know, Ethan. Have you asked her about it?'

'Not yet. She went back to work. At least, that's where I assume she went. But I'm scared to ask her because I don't want her to tell me our marriage is over. That she's in love with him. I mean, she might be trying to decide what to do, and I don't want to push her in his direction by acting like a . . . like a . . .'

'Bitch?'

'Yes.'

'Or a twat?'

'Either of those. I think maybe I should wait a little while, see if she comes to me.'

'Hmm. And what will you do if she tells you she's in love with him and wants to be with him?'

'Oh God, you put it so bluntly, Fiona.'

She shrugged. 'I can't help it. I had a strange day today too.'

'Really? What, with Rose? Did something happen?'

'Oh. No.' I could tell she regretted what she'd said. 'I . . . bumped into an old friend, that's all. Someone who reminded me of my ex. But let's not talk about that. I think there's a strong possibility you got the wrong end of the stick. Maybe this Mike guy contacted Emma, told her he couldn't stop thinking about her, insisted they meet – and she told him it was over, that she loves you and only you.'

'I hadn't thought of that.'

'Or maybe he came to tell her he's dying of cancer.'

'Oh Jesus.'

'Sorry, didn't mean to get your hopes up.'

I laughed, then realised she wasn't joking. 'I don't want him to *die*.'

'You don't? Oh. Well, anyway, I think . . . you should wait and see. Keep an eye on her. I don't think you should make a move until you know what's going on. What do they say? Knowledge is power.' She looked at me. 'Oh, Ethan, you look so sad. Come here.'

She held her arms out and I stepped into a hug. She was so warm, her body soft, her hair even softer against my face. She smelled a little sweaty, but not in a bad way. I probably smelled worse, but she wrapped her arms tightly around me and pulled me close.

Still hugging me, she whispered, 'Does that feel a little better?'

I moved my head back and looked into her eyes, our noses almost touching. I could kiss her, and I was sure, in that moment, that she would kiss me back. She was so pretty, and kind, and it would be revenge – sweet retaliation. And I felt it radiating through me: something dark and mean and lustful, and Fiona parted her lips and her eyelids flickered, waiting, breathing . . .

And, from the corner of my eye, I saw a figure.

There was someone watching us through the window.

I jerked away, stepping back, out of Fiona's reach, and she turned to follow my gaze. Tommy was standing on the other side of the hedge at the bottom of Fiona's garden. He was too far for me to make out his facial features, but not so far that he wouldn't have seen us embrace. He shook his head before turning and walking away towards the fields, his German shepherds straining on their leads.

'It was just a hug,' I said, as if he could hear. I wanted to run out and tell him. *Just a comforting hug because I thought my wife was cheating on me.*

But of course I wouldn't tell him that.

'I'd better get back,' I said.

'Yes. Of course.'

Fiona showed no sign that we had almost just kissed, to the point where I wondered if it had been a fantasy. But then I knew I hadn't imagined seeing Tommy; Tommy seeing us.

'What are you going to do?' she asked. 'Are you going to talk to her, or wait?'

'I think I'll wait.'

In fact, I had already decided. The money from Iris, that fat bundle of banknotes, was still in my pocket. I knew what I was going to do with it.

21

The holiday resort was so new it wasn't finished yet. I only knew about it because one of my regulars had a nephew who had helped build it. As we drove up the long, snaking lane that led to the accommodation, we passed JCBs and concrete mixers that stood abandoned as if the workers had gone on holiday themselves. Despite that, it was beautiful here; here being the Wales-Shropshire border, just outside the small market town of Ellesmere.

The cabins were arranged in a semicircle around what had been described as a lake, though it was actually a pond, surrounded by long grass that was dotted with wildflowers. We had a hot tub which had never been used before, and an outdoor table and chairs that looked like they'd come straight from a warehouse.

'So, what do you think?' I asked after we'd looked round the open-plan kitchen/diner/living room and checked out the three bedrooms.

'What's the Wi-Fi password?' Dylan asked, opening his phone and simultaneously turning the TV on to reveal the Netflix logo.

'It's small,' said Rose. She wrinkled her nose in her brother's direction. 'And have I got to share a bathroom with him?'

'That's what you do at home,' I said.

'Yeah, but he always stays in there forever – doing God knows what – *and* he makes it stink.'

'You're such a brat,' Dylan said.

Rose turned to me. 'Please, Dad. You promised we'd have our own bathrooms.'

'Did I?'

'I suppose she could have the room with the en-suite,' Emma suggested.

'But that's the only room with a double bed.' The others each contained two singles. Is that what Emma wanted? To sleep in separate beds?

'Oh my God, there's no need to look so horrified. It'll be nice for Rose to have her own bathroom.'

So we were rewarding bad behaviour now, were we? Rose had been awful since the moment I'd told the kids we were going away for a few days.

I'd texted Emma as soon as I'd left Fiona's house, sick with guilt and fear, asking if she could book a long weekend off work.

> *Iris gave me a commission for selling that record and I think we should all go away for a few days. Me, you and the kids. xx*

I had been surprised when she'd responded almost immediately, saying *Great idea x*. My instant, pleased reaction was very quickly replaced by an extra helping of paranoia. Did she think a break would give her the perfect opportunity to drop her bombshell, and tell me she was in love with someone else?

Now I couldn't help but think she was pleased about us sleeping in single beds. Was she worried I'd try to initiate sex? Rose had handed her a chance to put a physical gap between us.

'Are you all right?' Emma asked, tilting her head and studying me. 'We're on holiday. You're meant to be relaxed.'

Maybe I would be, I thought, *if I hadn't seen you hugging Mike.*

'Please don't argue,' Dylan said. 'I can't stand it.'

'We're not arguing.' Emma and I both spoke at the same time.

I forced myself to breathe. 'I'm going to unload the car. Do you want to give me a hand, Rose?'

'Do I really have to?'

I shook my head. 'What has got into you?'

'I told you,' said Dylan. 'She's a brat.'

Right now, it was hard to disagree. She'd been like this ever since she'd got home from her day trip to the countryside with Fiona. Different, somehow. Like she was holding herself straighter, or she'd grown an inch or two. She seemed more grown-up, like there was suddenly a young adult in the house instead of a child. Of course, when I'd asked her what she and Fiona had done on their day out, she had clammed up in typical tweenage fashion. Then she had been less than pleased when I told her we were going away for a couple of nights.

We had been in the middle of dinner. She'd been quiet, eating steadily. I'd been struggling a little because I felt so sick – afraid I was visibly trembling from the pressure of trying to conceal my unhappiness.

I'd thought that telling the kids about the holiday would be a bright spot in a shit week. But Rose had set down her fork.

'You're joking. I don't *want* to go away.'

'Why not? It'll be fun. We'll have a hot tub and there will be lots of places we can go for days out—'

'Just stop whining, Rose,' Emma said, interrupting me. She had been on her phone – *texting Mike?* – but she put it down now. 'Your dad has arranged for us to go away on a family holiday. You should be grateful.'

Rose glowered at her. 'It sounds lame. I want to stay here.'

'She doesn't want to be apart from Fiona,' Dylan said.

'Don't be stupid,' Rose said with a snarl. 'I just don't want to stay in a stupid cabin and play stupid board games.'

Emma leaned towards her, wearing her patented take-no-shit expression. 'You see Fiona every day and now you're going to spend some time with your family.'

While I took comfort from that remark – it seemed she still cared about our family – Rose muttered something under her breath. It sounded like: *With the herd.*

I tried to break the tension by making a joke of it. 'You're going to have fun even if it kills you.'

But Rose hadn't seen the funny side. She had left her dinner half-eaten and stormed out of the room.

And then there had been another incident. Emma had told Rose and Dylan to pack their bags and to ensure they had enough clothes for a few days, plus the gadgets and chargers and anything else they couldn't live without. Rose had stomped around the house gathering her stuff together while wearing headphones so she wouldn't have to talk to us. Finally, fed up of how long she was taking, Emma went into her room to help her, pulling clothes out of her wardrobe. I could hear everything from our bedroom, where I was packing my own bag.

'How about these?' Emma said.

'They're ugly.'

'But I thought you loved them.'

'Yeah, when I was *little*.'

I could picture Emma sighing. She said, 'What about—?' and then 'What's this?' A pause. 'Did you take this from my room? I've been looking for it everywhere.'

I left our bedroom and crossed the landing, standing in Rose's doorway. Emma was holding up a small object. A lipstick. Emma had asked me a week or two ago if I'd seen it, but I'd assumed she'd misplaced it and hadn't given it a second thought.

'I don't mind you borrowing my stuff, but you should ask first, not just go into my room and help yourself. Also, you don't need—'

'I didn't do it!'

'Then how did it get into your pocket?'

'I have no idea. Maybe you put it there.'

'Why would I do that?'

'Come on, Emma,' I said. 'It's not a big deal, is it?'

Emma wheeled around on me, annoyed. 'She shouldn't take stuff without asking.'

Without warning, Rose snatched the lipstick from Emma's hand and threw it against the wall.

'I *hate* you!' She yelled it at the top of her voice, drawing Dylan from his room.

'What's going on?'

'Dylan, just stay out of it,' I said, but Rose barged past me as I spoke, leaving Emma open-mouthed behind her, and locked herself in the bathroom. She didn't come out for an hour. In the meantime, Emma agreed to leave it. We would go away, enjoy the holiday. I was so tense because of my marital woes that I could barely function. I couldn't cope with a war between Emma and Rose on top.

All the way up the motorway Rose had sat there looking like she was being driven to a prison camp, complaining about the music, about feeling carsick, asking to stop so she could use the loo three times in four hours. She was hardly talking to Emma. Thankfully, the lipstick hadn't been mentioned again, but I had never seen Rose in such a foul mood.

'Rose,' I said now, determined not to lose my temper. 'You're going to help me unpack the car.'

She huffed and puffed as she carried small bags to and fro, stopping several times to look at TikTok on her phone. I was tempted to pluck it from her grasp and fling it into the pond.

'We're going to have a good time, I promise,' I said, knowing that shouting and playing the parent card wouldn't work. Much better to be positive and wait for the storm clouds to pass.

She grunted – and then, to my enormous surprise, she flung her arms around me, pressing the side of her face against my chest. She hung on for thirty seconds.

'What was that for?' I asked.

She looked confused, like she wasn't sure why she'd done what she'd just done. Like she was annoyed with herself.

'I love you, sweetheart,' I said, ruffling her hair.

She flinched away, irritated by my touch, and I thought she was going to storm off again, the most capricious creature on the planet, but instead she said, 'I love you too, Dad,' and of course I forgave her for everything.

ϖ

There was another family in the cabin next to ours with kids roughly the same age as Dylan and Rose. The son, Henry, was eleven, and the daughter, Keira, was fifteen. Their parents, Theo and Angela, came round a couple of hours after we'd arrived, and said that if our kids wanted to hang out with theirs, that was cool by them.

Dylan shrugged and acted nonchalant but I could tell he was keen – because Keira was a very pretty girl. They had brought their dog with them (we had only made arrangements to leave Lola behind because she hated car journeys), and Keira asked Dylan if he wanted to take the dog, a golden retriever, for a walk along the nearby canal. He agreed immediately.

Rose seemed far less enthusiastic about spending time with Henry, but there was something wrong with our hot tub – the temperature was too low – and when Henry, who was one of those kids who seemed to be completely lacking the shyness gene, suggested Rose use their tub, she allowed herself to be persuaded.

'Don't worry,' said Theo to Emma and me. 'We'll keep an eye on them.' He had a Manchester accent and we had a chat about music while Rose got changed. He seemed nice, as did Angela, who explained she was a child psychologist.

'That must be interesting,' Emma said. 'Except I guess you're constantly having to resist the urge to analyse your own kids.'

'Oh, I can't help it.' She laughed. We were standing on the strip of grass between our cabins. 'It's impossible not to mess up your children in some way or other. Luckily, ours seem to be doing pretty well so far. Henry is outgoing, like his dad.'

'And Keira is a brainbox like her mum,' Theo said. 'Beautiful like her too.'

'Creep.'

He put his hand on the small of her back and their lips met briefly. I felt a stab of envy. When was the last time Emma had kissed me or shown affection in front of others? I couldn't remember.

'Are you all right, mate?' Theo asked.

'Huh? I'm fine.' I knew I didn't sound it. 'I was just thinking . . . Rose has been quite moody and difficult the last couple of days.'

'"Quite moody" is an understatement,' Emma interjected. 'It's like someone came and body-swapped our lovely daughter and replaced her with a new, angrier model.'

'How old is she?' Angela asked.

'Just turned twelve.'

'And she's only just started to get moody?'

I was about to go into more detail when Angela put her palms up and said, 'It's not ethical for me to talk about a specific child, so don't give me any more information. But in general terms, my advice is simple.'

'Yes?'

She smiled. 'Chill out. *That's* my advice. A lot of parents get very het up about their child's behaviour in their tween years and when they hit puberty. They're like, "my child is suddenly so angry", or "my child hates me". But it's just normal childhood development. Moodiness, anger, being difficult. I'm sure you were both the same. I bet you went through it with Dylan a few years ago too.'

'Hmm. Not really.'

'He was a *bit* moody,' Emma said. 'And he still spends a lot of time locked away playing video games and listening to music.'

'And probably watching all sorts of muck,' Theo said with a laugh.

'I dread to think,' said Emma.

'The point is,' Angela said once we'd all stopped pulling faces, 'I wouldn't worry. As long as a child – a young adult – isn't completely unattached from his or her parents and isn't suffering from one or more of the mental health issues that are so common these days . . .'

'As long as she's not going round burning down houses or torturing cats, you're grand.' Theo winked at me.

Rose appeared, changed into her swimming costume and wrapped in a towel.

'What were you all talking about?' she asked, and for a horrible moment I thought she might have overheard us.

'Oh, nothing,' Emma said. 'I think Henry is waiting for you by the hot tub.'

We all looked over. There he was, a skinny eleven-year-old kid wearing a pair of goggles, waiting patiently with a big smile on his face. Rose looked at him and I couldn't help but laugh at her expression. She looked like the headmistress of a posh boarding school regarding a poor oik who had somehow won a scholarship. But she strode over to him and I heard her say, 'I hope it's not cold like ours.'

'Well,' said Angela. 'We'd better go and keep an eye on them.'

'You two should make the most of being child-free,' said Theo, winking again.

'Hmm,' said Emma. 'I think I'll go and read in the bath.'

She went inside and I thought, *This is the perfect opportunity to talk to her, while there are no kids around.* But by the time I went in she had locked herself in the bathroom and the taps were running.

Was she in there texting *him*?

My guts roiled from the stress of it all, and the only thing I could think to do was get a bottle of wine out of the fridge and take it outside. I stood on the decking and saw Dylan and Keira emerge from the woods in the distance, the dog trotting along beside them. As they came closer I heard laughter and wondered if this was going to result in a brief holiday romance. I guessed it was easier for teenagers these days. They could keep in touch and chat online, follow each other on TikTok or whatever. It would be nice for Dylan to make a new friend. And if he did like Keira, it was certainly a lot healthier than watching him eye up our adult neighbour – which, thankfully, I hadn't seen him do in a while.

You're the only one eyeing her up, said my conscience.

It struck me that Dylan was the easiest member of our family. The only one I wasn't worried about.

But what about my moody daughter? Was *she* making a new friend? I peered over the fence that separated the two cabins. Rose was in next door's hot tub, the bubbling water covering her shoulders, seemingly relaxed and happy. Strangely, Henry was standing beside the tub, holding his towel, goggles still on.

It was as if she had told him he wasn't allowed to get in with her. Was he *scared* of her – this little twelve-year-old girl?

Surely not.

But the more I looked, the more it seemed evident. He was afraid of her.

22

Fiona wished she didn't have to look after Lola, something she had only agreed to because Rose had asked her to and she knew how important it was right now to do everything she could to keep Rose calm. After what had happened in Wadhurst, the girl would be in a state of intense emotional turmoil. Hyperarousal, to use the technical term – with all her feelings heightened. Excitement, anger, fear, elation. All this would be tumbling through her blood, way beyond the cool, calm state she needed to be in right now. It was vital for Fiona to keep an eye on her, talk to her, help her understand who she was and what she was going to feel. It was important that Rose didn't do anything to draw attention to herself and her outings with Fiona, especially anything to do with the deaths of Max and Patrick. She was confident Rose wouldn't blurt out what they'd done, but it was possible she might behave in a way that would make her parents question what was going on while Fiona was looking after her.

This was the worst possible time for her parents to have taken her on a stupid mini-break.

'Come on, dog,' she said, attaching the lead to Lola's collar.

She stepped out into the afternoon light, squinting at the sunshine, wishing she hadn't drunk so much the last two nights. The problem was, *she* was in a state of hyperarousal too, and she had needed the alcohol to knock herself out. The first thing she'd done this morning, and the previous day, was check the news for reports of a death in Wadhurst.

She was confident no one had seen her and Rose leave the pub with Patrick – and, on top of that, no one who might have seen them playing chess in the beer garden would know who she was. Even if they'd been captured on CCTV somewhere along the route, she was confident they wouldn't be identified, partly because she didn't think anyone would look that hard. The plan had always been to make Patrick's death look like an accident, or possibly a suicide, and real life was not how it was in the movies. The police force wasn't full of tenacious detectives who smelled something fishy and dedicated their lives to uncovering the truth. No, the pressure on the police to hit targets and deal with their huge workload meant that, if something looked like an accident, it would stay an accident. No case to be cleared up. On top of that, Patrick didn't have any close relatives who might lean on the police to ask them to look closer.

However, she still wanted to double-check there were no reports of a suspicious death; of a man found dead after he'd been seen with a mysterious woman and girl. But there was nothing, and she could only assume he hadn't been found yet.

She flashed back to the immediate aftermath of the incident: Rose standing at the top of the staircase, Fiona several steps below – and, down in the darkness of the cellar, a dark shape on the concrete.

Fiona had crept down the steps, instructing Rose to stay where she was. She needed to make sure it was his neck breaking that she'd heard. He might be merely winded, still holding the gun. He might sit up when she reached the bottom of the steps and pull the trigger.

But all was well. He lay on his front, arms outstretched, his head bent at an unnatural angle. The small gun – it looked like something from an old Agatha Christie adaptation – was on the floor several feet away from his hand. Fiona looked down at it. It was a simple story: the octogenarian gets home from the pub, booze in his bloodstream, ventures into the cellar and trips over his own feet, falling to his death. Fragile bones breaking. Nothing to stop his fall. It fitted her plan perfectly.

The only issue was the gun. What possible reason could there be for him carrying that? It pointed to there being someone else in the house. An intruder. Patrick feeling threatened.

She needed to put it back where Patrick kept it.

Fiona jogged back up the cellar steps, ducking to avoid the cobwebs and being careful not to slip herself. Rose was still rooted to the spot, staring down into the darkness.

'Is he dead?' she asked.

'Yes.'

'I killed him.'

'You did.'

She wanted to ask Rose how she felt, what physical sensations were coursing through her. What emotions. Was she scared of being caught or punished?

Was there any part of her that felt bad?

There was no time for any of that now, though. They needed to get out of here.

She found the place where Patrick kept his gun: a cupboard next to his bed, the door hanging open to reveal a space where there were boxes of ammunition. Had he suspected she would come for him one day, or did he have other enemies? Perhaps he was simply serious about home security.

She went back down to the cellar and used the sleeves of her jacket to pick the gun up, taking it upstairs and returning it to its home. In the kitchen she found several cans of Guinness in the fridge. Still using her jacket sleeve to touch any surface that might hold prints, she emptied a can into a glass, then tipped most of it down the sink, leaving the foam-streaked glass on the counter. She emptied a few other cans and put them in the bin. After that, she went round with a cloth and wiped any other surface she had touched, although she had been careful since getting here, so it wasn't a big job. Rose's fingerprints and DNA wouldn't be in any databases, but Fiona still looked around to ensure they hadn't left anything the naked eye could see: no long strands of hair or items dropped from pockets.

All this took fifteen minutes, and then they exited through the front door, on to the empty lane and back to the train station.

'The painting,' Rose said suddenly as they walked through the village. 'That was a lie, wasn't it?'

'It was. But he took something else from me.'

'What?'

'Not what. *Who.*' She stopped, and put her hands on Rose's shoulders. 'I promise I will explain everything. Okay? And thank you. You saved me.'

Rose nodded, clearly still stunned by what she had done. But – and this was the best part, the part that made Fiona realise she had been right all along – Rose wasn't freaking out. She wasn't babbling with fear or regret. She wasn't showing any signs of regret at all.

She seemed excited.

Just like when Fiona had allowed Sienna to drown. Rose finally knew who, and what, she was.

ϖ

Lola wanted to stop every ten seconds to sniff for traces of other dogs. Passing the spot where Albie had smashed his head against the tree trunk, Lola pulled at her lead and Fiona wondered if the animal could scent blood or brains. Somewhere inside that fluffy head was the mind of a wolf. Lola's ancestors had run wild across this land, hunting in packs.

'Do you feel it?' Fiona said to the dog. 'Do you feel that connection?'

Lola squatted and peed.

It was another warm day and alcohol seeped from Fiona's pores, her armpits prickled, and nausea burbled inside her. She was gripped by an urge to rip off her clothes, to peel them all off, fling her bra and pants into the stinging nettles, and go running free and wild across the fields, screaming. Letting it all out. She pictured herself doing it, got deep into the fantasy, and when she emerged she didn't know how long she'd been in a fugue state; was afraid, for a second, that she might have actually done it, which wouldn't have been at all wise. But she was still dressed, still on the path, and Lola was snuffling obliviously in a bramble bush.

It wasn't surprising the pressure was getting to her. A lot had happened this week. Almost as soon as she'd got home from Patrick's there had been the encounter with Ethan – another part of her plan that was going exactly as she'd hoped, except the timing was slightly off. That was why she'd encouraged him not to confront Emma straight away. She wasn't quite ready yet for Ethan to step forward into her embrace. She had to ensure Rose was fully primed first.

Ready to play her role in the final part of Fiona's plan.

Rose.

This summer had been all about testing her, preparing her . . . and using her. Now everything had accelerated. By killing Patrick, Rose had begun to run before she could walk. Instead of a slow emergence and understanding of herself, she had come out too early. A butterfly smashing its way out of its chrysalis with a hammer, exercising no caution.

Rose had never been part of the original plan, of course. Fiona could never have predicted that she would find herself living next door to another of her kind. It was almost too perfect.

However, involving Rose added an extra layer of complexity, which had become even more complicated when the girl pushed Patrick down those steps. Fiona hadn't intended for that to happen. The plan had been for Rose to witness Fiona helping Patrick to have an accident, and the girl's reaction would tell Fiona everything she needed to know.

In taking action and saving Fiona by killing Patrick herself, Rose had exceeded Fiona's expectations. And it was exciting, sure, but it was also scary. With everything happening with Ethan and Emma at the same time, Fiona needed to pause. She still had to have that conversation with Rose about her true nature and the reason she had wanted Max and Patrick dead. She needed to ensure events didn't spiral out of control. To make sure that Rose didn't screw up the plan and that she was primed for what lay ahead. Rose needed, too, to understand how important it was for her to stick close to Fiona – to see the value of having a mentor.

Patience, Fiona, she told herself. *Don't rush things.* So far, it was all going so well. When she'd set out on this journey of revenge, she hadn't really thought much about what she would do when she was finished. Now she was able to see the future – a future in which Rose would help disguise her as well as giving her new purpose. She couldn't afford to mess it up.

She would talk to Rose as soon as she got back from her bloody mini-break.

She sighed.

And on top of all the stuff with the Doves, there was the delivery from Lucy.

For a short while, in prison, she'd felt a bond with Lucy. The thrill of discovering another like herself. Teaming up, working as a pair to get what they wanted. If Fiona had remained in prison, she had no doubt they would have gone on to be a power couple in there. A formidable alliance.

And yes, she had promised Lucy she would help make her nemeses' lives a misery, and she still intended to do it – but Lucy needed to understand that getting revenge for Maisie's death had to be Fiona's priority. She couldn't afford any distractions.

Unfortunately, Lucy was actually *increasing* the pressure on her. A couple of days ago, a woman had turned up on a motorbike and had handed Fiona a small package. Inside was a tiny mobile phone with one number stored in it.

'Keep it hidden,' the woman had said, not lifting her visor. Then she had ridden away, leaving Fiona wondering if this was another woman Lucy had met inside or if she was merely a professional courier. She had put the phone away, wondering if and when Lucy would call to hassle her.

Now, she and Lola passed through the gate into the first field and the dog immediately stopped, backing up and hiding behind Fiona's legs.

Tommy was in the middle of the field with his two German shepherds.

Fiona had long dreamed of being able to control animals with her mind. It was the superpower she wished for; much better than invisibility, or being able to fly. Now, she fantasised about silently commanding the two German shepherds to turn on their owner. Rip his nuts off. Tear his throat out. Lola would join in, and together the three dogs would feast, and Fiona would be there too, dipping her hands into the wounds, smearing herself with his blood, howling into the emptiness . . .

'Oi! You! I want a word with you.'

He strode towards her, the most inelegant man she'd ever seen, walking like his balls were too big. There was something, she supposed, brutishly attractive about him. Every now and then she would sleep with a man, and Tommy looked like he'd get the job done – the kind of bloke who'd screw you without worrying too much about your feelings.

She didn't want him to think she was waiting for him to reach her, so she walked along the edge of the field, saying, 'Come on, Lola,' and forcing Tommy to re-route, taking a diagonal path until he caught up with her, and even then she didn't slow down, so he had to walk beside her.

'Are you going to stop?' He was panting a little. Out of shape.

'I'm not planning to.'

He muttered something under his breath. 'I want to know if you saw anything. Before my son's accident.'

'Nope.'

'Because Eric told me what you said to him and Albie.'

'Oh yes? And what was that?'

He furrowed his brow. She was really annoying him, which sent a little ripple of pleasure through her. She remembered what she'd said to them that day: *Why don't you go back to your little house and do what you do best. Wank yourselves into a stupor.* Not her finest, wittiest moment, but it had had the desired effect.

And it delivered here once again, as Tommy was suddenly tongue-tied, not wanting to repeat the words back to this woman he didn't know or understand.

'You threatened them,' was what he settled for.

'No I didn't. They were harassing the children I was with. I told them to stop and go home. End of.'

She expected him to mention what he'd witnessed earlier this week: the hug with Ethan. Instead, he said, 'Who the hell are you? Where did you come from?'

'Ever heard of a place called Australia?'

'Nah. I looked you up online. There's no trace of you. Loads of Fiona Smiths, but none who look like you.'

'What the hell?' Her pulse was pounding in her ears. 'You've been looking me up? That's stalking.'

'No it's not. It's a free country. And I just want to know who I'm living opposite. Because there's something not right about you. Are you even an Aussie, or are you putting that accent on, eh?'

She increased her pace. 'Leave me alone, or I'm calling the police.'

'Go on then. I've been trying to get them to talk to you, because I *know* you had something to do with the accident.'

'You're a dickhead,' she said.

His dogs were right behind him, trotting along and watching like they understood what was going on. She was having to drag Lola, who seemed terrified, along on her lead. If it weren't for his massive German shepherds, she might punch Tommy. Most men, even morons like him, wouldn't hit a woman back, at least not in public. His dogs, though, if they had been trained to protect their master, wouldn't care.

Suddenly, Tommy was in front of her, with his phone out. He was trying to take her photo.

'What the hell?' She threw her spare hand up to cover her face and whirled around.

'Come on, hold still. I just want a picture.'

With her back to him she said, 'If you don't put that away right this second I'm going to start screaming.'

As she'd turned around, she'd noticed a young couple had entered the field with a couple of small dogs in tow. They were watching, curious. Tommy saw them too, and backed off, putting his phone in his pocket.

He pointed a finger at her. 'I'm going to find out who you are. I know you caused that accident. Maybe I'll ask Ethan. He seems to know you pretty well.'

She gave him the finger and he laughed and walked away, the dogs trotting beside him, their tails wagging like they'd seen a fun show.

Fiona stopped walking and bent over, hands on her knees, sure she was going to throw up. The feeling passed, but her head still spun and her heart was hammering.

Had he managed to get a photo of her face? She hadn't heard a click, but that didn't necessarily mean anything. And if he had, what would he do with it? Who would he show it to?

A horrible realisation dawned.

He could reverse image-search it.

There were news stories out there on the internet with her picture, and even though she looked different now she thought Google's algorithms would probably match any photo Tommy had taken with the images of her online. After all, Patrick had recognised her. A computer system surely would too.

She had to do something.

Without hesitation, she hurried after him, calling, 'Tommy. Hey, stop.'

He carried on for a few more steps but couldn't resist. He turned his head.

'Listen,' she said, adopting her most rehearsed smile. 'I'm sorry for going off on you like that. We've got off on the wrong foot. I think I might be able to help you figure out what happened with Albie.'

He turned fully now, the dogs either side of him. Lola cowered behind Fiona.

'What are you going on about?'

'I might know what happened. Just . . . something I saw the day before the accident. I don't want to talk about it out here in the open, though, in the middle of a field. Why don't you come back to my house and I can explain? And I'll answer all your questions about me too.'

He narrowed his eyes at her. He was suspicious, of course he was. But he was desperate to know. Also, this would feel like a victory to him. Her capitulating. And why would a big, macho bloke like Tommy be scared of a little woman like her?

23

The laser tag venue was on an industrial estate – as fun children's activities often were – on the outskirts of Oswestry, a short drive from the cabin resort. The idea to go there had come up when we woke to find it was raining and Emma had searched online for indoor activities.

'Bowling?'

'So boring,' said Rose.

'The cinema?'

'Nothing on,' Dylan protested.

'Trampolining?'

'I'm *not* a baby.' Rose didn't even crack a smile.

'How about laser tag?' Emma said eventually. 'That might be fun. Ethan? What do you think?'

I had been distracted, hungover after polishing off a bottle of wine by myself and staying up to watch Netflix after everyone else had gone to bed, drunkenly falling asleep on the sofa. I had woken up in the morning to find that someone, presumably Emma, had draped a blanket over me.

'Hmm?' I said.

'Laser tag? Do you fancy it?'

With my hangover, I couldn't think of anything I'd like less than running around an indoor play area with laser-gun noises ringing in my ears. I would have preferred to lie on the couch all day and wallow.

Except that was pathetic, wasn't it? Part of the reason for this trip was to remind Emma that we were a strong family unit, better together. And here she was, wanting us all to do something. Acting, I had to admit, as if her family was all she cared about.

Was she pretending? Thinking about it, I realised her prime motivation was likely trying to build bridges with Rose after all the tension of the past few days.

'Maybe Keira would like to come,' Emma suggested to Dylan, who immediately seemed excited about this idea.

'Oh God,' said Rose. 'If she comes, her dumb little brother will have to come too.'

'Has the real Rose been body-snatched?' Dylan asked. 'Or were you always this annoying?'

'You're the annoying one,' Rose said, glaring at Dylan. 'Keira isn't even pretty. You're just desperate.'

Dylan looked like he'd been slapped.

'Oh my God.' That was Emma. 'Rose. Apologise to your brother.'

Rose narrowed her eyes, and I was certain she was going to swear at Emma. I was horrified but mesmerised – this behaviour was so unlike the Rose of old – and I braced myself for the fallout. But then Rose blinked and rubbed a hand across her face, and her expression completely changed. Became pleasant again.

'I'm sorry, Dylan. I didn't mean it.'

He stared at her for a second, shocked by the change, before finally saying, 'Whatever.'

In the end, Theo and Angela decided they wanted to come along too. So here we were, the two families, pulling up outside what looked like a 1960s warehouse.

We went inside and the instructor, a broad-shouldered man called Dave who clearly loved his job, showed us how everything worked before handing out the guns and helmets, which he explained were necessary because the ceilings were low in places.

'You're lucky, you've got the whole place to yourselves,' he said, taking us into the arena – a large space that had been turned into a kind of maze across two levels, with ramps and steps leading up to higher platforms, all decorated to look like something from a future war. There was a 'control tower' at the centre of the ground floor where Dave based himself, with a number of screens that would display our scores. The guns kept track of how many hits we achieved and received. At either end of the arena were two sheltered areas that Dave described as 'camps'.

'We'll start with a team game. Family versus family. The Doves and the Gallaghers.' He smiled at Theo and Angela. 'Shame your surname isn't Hawk, right?' When they just nodded, he sighed and said to them, 'If you go over to the camp at the other end of the arena, we can make a start.'

I crouched in the camp with Emma, Dylan and Rose. Emma looked weirdly sexy in her army helmet – did I have some kink I hadn't previously known about? – and Dylan wore a look of rapt concentration. I'd observed him flirting with Keira in a way I'd never seen him do before, the two of them teasing each other about how they were going to get murdered. It was sweet. Dylan had never had a girlfriend before. He'd been on a couple of dates, but then we'd never heard about the girls again.

Rose seemed quite excited too, her filthy mood from earlier having evaporated, although I'd seen her bristling with irritation when Henry tried to talk to her. The poor kid gazed at her like she was the loveliest thing his eleven-year-old eyes had ever seen, but she just wasn't interested, although I didn't blame her for not finding his chat about how he and his friends 'slayed at Fortnite' appealing.

'We ready, team?' I asked. 'Are the Doves going to show we're not all about peace?'

Dylan groaned. 'Dad, that's so cringe.'

'The Deadly Doves, that's what we should call ourselves.'

'No More Lovey-Dovey,' suggested Emma.

Both kids made noises like they were being tortured.

'Okay!' called Dave from the control tower. 'Let's go.' He pressed a button, a siren wailed, and we were off.

It was fun. A little stressful, running around the course, trying not to bang my head on the low ceilings. There was lots of dashing around, attempting to hide, the guns spluttering and beeping and the kids yelling at each other as the time ticked down. The problem for the Deadly Doves was that the Gallaghers were much better than us. They'd obviously done this before, and both adult Gallaghers and kids kept popping out and shooting me in the head, then vanishing before I could reciprocate. If this were a real battlefield, I'd have lasted five seconds. The only member of our family who was any good was Dylan, having poured thousands of hours of his life into playing first-person shooters on his Xbox. But I noticed he was reluctant to shoot Keira.

Rose noticed too.

'Why are you letting your girlfriend off the hook?' she asked during a timeout.

'I'm not. And she's not my girlfriend.'

'She's not going to hate you for shooting her. It's the *game*. If you don't try to kill her, she'll have no respect for you.'

'Where on earth is this coming from?' Emma asked. She, like me, was sweaty and out of breath, her helmet askew, damp tendrils of hair sticking to her forehead.

'Rose has been watching relationship videos on YouTube,' Dylan said. 'What about you and Henry? You've hardly landed a shot on him. Or is that just because you're rubbish?'

'Please, both of you.' I put myself between them. 'Let's not argue again.'

'Henry's so annoying,' Rose said.

Dylan smirked. 'There's a thin line between love and hate.'

'Shut *up*!'

A few minutes later, Rose got Henry in a corner and blasted him with every piece of virtual ammo she had.

Maybe it's good for her, I thought, watching her as she squeezed the trigger over and over and Henry cowered before her. *Help her get some of that aggression out. Do what her hormones are telling her to do.* I couldn't help but feel sorry for Henry, though, watching him finally duck and weave away after Rose temporarily ran out of shots.

I turned to see Angela watching, shaking her head before remembering the game and aiming her gun at me.

ϖ

By the time the final game of the hour-long session arrived, I was shattered. I'd banged my head a dozen times and my clothes were soaked with sweat. I was suffering with my hangover too, and in dire need of water. But I was enjoying myself. We were doing something together, as a family. And as a couple too. Emma had called out a warning when Theo was about to snipe at me from one of the raised areas, and we'd exchanged a grin after Emma shot our adversary.

'The last game is a battle royale,' Dave declared. 'Every person for him- or herself. Let's see who's the top player out of all of you.'

He explained that, once you took three shots, you were out.

I was eliminated by Dylan pretty early. I retreated to our camp and sat waiting for the rest of them. Theo, Angela and Emma soon joined me. Our kids were far better than us. Then Dylan, surprisingly, was eliminated, leaving just Rose, Henry and Keira.

'If Rose wins, she's going to be a nightmare,' said Dylan. 'She'll never stop going on about it.'

'She's not like that,' Emma said, with little conviction.

'Huh. Not before this summer. But since she's been hanging out with Fiona . . .' He trailed off.

Angela was listening with interest. 'Is Fiona a new friend? A bad influence, perhaps?'

'She's our childminder,' I said. 'Well, of sorts.'

'Our next-door neighbour,' Dylan said. 'She's weird.'

'What makes you say that?' I asked, surprised. In that same moment, I saw myself and Fiona hugging. Almost kissing. I was glad I was already flushed from all the exercise.

Dylan didn't get the chance to answer, because somewhere close by there was a loud thud and a child screamed. All of us adults jumped up and ran towards the noise, Angela and Theo leading. Dave came rushing down from the control tower too, and was the first to reach the scene.

Henry lay on the ground, clutching his upper arm and wincing with pain. His helmet had come off, and tears ran from the corners of his eyes down towards his ears. His gun was nowhere to be seen.

Angela and Theo rushed over to him, throwing themselves down beside him. Dave was saying, 'He's okay, nothing broken, I told all of you to be careful and not to come running down the ramps.'

'I . . . didn't,' Henry hissed.

'Where does it hurt, darling?' Angela asked, checking him over while Dave went on about how they'd all signed a legal disclaimer. 'Oh, shut up, Dave,' she said, just as Rose and Keira appeared from around the corner, both holding their guns down by their sides. Rose, I noticed, had two guns, presumably hers and Henry's. Keira headed straight over to her dad and said something into his ear which made him frown.

I couldn't take my eyes off Rose. She looked like she was fighting to suppress a smile, the muscles at the edges of her lips twitching. She set Henry's gun on the floor but kept hold of her own.

'He's okay,' Angela said, helping Henry into a sitting position. 'He doesn't appear to have broken anything.'

Theo crouched beside him. 'Tell us what happened, son.'

Henry shook his head, but he looked at Rose, his lower lip quivering. 'I fell down the ramp.' His voice was very high. 'It was my fault.'

Keira made a disgusted noise.

'Did you see something different?' Angela said to her. 'Keira? What happened?'

Keira recounted what she'd seen. 'Henry was up in the crow's nest.' That was a point on the higher platform, over in the corner. The Gallaghers had commandeered it and used it to snipe from when they were playing as a team. 'Rose was up there too, talking to him. I didn't see what happened next because I assumed they were forming an alliance, so I went and hid.'

'Were you forming an alliance?' I said to Rose.

She folded her arms. 'I was telling him to surrender.'

'And then what happened?' Emma asked, going over so she was standing close to Rose, protecting her from the glares of Theo, Angela and Keira.

'Tell them, Henry,' said Rose.

I saw it then. He wasn't merely afraid of her. He was terrified. He swallowed and stuttered as he tried to get the words out. 'I . . . I didn't want to surrender, so I – so I jumped out of the crow's nest and ran down the ramp, but I slipped and fell down.'

'See?' said Emma. 'An accident.' She turned to Dave. 'I'm amazed you don't have more of them in this place.'

'I'll have you know that we have been ranked the safest laser tag place in . . .'

No one was listening to him. We were all watching Angela help her limping son out of the arena, Theo and Keira walking behind them. Outside, we went back to our cars in silence, except for Keira, who approached Dylan and whispered something to him which made him look at Rose as if she were a stranger.

I got behind the wheel as everyone else climbed in. I couldn't get the image out of my head: the terror on Henry's face. It conjured an echo from years ago. An incident at nursery and a streak in my daughter that I had thought was long gone.

Driving back from the laser tag, with my family sitting in silence in the car, I felt deeply unsettled.

I looked in the rear-view mirror at Rose on the back seat. At first glance, her face was blank, her expression neutral. But then I looked again. There was something else there, just beneath the surface. Something similar to what I'd seen after Albie had his accident. A glimmer of joy.

Of satisfaction at a job well done.

24

It was the day after her encounter with Tommy, and Fiona wondered what Rose was doing now. She could text her, of course, but she didn't know if her parents monitored her phone, and she was unsure if Rose would know how important it was to be discreet in her replies. That was one of the things she needed to teach her: that in order to survive and keep their freedom, people like them needed to know how to hide, how to operate in darkness. It was something Maisie had taught Fiona shortly after she'd come to the UK.

The importance of hiding. And the importance of teaming up to help each other.

Fiona had only been twenty-three when she fled Australia, leaving behind the mess and chaos of her early adulthood, the years when she'd struggled to control her desires. She had only survived because she had stumbled into an underground scene where she'd found people who wanted to be hurt – people who threw themselves into victimhood, their lives even messier and less controlled than Fiona's. Emotional masochists. Willing participants. The problem was, the initial thrill didn't last. There was little satisfaction in hurting those who wanted to be hurt. Fiona had taken risks, been reckless. After a bad scene that led to a woman almost suffocating to death, she'd bought a one-way ticket to London.

She spent her first year in the city feeling even more lost than she had in Perth, and she almost went back several times. She had come to London dreaming of getting rich. Wasn't this still the city where the pavements gleamed with gold? She got involved with a guy who worked in the City and was ten years older than her – a hedge fund manager called Gareth. He was loaded, generous, wild. They spent their weekends doing lines of cocaine and having the kind of sex that left them both covered with bruises and scratches, the expensive lingerie he'd bought her ripped and stained with blood; deep wounds in his flesh. During the week, when he was working, she would cruise lesbian bars, looking for soft, gentle women who would fall in love with her on Monday before she broke their hearts on Thursday.

A few months into their 'relationship', Gareth got coked up and bragged to her about how he was about to make millions. A 'risk-free' insider trading scheme that he and some of his posh friends had dreamed up. By this point, she was sick of him. She no longer enjoyed sleeping with him; was genuinely scared that one day he would really hurt her. Maybe even kill her. Or perhaps she would kill him. Mulling over the best way to dump him, she saw an opportunity.

Pretending all his talk about insider trading turned her on – in reality, she found it pitiful, pathetic – she asked him to explain it all to her again, and secretly videoed the whole thing. She also had access to his home computer – she'd watched him type in the password many times – and she found some messages between Gareth and his co-conspirators, which she took photos of.

The next day, hiding in a hotel room so he wouldn't find her, she messaged him. If he didn't pay up, she would send the video and other evidence to his bosses and the police.

He threatened her. He begged. But in the end he knew he was beaten. He paid up and she lived off that money for a year.

At the end of that glorious year, during which she travelled, stayed in luxury resorts, broken more hearts and helped herself to expensive jewellery and watches her victims left lying around, she reconnected with Maisie. Fiona hadn't seen her since Maisie left Perth and returned to the UK, back before Fiona's dangerous spell. They hadn't fallen out; the parting had been purely geographical. That, and Maisie telling Fiona she needed to spend some time on her own, finding her feet.

'Look me up when you're ready,' Maisie had said when she'd left Australia.

In the aftermath of the Gareth situation, Fiona reached out.

Maisie immediately told her how risky Fiona's actions had been. Gareth might have murdered her. Fiona was a young Aussie girl with no friends or family to look after her. If she'd gone missing, no one would even have noticed.

'Alone, we're vulnerable,' Maisie said. 'But together, as a little pack, we're strong, and not least because together we can hide in plain sight.'

Rose needed to learn that too. But Fiona knew that if Tommy found out who she was, she wouldn't be around to pass on any more lessons.

Standing in that field yesterday afternoon, she had remembered Gareth. And she had suddenly known what to do.

She thought back to the events of yesterday afternoon, after she had invited Tommy back to her house. It had been dangerous, just as it had been with Gareth. But she hadn't had any choice.

Besides, she liked danger.

It was one of the few things that made her feel anything.

ꙍ

Tommy had dropped his dogs at home, letting them in through the back door. It was the middle of the afternoon, and Tommy said something about how his wife had taken Albie to the hospital for a check-up. Eric, the younger boy, was with his grandparents.

Fiona heard Tommy order the German shepherds to lie down, then he followed her over to her house. It was peaceful. Birds were singing. There was a delivery driver dropping off a parcel further down the street, and music drifted out of an open window several houses down. Apart from that, none of the other neighbours were around.

'This had better be good,' Tommy said as they entered her house.

'It will be. Can I get you a drink? A beer?'

'Let's just get on with it.' They stood in the hallway and he looked around very briefly. Lola stood by his feet and he glanced down at her.

'Does Emma next door know about you and her husband?'

'I know what it looked like, but I was seriously only comforting him, that's all. Giving him a hug because he'd had some bad news.'

'Oh yeah? What bad news?'

She shook her head to indicate it was none of his business. '*I'm* going to have a beer. Sure you don't want one?'

He raised his eyebrows. A woman having a beer in the afternoon? *Well,* she could hear him thinking, *she* is *Australian.*

'Go on then.'

'Why don't you go into the living room?' she said with the warmest smile she could fake. 'Make yourself comfortable.'

When she came back, holding two bottles of lager, he was on the sofa, knees spread, scrolling through his phone.

'News from the hospital?' Fiona asked, handing him a bottle. 'About your son?'

'Yeah. We got the results from the latest scan. Looks like it might not be as bad as they first feared.'

Shame.

'Wow, that's great.'

'Yeah.' His eyes filled with tears and he swiped at his face with one of his massive paws, then appeared to remember who he was talking to. 'It's still gonna be a long process, though, they say. And someone did it. *Someone* put nails or glass on the path.'

He really was tedious. She watched him, keeping her face neutral to disguise her loathing, while he took a long swig from the beer bottle.

'I'm really sorry we got off on the wrong foot,' Fiona said.

'We're still on the wrong foot, and will be until you tell me what you saw.'

She switched on her most obsequious smile, mixed with an apologetic head-bow. 'I will. I just want to explain why I acted so aggressively. You see, I haven't been sleeping very well recently, and the doctor gave me these tablets to knock me out, but I think they have side effects because I wake up feeling like a bear who hibernated too long . . .'

She talked for a while, giving him an entire invented history of her insomnia and her attempts to cure it naturally before resorting to drugs, not pausing for breath or giving him any room to interrupt, killing time but also deliberately speaking slowly, monotonously, making her voice as close to a drone as possible. She enjoyed watching him squirm impatiently, although she noticed his movements slow as she went on. She used the same words over and over: tired, pillow, bed, dream, *sleep*. He bit down on a yawn.

'Oh, sorry, am I boring you?'

'Yeah. Actually . . .' He trailed off, looked confused, shook his head. Looked into his beer bottle and realised it was empty.

'Would you like another?'

'No. I'm . . . good.'

He yawned again and his eyelids fluttered, looked heavy, like there were tiny weights attached to his lashes.

'It's the weather,' she said, in a slow, dreary tone. 'It makes you feel *drowsy*, doesn't it? *Sleepy*.'

'Huh? Yeah, I guess.' His eyes closed for a couple of seconds.

'Maybe I should make you a coffee?' she said. 'Do you take milk? Sugar?'

She didn't give him a chance to respond. She went into the kitchen and filled the kettle, then stood next to it, letting it boil. She checked the time on her phone. Waited until five minutes had passed.

When she went back in, Tommy was asleep.

The sedative she had put in his beer had done its job. She'd procured it a while back, from a woman she'd met in prison, knowing it would come in handy at some point. She'd discovered it years ago, during her year of travelling and sleeping around. Had regularly slipped it into the post-coital drinks of her partners so she could make an exit with whatever belongings took her fancy. Then she'd move on to the next place, the next bed.

Tommy was passed out on the sofa, his head resting on the back, his mouth open. He wasn't quite snoring but his breathing was wet and heavy. Why had she thought he was brutishly attractive? Close up, he truly was a disgusting specimen of a man. If she could slit his throat right now – put a blade through that bulging Adam's apple – and get away with it, she wouldn't hesitate. All that blood and DNA, though, and that was before she even considered the practicalities of removing his heavy body.

She had a much better idea.

Unfortunately, it involved taking his underpants off.

She crouched on the carpet by his feet and undid his shoelaces, then tugged at his trainers, recoiling at the smell of his socks and struggling not to gag. Muttering to herself, a steady stream of insults and curse words, she hooked her fingers into the waistband of his jogging bottoms and dragged them down to his knees, exposing his underpants. He was wearing tight little briefs, navy blue. She took a deep breath then pulled them down too. Finally, she pulled his T-shirt up to his chest so it wasn't anywhere near his naked groin.

It was, she supposed, unfortunate that he was flaccid, because it made the story she was concocting slightly less plausible. He was still quite big, though. Circumcised. She went out to the hallway and fetched some gloves so she wouldn't have to touch him with her bare hands. It was still gross, but she manoeuvred him so it looked like he at least had a semi. Then she picked up Tommy's phone, which was lying beside him on the sofa, and held it in front of his face to unlock it before taking several dick pics.

Then she sent them from his phone to hers, along with a string of messages.

> *Fiona. I want you to imagine how big I'm going to be when I'm naked with you. So big you're going to gasp with shock. I'm going to ruin you.*

Too much? No, it was the kind of vile message she'd received in the past from men on social media.

She typed out some more – a load of crap about all the things he wanted to do to her. *My wife doesn't turn me on anymore. I have to think about you to get hard with her. You're so much hotter than her.*

She thought about adding some more. Making up a confession that it was his fault that the bike's tyre had burst and that he knew Fiona wasn't to blame. But she decided to keep it simple. A bloke lusting after his neighbour. What could be simpler and easier to believe than that?

She messaged back from her own phone: *Leave me alone. You're married. Come near me again and I'll show this to Nicola. I can't believe you could be thinking about cheating when your poor son is still getting better.*

Then she fetched a knife from the kitchen and sat in the armchair across from him, waiting for him to wake up.

It took thirty minutes. Going mad with boredom, she considered chucking a glass of water in his face. But finally, he stirred. It took him a minute to figure out that he was sitting there with his underpants and joggers pulled down; another few seconds to see Fiona with the knife.

'Do what I say or I'll cut your cock off,' she said flatly, once she had his attention. 'Now, pick up your phone – it's right there – and look at your WhatsApp.'

Eyes wide, he wiped drool off his chin with the back of his hand, then opened the phone, all fingers and thumbs, taking a long time to navigate to WhatsApp. But when he did, it woke him up properly.

'What the hell?'

He tried to stand up, but she pointed the knife at him. 'Stay there and listen to me. I didn't have anything to do with your brat's accident, even though I might wish I had.' She spoke the lie with conviction. 'You're going to leave me alone. You're going to stop asking questions about me. Otherwise I'm going to show the pictures and messages you sent me to your wife. Got it?'

'You bitch. You drugged me!'

'Shut up. Tell me you understand. Or I'll go over there the moment she gets home and tell her how you've been harassing me. I'll tell the whole neighbourhood about what a disgusting pervert you are. Everyone will also know that you're so pathetic you can't even get a proper hard-on when you send a dick pic.'

He seemed even more concerned about that than he did about the prospect of his wife finding out.

'One more thing: you don't say anything to Emma about seeing me with Ethan, all right?'

'So are you shagging him?'

'Shut up, and tell me you understand.'

'I understand.'

'Good. Now pull your undies up and get out.'

He did exactly as she asked, glancing at the knife one more time before getting up and rearranging himself.

'I know what you're thinking,' she said. 'You're wondering how you can get my phone, delete the photos and messages. Well, they're already backed up and I've sent everything to a friend. If anything happens to me, she'll send everything to the police – and to Nicola.'

ϖ

So that was it. Tommy's threat had been eliminated – for now at least. She didn't think he would let this go forever, especially if he didn't believe her denials about her involvement in the accident. She might still have to do something about that.

For now, though, she had given herself breathing room.

'We're almost there,' she said, as if Maisie were there in the room with her. 'Just one to go.'

This was it. The final stages of the plan. And the person she needed to complete her plan – and move into the next stage of her life – would arrive home tomorrow.

25

I checked Rose's room in the holiday cabin to make sure she was asleep, then looked in on Dylan. He was sitting up in bed, playing on his phone, headphones on. I gestured to ask him to lower them.

'You okay?' I asked.

'I guess.'

'Pretty dramatic today, huh?'

He shrugged.

'Did you . . . see anything? Between Rose and Henry, I mean? Before his accident.'

'I just know that she hates him. Like she hates everyone at the moment.'

'She doesn't hate you.'

'Huh.' He was looking at his phone screen, rather than me. Avoiding eye contact. 'She's so angry with Mum. I think the only person she cares about right now is Fiona.'

I sighed. 'I'm sure that's not true. But . . . you're not a big fan of Fiona's, are you? Why is that?'

He didn't reply straight away. He fiddled with his phone, tapping at it, and I wondered if he was too distracted by his game to answer. But then he said, 'There's something sketchy about her. Like, when she doesn't know you're watching her, she changes.'

'What do you mean?'

'I can't explain it properly. But it's like, all the emotion disappears from her face and she goes blank. Like, I dunno, a robot or something.' He went a little pink as he said this, and I wondered if it was because, in order to make this observation, he must have spent a lot of time looking at her. 'Also, the other day, when Rose got back from their day out in the countryside, I saw them outside whispering to each other before Rose came inside, like they had a big secret.'

'What kind of a big secret?'

'How am I supposed to know? I just think . . .'

I waited.

'You always tell us to be wary of strangers. To not talk to people online or share our address or accept gifts. You taught us to be vigilant when it comes to people we don't know. But with Fiona, it's like all that went out the window.'

'We do know her, though. She's our neighbour.'

'For, like, five minutes!'

He put his headphones back on, signalling the end of the conversation. I left his room, feeling discombobulated. All this stuff about her face going blank when no one was looking was bizarre – and, frankly, hard to believe. I hadn't seen that side of her at all – had I? I racked my brain for any signs that she was anything other than completely nice and normal. All I could think of was that she hadn't told us about Rose seeing a man die in the park, and she'd let Rose watch a horror movie. There was Tommy's weird conviction that she'd had something to do with his son's accident, but I was sure that was nonsense.

You like her because she flirts with you, flatters you, said a little voice in my head. *You can't see beyond her pretty face and her body.*

But Emma liked her too. Trusted her enough to let her look after our daughter.

Dylan had to be imagining it. Misreading Fiona. He was only fifteen, after all, and he spent half his life in imaginary worlds where at least half the people you encountered wanted to kill you.

But even as I tried to reassure myself that Rose's character hadn't changed, I couldn't shake the sensation of unease – and the root cause of that was obvious. My discomfort whenever Fiona was mentioned. My guilt.

Playing laser tag with Emma earlier, being a team, having fun outside our domestic environment – it had brought it home to me how much I not only loved her but liked her. She was not just my wife and the mother of my children. She was my favourite person. She was cool and capable and game for a laugh. She was compassionate and clever. Fiona was nothing compared to Emma.

And I was in terrible danger of losing her.

I took a deep breath and steeled myself. It was time we talked.

ϖ

I found her sitting at the table outside, looking out at the lake, or pond – whatever it was. She had a bottle of wine in front of her, her glass half full. She poured one for me and pushed it in my direction as I sat down.

'Do you ever wish we still smoked?' she asked. We had both quit when she got pregnant with Dylan. 'I was just thinking how delicious a cigarette would be right now.'

'I could go and buy some if you like.'

'Ha.'

'I need to talk to you,' I said, at the same time that she said, 'We need to talk.'

I made a zipping motion across my lips and nodded for Emma to go ahead, a little dagger of dread pressing into my heart. Was this the conversation where she told me she was leaving me, that she was in love with someone else?

She took a deep breath.

'I saw Mike,' she said.

This of course delivered an electric charge, but I retained enough presence of mind to weigh my options: tell her that I knew this, that I'd seen them, or act surprised. In the end, my reaction was somewhere in between. I waited, heart thumping, bracing myself for what came next.

'It was the other day, before Iris gave you that money and you booked this holiday. I . . . It's hard to explain, and I need you to listen without interrupting or getting angry or upset, okay?'

I nodded. My insides had gone cold.

'Last year, when you found out about my friendship with him and forced me to end it, I knew it was the right thing to do because I valued our marriage and our family above everything else. I loved and love you, and didn't and don't want to be with anyone else.'

I could sense a 'but' coming.

'But . . . and please don't freak out, let me finish . . . I was a little bit in love with him. That infatuated, new-person kind of "in love", when you meet someone that you feel you have a connection with. Do you understand?'

I nodded. My mouth was too dry for me to speak.

'Nothing physical happened between Mike and me. I've told the truth about that. I never kissed him. We never touched each other. We didn't talk about sex or exchange sexual messages or anything like that.'

'But that . . . that might have happened,' I said, 'if you'd carried on seeing him.'

She hesitated, took a sip of wine. 'It might. I don't know. There was tension. I did think about it. And before you get upset, can you deny that you've ever fantasised about someone else since we've been together?'

I couldn't deny it.

'It's normal,' she said. 'But what wasn't normal, what wasn't right, was how addicted I felt to his company. How often we would meet up, even if it was just talking. It was dangerous. And I think I wanted you to find out, to put a stop to it before anything more happened. I was scared to tell you about it, but I made it easy for you to discover what was going on.'

I nodded, remembering how she'd left her phone out, unlocked, so I could see she had added the extra layer of security to WhatsApp. How she had immediately caved when I'd demanded to know why.

'So when you found out what was happening and went ballistic, I was relieved. It was horrible, yes. I hated how hurt you were. I hated all the arguments. And I was shocked when you said we needed to move, that I needed to be out of sight of Mike, even though I knew you were right. So I agreed with you. I did it because I knew it was for the best, and it *was* what I wanted.'

'I can feel another "but" coming.'

'*However . . .*' She smiled, breaking the tension, but just a little. 'I couldn't shake this feeling that everything had happened on your terms, and after we moved to our new place, where I didn't know anyone, in a new house that I still don't like as much as our old one, I started to feel resentful. I told myself I hadn't really done anything wrong. I'd been friends with Mike, that was all. Would you have minded if he was a woman? What even *is* an emotional affair, anyway? I started to think it was a ridiculous term. And I brooded over it, feeling dissatisfied and hard done by. And I was sick and tired of you making me feel guilty, like I was a child who'd done something wrong.'

I had to fight the urge to say *But you* did *do something wrong.* Some of the stuff she was saying hurt. But, somehow, knowing that I needed to push that hurt aside – or we would never get anywhere, never get through this – I bit my tongue. After a moment, I was able to say, 'Emma, you should have talked to me about all of this. Told me how you were feeling.'

'I couldn't. Because I was sure you would just tell me that I had no right to complain, that it was me who'd almost wrecked our marriage, that I should suck it up and get on with it.'

I was shocked. 'I never talk to you like that.'

'No. But I'm sure that's what you think. Maybe in milder terms, but I'm in the right ballpark, aren't I?'

It was hard for me to deny.

'Anyway, that's why I decided to see Mike. I wanted that chance to do things on my terms. To see if I did still have feelings for him.'

That made me flinch. 'And . . . do you?'

'No. Oh, Ethan, don't look so worried. You know what? I didn't even have platonic feelings for him. I realised that I didn't even like him that much – that he's boring. Big-headed. Not funny. I have no idea what I was even thinking last year . . . Except, and this is something we are going to need to talk about, I think I was trying to fill a gap in my life, something I wasn't getting from our marriage.' Another gulp of wine. 'This is all hard to say and hard to hear, I'm sure. I'm just trying to be totally honest.'

I nodded. I felt sick. But my overwhelming sensation was relief. She hadn't told me she'd realised she loved Mike and wanted to be with him.

'I am almost certain now that whatever was going on between Mike and me would have burned itself out. I would have come to my senses. Because I do love you. Maybe I was feeling neglected because you were putting so much energy into the shop. Maybe it was just a twenty-year-itch thing. I don't know. Marriage is hard, isn't it, especially when you live in a world full of other people. So yeah, that's what I wanted to say. I feel like a great weight has lifted off me. That the sense of injustice and of unfinished business has gone. Oh my God, Ethan, is that a tear?'

I wiped my cheek. 'I'm just so relieved. I thought you were going to tell me you wanted a divorce.'

'And claim half your record collection.'

'I knew I should have got you to sign a pre-nup.'

We both laughed and I rubbed my eyes, blinking away more tears. I took her hands and we leaned forward, putting our foreheads together. Some of what she'd said had been difficult to hear and I knew there were some issues we were going to have to deal with. On top of that, I could see how wrong I'd been to keep punishing her, and to brood over my own resentment.

We should've talked more. Should have been more honest.

We both stood and embraced. I kissed her. She kissed me back. And then we sat down again and talked more. We talked about things we were going to do to make sure we felt close to each other. More time together. Date nights. I would spend less time at the shop. We'd do more things with the kids, as a family. Most importantly, we would check in with each other. Talk more. Not hide things. It was the most constructive, honest conversation we'd had in a long time.

Except I didn't tell her about how I'd almost kissed Fiona. I didn't see the point. I had only gone round to see her because I thought Emma was seeing Mike again, and nothing had happened really. It wasn't important. I could honestly say that I had no feelings for Fiona whatsoever.

Then Emma startled me by saying, 'I actually have Fiona to thank.'

I pulled back. 'What? Why?'

'We had a chat the other day, when she dropped Rose home. She asked me if I was okay, and then started telling me about her ex-girlfriend, about how it would have been their anniversary, and then we ended up opening a bottle of wine and having a bit of a heart-to-heart.'

'And you told her about Mike?'

I felt something cold creep through my veins. I had already told Fiona about Emma's 'emotional affair' before this.

'Yeah. Not everything, but enough. Including what I just told you about feeling like it had ended on your terms. And she recommended that I get in touch with him, meet up with him, prove to myself we could just be friends. Of course, she didn't realise it would end with me not wanting to even be that.'

I was stunned. Fiona had known Emma was going to see Mike, but had acted like she was surprised when I told her.

What was she up to? And now, of course, it was too late to talk to Emma about this, because I'd failed to tell her about my encounter with Fiona.

'Ethan? Hello?' Emma was speaking. 'What was it you wanted to talk to me about?'

I blinked at her. 'Huh?'

'When you first came out here, you said you wanted to talk.'

'Oh.' I didn't want to go into it now. I needed time to process what I'd just learned. 'I was going to talk to you about Rose and this incident with Henry, and her behaviour recently, but it can wait.'

'Yeah. I've decided to try to go a bit easier on her. Like Angela said, she's growing up. It's all normal. I just don't want her to turn into a complete devil.'

I laughed, and said, 'Amen to that.'

I leaned forward and kissed my wife. 'I love you,' I said. 'Let's go to bed.'

26

Fiona watched from her upstairs window as the Doves' car rolled to a halt outside their house. They were back. At last! Lola, sensing her owners, had already begun to bark, and she rushed out to greet her humans the second Fiona opened the door, tail whipping back and forth as she ran up to Emma, then Ethan.

Fiona slipped out quietly, heading straight to the car, to Rose.

As soon as the girl got out of the back seat, she lifted her face towards Fiona's and their eyes met, held contact, and there it was. The connection. The recognition. Unmistakable. It was like the ugly duckling looking at his reflection and realising he was a beautiful swan. That moment of recognising your true nature and seeing it mirrored back at you. If Fiona had harboured any final doubts, even after witnessing Rose launch Patrick down the stairs, they were gone now.

'Have a good time?' Fiona asked, heading back towards Ethan and Emma, who were being licked to death by their cockapoo.

Emma laughed. 'Yes, beautiful place. We had fun.'

Fiona looked Emma up and down. She had a lightness about her. A different energy. Glancing over towards the car, where Ethan was struggling with the suitcases, Fiona whispered to her, 'Did anything happen with Mike? Did you contact him?'

'It's okay,' Emma said, stepping out of her children's earshot. 'Ethan knows. And it's all sorted. Seeing Mike made me realise there was no real connection between us. Not even friendship. Ethan and I had a really good talk and cleared the air.'

'Oh. That's great.'

Fiona glanced towards Ethan again and caught him looking at her, wearing a sheepish expression. He immediately looked away.

'I guess I have to thank you for your advice,' Emma said. 'And thank you so much for looking after Lola.'

The dog was running around in circles now, whimpering with excitement, and Emma scooped her into her arms, turning to go.

'Ethan will pop round later to pick up Lola's stuff. That okay, Ethan?'

He had that rabbit-in-the-headlights look. 'Huh? Oh yeah. Of course.'

'Shall I pick Rose up at the usual time tomorrow morning?' Fiona asked.

'Oh, you don't need to,' Emma said. 'I've taken the rest of the week off work.'

The whole family trooped into their house, Ethan avoiding her gaze, only Rose turning to look back at her. Their eyes meeting. It was clear she had changed, was fully out of the chrysalis now. But when was Fiona going to be able to spend time with her? It was frustrating as hell.

On top of that, Ethan and Emma had made up; and that had not been part of the plan. Right now, the broken-hearted Ethan – realising his marriage was over, full of hatred for his wife – should be running into Fiona's arms.

As she closed the front door, a phone rang.

She went into the living room and grabbed her mobile. Except the ringing wasn't coming from this phone. And she didn't have a landline. Then she remembered: Lucy's phone. God, no. Where had she put it?

She followed the ringing and found it in her bedroom cupboard. Pressed the answer button.

'Fiona.' Her voice was icy.

'Hello Lucy. Where are you. In your cell?'

'My *room*, yes.' As if the prison were a hotel that she'd chosen to book into permanently. 'We're all in lockdown because there was a fight this morning. Some drama caused by this new woman who really ought to be in a psychiatric hospital.' She sighed. 'I'm going to have to deal with her.'

'But that's not why you're calling?'

'No. I just wanted to catch up. What's been happening out there?'

Fiona was hesitant. Could Lucy have been offered some sort of deal? Were the police listening in to this call? Four days had passed now since Patrick's death, and there still hadn't been anything on the news about it. That didn't mean, though, that they hadn't found him. Fiona was sure she hadn't left any evidence behind and that no one had seen her and Rose go to his house. But might she have made a mistake she wasn't aware of? And might Lucy have been told she'd get special privileges if she helped entrap Fiona?

'Nothing's been happening at all.'

'Really? Not been working on your mission?'

Fiona didn't respond. Through the window she could see that Ethan had gone back outside to unpack the car. She wondered what Lucy would make of him. He was exactly the kind of naive, good-natured person she enjoyed tormenting.

'What about the girl? Did you take my advice and ditch her?'

'I'm still spending my days looking after her,' Fiona said.

'Huh. Well, you do you, as they say. I'm really calling to find out what progress you've made with my old friends.'

Of course she was. Irritating, but better than an attempt at entrapment.

'You mean Jamie and Kirsty?'

'Urgh. It still makes me feel ill when I hear their names. But what have you done? I've been going crazy here, waiting to hear about the suffering you've caused them. I've decided for certain, Kirsty's daughter should be the target . . .'

'Lucy, I haven't had a chance. I've been too busy.'

'What, looking after that girl?'

'Among other things.'

Lucy's voice could have frozen lava. 'You promised me, Fiona. When you were in here, you told me you were going to help me. I thought we had a bond.'

'We do. And I will get round to it. You just need to be patient.'

Lucy's voice went from icy to Arctic: 'Do *not* tell me to be patient.'

'Or what?' The words emerged before Fiona could worry about the consequences. Oh well. The page had been turned. 'What are you going to do about it?'

There was a long, outraged silence before Lucy said, 'How dare you.'

Fiona could hardly believe it herself. But she was sick of Lucy trying to order her around. And she was in a bad mood after hearing about Ethan and Emma, and being told she would be kept from Rose this week.

'You're going to be in prison for the rest of your life, Lucy. Maybe it's time you made peace with it. Jamie and Kirsty beat you. Accept it and move on.'

Lucy screeched, 'You b—'

Fiona hung up, trembling as adrenaline coursed through her.

She and Lucy might have a bond, but Fiona would *not* let someone boss her about. Besides, she had a new connection now. With someone at the start of her career, not the end.

She watched as Ethan finished unpacking the car. She noticed that he deliberately didn't look in the direction of her house. Such a coward.

In her original plan, she had thought that driving a further wedge between Ethan and Emma would make everything easier, with both her mission and its aftermath. But thinking about it, she decided it didn't make too much of a difference. The important thing was that Rose was fully ready now. It was time to speed things up.

Very soon, she would have Ethan exactly where she wanted him.

27

I returned to work the day after we got back from Shropshire. The shop was busy, which helped to distract me, and I should have been happy. Emma and I were getting along better than we had in years. Even Dylan had commented on it: 'What's up with you two? Anyone would think you actually like each other.'

We knew we still had work to do. There were a lot of wrinkles that needed to be ironed out. But I was confident it was going to be okay between us.

There were, however, two things gnawing at my good mood.

First, Rose's behaviour on the trip and the continuing tension between her and Emma. I couldn't work out if it was emotional growing pains or something more. I did hope, though, that the two of them spending this week together would help, and I had my fingers crossed that by the weekend they would be best friends again, and we would be reassured that our daughter wasn't growing devil horns and a pointed tail.

The second thing playing on my mind was my growing worry about Fiona. Not the hug I'd exchanged with her – because that's all it had been, a comforting hug – but my concern that, well, to use Dylan's words: there was something sketchy about her. *Like, when she doesn't know you're watching her, she changes.*

Last night, I had gone round to pick up Lola's stuff. Fiona was friendly, relaxed, asking about the trip, wanting to know if Rose had enjoyed herself. I wanted to get out of her house quickly so didn't tell her about the incident at laser tag. But while we chatted I tried to surreptitiously study her. Had she deliberately tried to break me and Emma up, encouraging her to contact Mike while flirting with me? If I'd thought she wanted me, and that the stuff with Mike was part of a scheme to send me into her arms, I would have understood it. Seeing her after the trip, I was nervous, worrying she would be all over me. But she showed no signs of liking me in that way at all. She acted like we were nothing more than neighbours. I was simultaneously relieved and confused.

But *why* had she led Emma towards the meet-up with Mike and then acted as if she knew nothing about it? There was something devious about her behaviour.

It played on my mind all day at work. So much so that, when I got home, instead of going into my house, I headed over to see Iris.

She invited me in and I immediately spotted the suitcase in the hallway.

'Oh, you're going away?'

'Yes.' She beamed. 'I'm off to Canada. I'm going to visit my son and see my grandchildren.'

'That's so lovely. Are you on your way out right now?'

'No, I've got a taxi picking me up at one. Early-morning flight from Heathrow. I'm so excited, Ethan! And I wouldn't be able to afford it without you.' I followed her into the kitchen. 'I was actually going to come over and ask if you could keep an eye on the house for me.'

'Of course.'

We were standing by her kitchen window, which gave me an excellent view of both my house and Fiona's. Iris followed my gaze.

'Everything all right?' she asked. 'You seem like there's something on your mind.'

I hesitated. This was why I'd come over here. 'I don't suppose you've remembered where you know Fiona from, have you?'

She exhaled with frustration. 'No. It's been driving me crazy. I can feel it right there, just beneath the surface. I probably need to be hypnotised to free the memory.'

I looked at her and she laughed.

'That wasn't a serious suggestion. A friend of mine was hypnotised and she still thinks she's a chicken.'

'Really?'

Another laugh. 'Oh, Ethan, what's happened to your sense of humour? Tell me again what you know about Fiona. Perhaps it will shake something loose.'

We sat at the kitchen table and went through it all again. She had grown up in Western Australia but moved here when she was in her early twenties. She used to work in Canary Wharf, something to do with banking.

'Has she ever mentioned any friends?' Iris asked. 'Boyfriends or ex-husbands?'

'No, though I think she's bisexual. And, as far as I've seen, she doesn't have any friends.'

This had only just struck me. It was odd, wasn't it? It wasn't as if she was completely new to the Greater London area. But I hadn't ever seen anyone visit her house and she never appeared to go out, unless it was with Rose. She had never mentioned any friends either.

Iris fetched her iPad and her reading glasses. 'Let's have a look and see if we can find her online. Fiona Smith, yes?'

She typed the name into Google and we scanned through the results. There were, of course, seemingly thousands of them.

Academics, lawyers, doctors, councillors, a woman who did make-up tutorials on YouTube.

'Search for "Fiona Smith banker",' I suggested.

Iris tried that and there were a number of results, but none of them were my next-door neighbour.

Next we tried Facebook, where Iris had hundreds of friends, far more than me. Again, there were many Fiona Smiths but none of them looked like the person we were looking for.

'Why can't she be called Moonbeam Skyrocket or something?' Iris asked. 'Fiona Smith is a bit like being called Jane Smith, isn't it? Or John Smith.'

'You think it might be a fake name?'

'Hmm. That wasn't what I meant. But . . . do *you* think it might be? No job, no friends, a name that is unsearchable . . . Oh my goodness.'

'What?'

Her voice was hushed, as if there might be criminals at the door, listening in. 'Do you think she might be in witness protection? Maybe she's due to give evidence against some dangerous people.'

'I hope not! I can't imagine her volunteering to be a childminder if she had people after her.'

'True.'

At that moment a car pulled up outside and, through the kitchen window, we watched Tommy get out, heading towards his house.

Iris got up. 'Wait there. I just need to tell him I'm going away.'

She went to her front door and I watched Iris chatting with him. I had heard that Albie's long-term prognosis was much improved, which was a big relief. Then something else came to me and I went out on to the front lawn where Iris and Tommy stood.

I was quite shocked by his appearance. He had dark shadows under his eyes and looked like he was coming down with something nasty.

'Hey Tommy,' I said. 'Can I just ask you something?'

'I'm in the middle of a conversation.'

Iris stepped back and said, 'It's fine. I need to water the garden before I go away anyway.'

Tommy said, 'Have a wicked holiday, Mrs B.' Then, as she went through the side gate towards the garden, he turned to me. 'What is it?'

I flicked my eyes across to Fiona's place and spoke quietly, as if she'd be able to hear me from across the street. 'Do you still think Fiona might have had something to do with—?'

He cut me off. 'Nope. No way.'

'Oh. Because last time I was here, Eric said something about you having your eye on her.'

'Did he?' Why did he seem so flustered? Spots of pink had appeared on his neck. 'That kid doesn't know what he's talking about. Albie's accident was just that. An accident.'

'But—'

'I've gotta go, yeah?'

He vanished into his house and I turned to find Iris standing just beyond her gate. She had clearly been eavesdropping.

'Is it me,' I asked, 'or did he start acting extremely weird when I mentioned Fiona's name?'

'It's not you.'

I could see movement behind the windows of my house. I hadn't been home yet. 'I'd better get back. If you think of anything while you're in Canada, will you call me?'

'Of course. Take my advice, Ethan. Don't get old. It does terrible things to the memory.'

'Getting old is better than the alternative.'

'Ha. Very true.'

I walked back to the house, wondering what to do. It was only a fortnight until Rose went back to school, and she would be spending this week with Emma, but should we stop Fiona from looking after her for the final week? I knew Rose would protest vehemently if we did.

I went through the front door, intending to talk to Emma about it, and found her in our bedroom. She was wearing a dress and putting her make-up on in the mirror.

'What's happening?' I asked. 'Have I forgotten something?'

She kissed me. 'No, I decided to surprise you. I've booked us a table at this new place in Wimbledon. The one that was in the *Guardian* a couple of weeks ago.'

I had a vague memory that I'd read the review out to Emma, saying how much I'd like to go there. A new Indonesian place that sounded amazing.

'I was about to call you to find out where you were. You'd better start getting ready.'

'What about the kids? Are they coming?'

'To our romantic evening out? No, I've sorted it. Fiona's coming round.' The doorbell rang. 'That'll be her now.'

I heard footsteps on the stairs. Rose running down to open the door.

'What's the matter?' Emma asked.

'I . . . Nothing.'

It was too late to do anything now. Fiona was already here and I could hear her and Rose talking in the hallway, Rose speaking quickly, excitedly, thrilled to be reunited.

I went to the top of the stairs and looked down. There was Fiona, wearing jeans and a baggy T-shirt. From here, I could see the dark roots of her hair. It hadn't struck me before that she wasn't a natural blonde.

She sensed me looking and glanced up.

'Hi Ethan.'

Our eyes met and she held my gaze, and it was like she was looking right into my brain, reading my thoughts. I forced myself to smile and she smiled too, though hers looked as fake as mine felt.

It was as if we were playing chess and she'd realised I'd figured out she was about to attempt to checkmate me. Like we were entering some sort of endgame.

The problem was, I had no idea what that endgame was.

28

Rose's bedroom was different. The room of an adolescent rather than a little girl. The walls were bare, apart from a picture of a beach that looked like it had come from IKEA.

'What happened to the Taylor Swift posters?' Fiona asked.

Rose shrugged. 'Got bored of them.'

'And your Barbies?'

'I put them out with the bins.'

Fiona was shocked. 'What did your parents say about that?'

'They don't know yet. I just did it.' Her voice was flat. Emotionless.

'Rose . . . It's a good idea to pretend. To be into the kind of stuff twelve-year-olds are meant to be into. For protection.'

Rose frowned like this annoyed her. 'Twelve-year-olds aren't meant to like dolls. They're stupid. I'm leaving all that behind.'

Fiona had been expecting something like this. The change, hastened by what had happened at Patrick's house. The accelerated pupation. Still, it was unsettling. Here was the butterfly, perched on the edge of her single bed, no expression on her face.

Fiona took a deep breath. Dylan was in his room but had music playing – some discordant rock racket – so Fiona was confident he wouldn't be able to eavesdrop. 'They found him today,' she said. 'Patrick. There was a piece on the local newspaper site.

Former journalist dies in domestic accident. There doesn't seem to be any suspicion that it was anything other than a fall.'

Rose nodded as if she hadn't expected anything else.

'He worked for a national paper, so I expect there'll be some coverage there, maybe an obituary, but I don't think we have anything to worry about.'

'I wasn't worried.'

Of course. Nothing had gone wrong in Rose's life yet. She thought she was invincible. 'I'm glad to hear it. Tell me about your holiday. How was it? Anything interesting happen?'

Rose sighed like Fiona had asked her how her day at school had been. 'There was this really annoying boy called Henry who followed me around everywhere. We were playing laser tag, my family and his, and I wanted to win.'

'Of course you did. What happened?'

Rose swung her legs, bouncing her heels on the carpet. 'There was this raised area, the crow's nest they called it, and I couldn't get Henry out of it without getting shot. So I talked to him. I told him how repulsive he was. How his ears stuck out and he had bad breath. I told him he was ugly and stupid and that his parents didn't really love him. I said I'd overheard them talking about how they wished he'd never been born. I said that I'd heard his sister say that he still wet the bed.'

Fiona laughed. 'Wow. You laid it on thick.'

Rose didn't crack a smile. 'I thought he was going to yell at me, that I'd make him angry and he'd expose his position, allow me to shoot him. But he melted down, started crying. He jumped out of the crow's nest and tried to run down this ramp, which was when he slipped and fell.'

'Was he hurt?'

'Not that badly.' She sounded disappointed. 'I think he was bruised, that was all. But he didn't snitch on me. Too scared.'

Fiona made another mental note to warn Rose that normal people often told tales later, that she should always be careful. Have plausible deniability, and be prepared to use blackmail if that failed.

'Did anyone overhear you?'

'Maybe his sister. Dylan's new girlfriend.' She said the last word like it tasted rotten.

'Girlfriend?'

'Yeah. They've been messaging non-stop since we got back. Keira. She heard me talking to Henry, but she doesn't have any proof.'

Fiona was excited. She had feared that Rose might be freaked out by what had happened in Wadhurst, feel the need to confess, reveal that she wasn't like Fiona after all. But Rose was acting exactly as Fiona had done after Sienna drowned, all those years ago. Fiona hadn't yet met Maisie then; hadn't understood her own feelings – or lack of them – and had no one to guide her. Rose was lucky. She was about to get the education Fiona had only had later.

Rose lifted her gaze to meet Fiona's. The girl's eyes shone like dark pebbles. 'What I did to Henry. I'm supposed to feel bad, aren't I?'

'Are you?'

Rose got up and walked across to the window. She seemed so much older than she was. Fiona remembered that she had been the same. When she was eleven or twelve, everyone had said she was an old soul. Adults would compliment her on her maturity. 'She's very serious, isn't she?' people would say, after which Fiona learned how to copy smiles and laughter, to make them look and sound real. Normal society didn't like girls who didn't smile, who didn't appear to be soft. This was another lesson she was going to have to teach Rose.

'When I was a little kid,' Rose went on, 'at nursery, they had this big soft-play room. There was a tower and chutes you could slide down and all these things you could climb. One day I pushed this other kid off this big tower because I wanted this cuddly animal she had. She sprained her arm and everyone went crazy. The girl's parents, the nursery staff, my mum and dad. I kept saying sorry. But I don't think I did feel sorry. I wanted that cuddly toy. I didn't care if I had to hurt her to get it.'

Fiona nodded for her to go on.

'But I think I realised that if I kept doing what I wanted, I'd get into trouble. I liked the nursery. It was fun. I liked playing on the tower. They gave us treats. So I learned to follow the rules. That made people happy. All the adults smiled and told me I was a good girl and gave me the things I asked for. I learned to camouflage myself. I learned how to blend in.'

Fiona had that tingle. This was so familiar. 'But sometimes your nature shone through?'

Rose turned away from the window. Behind her, it was growing dark. Autumn would be on its way soon. Fiona's favourite season. Leaves dying, black nights, less imperative to fake happiness.

'I had this best friend. A girl called Jasmine.'

'You've mentioned her.'

'Yeah. Well, when we started school she was, like, the weirdo. The kid whose parents sent her to school in the wrong uniform, who had nothing in her lunchbox except a chocolate bar. She always had dirty fingernails and you'd see the teachers whispering about her. I decided to be friends with her because I didn't want to be on my own.'

'The pack instinct,' Fiona said.

Rose frowned. 'Jasmine was so annoying. She was weak. She let the other girls upset her. They called her Jas-minger.'

Fiona hadn't encountered the word 'minger', meaning an unattractive person, until she'd come to the UK.

Rose went on: 'And she let them. There was this group of popular girls who really bullied her and made her do jobs for them, or do their homework, clean their shoes at breaktime. It was so embarrassing. She'd do everything they asked and then they'd shout, "Thank you, Jas-minger!" and run off laughing, ignoring her. It made me hate her. The way she refused to stand up for herself. She was so weak.'

'So what did you do?'

'I guess I started being horrible to her. I called her Jas-minger too. I made her shoplift chocolate bars from the corner shop, even though she was terrified of being caught. I wrote a fake love letter to this boy and signed it from her, so then all the boys started teasing her. I stole her schoolwork from her bag so she'd get into trouble with teachers. And all the time I knew I was meant to feel bad, but I didn't. It made me happy. I had power over her. And she was so pathetic, she deserved it.'

'Like Henry.'

'Yeah. Just like Henry.'

There was a long pause.

'I know why you took me to that museum to see the wolves and the walrus and all the predators. Because that's what I am, isn't it?'

'It's what *we* are, Rose. Apex predators. And people like Jasmine and Henry are prey. It's the way the world is supposed to work. Some people – like a friend of mine called Lucy – get nourishment from tormenting and hurting others in the same way wolves obtain nourishment from meat. It's a kind of pure pleasure for her. A need. Some of us aren't that . . . sadistic. But we don't let others stand in the way of what we want.'

'Is that what Max and Patrick were? Prey? Or were you trying to get something from them?'

Rose's pupils were dilated. She was excited by all this. Happy to hear she was different. To understand why she felt the way she did.

To know she was special – and not alone.

'With Max and Patrick it was different. That was vengeance – another understandable motivation for us. It was because of what they did to me. It was because of them that I spent some time in prison.'

Rose's eyes went wide. 'You were in prison?'

'Yeah. Max was our lawyer and Patrick was the one who figured out what we were doing. Who exposed—'

'Wait. Who's *we*?'

'Ah. Maisie and me. Maisie was my partner.'

'Your *girlfriend*?'

'I suppose you could use that word, but it doesn't really describe it.' She really didn't want to go into all the details of her relationship with Maisie with a twelve-year-old. 'We were a team. A little pack. We lived together, did everything as a couple. And we were going to get rich together.'

29

It was Fiona's turn to get up and cross to the window. The street lights had come on, casting a soft glow across the estate. As she watched, Tommy came out of his house and lurched off down the road, walking unsteadily. Drunk, Fiona assumed.

'We had a scheme to make a lot of money,' she said to Rose. 'Enough to allow us to move out of London into the countryside. There's this house . . . Well, we'll come to that. It's the kind of property neither of us could ever afford through so-called honest means. But the world is full of people who have inherited their wealth, been handed everything by Mummy and Daddy. My parents had nothing to give me and neither did Maisie's. So we found someone who would be generous.'

'A rich person?'

'Oh yes.' The thought of all the money in Dinah Uxbridge's bank account still made her blood grow hot. 'Filthy rich. And all alone. She lived in this ridiculous, huge house in Dulwich, not far from where Maisie and I had our little flat. Maisie met her first. Got chatting to her in this cemetery in West Norwood, where Dinah was visiting her husband's grave. He was a former Member of Parliament. Old Etonian. Born with a silver spoon rammed right up his . . .' She trailed off, remembering who her audience was.

'And he left his money to his wife?'

'Yes, exactly, although she already had family money of her own. Honestly, Rose, these people . . . They were old money through and through. So *British*. Dinah said that she'd been a "party girl" in New York. Run away from home, hung out with a wild crowd. Andy Warhol and his superstars.' Rose's reaction told Fiona that she didn't know who that was. Of course she wouldn't. Ancient history. 'Once she'd got that out of her system, she came home and married a rising star of the Tory Party. They had a daughter but she died when she was young. Drug overdose. All very tragic, blah blah.'

Rose nodded.

'Anyway, to cut a long story short, she was in her early eighties when Maisie met her. Still quite healthy, but living all alone in this house that was too big for her to take care of. She'd had a housekeeper and a gardener but they'd both retired recently, and she didn't have a clue about how to hire new ones. You should have seen the place. The garden looked post-apocalyptic and the house was crumbling from the inside, mice everywhere, damp coming through the walls. Worth a mint, though. An absolute mint.'

'A million?'

'Oh, more. Much more. Plus she had all this money in her bank account that she refused to spend because she was supposedly saving it for a rainy day. She was in her eighties! It was already pissing down.' Fiona chuckled. 'Maisie saw the opportunity immediately. Dinah was exactly the kind of person we'd been looking for. Loaded and clueless and lonely. Most importantly, she had no immediate family. There was a sister who was in a nursing home. A niece and her offspring. But that was it.'

Fiona was enjoying this. The only other person she'd told this story to was Lucy, huddled together in Lucy's cell – sorry, *room*. 'Maisie told Dinah she had a friend who was looking for somewhere to stay, then took me round to meet her. I thickened my accent, which she loved because she'd spent some time in Australia when she was young. She talked at length about the wonderful vineyards in Margaret River. *My* family used to buy cheap crap from the bottle-o. We came to an agreement. She would provide me with lodgings, and in return I'd keep the place clean and do some gardening.'

Rose was beginning to fidget, so Fiona hurried up.

'The point was, I wanted Dinah to change her will so when she died everything went to me. Early on, she'd told me she was going to leave her estate to her niece, Verity, and her children. Verity would pop round every now and then, have a nose round, examine the valuables, check the house wasn't going to fall down. I could see the pound signs in her eyes, even though she was already well-off and would never want for anything. One day I found her taking photos of the paintings on the wall. Dinah also had this sketch that Warhol had given her, which Verity was always asking to look at. She asked if she could take it to get it valued, but Dinah wouldn't let her remove it from the house.

'I had three objectives: One, let Dinah know that Verity was a gold digger and drive a wedge between them. Two, take Verity's place in the will. And three, because Dinah was in annoyingly good health and could easily have lived to a hundred, help her get on with shuffling off this mortal coil.'

'This mortal what?'

'Coil. I needed to help her cark it.'

Rose still looked confused.

'*Die.*'

'Ah. Got it.'

Fiona smiled. 'The first and second parts were relatively easy. Dinah already knew Verity only loved her for her money, and she accurately thought the great-nieces were a pair of spoiled brats. I kept telling Dinah that if I were her, I would leave my money to charity. A cats' home, or something in her daughter's name: a drug rehab centre, maybe. I knew she'd hate that idea because she didn't want her family name forever associated with heroin. She didn't like cats either. But it was all designed to make her think about changing her will.

'I used all my charm' – everything she had learned about normal human behaviour – 'to win her over. I would hide her favourite pieces of jewellery or her purse so she thought she'd lost them, then miraculously find them, showing how honest I was and how she couldn't live without me. I pretended to be devoutly religious and went to church with her every Sunday. I cut her hair for her and did revolting things like massaging her bunions.' She shuddered at the memory. 'Finally, I saved her life.'

Rose, who had appeared to be drifting into a daydream, suddenly paid attention. 'How?'

'I knocked over a candle that Dinah had lit downstairs. She had actually snuffed it out before going to bed, but I relit it and used it to start a small fire. Then I rushed into her room and told her we needed to get out. It was a gamble. If the fire had spread and destroyed the house, I'd have had nowhere to live, not to mention the effect on the inheritance I was banking on. But I called 999 almost as soon as I lit the candle, so they arrived quickly and put it out before too much damage was done. Dinah was, as you can imagine, supremely grateful. Also, Maisie phoned, pretending to be Verity, calling not to check on her aunt but to ensure the Warhol sketch and all the other valuable possessions were okay.' Fiona laughed at the memory. Maisie had been so deliciously devious. 'Shortly after that, Dinah changed her will to leave everything to yours truly.'

'Wow.'

'Yep. And that meant it was time for the third part of the plan.'

'Pushing her off this mortal coil.'

'Exactly. Which is where Maisie really came in. She'd done this before, you see. She knew all about poisons. Drugs. Things you could slip into someone's food or drink, to slowly poison them over an extended period. Thallium, mostly. I was cooking Dinah's dinner every day, so it was easy to add it to her food. Tiny amounts that only had a big effect over time. We wanted it to look like she'd died of natural causes. And it would have worked, if it wasn't for Patrick.'

Rose had become far more attentive once Fiona had started talking about poison. 'That's why you wanted revenge on him?'

'Yep. He was an old friend of Dinah's late husband, the Tory MP. Often quoted him in stories about the soaring crime rate. He popped round unannounced one afternoon, because he was visiting a friend in the area. At this point, Dinah was in a bad way. Her hair was thinning, she was delirious half the time, and she had awful stomach pains. She was so delirious that she didn't notice that the doctor who kept visiting her was actually Maisie in a white coat.'

She sighed. 'I wasn't there when Patrick came round. I'd popped out to do some shopping. Dinah let him in, apparently convinced he was some lover she'd had in the sixties, and tried to slobber all over him. When he saw the state she was in, he rushed her to the hospital. He'd seen thallium poisoning before, reported on a case of it, so he was sure he knew what it was. They treated her and she made a full recovery. Told all about her lodger.'

'And that's when you went to prison?'

'Yes. Well, after a while. There was an investigation. Interviews. Evidence had to be gathered. It took a while. And then, one morning, the police turned up. We tried to get away but were arrested.' She glowered at the memory of it, then hurried through the rest of the story.

'We hired Max as our lawyer. He told us the police's evidence was overwhelming. The niece, Verity, was ready to testify, as was

Dinah herself. Max advised us to plead guilty. The arsehole. Then he brought me a letter from Maisie. We weren't allowed to see each other, you see.'

Rose was leaning forward now, gripped. 'What did the letter say?'

'She told me to read it, then destroy it. The letter said that she wished me luck. That she had written another letter confessing to the poisoning, saying I wasn't involved at all and hadn't known about it. And at the end she said that she had decided she couldn't face prison, even for a few years. *I was born to be free*, she wrote. *I can never be caged.*'

Rose's mouth hung open. 'What did she mean?'

Fiona didn't really feel emotions towards other people. Concern, pity, love: they were alien to her. But this was the closest she had ever come to feeling upset about something that had happened to someone else. Perhaps it was self-pity – the sensation that she'd been abandoned, left alone. But she had yelled at Max, told him to call the prison where they were holding Maisie. While he did that, she ripped the letter up into tiny pieces, chewing and swallowing it.

Max had returned just as she forced down the final shred, his face ashen, to tell her that Maisie had provoked the hardest, most violent criminal in the prison into a fight. The woman and her cronies had beaten Maisie to a pulp. She was in a coma.

Two days later, she died.

Rose's voice was hushed. Awestruck. 'She sacrificed herself. For you.'

Maisie had saved Fiona from a much longer prison term with her fake confession, which she had done not out of the goodness of her heart but because she enjoyed getting one over on the authorities, and Dinah had been so addled and confused that she didn't know who had been cooking her meals; she just remembered both women being in the house at various points. The CPS decided to go for the easy conviction: Fiona pleaded guilty to will fraud and was given three years, serving two of them.

Fiona had heard that line before, about Maisie sacrificing herself. But she didn't agree. Maisie had taken the coward's way out. She had abandoned Fiona, left her all alone in the world. Maisie hadn't even managed to conjure any emotions about her own life, making the cold, rational decision that she would rather be dead than in jail. Lucy, when Fiona had told her what happened, had put it best: *She was a quitter. A weak, pathetic quitter.*

'But,' Rose said, 'you wanted revenge for her death?'

'It's complicated. This is about being beaten. About having all my dreams snatched away from me, having to literally start again from scratch. I don't like losing, Rose. Max's incompetence and Patrick's sticky beak . . .'

Rose looked confused.

'Sticking his oar in. Interfering. If Max hadn't told us to plead guilty, that we stood little chance of acquittal, perhaps Maisie would have chosen to fight. Between the two of them – and the last person left on my shitlist – Max and Patrick destroyed all the work we'd done. I'm not going to let anyone get away with that.'

Rose started to ask something but Fiona talked over her. 'I was furious with Maisie too, even if she wrote that letter to absolve me. She left me on my own. Abandoned me.'

The one good thing Maisie had left Fiona was money. There was nothing in the law to stop Fiona inheriting Maisie's flat and her possessions. It had sat in a bank account until she'd got out of prison and had eventually allowed her to buy her new home here.

It was almost two years since she'd left prison. She'd had eighteen months of having to see a probation officer, of biding her time, and then she had moved here, free at last, and begun her mission. Max and Patrick were dead now. Dinah had died too, of natural causes, while Fiona was inside. Verity had inherited everything, including that Andy Warhol sketch. Fiona wished she'd ripped it up and eaten it, just like she'd eaten Maisie's letter.

'I'm thirsty,' Rose said.

'Me too. Let's get a drink.'

They passed Dylan's room and Fiona paused at the door. She could hear the low rumble of his voice. Talking to his new girlfriend? Or chatting with his gamer pals?

Downstairs, Fiona said, 'Can you grab me a Diet Coke? I need the loo.' She went into the toilet, which was right by the front door. As she sat down, the doorbell rang.

She heard Rose come into the hallway and call out, 'Hello?'

'Rose? It's me. Iris from across the road.'

Fiona listened as the front door opened, picturing the scene: the older woman standing there on the doorstep, street lights glowing behind her.

'Is your dad here?' Iris asked.

'They've gone out.'

'Oh . . . Damn. Can you give a message to him as soon as he gets home and ask him to come and see me? I have a taxi picking me up at one in the morning to take me to the airport, so any time before that is fine.'

'What shall I say it's about?'

In the toilet, Fiona was enrapt, waiting for the reply.

'Tell him I've remembered where I know Fiona from. She's not . . .' She didn't finish the sentence. *Not what?* 'Don't talk to Fiona, Rose, not until after I've talked to your dad. Do you promise me?'

'Sure.'

'Don't forget, Rose.'

The door closed, and Fiona flushed the toilet before emerging.

'Did you hear that?' Rose asked. 'She remembers you. Do you know *her*?'

Fiona shook her head, impatient, thrumming with stress. But if Iris knew *her* . . . This was bad. This could mess everything up.

She looked out through the front window and watched Iris cross back to her house. She glanced up the stairs. There was no sign of Dylan emerging from his room. Iris went inside and Fiona made an instant decision, speaking in a soft voice to give Rose instructions.

Putting the front door on the latch, she gestured for Rose to follow her across the street. It was fully dark now, all the street lights on. Quiet. Looking back over her shoulder, she could see a green-tinted flicker coming from Dylan's bedroom.

She stood to one side of Iris's door and whispered to Rose, telling her to knock.

Rose rapped gently on the door and Iris opened it almost immediately.

'Rose? Everything okay? Is your dad home now?'

Rose shook her head. 'Can I come in? I need to talk to you about Fiona. I'm . . . I'm frightened.'

'Of course. Come in, come in.'

Iris opened the door wide and Fiona stepped on to the front path.

'Hello Iris,' she said.

Iris looked like she was going to have a heart attack. She tried to shut the door but she was too slow. Fiona pushed through, shoving the old lady as she went, sending her stumbling into the hallway, banging a hip against the wall, crying out with pain. Rose followed, closing the door gently behind her. Fiona could sense her excitement.

'I'm calling the police,' Iris said, trying to get to the kitchen.

Fiona blocked her.

'Oh no,' she said. 'You're not calling anyone.'

30

'I don't think we should let Rose spend her days with Fiona anymore,' I said.

We were halfway through our main course. The restaurant was busy, the food a little disappointing after the hype, but it was still good to be out with my wife. There was a candle on the table, the lights were low, and it was romantic. We were reconnecting and, with the candlelight casting a glow upon her skin and hair, Emma was as beautiful as on our very first date, all those years ago.

It might have been romantic, but we were still talking about our offspring.

Emma put her fork down. 'Why? Has something happened?'

I outlined my worries. My growing concern about the influence Fiona was having on our daughter, including what Dylan had said about our neighbour.

'I mean, look at Rose's behaviour recently. Her moodiness. The way she talks to you in particular. She's even changed her bedroom. She told me she was going to get rid of her Barbies.'

'But that's just her growing up! I know as her dad you find it hard to accept, but that's all that's happening.'

'So how do you explain what Dylan said? About how Fiona's face goes blank when she doesn't think anyone is looking?'

'That just sounds like Dylan's imagination running riot to me. Too many video games and horror films.'

'Dylan's not the one who watches horror films. Fiona let Rose watch that *M3GAN* movie. God knows what else she's been showing her.'

'Didn't you tell me you started watching scary movies when you were eleven?'

'Yeah, but—'

'What, it's different for boys?'

I had stopped eating, suddenly no longer hungry. I really didn't want to argue, not when we were finally getting along again. But I couldn't let the subject drop.

'She let Rose see someone *die*. That man in the park.'

'That wasn't Fiona's fault.'

'I know, but she neglected to tell us about it. There was the whole thing with Albie and Eric too, back at the start of the summer. She didn't tell us about that either. What if we made a big mistake letting Fiona look after her? What if Fiona brings out Rose's bad side?'

'What are you talking about?'

'Remember when Rose pushed that girl off the tower at nursery?'

'What, when she was four?'

'Yes. I know it was a long time ago, but don't you remember how concerned we were at the time? About how she showed no remorse?'

'She was four!'

'You've obviously forgotten how worried about it we were. How we wondered if we were doing something wrong with our parenting. Don't you remember how we talked to her about the importance of being kind?'

'Of course I remember. And it worked. She's been absolutely fine since then.'

'She *was* absolutely fine.' I sighed. 'Maybe I'm being stupid. But her behaviour has definitely changed recently. You can't deny it. This incident with Henry, her bad temper, taking stuff without asking . . .'

'You really think that's because of Fiona? You heard what Angela said. She's a child psychologist. She knows what she's talking about. It's normal, Ethan. We don't know what happened with Henry, and it's completely normal for there to be conflict between me and her – though I'm going to do what I can to smooth things over. That's why I took this week off work, so I can spend some time with her, show her I'm not a bad guy.'

'That's good. I'm really pleased you're doing that. Maybe I could take a week off too, look after her for the final week of the holidays. Then Fiona won't need to do any more childminding, Rose will be back at school, Fiona will presumably start her job – if it even exists.'

'What makes you say that?'

'Well, she never mentions it, does she? And she's extremely vague if you ask her about it. Plus I searched for her name in relation to banking and nothing came up. I checked Google, LinkedIn, all the social sites. It's weird. I'm not even sure if Fiona Smith is her real name.'

'What?'

'Iris is sure she knows her from somewhere.'

'Right.' Emma looked at me as if waiting for more.

'She gets a bad vibe from her too.'

Emma laughed. 'Oh my God. The woman across the road gets a bad vibe from her. We'd definitely better stop our daughter from seeing her.' She picked up her fork again. 'I am so tired of this subject, Ethan.'

'So you're not going to listen to my concerns?'

She sighed heavily. 'Rose loves her. If we stop her seeing her – based on some hunch – then, well, if you think Rose has been difficult recently, you'll be in for a nasty surprise. Because, believe me, she could be a *lot* worse.'

'We shouldn't allow the fear of Rose's moods to dictate our parenting decisions.'

This time the sigh was both heavy and deep. 'We're going in circles, Ethan. Look, if you bring me one piece of proof that Fiona is a bad person or a malign influence, then of course I'll stop Rose from seeing her. In fact, if she's done anything to harm Rose, I'll punch her bloody lights out. But this is all starting to seem like a one-man witch hunt, and I don't get it.'

'But—'

'Let's change the subject. What vinyl is coming out next week?'

I had to laugh at that. 'Wow, you really *are* desperate to talk about something else.'

We finished our meal, paid the bill. Chatted about the shop and Emma's job and some home improvements we wanted to get done before Christmas. We talked about Lola and the possibility of getting another dog, or even a cat.

I didn't mention Fiona again.

ϖ

We got off the train and decided to walk the rest of the way home, because it was such a warm evening.

There was a row of shops between the train station and the estate, all of them shut except for the kebab shop and the convenience store that sold, along with milk and bread and cigarettes, a selection of cheap alcohol. As we passed it, a familiar figure came out. Tommy.

He was carrying a flimsy bag, a six-pack of lager visible through the plastic.

'You,' he said when he spotted us, and I immediately got a feeling of foreboding.

He was drunk. Properly wasted, standing on the spot but swaying like he was being buffeted by strong winds.

I tried to hurry on, but Emma stopped. 'How's Albie?' she asked.

'He's getting better.' He tapped the side of his head. 'His brain. They reckon he's gonna make a full recovery.'

'That's amazing. What a relief.'

'Too right.' He belched, then his eyes focused on me. I thought he might vomit on my shoes, so I took a step back. It seemed he had something to say.

'You let her look after your kid, don't you?'

I found myself frozen.

'Whatever she says about me, it's a lie.' His words were slurred, his S's coming out with a *shh* sound. *Ish a lie.* He jabbed a finger towards us. 'Don't ever try to take her photo. She'll freak *right* out. And I don't care what she says. I wouldn't touch her with a barge pole. With somebody else's barge pole. Not like you, eh, Ethan?'

This was the moment I'd been dreading.

'What's he talking about?' Emma asked.

I shook my head, trying to act ignorant, wanting to push Tommy in front of a passing bus.

Tommy belched again, pressing his fist to his lips.

'If I lived next to that psycho, I'd move out. And I wouldn't let my kids anywhere near her. *I* certainly wouldn't shag her.'

With that, he staggered away, into the road, a taxi swerving to avoid him, the driver sounding the horn furiously.

I turned to Emma and, to my horror, saw fury on her face.

'What the hell was he talking about? You've gone completely pale, so do not try to tell me you have no idea.'

All I could do was be honest.

'He got the wrong end of the stick.'

'Which stick?'

'He saw Fiona give me a hug, that was all. In her kitchen.'

'What? Why the hell was Fiona hugging you in her kitchen?'

'Because . . . because I saw you with Mike. I was upset, needed comforting . . .'

I knew that was a poor choice of words, but it was too late. 'Wait. Why didn't you tell me you saw me with Mike? We had a whole big heart-to-heart about that very subject and you didn't mention it?'

'I was about to when you brought it up.'

'Hold on. It sounds like you didn't mention it because it led to you going round to Fiona's so she could "comfort" you. Oh my God, this is the real reason you want Rose to stop seeing her, isn't it? You're afraid Fiona will let it slip there's something going on between you.'

'No! Emma, that's not right. It has nothing to do with that. And there isn't anything going on between us!'

But she had stopped listening, was already walking away. I hurried to catch up with her. 'It was a *hug*. That's all. And I didn't want you to think I'd been watching you. I was so relieved when you told me there was nothing between you and Mike, I didn't see the need to tell you I'd seen you.'

She kept walking.

'Emma. What about what Tommy said about Fiona?'

'He's just a drunk idiot. Probably tried it on with her and she rejected him. Trying to take her photo? Probably leaning over her fence when she was in her bikini. Or pointing his phone at her bedroom window when she was getting dressed. And she caught him and called him out for it. Now stop talking to me.'

We walked the rest of the way home in silence. When we reached our house, I looked over at Iris's. The downstairs lights were on, and I remembered a taxi was due to pick her up at one to take her to the airport. I was chuffed for her, and proud that I'd helped her afford the trip.

We found Fiona and Rose in the kitchen, playing chess.

'Everything been okay?' Emma asked, her voice clipped.

Fiona looked up from the board. Half the pieces had been taken, the endgame approaching. 'Yep. It's all been quiet, hasn't it, Rose?'

Our daughter didn't remove her eyes from the game. 'Uh-huh.' She moved her knight and sat back.

I couldn't stop staring at them. It was such a wholesome scene. The babysitter and my daughter quietly playing chess in the kitchen. Was I going crazy, imagining everything? Was I completely wrong to worry about Fiona? Creating problems that didn't exist?

I should dismiss my fears as paranoia, I thought. I should definitely dismiss the drunken ranting of my most unpleasant neighbour who'd called Fiona a 'psycho'.

Except I couldn't. And, apart from making Emma think there was something going on between me and Fiona, Tommy had actually given me an idea.

'I'm going to bed,' Emma said, not looking at me as she left the room.

Fiona raised an eyebrow. 'Trouble in paradise?'

I kept calm, smiled, said, 'No, everything is fine. Who's winning?'

Fiona and Rose exchanged a glance that, for some reason I couldn't understand, sent a shiver along my spine.

'We both are,' Fiona replied.

31

One in the morning. Fiona watched from her upstairs window as the taxi pulled up outside Iris's house. It was an electric vehicle, almost silent as it glided to a halt beneath a lamp post. Fiona could see the driver in the cabin, reading something on his phone while he waited for his fare to emerge.

After five minutes, when she hadn't appeared, he got out of the car and knocked on the door. Waited some more, then knocked again. Looked at his watch and stood back, peering up at the house, hands on his hips. A shake of the head, then he stomped back to the taxi.

Drove away.

He would let his controller know that the fare hadn't been at home. This kind of thing must happen all the time. They'd assume she'd decided to drive herself or take an Uber, forgetting to cancel.

At the airport, when the plane was being prepared for take-off, perhaps someone would notice a passenger hadn't checked in – but that must happen all the time too.

It would only be eight hours later, when the plane landed and Iris didn't appear, that anyone would notice she was missing. Fiona didn't know who Iris had been intending to visit in Canada. A sibling? A son or daughter? Old friends? Whoever it was, they would try to phone her, text her. They might check with the airline to ask if she'd showed up. Then, when Iris never got back to them, they would call the police.

By then, Fiona would have disposed of the vinyl records she had taken from the house – the ones Rose had seen her dad describe as valuable. She would have got rid of the jewellery too: the wedding ring she had yanked from Iris's finger; the diamond earrings and necklaces and other expensive rings she'd found in the old woman's bedroom. She'd have burned the Canadian dollars.

A burglary gone wrong. That's what it would look like. A burglar disturbed by the homeowner, panicking, grabbing a heavy brass candlestick from the mantelpiece and smacking the poor woman over the head.

That had been the messy bit. Fiona hadn't hit her hard enough to kill her instantly. Instead, Iris had gone down on her knees. She had pleaded with Rose to help her, unable to understand why the girl was just standing there, expressionless, as Fiona hit her again, and again, until understanding anything was beyond her. Fiona was annoyed with herself for getting blood spatters on her clothes and hands. She'd had to get changed, but she didn't think Emma or Ethan had noticed when they got home. She was annoyed because there was blood on her new trainers too. All of it would have to be destroyed, and the candlestick would have to be dumped with the other stuff.

A lot of work, and something that brought the police uncomfortably close to Fiona's door, but she hadn't had much choice, had she?

It turned out Iris had known Dinah. Not at the time Fiona had lived with her, but years before. When Fiona and Maisie were arrested and the story was in the papers, Iris had paid particular attention because she had once served on a charity committee with the victim. She had looked at the photos of the perpetrators, finding it hard to believe that someone as young and pretty as Fiona could be guilty of something so heinous.

'You look different now,' she had said, as Fiona stood before her in the hallway of her house. 'You've changed your surname too, haven't you? But your eyes. You can't change your eyes.'

Patrick had said something similar, and Fiona had made a mental note to do something about it. Contact lenses, maybe. Or spending more time practising, gazing into the mirror. Perfecting her lifetime's effort to pass for normal.

Afterwards, she and Rose had strolled back across the road. If anyone had spotted them, Fiona would say they had gone to see the old woman to wish her a good trip. No one would suspect a twelve-year-old girl of being involved. She was like armour.

This was what it was going to be like from now on, at least until Rose grew up – and Fiona had plenty of time to figure out what would happen then.

It was so easy.

Fiona had deposited the items she'd taken from Iris's here, in her spare room, got changed, then gone back to the Doves' house, where Rose had asked if she wanted a game of chess.

She hadn't said anything about the murder. Hadn't mentioned Iris at all.

But five minutes before her parents had got home, Rose had said, 'Can I ask my question now? The one you owe me.'

'Of course.'

Rose had picked up her queen and turned it over in her small hands.

'Who's next?' she'd asked. 'You said there are three people who need to pay for Maisie's death. Who's the third one?'

Now, Fiona turned away from the window as the taxi's rear lights vanished into the distance. She was sure there were still specks of blood, maybe pieces of skull, of brains, on her skin. Fragments of

Iris's DNA. She went to the bathroom and turned the shower on, shedding the fresh clothes she'd put on before the chess game. She scrubbed herself clean, really getting under her fingernails, shampooing her hair, then doing it again. Only when she was confident there could no longer be any traces of Iris on her did she get out.

She wrapped a towel around her and turned to the steamed-up mirror.

Did she really need to do it? Write the remaining name there in the condensation? She decided yes, one last time, putting her finger to the glass and etching the name of the third person on her list.

Her next-door neighbour.

PART THREE

32

April 2019

'We need to go. Now.'

The tip-off had come in from a civilian member of staff at the nearest police station, a woman called Kia who Fiona had picked up in a bar several months before, stringing her along ever since. Kia had sent a text from the phone she used to arrange their occasional liaisons.

> *They're going to arrest you both this morning. Sorry. Good luck! Xxxx*

Fiona had stared at the text for too long, hardly able to believe it. She hadn't seen this coming.

But she knew what they needed to do.

'Maisie.' She shook her shoulder. 'Maisie. We need to get going. Right now.'

She showed her the text from Kia and Maisie sat up like a toy whose power button had been pressed. Wide awake. Ready. It was one of the things Fiona liked about her – this ability to shake off sleep in an instant, so different to the sloth-like masses. If she'd known this would be the last hour they'd ever spend together, she might have taken more time to mull over Maisie's finest attributes. Her ambition and single-mindedness. Her wonderful, creative cruelty. Fiona wondered if the emotion she experienced when she and Maisie were alone was similar to what the herd called love, or if it was only recognition. Her own reflection in the dark glass of Maisie's regard.

'What time is it?' Maisie asked. She was already out of bed, combing her fingers through her hair as she headed to the en-suite to pee.

'Quarter past eight.'

Above the trickle, Maisie called out through the open door. 'How long have we got?'

'I don't know. But we have to assume they could be here any second.'

As she spoke, she took down a suitcase from on top of the wardrobe and began to throw clothes into it. Underwear. Chargers. The spare phones they kept for emergencies. She marched into the bathroom, where Maisie was now cleaning her teeth in front of the mirror, and swept a load of toiletries into a bag. 'Please, hurry up and get dressed.'

'Fiona? Just relax, okay? We're going to be fine. We're smarter than them.'

'Different, special, better?'

'Exactly.'

Most of the time, Maisie's sense of superiority, her confidence, gave Fiona goosebumps. The cold glow of her arrogance; Fiona loved to bask in it. But it was also a flaw, and Fiona had warned her it could one day be a fatal one.

She snatched the toothbrush from Maisie's hand. 'We have to run. Now.'

Fiona strode back into the bedroom and dropped the toiletries into the now-full suitcase, then grabbed some clothes and threw them to Maisie as she appeared in the bathroom doorway. 'Get dressed.' She hefted the suitcase. 'I'll see you downstairs.'

She carried the case to the ground floor and grabbed the car keys, then opened the large food cupboard. On the second shelf down there were a dozen tins of peaches. She moved them aside, reached in, and pushed at the wood at the rear of the shelf, revealing the secret space behind. She pulled out six bundles of cash, secured with rubber bands. Enough to see them through for a while, while they were hiding out. But still a long way from the life-changing sum they'd set their sights on. The sum they were so close to. Or had been.

She stuffed the money in the suitcase, then took it out on to the street where the car was parked. She felt sick with anger and disappointment. Who had discovered what they were up to? It couldn't have been Dinah herself. The niece, Verity? She had to be the prime suspect. The nausea was replaced by the urge to scream. The house of her dreams had been so close. Now they were going to have to start all over again.

Where the hell was Maisie?

She went back inside and found her in the kitchen, waiting for the kettle to boil.

'What the hell are you doing?' Fiona said.

'I'm not leaving here without a cup of tea.'

'For God's sake.'

She tried to grab Maisie's arm but Maisie was surprisingly quick, slipping out of reach. She picked up the kettle, wielding it like a weapon.

'I can't be locked up.'

'Maisie, please, make your tea and let's go.'

'I have to be free. I wasn't born to be kept in a cage.'

Fiona wanted to grab hold of her and drag her out the door. She could be maddening. 'It's not going to happen. We're faster and cleverer, remember? But we need to prove it by getting in the car and getting out of here *right now*.'

'Okay. But I mean it. I'm not going to prison.'

There wasn't time for a last look around. She got behind the wheel and Maisie sat in the passenger seat, clutching her travel mug. Since she'd come out here to deposit the suitcase, it had started raining. Fiona cursed, because she knew that meant the roads would be busier, all the school-run parents jumping in their Chelsea tractors instead of walking.

And she was right.

The traffic started at the end of their road. This was another issue with living out here in the suburbs, in an area with several 'outstanding' schools. The road was gridlocked, cars and buses and the dreaded four-by-fours. Ubers and black cabs. The rain was heavier now, beating against the windscreen, the wipers hardly able to cope.

Maisie reached over and pressed the horn.

'What are you doing?' Fiona said. 'You're going to draw attention to us.'

But she wanted to hit the horn herself. She wanted to scream. She pictured herself dragging whoever was at the front of this queue out of their vehicle and slitting their throat, then taking their car. She imagined herself with a rocket launcher, blasting away that bus full of schoolchildren, clearing a path before driving through the smoking wreckage.

She forced herself to breathe. In. Out. In. Out.

It almost worked.

Finally, the lights up ahead changed and they began to move forward. A couple of buses turned the corner, freeing space ahead, and then there was only one car between them and the traffic lights.

A white Land Rover, almost as old as this car. The lights turned amber and Fiona expected the Land Rover to sail through – no one around here ever stopped on amber – but to her horror the driver's brake lights came on, then the lights turned red and they were stuck.

'Morons!' she shouted.

She breathed in and out again. And then she saw it, in the rear-view mirror. Flashing blue lights. A police car. No – two police cars. One of them was a marked car but the other was plain, with the blue light strapped to its roof. They were about seven cars back, and on this tightly packed street there was no room for other vehicles to move to let them through. A small blessing. She glanced at Maisie, who was staring ahead, in a trance. It seemed she hadn't seen the lights. Better to let her remain ignorant of them.

Fiona's knuckles were white on the wheel. Why weren't the traffic lights changing? Come on. Come *on*. Maybe they could still get out of this even if they were caught. Find a good lawyer. Impress a jury. They looked good. They knew how to charm people. It might all be okay.

But she didn't want to risk it. She wanted these lights to turn green before the cops behind spotted them. There was a quieter road over to the left, just beyond this crossroads. Her plan, as soon as the lights changed and the traffic parted, was to head there, get off the main street, take the back roads out of town and on to the motorway.

The cars flowing left and right stopped and Fiona readied herself. She hoped the driver of the Land Rover was ready too. With the rain bouncing off the glass, it was too hard to see them.

The lights turned amber, then green. Fiona put the car into first gear, prepared to ease away.

The Land Rover didn't move.

What the hell?

'They've stalled it,' she said aloud. 'They've bloody stalled it!'

Of all the stupid drivers in south London, why did Fiona and Maisie have to get stuck behind this one? Why wasn't the Land Rover moving? What the hell was the driver doing? The lights were about to change again. Fiona tried to pull out to the left, to manoeuvre her way past the bloody Chelsea tractor, squeeze through, but there was no room. A bus had pulled up beside them now, just two feet away, and a teenage boy stared at her through the window, so close she could see his zits.

She leaned on the horn, even though she knew this would only put more pressure on the person ahead, fluster them further and render them less likely to get the car started. The cars behind were hitting their horns too, and the police lights were still flashing, turning the raindrops on the windscreen blue, and then she saw it. As the traffic light turned red, she watched both front doors of each of the police cars open behind her, and a mix of uniformed and plainclothes police started making their way through the stationary traffic towards them.

She opened her door, ready to run, but Maisie didn't move.

'Let's be dignified,' Maisie said, and then a cop, a man with a patchy beard, was tapping on her window.

It was too late.

As they were arrested, standing in the street with the rain beating down on them, drivers rolling down their windows to stare, Fiona concentrated on the licence plate of the Land Rover. She still couldn't see the driver properly, rain obscuring the reflection in the wing mirrors and making it too difficult to see clearly through the rear windscreen.

She memorised the number plate, repeating it over and over so it would be there the moment she got access to a pen and piece of paper.

She watched the traffic lights change as the cop read her rights. This time the Land Rover's driver didn't stall. This time they sailed through the lights and across the junction.

It made her even more enraged.

Even more determined to get revenge.

ϖ

It wasn't until three years later, when Maisie had been dead for a long time, and Fiona was on probation after being let out of Franklin Grange, that she was able to find out the name and address of the person who had owned the Land Rover, though it had changed hands since.

The owner in 2019 was Ethan Dove.

She got the information from the same friendly civilian member of staff at the police station who had tipped her off before they got arrested, Kia. Ethan Dove didn't even know what he had done, might not have even followed the news story about these two women who had attempted to defraud and murder an elderly lady. But that didn't make Fiona hate him any less.

Once she had the name and address, it was easy to keep track of Ethan Dove. She found his social media accounts, which led her to his shop. She went in a couple of times, browsing through the vinyl, the appeal of which she would never understand – well, apart from the monetary value. Through his social media accounts she learned the names of Ethan's wife and kids. And she bided her time. She couldn't afford to risk getting into any kind of trouble while she was on probation, and she kept having to check in with her probation officer, which restricted her movements.

By the time Fiona's probationary period ended, the Doves had moved house; and, after trawling back through Ethan's Twitter and Instagram accounts, she had found out some interesting, surprising stuff – one or two facts that made a significant difference to her plan, in fact. Then something else happened: Fiona had followed Ethan home one day – he always left the record shop at the same time – and there, next to the new-build semi they had moved into, was another brand-new home with a 'For Sale' sign outside.

Fiona didn't hesitate. She had the money Maisie had left her, enough to buy this house outright with some left over to keep her going for a couple of years. She had already come up with a new backstory. She was a single woman who had worked in banking and who was going to return to that industry soon. She was going to befriend the Dove family and figure out the best form of vengeance – something that would scratch the itch that had tormented her for years. Because the loathing she felt for the driver of that Land Rover was even greater than her hatred of Patrick and Max. It was the stupid randomness of it, the sheer incompetence which had led to Fiona's arrest and Maisie's death. They would have got away, she was sure of it.

There was something else, too, that made her decide to put more energy into this act of vengeance than the others. When she looked at them – Ethan and Emma and Dylan and Rose, plus their dog – she saw this happy, normal family, like the one she'd never been part of. They were the epitome of normal. And when she looked at their perfection, she wanted to destroy it.

It would be a fun, deeply satisfying project.

But what Fiona didn't expect was Rose. The first time Fiona met the girl, it confused and excited her in equal measure. She didn't believe in fate or destiny. It was luck, that was all. Great luck, for both Fiona and Rose. And bad luck for Ethan and Emma.

Now, she had tested Rose. She had educated her, trained her, made her understand what she was. She had seen how Rose reacted to pressure.

Rose had already smashed her way out of her chrysalis.

Now it was time for her to prove she could fly.

33

Wednesday morning and Rebel Records was heaving, the aisles crammed with the usual mix of middle-aged men purchasing deluxe reissues of albums they'd loved when they were young, and the new generation of record buyers, many of whom were buying classics too. Fleetwood Mac, The Cure, Marvin Gaye. It was the busiest we'd been since Record Store Day in the spring, almost as if everyone was doing their Christmas shopping three months early.

It didn't matter that business was booming, though. My insides were still twisted with anxiety after our encounter with Tommy the night before. This morning I'd woken up to find that Emma was already in her sports kit and on her way out for a run. I'd asked her if we could talk and she said, 'Tonight.' Her tone was ominous, like it was going to be a serious conversation. Before I could say anything more, she headed out and I watched her run up the road, towards the footpath where Albie had come off his bike, and the fields beyond. Watching her go, I felt a surge of emotion. I had been convinced I was going to lose her, had done something stupid then compounded that mistake by not being honest about it. This evening, I decided, I would tell her everything.

As she'd vanished from sight, I had looked across the street to Iris's place. She'd be on her way to Canada now, to see her son and grandchildren. I was happy for her; it was just a shame she'd gone before remembering where she knew Fiona from.

I had just sold a copy of the new Madonna box set when I heard a male voice say, 'Dad.'

The customer stepped out of the way and I saw my son standing there.

'Dylan. I didn't know you were in town.'

He wasn't smiling. 'I need to talk to you. I've been texting and calling you but you didn't answer, so I came here.'

My phone was charging in the back office. 'What is it?'

A customer was watching us, which made Dylan say, 'Can we go somewhere quieter?'

'Of course.'

I led him into the back room. What was going on? Dylan had never come into the shop like this before. I could hardly remember ever seeing him look so agitated.

He ran his hands through his hair. 'The estate is full of cops, parked outside Iris's house. I went over to try to see what's going on but the police are making everyone stay away. They've strung up crime scene tape all around the house. All the neighbours are going crazy and I heard one guy say that Iris had been murdered.'

It didn't sink in for a second. '*Murdered?*'

'Yeah. He said he'd spoken to one of the cops and they'd told him it looked like a burglary, but Iris must have disturbed them and they . . . they killed her.'

'She can't be dead.' What he was saying didn't make sense. 'She's meant to be in Canada.'

Dylan opened his mouth to say something but I interrupted him.

'Where's your mum? Why have you come here on your own?'

'If you'd read the texts I sent you . . . She and Rose have gone out.'

'Gone out? Where?'

'I don't know!' He was raking his fingers almost maniacally through his hair now. I wanted to grab his wrists, make him stop. 'You're not allowing me to speak.'

'Okay. I'm sorry. Go ahead.'

Iris. *Murdered?* It still wouldn't sink in. I'd stood with her in her house less than twenty-four hours ago. She was meant to be on a plane.

Dylan sat down in a chair that was surrounded by piles of boxes, gathering himself before he spoke. He looked like someone who was about to confess some terrible crime.

'Last night, when you were out, I was in my room chatting with Keira on Discord, and I don't know what Fiona and Rose were doing but at about ten someone knocked on the front door. I was going to go down but Rose answered it. I could hear her talking to someone. A woman. Ten minutes after that, I heard the front door close again and . . . You know how you can tell when you're suddenly on your own?'

'I do.'

'Well, it was like that. I went into your room and peeked out and I saw them.'

He stopped.

'Who?' I asked.

'Rose and Fiona. They were outside Iris's house. Fiona was kind of standing to the side, like she was planning to jump out and say "Boo!" – and when Iris opened the door, that's exactly what she did.'

'She jumped out and said boo?'

He huffed. 'I couldn't *hear* her, and it was too dark and too far across the street for me to see Iris's face, but I got the impression she was freaked out. And then they all went inside.'

'And then what happened?'

'I don't know. Keira was messaging, asking where I was, so I went back to talk to her and got distracted. A bit later I realised I wasn't on my own anymore, that Rose and Fiona were back in the house. And I didn't think anything more about it until all the police turned up this morning.' He blinked at me. 'Dad, you don't think . . .'

'That Fiona and Rose had something to do with Iris's death? Of course not. Rose? Don't be silly.'

'But . . .'

I waited.

'Rose *has* been acting weird, and I told you what I think of Fiona.'

She's a psycho, said Tommy's voice in my head. At the same time, I wondered at my reaction to what Dylan had said. Of course I had immediately rejected the idea that Rose had done Iris harm – she was my daughter, my little girl – but my gut hadn't done the same with Fiona.

'Keira says that her mum said that Rose shows all the signs of having the dark triad of personality traits. After what she did to Henry.'

Dark triad? 'What are you talking about?'

'Do you not remember what happened at laser tag?'

'We don't know what happened. He told us he jumped out of the crow's nest and fell down the ramp.'

'Yeah, but only because of all the things Rose was saying to him. Keira heard all of it, and she told her parents, and her mum almost made her stop talking to me. Henry is still having bad dreams, apparently, and has started wetting the bed. He's convinced Rose is going to turn up at their house and kill him.'

I flashed to an image of another incident I hadn't witnessed. A four-year-old Rose pushing that kid off the tower at nursery. Then:

her face when Albie had his accident. That I *had* seen. And the fear on Henry's face when they'd been using the hot tub.

I still felt the need to defend her.

'But that's crazy. Maybe she said something mean to him – kids do that all the time – but he must have overreacted.'

Dylan shook his head. 'I knew you'd be like this. You think Rose is all sweetness and light—'

Except I didn't, did I?

'—but she's always been a bit weird. More than a bit, if we're honest. You know she's never had any proper friends? It's because she's horrible to anyone who tries to get close to her. Like that friend she had at school. Jasmine. Her brother told me Rose really bullied her, made her life hell until Jasmine finally got the guts to tell her to eff off.'

'You never told us that.'

'I tried, but you didn't listen.'

Was that true? I had no memory of it.

'She's been much worse recently. I see her and Fiona all the time, whispering. Also, she barely even reacted when that guy died from eating those cookies. I'd be traumatised if I saw something like that. Just about anyone would. But Rose acts like it was something she saw on telly.'

'But . . .' I couldn't think of an excuse. Last night it had been me arguing that Rose's behaviour was down to more than growing pains. Now my instinct was to defend her, to argue the other way.

'Keira says you're in denial. Parents of kids with psychological issues often are. Rose always used to put on this act at home, pretending to be an angel. It's only the last few weeks that she's stopped acting. Keira says it will be because her hormones are surging, making it harder for her to keep everything under control.'

'But . . . that's normal, though. It's called growing up.'

'No, it's more than that. Keira says—'

'Oh my God. Keira. She's filling your head with nonsense.'

'Yeah, she also said you'd say that. You're in denial. I was in denial too, for ages.'

I leaned against the wall. There was a churning sensation in my guts and my heart was pounding. Dylan sounded so mature, as if there had been this grown man living in my house all this time and I'd never noticed. And I could feel myself splitting in two: the part of me that refused to believe my precious daughter could ever do anything awful, and the part of me that had suspected something was wrong. That she had changed.

But she couldn't have hurt Iris. No way. She was a twelve-year-old girl. She wasn't capable of being involved in *murder*.

'I need to talk to your mum,' I said, crossing the office to where my phone was plugged in. As I picked it up I saw all the missed calls from Dylan and, among them, a text from Emma, who was still off work.

> *Hey. Rose and I are going out for the day with Fiona. Be back around dinner time.*

With Fiona?

'What is it?' Dylan said, seeing my reaction.

I showed him.

'Shit. I mean . . . Sorry.'

'You swearing is the least of my worries right now,' I said, lifting the phone to my ear and calling Emma.

It went straight to voicemail. I tapped out a text: *Where have you gone? I need to talk to you urgently.*

The status quickly displayed as 'delivered' but didn't change to 'read'.

I texted Rose, who always saw her messages and responded to them quickly. *Hi Rose, can you ask Mum to call me ASAP?*

This time the status didn't even change to delivered.

Dylan was on his phone too. 'What are you doing?' I asked.

'Telling Keira what's happening.'

I didn't know what to do, except that I needed to head home. I grabbed my car key off the desk and said, 'Come with me.'

On the way out, I told my assistant there was an emergency and that she'd have to run the shop for a little while.

I drove us home on autopilot, waiting for my phone to ping to tell me Emma or Rose had responded. Dylan attempted to contact them too, but with no joy. I tried to convince myself that I was overreacting, that even if Iris had been murdered – and this still seemed too outlandish to believe – that I didn't need to worry about my family. It must have been a burglary gone wrong, just as the police had said. Sickening, but nothing to do with Rose.

I entered the estate to find the road blocked by police cars and rubberneckers who had come to look at the crime scene. A BBC news van idled by the kerb. As Dylan had said, police tape was strung up around Iris's house and there were half a dozen cops standing on her front lawn.

I parked as close as I could to our house and hurried up the street. As we neared Iris's, a CSI came out wearing all the gear, just like on TV. This was surreal. *Un*real. I had to say 'Excuse me' to numerous onlookers, a mix of neighbours and strangers, to get to my house. As I reached the drive, I saw Tommy and Nicola standing outside their house, watching the comings and goings next door.

I crossed the road to them, Dylan at my heels.

'Tommy,' I said.

He looked startled to see me, and as I got close I caught a whiff of him. He still smelled of alcohol. Inside his house, his dogs were going crazy, barking in tandem. I realised Eric and Albie, who looked a lot better than when I'd last seen him, were in the back of their car.

'Do you know what's going on?' I asked, a little breathless. 'Did you see or hear anything?'

'She's dead,' said Nicola. 'That cop over there said her head was bashed in, and the place looks like it's been ransacked.'

'Oh Jesus.'

'We thought this was going to be a nice neighbourhood but we've had enough. We're going to put our place on the market. You should too.'

They both went to move towards their car but I stopped Tommy and gestured for him to accompany me out of Dylan's earshot. Speaking quietly, I said, 'There's nothing going on between me and Fiona.'

'None of my business, mate.'

'It was just a hug. But I want to ask you about the other stuff you said last night. What were you talking about? Have you seen Fiona do something?'

He flicked a glance at Nicola, who was squinting in our direction. 'I don't know what you're on about.'

'You said not to try to take a photo of Fiona, and that she's a psycho.'

His face contorted. 'I was wasted last night. I don't even remember seeing you. But it's not safe round here anymore.'

'Because of Fiona?'

He shook his head, wincing in pain. 'Albie's going to be all right, but we're not staying here and risking something else happening to him or Eric. Not while that lunatic is around.'

With that, he pushed past me and they both got into their car, Tommy sounding his horn until the police let him past.

Should I go and talk to the police? Tell them what Dylan had seen last night?

After forcing myself to calm down, think it through, I decided I couldn't. My first instinct was to protect my daughter, and that meant I didn't want to do anything until I'd spoken to her and Emma. I wanted to talk to Fiona too. Find out why she'd been at Iris's yesterday night, confident I would know if she was lying. Only then, if I thought I knew what was going on, would I talk to the police. Despite the whispering voice in my head, I was sure Rose and Fiona must have gone to wish Iris a good trip, that was all. A coincidence. They'd probably had a lucky escape, getting out before the violent intruder turned up.

I tried ringing Emma again as we walked over to the house but, again, it went to voicemail. I tried Rose too, and got the same result.

We entered the house and Lola ran up to us, tail wagging furiously.

'Did they not give you an indication where they were going?' I asked Dylan.

'No. Mum just said they were going out. That was it.'

'What time was this?'

'I don't know. I was still in bed. She spoke to me through my bedroom door and then I went back to sleep.'

This was what he did pretty much every day in the school holidays. I'd been the same when I was his age. A nocturnal animal.

I paced around helplessly.

'Don't you have us all on that family location app?' he said.

'Oh my God. Of course.'

When we'd bought Dylan and Rose their phones, I had installed an app that meant Emma and I could see where they were. All the parents I knew were the same. It was one of the positive things about teenagers and phones; we parents didn't have to rely on them letting us know their whereabouts. Emma and I both had the app, which meant we could also both tell where the other was.

I had very rarely used it to locate Emma, even at the darkest points of my paranoia about Mike, because it told the other person if you'd checked up on them. Now, though, I had good reason to look.

I opened the app.

'What the hell?' Dylan and I were listed as part of our family group, but Emma and Rose were missing. I handed my phone to Dylan, deferring to his teenage technological superiority. 'Does this mean they're offline?'

He scrutinised it. 'No, it means they've deleted themselves.'

'But Rose can't delete hers without the password, can she?'

He shook his head. 'Mum could do both, though.'

Dylan handed the phone back and I stared at the screen. 'Why would she?'

'I don't know.'

I thought I might be sick. Maybe now was the time to go out and talk to the police. I was still reluctant, though, just in case Rose was involved with something criminal. I needed to do more to figure out what was going on first. Also, I felt certain the police wouldn't take it seriously yet, not unless I told them I thought Fiona and Rose might know something about Iris's death.

I took deep breaths to try to calm myself down, then went to the tap in the kitchen to fill a glass of water, taking it into the living room. From there I could see Iris's house, the cops swarming around. The space where I'd stood talking to Tommy and Nicola.

What exactly had he said about Fiona last night? *Don't ever try to take her photo. She'll freak right out.*

Emma had speculated this was because Tommy was a creep who'd tried to spy on his female neighbour, a perv taking pics over the fence. But what if it was something else? I remembered my own attempts to research Fiona Smith online and my efforts to jog Iris's memory.

'She doesn't want anyone to know who she is.'

'What?' Dylan said.

I hadn't realised I'd spoken out loud, but now that I'd said it a terrible notion struck me. Had Iris remembered who Fiona was? And revealed this to Fiona?

Had Fiona murdered her to keep her real identity secret?

Still unable to believe this might actually be the case, I said, 'If you wanted to find out who someone was, how would you do it? Apart from searching for their name, I mean?'

Because I was almost certain now that Fiona Smith was a fake name.

I didn't need to wait for the answer. Tommy had provided it already. I said it aloud: 'You'd take their photo. Show it around, maybe put it on social media . . .'

'No, you wouldn't need to do all that, Dad. You'd just have to put it into reverse image search.'

Of course.

'Except we don't have any photos of Fiona.'

'Rose might.'

I immediately headed upstairs to Rose's room, with Dylan following. Rose might have her phone with her, but her laptop, which she used mostly for homework or to play Roblox, automatically synced with her phone, so all her photos would be on there.

'Do you know the password?' I asked.

'It always used to be Lola123. Capital L.' Dylan had helped her set the laptop up when she'd first got it. 'I told her to change it to something harder to guess, but don't know if she did.'

I tried it and thanked the gods Rose had never got round to updating it. I was in, and navigated straight to her photos app.

There were very few photos taken in the last few months. Ninety per cent of them were of the dog – which, to be honest, wasn't dissimilar to my own photo reel. A few landscape pictures she'd taken on holiday. My eyes were immediately drawn to some pictures taken at what I recognised as the Horniman Museum. Dog and wolf heads mounted on a wall. A gigantic stuffed walrus. There were some pictures of Rose taken on this trip. A few of her in a park too.

But no photos of Fiona.

'Fiona must have some photos of herself,' Dylan said. 'In her house, I mean.'

I looked towards the wall. Fiona's house was on the other side. If only I could walk through it.

'I can't break in to her house,' I said. There was nothing else for it. I was going to have to talk to the police.

'We don't have to,' Dylan said.

'Go to the police?' I was losing track of what I'd merely thought and what I'd said aloud.

'No, Dad.' My fifteen-year-old son was looking at me like he was worried I'd lost my mind. 'Break into her house.'

He went over to Rose's bedside drawer, opened it and rifled around inside. I was about to say something about his sister's privacy when he turned around, proudly brandishing a key. 'Rose told me Fiona gave her a key so she could go in and feed the cat when Fiona was away that time.'

'Of course.'

We headed downstairs. Leaving the house, I heard Tommy's voice in my head again, calling Fiona a psycho. I braced myself, terrified of what we might find next door. Increasingly scared that I was going to find something in there that would prove Dylan was right.

That not only did we live next door to a psychopath, but that my daughter was one too.

34

Fiona's place was the kind of neat and clean you could only achieve if you didn't have children. A house where you could leave a room tidy knowing that next time you walked back in that room it wasn't going to have been trashed.

Dylan and I had let ourselves in through the front door, and the kitten had immediately come running up to us, meowing and rubbing around our ankles. The cat's presence gave me some comfort. Surely Fiona wouldn't leave it on its own for too long? She genuinely seemed to like animals, which was one of the reasons I found it hard to believe she was a psychotic killer. Didn't most serial killers start off by torturing animals? Maybe that was just a pop-cultural belief.

Or perhaps she had only acquired Karma the kitten to lure Rose into her house. Maybe when there was no one around, she mistreated this poor animal.

'Rose genuinely loves cats and dogs,' I said.

'And that means she can't be a bad person?' said Dylan. Again, I hadn't realised I'd spoken aloud. 'Keira told me it's a myth that dark triad people can't like animals. Harold Shipman used to cry over dogs that were being used for medical experiments. Dennis Nilsen loved his border collie. Even Ian Brady liked pets, and asked for the proceeds of his memoir to be split between several animal charities if it was ever published.'

'How do you know all this stuff?'

'Keira.' Of course. 'She wants to be a psychologist like her mum, but specialising in the criminally insane.'

'Why would she want to do that?'

He shrugged. 'It's interesting. Even you find that stuff fascinating. I remember you going on about how Charles Manson was influenced by the Beatles.'

'Yeah, but that's music history. If my specialist subject was serial killers, I'd be extremely worried about myself.'

He frowned, and I realised I needed to leave off criticising Keira. He liked her. And I was certain this was one relationship I didn't need to be worried about.

We went into the kitchen, which was the only room I'd ever spent any time in. There was no sign of a laptop or tablet, and the drawers contained nothing but the things you would expect to find in a kitchen. She didn't have a 'man drawer' like in our house, full of old batteries and takeaway leaflets. The contents of her cupboards and fridge told me she liked plain food: pasta, mild cheddar, chicken, tomato soup. There was a rack full of decent wine, though.

No photographs.

We went into the living room, where there were no photos on display, not of Fiona or anyone else. That was unusual. She had a bookcase which didn't contain a single novel or interesting non-fiction book, just a medical encyclopedia, a book about interior design and a very dry-looking tome called *The Diagnostic and Statistical Manual of Mental Disorders, Fifth Edition*.

'She's got the DSM-5,' Dylan said, taking it down off the shelf.

I stared at him.

'Keira has a PDF of this. It's used to diagnose people with psychological issues. I bet Fiona has it so she can read up on herself.'

He opened it and read out the handwritten dedication at the front: '*To Fiona, from Maisie. Interesting bedtime reading!*' He turned to me. 'Who's Maisie?'

'I think that might be her former partner,' I said.

He had got out his phone and was taking photos of the book, presumably to send to his new girlfriend. I looked over his shoulder at the text on the page. 'Does this book talk about this "dark triad" you keep mentioning? You never really explained what it means.'

He looked up from his phone, then put the book back. 'It probably covers it. But I can tell you: it's psychopathy, narcissism and . . . How do you say it? Machiavellianism. Is that right?'

'Yeah, I think so. Enjoying manipulating others?'

'That's it.'

'Narcissism' had become one of those words, like 'genius' or 'tragedy', that was so overused that it was now almost meaningless. Everyone in the world thought their ex was a narcissist. Did it describe Fiona? Was she overly obsessed with herself?

'I can't see Fiona as a narcissist,' I said. 'She seems way too interested in other people, namely our family. Would a narcissist spend so much time teaching the girl next door how to play chess, or taking her on day trips?'

'That's her being manipulative. Making us think she's *not* self-obsessed. Plus, she must be getting something from it. Something that's helpful to her.'

'Like what?'

'I'm not sure. I don't think it's a pervy thing . . .'

'Oh God.'

'But maybe she just likes having someone who looks up to her. Rose hangs off Fiona's every word. That's going to appeal to Fiona's narcissism. And maybe, I don't know, she's training her up.'

I stared at him.

'If she thinks Rose is a dark triad person too, then maybe she's treating her like an apprentice. Showing her the ropes.'

'Dylan, that's mad.'

'Is it? It makes sense to me. It's like a mother animal teaching her offspring how to behave.'

'Fiona isn't Rose's mum.'

He shrugged. 'Maybe she sees Rose as the daughter she never had.'

Could any of this be true? Despite all my worries about Rose's recent behaviour, I couldn't accept it.

'What's the definition of a psychopath?' I asked. 'According to Keira and her extensive knowledge.'

He scowled at me.

'Sorry. I'm finding all of this hard to take. The idea that your mum and sister might be with someone like that.' Not to mention the accusation that Rose was like that too.

'The DSM doesn't have a diagnosis for psychopathy,' Dylan said. 'But Keira – yes, *Keira* – told me that the closest thing is called something like "conduct disorder".' I could almost hear his brain whirring as he recalled what she'd told him. 'Traits include a lack of remorse and feelings of guilt, callousness, a lack of empathy . . .'

'But they learn to mimic emotions, right?' This was the kind of pop psychology I'd heard before. A staple of true crime documentaries and movies in which cops discussed the behaviour patterns of vicious serial killers.

'Yeah, exactly.'

I shook my head. None of this was helping us find my wife and daughter, and it definitely wasn't making me feel any better.

There was little else in the living room. A TV and a generous pile of magazines on a coffee table. *Country Life* and *Tatler*. Various others that focused on posh houses and luxury travel. I flicked through them and saw that they were well thumbed. Fiona had torn some pages out too, and made notes on others, circling items in lists of expensive furniture and fittings. Was this how she spent her evenings? Flicking through magazines dreaming of a five-star existence?

We went back into the hallway. Again, there were no pictures on the walls. No photos. Nothing personal at all, apart from a couple of coats hanging from hooks. It was like wandering through a show home, or a place someone had just moved into the day before. Dylan, who was texting Keira as he walked up the stairs behind me, didn't seem to be impacted in the same way, but I found it deeply unsettling. Outside her home she seemed so normal. Friendly and full of opinions and interests. But if a person's home reflects their personality, she was less than vanilla. She was blank.

Upstairs, we encountered more blankness. The landing also had plain walls. There were two rooms, the mirrored equivalent of Rose and Dylan's rooms, that were completely empty apart from a few packing boxes that proved to have nothing in them. There had been part of me that had wondered if we might find possessions taken from Iris's, but there was nothing here. No smoking gun that told me Fiona was a killer.

'Not exactly a serial killer's lair, is it?' I said. 'No photographs of victims pinned to the walls. No scrapbooks full of crazy scrawlings. No heads in the fridge.'

Dylan side-eyed me.

'Sorry. It's the tension. I can promise you I'm not actually finding any of this funny.'

'I get it, Dad.' He'd put his phone away. 'I just want to know where Mum and Rose are, though.'

We were both silent for a minute, looking around the empty room we were in. There was a hollow, cold sensation in my stomach, and I kept thinking this must be a dream I was going to wake up from. The kind that makes you laugh with relief when you re-enter the real world. *I had the weirdest dream . . .*

'Come on, let's check the other rooms, and then I'm going to go and talk to the police.'

I poked my head into the bathroom, which actually looked used, with numerous bottles of shower gel and shampoo and creams. It was the only room that wasn't spotlessly clean. The mirror was smeared, like someone had been writing on the glass with their fingertip, but I couldn't make any sense of it.

Finally, we went into Fiona's bedroom. I couldn't help but feel guilty, invasive. If she was completely innocent, this was not cool of us. But the bedroom was as devoid of personality as the rest of the house. A double bed, plain white sheets; a bedside table with nothing on it except a lamp and a box of tissues. No books, no photos. I opened the drawer beside her bed, flushed with shame, aware that Dylan was watching me – a child, my son, being set this example. But the drawer had nothing in it except some mysterious tablets in a plain brown bottle, some lip salve, and some of the pages that had been ripped out of the magazines. I unfolded them, hoping they might tell me something useful, but they were just glossy photoshoots of expensive houses. The kind of places you see on *Grand Designs*, with glass walls and gleaming surfaces. An underground swimming pool and a garden full of bonsai.

There were no photos here. Nothing that would tell me who Fiona really was. I still didn't even know for certain if Fiona Smith was a made-up name. This had been a wasted intrusion into her life and, although we hadn't found anything embarrassing or private, I still felt dirty.

'Let's get out of—'

I froze. A phone was ringing.

'That's not your phone, is it?' I asked, although I already knew the answer.

Dylan shook his head. 'No.'

It was a noise that had once been omnipresent, but one I hadn't heard in a long time: the old Nokia ringtone. It was faint, but the high-pitched beeps were still distinct. It kept ringing.

'I think it's coming from downstairs,' Dylan said.

He was right. We both left Fiona's bedroom – having refolded the magazine pages and put them back where I'd found them – and went back to the ground floor. I stood still for a moment, trying to figure out where the ringing was coming from.

'The kitchen,' I said.

We went in. The ringtone was muffled, indicating the phone was inside something or behind a door. I opened all the cupboards, including the ones I'd looked in earlier, and peered in. Same with the drawers.

Dylan looked up and said, 'I think it's coming from above our heads.'

There was a smoke alarm attached to the ceiling. I squinted up at it, confused. Was this smoke alarm ringing like a phone instead of emitting the usual shrill beeps that came out of them? I grabbed a chair, positioned it beneath the alarm and stood on it, reaching up to remove the cover.

Something dropped out. I tried to catch it but my reactions were too slow. Fortunately, Dylan had more time to see it and his reflexes were better. He caught it before it could hit the ground.

It was a tiny mobile phone that fitted in the palm of his hand. It did indeed look like an old Nokia, the kind everyone had once had, though I didn't remember them being this small. And it was still ringing.

Dylan and I looked at each other, then I grabbed the phone and – carefully, because the buttons were so miniscule – answered it and put it to my ear.

'At last,' said a woman's harsh voice. 'Where the hell were you?'

35

I held the tiny phone against my ear, unsure what to say. I didn't recognise the voice of the woman at the other end, but it wasn't Fiona. Dylan was gawping at me, his palms out, desperate to know who it was.

'Hello?' said the woman, in a sarcastic sing-song voice. She was English. Southern. She sounded about my age. She also sounded extremely pissed off. 'Lucy calling Fiona. Come in. Helloooo?'

'Fiona's not here at the moment,' I said.

There was a sharp intake of breath at the other end. Sensing she was about to hang up, I said, as rapidly as I could, 'Fiona has gone off somewhere with my wife and daughter and I need to find them urgently. If you know anything, please help me.'

I waited. I could hear breathing, so she hadn't hung up yet.

'I don't know who you are,' I said. Except she had given away that her name was Lucy. 'But I'm desperate. Worried Fiona is going to do something to my family. If you've got any idea where she might be, please tell me.'

I heard her breathing quicken, her mouth come closer to the phone. Was she *excited*?

'You're the dad,' she said. 'The neighbour.'

This Lucy knew who I was. Dylan was still staring at me, eyes stretched wide, frustration pouring off him.

'That's right. I'm Ethan Dove.'

'Rose's dad. Well well.'

'And who are you?' I asked.

She made a noise reminiscent of a laugh, but with no trace of humour in it. 'You don't need to know that. What are you doing in Fiona's house?'

'I told you. I'm trying to find Rose and my wife. I have Fiona's spare key, so we didn't break in.' I wasn't sure why I felt the need to tell this woman about that.

'Good for you,' she said. There was a pause. 'So you know Fiona's dangerous. Does that mean you know who she really is?'

Even though I was in Fiona's house searching for a photo of her so I could find out her real identity, this still sent a chill through me. My mouth went dry, so when I spoke, the words almost got stuck. 'No, I don't. She told us her name is Fiona Smith.'

'Ha. Well, the first name is real. I'm not sure why she didn't change that too.' She made a noise like she was musing over this. 'I guess she was attached to it.'

There was a long pause, then she said, 'I can help you, Ethan Dove, but I need you to do something for me first. I'm going to give you two names and an address. I want you to pay them a visit, see how they are, then report back to me.'

'What? I don't have time—'

'*This* is the deal, Ethan. I need to know—' She stopped herself, obviously deciding not to share whatever it was. 'I just want you to ask these people if everything has been going well for them recently. Do not tell them you've been talking to me, even if they ask. Got that? If you do, if I think you're lying, I won't help you find Fiona and your wife and the famous Rose.'

Famous? What the hell had Fiona said to this woman about my daughter?

'Also, if you go to the police and tell them about me and this call, you'll never find Fiona in time.' She chuckled. 'I'm your only hope.'

'Is she going to hurt her?' I asked.

'Hurt who? Rose? Oh no.' There was that approximation of a laugh again. 'Now, the address of the people I want you to go and see is . . .'

She gave me an address in north London.

'And their names are Jamie and Kirsty Knight.'

ϖ

I took the little phone with me, tucking it into my pocket as I marched out of Fiona's house, gesturing for Dylan to follow me.

'Where are we going?' he asked as I headed towards the car.

Lucy had given me a few questions to ask this couple. Jamie and Kirsty Knight. The names weren't familiar, but I asked Dylan to look them up on Google while I drove off the estate, leaving the police cars and rubberneckers behind. I stuck the address Lucy had given me in the satnav. Finsbury Park in north London. Twenty miles away. I knew that every red traffic light would make my nerves jangle, every clogged street would tempt me to thump my horn. I took deep breaths, telling myself to stay calm. The last thing I needed was a road rage incident or, God forbid, an accident.

'Jamie Knight, Kirsty Knight.' He tapped the names into his phone along with the area where they lived. 'Um, something about a home security company. Looks like it was based in Australia but is over here now.'

Australia? Was that the connection with Fiona? 'Are they Aussies?'

'Hang on. Hmm, neither of them seem to be on social media. There's an "About Us" page on the security company site with a letter written by Jamie Knight. Listen to this: *My own personal experiences led to me understanding how dangerous the world can be and how vitally important it is to feel safe in your own home.* Sounds like he's been through some shit.'

'Add Lucy to the search,' I suggested.

He thumbed his phone and then, seeing the results, said, 'Bollocks. I mean . . .'

'I told you, I don't care if you swear. What does it say?'

We had left the estate behind and were heading out of South Croydon, through Addington towards Bromley. From there we would head through Greenwich, across the river and into north London.

'It's a news story from 2013. *IT worker not guilty in "Magpies trial"*. They're all mentioned here. Jamie and Kirsty and Lucy. Her surname is Newton.'

'Oh my God. You. Are. Joking.' I glanced at him. 'Are you saying you haven't heard of her? I bet Keira has! Lucy Newton's a serial killer. The Dark Angel, I think that's her nickname. She murdered loads of elderly people in this nursing home where she worked. She would have been sent to prison shortly after this trial.' It was coming back to me now. 'This Jamie guy was her neighbour, and I think he was accused of murdering Lucy's husband.'

'Chris Newton.'

'Yeah, that was it. But Jamie Knight was found not guilty because of extreme provocation. Something like that. Then Lucy went to prison for the murders, got out on appeal because of a technicality and then killed someone else. Maybe several people? I can't remember, but I definitely heard about it a few years ago. She was arrested again and given a whole life sentence.'

Dylan's mouth hung open. 'A serial killer? And you were just talking to her on the phone? And she's friends with Fiona?'

It was the kind of statement that, typed online, would require several exclamation and question marks.

'Do you think Fiona is a serial killer too?' He had gone ghost-white, his voice an octave higher than normal. 'Dad, she's got Mum and Rose. What's she going to do to them?'

'We're going to find them.'

'We need to go to the police, *now*. If this Lucy knows where they are, the cops can make her tell, can't they?'

'I don't think it works like that, Dylan.' I reached across and squeezed his shoulder. 'They certainly wouldn't be able to get the information out of her quickly, not if she didn't want to give it. Right now we have to go along with what Lucy asked. But at the first sign she's lying or messing us around . . .'

He was silent for the remainder of the drive. We were lucky with the traffic, which actually put me more on edge. Were we using up our good luck with these green lights and relatively clear roads? We found the address, then drove around for five minutes looking for a parking space. But in the end I thought, *So what if we get a ticket?* I pulled up on the kerb, on double-yellow lines, outside the Victorian house – converted into flats – where the Knights lived, and Dylan and I approached the front door.

I pressed the buzzer. They had something similar to a Ring doorbell, but off-brand, with a camera and microphone. It was the middle of the afternoon and I was worried they'd both be out at work, but a man's voice said, 'Hello?'

He sounded wary. Suspicious.

I considered lying, telling him I had a package for him, to get him to come to the door, but if this was going to work – if we were to get information that would satisfy Lucy – I judged I needed to be honest. There could be too many unforeseen consequences once I launched into fabrications.

I knew he could see me and Dylan through the camera, and hoped the presence of my teenage son would reassure him.

'My name's Ethan Dove,' I said, 'and this is my son, Dylan. I know you don't know who we are, but my wife and little girl might be in trouble and I need your help.'

Did I imagine the intake of breath?

He went silent. Had he gone?

'Jamie? Mr Knight?'

I heard footsteps, and seconds later the door flew open to reveal a man a few years younger than me. Brown hair, average height and build, quite good-looking except there was something about his eyes. A haunted look.

'Who are you?' he demanded, peering over our shoulders.

'I told you, I'm Ethan—'

'Has this got something to do with Lucy? Jesus Christ, don't tell me she's got out again.' He sucked in a breath. 'No, the police would let me know straight away.'

Lucy had instructed us not to mention her to Jamie.

'I just need to ask you,' I said, 'has everything been all right? Recently, I mean. Have you had any problems?'

Jamie stared at me. 'What's that supposed to mean?'

'I can't tell you. I'm really sorry but I've just been told to find out if you're okay.'

He took half a step back. He was a mixture of terrified, angry and confused. 'Everything *was* fine – until you turned up asking stupid questions.'

Dylan tugged at my elbow. 'Dad, that's all we need to know.'

'Thank you,' I said to Jamie. 'And I'm sorry.' I dropped my voice, as if Lucy might be watching. As if she had spies everywhere. 'I'll come back and explain everything once my family are safe.'

I turned away from him, intending to keep my promise, and jogged back to the car with Dylan beside me. Jamie called out after us but I kept going, head down. I was worried he might follow us and demand to know what was going on, so instead of sitting in the car to call Lucy, I drove up the road until I found a petrol station and pulled in.

I took out the miniature phone and dialled the only number that was stored in it.

Lucy answered immediately. 'Well?' she asked.

'He had no idea what I was talking about. Said everything was fine.'

A sound that might very well have been a growl came from the other end of the line.

'I knew it. That bitch. She's been too busy mentoring your daughter to do what she promised.'

Mentoring her? That was exactly what Dylan said she'd been doing. Training her up, like an apprentice. 'Lucy, you promised you would help us.'

'And I'm a woman of my word. Firstly, you might want to know that Fiona's real surname is Woodfield. Secondly, she's obsessed with you. You're on her list.'

'Her *list*? What list? And why am I on it?'

She laughed. A cold sound, devoid of humour. 'Something to do with her failed getaway, but you'll have to ask her. I would also advise you to continue to stay away from the police – if you don't want to get Rose into trouble. Fiona told me she was going to take Rose under her wing, that she recognised the same thing in her that we have.'

'What does that mean?' I asked, but my blood, my organs, my flesh – all of it had gone cold. I already knew what she was going to say.

'We're special,' said Lucy, and she hissed with laughter. '"Different, better, special," as Fiona always says. People like you and your wife, and Jamie and Kirsty, are like sheep. Born victims, herd animals, not capable of—'

'Oh, just tell me where I can find them,' I snapped.

There was a pause, and I was about to yell at her, scared she was going to go back on her word, when she said, 'There's this place Fiona is obsessed with. It's called Ravenhill . . .'

36

'I can't wait for you to see it.'

Emma was behind the wheel, Rose beside her in the passenger seat. Fiona leaned forward, head between the two front seats. She was finding it hard to keep her enthusiasm in check – both for the place they were going to visit, and for what was going to happen later. Her insides fizzed and her palms hurt from where she kept clenching her fists, fingernails digging into her flesh.

'It's so nice to have a day out, the three of us,' Emma said. 'Maybe I should ask my boss if I could take the rest of the summer off, take a sabbatical. Would you like that, Rose?'

'Maybe.'

'Thanks for the enthusiasm.'

So far today, they'd driven out to Bluewater to do some shopping, which had been fascinating and educational for Fiona. Rose needed new stationery for the coming school term, plus new shoes and a few items of uniform. She'd dragged her feet around the enormous shopping mall, complaining about the uniform she had to wear – the clumpy, unfashionable shoes. She begged Emma to buy her Doc Martens but Emma said they were too expensive and non-regulation, and then Rose wanted an extortionately priced Swedish backpack because all the other girls at school had them, but Emma told her she should be happy with the one she already had, which led Rose to make the statement: 'You're the worst mother ever.'

When she's mine, Fiona thought, *she'll get a slap if she talks to me like that. More than a slap.*

Rose went off to buy a bubble tea and Emma let out a deep sigh. 'She's hard work at the moment. Flipping heck.'

'I'd have been grounded for a month if I'd spoken to my parents like that.'

'Yeah. Me too. I'm trying to cut her some slack. The house move was difficult for her and we haven't spent that much time together recently. I have to remind myself how awful it was being twelve with all those hormones wreaking havoc.'

'Hmm.'

If only Emma knew. It was a lot more than hormones. It was brain chemistry. It was nature.

It was the way things were meant to be.

'You know,' Emma went on, 'I found one of my lipsticks in her pocket. I don't mind her borrowing my stuff, but it was the fact she did it without asking and then lied about it. I guess I have to put that down to hormones too.'

Fiona pulled her sympathetic face. She'd slipped that lipstick into Rose's pocket for no reason other than to cause mischief, hoping it would create tension between mother and daughter – presuming Emma did the laundry and checked her kids' pockets before putting stuff into the washing machine. It seemed like her plan had worked perfectly.

After the shopping trip, Rose was starving, so they went to her favourite chain restaurant, Wagamama, but there was an enormous queue to get in and then service was excruciatingly slow. Rose complained throughout, especially when Emma and Fiona's food appeared first, by which point Rose had already finished the expensive glass of juice she'd ordered.

'I'm thirsty. I want another one of these.'

Fiona watched Emma's grip on her chopsticks tighten. 'Rose, just have some water.'

'But I want the juice. Oh God, I'm so hungry, I'm actually going to die.'

Fiona glared at her, trying to communicate silently, to tell her to cool it. She needed to be chilled out today. Calm. But Rose glared back and said, 'It's all right for you. You've got yours.'

Emma said, 'Rose, don't talk to Fiona like that. You're so rude.'

'She doesn't care. Do you, Fiona?'

Fiona pictured herself emptying her bowl of ramen over the girl's head. She really was going to get a shock in the near future. She had a lot to learn about blending in.

'I want you to apologise,' Emma said.

'No.'

'Say sorry, now!'

'It's okay,' Fiona said. 'She's tired and I'm fine.'

'I want her to apologise. She's been acting like a brat all day and needs to stop talking to people like that.'

'But I'm starving!' Rose cried out, throwing out her hands as she said it and knocking over Emma's drink, a non-alcoholic beer. The liquid sploshed across the bench and Emma leapt up, swearing, then went in search of napkins.

Fiona leaned across the table and hissed, 'Calm down. Stop acting like a little bitch.'

At that, Rose shot her daggers. But she did seem to cool down.

Now, in the car, Fiona wondered what was happening back on the estate – if Iris's body had been found yet. Overnight, she had disposed of the clothes she'd been wearing when she and Rose visited the old lady, along with all the stuff she'd taken to make it look like a burglary. It almost made her sad, watching the jewellery and records as they sunk into the dark water, thinking about how much money she could have got for them. The engagement ring she'd pulled from Iris's cold, bony finger must have been worth at least a couple of grand on its own. A shame.

She couldn't help but smile, though, thinking how horrified Ethan would be if he knew the vinyl he loved so much was lying at the bottom of a lake, the sleeves turning to mush, all that money dissolving in the cold depths.

She hadn't yet decided what she would do with his record collection.

'How much further?' Rose asked.

'Just half an hour, according to the satnav,' Emma said. She turned her head for a second to glance at Fiona. 'We really are out in the sticks here. Would you really enjoy living this far out in the countryside? I don't think I could bear it. In fact, when the kids are grown-up I'm planning to persuade Ethan to move back into London, if we can afford it. I want to be able to walk to a decent coffee shop or a theatre or some nice shops. A place where I don't have to drive.'

Fiona tuned out, even though she knew on an intellectual level it was kind to allow Emma to fantasise about a future with Ethan.

'There's going to be a storm,' Rose said, out of nowhere.

'Are you sure?' asked Emma, gesturing out the window at the blue sky. The fluffy white clouds. 'It's a lovely day.'

'I'm sure. I can feel it.' A pause. 'Can I use your phone to take a photo? You know the camera on mine is rubbish.'

'Sure.' Emma passed her phone to Rose. This, Fiona was confident, was where Rose would do what they'd arranged earlier, and delete herself and her mum from the tracking app the Dove family used. *We don't want your dad turning up during our outing, spoiling everything*, she'd explained.

While Rose took some photos of the sky and did what they'd arranged, the satnav instructed them to take the next left, and

Emma turned off, driving through a small village with narrow streets that was dominated by a huge church. Fiona spotted a black dog sitting alone in the churchyard, watching them as they went by.

Soon, they found themselves driving past fields full of cows, most of them lying down, which made Rose say, 'I told you,' although the sky was still clear and blue.

'You're going to have to direct me now,' Emma said, because Fiona hadn't been able to give the exact address. 'Do you know how to find it?'

'Of course. Take a right here.'

They drove up a lane that was only wide enough for a single vehicle, with farmland on either side, one containing more resting cows and the other lying fallow. The lane curved around blind corners, with mirrors in place to avoid collisions.

'You're actually a good driver,' she heard herself saying as they continued along the lane.

Emma laughed. 'Er . . . thanks. Did you think I wouldn't be?'

'Oh. No, I just think I heard Ethan say something about your driving once.'

'What? Really? That's a bloody cheek. Though I guess it's from when we had our Land Rover. It had really awkward gears – there was something wrong with the transmission – so I was always stalling it coming out of neutral into first. But he did too. We only had that stupid car for a couple of months.'

A couple of months. A faulty transmission. *Such bad luck.* Somehow, this made it even worse. They had known the vehicle was faulty, yet still chose to drive around in it without caring about how much inconvenience, disruption or – in Fiona and Maisie's case – life-changing catastrophe they caused.

'We're almost there. You'll reach a crossroads in a minute. Go right.'

The crossroads appeared. A faded wooden sign pointed in three directions, the kind of place where one might do a deal with the Devil. Straight ahead and right would take you to a pair of hamlets. The left pointer was marked *Ravenhill 1m.*

'Ravenhill?' Emma said. 'Is that the name of the nearest village?'

Fiona made a non-committal noise, not wanting to spoil the surprise. She genuinely wanted Emma to see the place that she had fantasised about so much. Mostly, though, she wanted Rose to see it. Rose who, she knew, was still itching to hear the answer to her question from last night. Because Fiona had promised to reveal all on this trip.

It was going to be such a surprise.

And then they were driving into the woods, all the trees with their leaves in their finest green splendour. To Fiona, it was like entering a fairy tale, one in which she was sometimes the princess, sometimes the wicked queen. A place of poison apples and hidden treasure; of beasts and beauty. The road narrowed even further until it was little more than a track, foliage crowding in on either side, and Fiona said, 'Pull up here. We'll have to go the rest of the way on foot.'

Emma stopped the car and turned her head. 'You're joking.'

'No. It's overgrown and not suitable for cars at the moment.' She opened the back door. 'Come on. You're going to love it.'

Rose opened her door at the same time and got out, standing beneath the trees and looking around. Fiona wondered if she could feel it too – the charge that hung in the air here, the dark energy. It caressed her, like fingertips stroking her skin and making all the tiny hairs stand on end.

Emma sat behind the wheel for a few more seconds, shaking her head, then got out. She looked at Fiona like this was a strange practical joke of which Emma was the victim.

'The place you wanted to show me is *here*? You said it was your dream home.'

'Oh, it is,' said Fiona. 'Follow me and I'll show you. Amazing here, isn't it?'

She pushed aside a low-hanging branch, ducking beneath it so she could follow the path, with Rose and Emma behind her.

'Amazing?' Emma sounded incredulous. 'It's creepy AF. Also, you could have warned me. I'm not wearing the right kind of shoes.'

Fiona looked back and down at Emma's Converse. 'They're fine. The ground is dry.'

'I think Rose is right, though,' Emma said. 'It's going to rain.'

The sky was hardly visible above the canopy of trees, but the slivers of blue between the branches had been replaced by glimpses of deep grey clouds. Fiona wasn't bothered by that. In fact, heavy rain might help her. Making surfaces slippery. Accidents more likely to happen.

They continued along the overgrown path, Fiona pushing aside vegetation, occasionally stopping to hold a branch so Rose could get by without scraping her head. The further they went, the stronger the charge of dark energy. She felt it enter her, slide beneath her skin and heat up her blood. She had to be careful: Maisie always told her that when she got overexcited she would make low, animal noises in her throat, ones she wasn't even aware of. She didn't want to freak Emma out and make her turn tail.

She glanced back at Rose, wondering what she was thinking. She looked grumpy, like any child forced to go on a hike by her parents. It was a shame she couldn't feel the energy of this place too, though one day she would understand. After today, it would always be special to her.

'I can see light,' Emma said from behind Fiona, and she was right. The path opened up and suddenly they were standing in a clearing – and looking at a wire fence that blocked the way. The fence was almost completely covered with creepers and long green tendrils that had wrapped themselves around the metal, obscuring the view beyond.

'Oh,' Emma said. 'What a shame.'

But Fiona had already moved to the left. It had been years since she'd come here, but she would be amazed if they'd fixed the fence. She just needed to remember where she had cut through last time. She patted at the vegetation, pulled some away, searching for the spot, remembering it was low down . . .

Here it was! She yanked at the creepers, then lifted the section of fence to reveal a gap, big enough to crawl through. She grinned at Rose and said, 'After you.'

'Rose,' Emma said. 'Wait . . .'

But it was too late. Rose had pushed her way through and now stood on the other side, taking a few steps up a steep slope.

Now Emma looked pissed off. 'Rose, get back here. You can't . . .' She turned to Fiona. 'What is this place? It must be private property. This is trespassing. Did you cut this hole in the fence?'

'Stop stressing,' Fiona said. 'The company that owned this place went bankrupt during the pandemic. It's public land now.'

Emma looked sceptical, as well she might. As far as Fiona knew, ownership of this land had passed back into the hands of the local council. Though didn't that mean it belonged to the people?

'I just want you to see it,' Fiona said. 'Come on. We've come all this way.'

Tutting, Emma put her hands on her hips. 'I'm not happy about this. I'm going in there to get Rose and then we're heading back.' She crawled through the gap, complaining about the dirt as she went, then stood and called for Rose, who had disappeared from sight.

Fiona watched Emma climb the bank, still shouting her daughter's name, then scrambled up after her.

Emma had caught up with Rose and they were standing at the crest of the slope, looking at the huge, crumbling building before them, with its half-collapsed roof and smashed windows and peeling paintwork and the ivy creeping up the red brick. As they stared, a pigeon emerged from one of the windows and flew into the trees. The once-pristine lawn was a tangle of weeds and knee-high grass. The front door hung off its hinges. And the sign that read *RAVENHILL* was thick with moss, obscuring most of the letters.

'What the hell is this place?' Emma asked.

A beatific smile lit up Fiona's face.

'Home,' she replied.

37

The long-closed-down Ravenhill Psychiatric Hospital – the very name sent an icy cascade of goosebumps across my flesh – was located in Essex, on the outskirts of Epping Forest. Again, as the crow flies it wasn't too far, but with London traffic it would take about an hour to get there, less if I broke the speed limit – which I intended to do, as aggressively as possible, as getting points on my licence was the least of my concerns.

'Are you okay?' I asked Dylan as we headed back into the traffic.

'Yeah.'

His voice and the paleness of his face betrayed how he really felt. He looked so sick with fear that I wished I didn't have to bring him with me, but what choice did I have? He was in no fit state to be dropped at a train station and told to go home. Besides, two members of my family were missing; I didn't want to risk losing another one.

Again, I wrestled with the idea of going to the police and handing everything over to them. But Lucy's words about Rose getting into trouble rang in my ears. Besides, I knew I would have to persuade the police to act – that they'd want to talk to me at length, and that it would take ages for them to mobilise.

There was no time for that.

'Fiona Woodfield,' I said. 'Can you look her up on your phone? See if there are any news stories about her?'

I thought there must be, if she had been in prison with Lucy – and I was right.

'Oh my days,' Dylan said. He had found something immediately. A news story from four years ago.

'She was done for will fraud,' he said, quickly scanning the article and summarising it for me. 'The prosecution said she formed a fake friendship with this wealthy elderly lady, moved in with her and persuaded her to change her will. She was sentenced to three years in prison after pleading guilty.'

I was actually slightly relieved. Will fraud was a long way from murder. Sure, it was a despicable crime and it was exactly the kind of thing I could imagine a psychopath – who saw other people as inferior and who had no conscience, no feelings of guilt – doing. But it was a financial crime, not a violent one. I wondered briefly if Fiona was planning to try to con me and Emma, though we would be unusual targets. We were far from rich. We were just a normal family living in suburbia. Why on earth was I on the list Lucy had mentioned? Or maybe Lucy, being a solid-gold psychopath herself – manipulative and cold-blooded, famous for her cruelty – had been lying. I found it reassuring to think this.

'Dad? Hello? Are you listening?'

'Sorry. I was deep in thought.'

'Okay, well, please concentrate. Listen to this. *Woodfield's partner in crime, Maisie Smith—*'

'Smith. That's where she borrowed the surname from.'

'*Maisie Smith died by suicide in her cell shortly after her arrest, leaving a full written confession for the attempted murder of Dinah Uxbridge. In the letter, she said she had acted alone and that Woodfield was not involved in giving Mrs Uxbridge thallium and attempting to poison her. Despite the protestations of Mrs Uxbridge's remaining family, who believe Woodfield was a full and active participant in the scheme, the Crown Prosecution Service decided only to charge her for the lesser crime of will fraud in light of Smith's confession.*'

Dylan looked up from his phone. 'There's a quote from Dinah Uxbridge's niece here. *I understand the CPS doesn't want to spend money on a trial, but as far as I'm concerned this is a gross miscarriage of justice. I believe Fiona Woodfield and Maisie Smith worked together to attempt to poison my aunt because, even when she'd changed her will, they couldn't wait for her to die of natural causes. Also, Aunt Dinah was so strong she might even have outlived Maisie Smith.*'

'Why would she say that?' I asked. Fiona would only have been in her mid-thirties then, and I assumed her partner would've been about the same.

We were stopped at a traffic light, in a queue of cars, so Dylan held his screen up for me to see. There was a woman on the screen in late middle age. Short, grey hair, probably in her mid-sixties. Quite attractive, with charisma shining out of the photo. The female equivalent of a silver fox. Silver vixen?

'Who's that?' I asked, expecting him to say it was Dinah Uxbridge, the victim.

'That's Maisie Smith.'

I did a double take. 'What? Are you sure?' She must have been at least thirty years older than Fiona.

'Hold on. There's another piece here about Fiona and Maisie,' Dylan said. 'At the time they were arrested, Fiona was thirty-five and Maisie was sixty-four. It says here that the couple met when Maisie lived in Australia when she was in her mid-forties.'

'Wait. So twenty years before? That means—'

'Fiona would have been a teenager. If it was twenty years earlier, she would have been fifteen.'

But it could have been even earlier. She could have been thirteen or fourteen. Barely older than Rose. And an older woman had come along . . .

'She groomed her,' I said.

I thought I might actually be sick.

'Have you ever seen . . . anything like that between them?' I asked.

'What? Like Fiona touching Rose?' He grimaced. 'No. Whatever she is, I'm sure she's not a paedo. This isn't about that, is it? It's about training her, like I said. Like Lucy said.'

Lucy's exact words came back to me.

Fiona told me she was going to take Rose under her wing, that she recognised the same thing in her that we have.

'But the article you read out, it describes Fiona and Maisie as a couple. And Fiona told your mum that her girlfriend had died.'

'I guess they must have got together once Fiona was grown-up.'

'But that's still grooming, isn't it?'

Teenagers today were taught all about this stuff. When I was a kid I was warned about strangers in cars with puppies and candy. Now, they were told to be careful of online predators and catfish and strangers who lurked not in playgrounds and near schools but in multiplayer games and on social media.

Was Fiona something more old-fashioned than what we warned our digital-native children about? Not a stranger on the internet, but the stranger next door. Who we had allowed into our lives; trusted. And we had let her groom our daughter – in the same way it appeared Fiona had been groomed.

'Is there any more?' I asked, afraid of what Dylan might find next.

'No. Just a final statement from this niece. She says if it were up to her, Fiona would be locked up for the rest of her life. Oh God, listen. This is a quote from her.'

My knuckles were white on the wheel.

'She looks like a human being. She smiles and talks and laughs like one. But she isn't. She's like an alien in a human suit. A devil. I hope people will remember her name and the mask she wears so she can never fool anyone again.'

ϖ

As we approached the spot the satnav had sent us to, the site of the former psychiatric hospital, the sky darkened rapidly and the heavens opened, fat raindrops bouncing off the windscreen, so hard the wipers couldn't cope.

Into the forest, along a dark path, a dirt track that ended suddenly on the edge of some trees. There was Emma's car, pulled over on the side of the road.

I parked behind it and told Dylan to stay in the car while I checked it. It was empty.

I returned to our car and gestured for Dylan to wind down the window.

'I want you to stay here while I go and find the hospital.'

'No way.'

'I'm not going to argue. Lock the doors, stay in the car, don't even open the windows for anyone you're not related to. You've got your phone. If I'm not back in thirty minutes, dial 999. Okay?'

He stared at me.

'Okay?'

A slow nod. I moved to get out of the car.

'Dad, wait.'

I turned back.

'Please, let's call the police now. It's not safe. I don't want anything to happen to you.'

'I'll be careful. I promise. Stay here, do not move. And close this window.'

I headed into the trees before he could try to persuade me to let him come. Maybe it was too little too late, but I was determined not to put any more of my children in danger.

Beyond the trees, I found a fence. I felt along it, looking for a way in, wondering if I'd need to scale it, and found a section that had been cut away. I slipped through and climbed up the steep bank beyond.

There it was, the silhouette of a huge house beneath the darkening sky.

Ravenhill.

38

'Maisie always said I was a dreamer,' Fiona said, leading Rose and Emma into what had once been the reception area. It hadn't changed since she'd last come here, a few months before her arrest, back when she'd thought she was about to be rich. There was still a desk in the corner, rotten and infested with woodworm. 'But the moment I laid eyes on this place, I knew it was perfect.'

Rose was looking around, peering through doors, reading the peeling signs on the damp-mottled walls. She seemed interested, open-minded. Emma, on the other hand, was goggling at Fiona like this might be a wind-up.

'It stinks in here. What is that?'

'Pigeon shit, probably. It's not that bad. It'll soon fade once the birds have been rehomed.'

'Rehomed . . . What actually *is* this place? Some kind of hospital?'

'Ravenhill House,' Fiona said. 'Formerly one of Britain's finest psychiatric institutions. Or lunatic asylums, as they used to call them.'

'Sweet Jesus.'

Fiona noticed that Rose was paying attention now, and Fiona couldn't help but play to the crowd. 'There were few signs of Jesus here, Emma. People, mostly women in fact, could be locked away for anything from depression caused by losing their son or husband in the war, to leading an immoral life. Hysteria was a big one. The wandering womb, causing all sorts of trouble as it roamed around the female body. You could be locked up for adultery, jealousy, nymphomania.'

'The bad old days,' Emma said.

'Maybe. I expect having an emotional affair with one's neighbour qualified too, not that anyone used such ridiculous language in Victorian times. A cheat was a cheat.'

Emma's face had gone pink. 'What the hell?'

Fiona waved this away. 'I'm messing with you. Yes, it was a terrible time. Guess what? I found out that my own great-grandmother was a patient here.'

Emma still looked shell-shocked from what Fiona had said, and Fiona realised she needed to be careful for a little longer. She didn't want Emma marching out of here, attempting to drag Rose with her.

'I'm sorry about the affair comment,' she said. 'Bad joke.'

'It didn't sound like a joke.'

'Why was she here?' Rose asked, ignoring this brewing argument.

'Unsociable behaviour, apparently,' Fiona said. 'She was accused of being a "loose woman" who damaged the reputations of several high-ranking gentlemen.'

'Typical,' Rose said.

'Also, she murdered her husband.'

'Oh. Wow.'

'Cut his head off with an axe, then carried it into town and handed it to his mistress, who worked at one of the more popular inns.'

Emma stared at her, then said, 'You *are* joking, right?'

'Why would I joke about that? Her name was Emma, in fact. Isn't that a coincidence?'

'It's a common name.'

'Hmm. Have you ever had the urge to chop anyone's head off?' Fiona giggled. 'Sorry, I'm messing with you still. How would you like a tour?'

Before Emma could reply, Fiona went through the door behind the reception desk into the corridor. There were no windows here, and it was almost too dark to see your own hand in front of your face. Fiona, knowing Emma wouldn't be able to see her, felt her inside pocket, checking the flick-knife was still there, and took her phone out of her pocket, switching the torch on.

'Isn't it amazing?' she called out, her voice bouncing between the walls.

Using her phone to light the way, Fiona went through a door into the washroom, brushing a cobweb from her cheek as she entered. This was where new patients would be cleaned, often with freezing water delivered by a hose, although this – by all accounts – did nothing to quash the lice that had infested this place. Several tin bathtubs, encrusted with dirt and brown rust, lined the wall. To the right of the corridor were several smaller rooms which might have been used for relatives, usually husbands, who were waving goodbye to their loved, or despised, ones.

'Why did you refer to this place as home?' Emma asked.

'Because that's what it's going to be one day.'

Emma was incredulous. '*Your* home? It would cost millions to buy this place and do it up. Are you secretly rich?'

'Not yet. But one day.'

'When you win the lottery?'

Fiona didn't smile. 'There are other ways to get rich, Emma. I almost managed it once. But you know what? Going forward, I won't make the same mistakes again. And I'll have a better disguise next time. Everyone trusts a mother.'

'Wait. Are you having a baby?'

Ignoring Emma's question, Fiona tried to catch Rose's eye, but she was busy inspecting the dilapidated bathtubs, taking photos of them on her phone. She had her own torch on too.

'What do you think of it, Rose?' she asked.

'It smells bad.'

'Yes, but apart from that?' Fiona tried not to let her irritation show. At the same time, she heard rain drumming against the remaining windows. The storm had come.

Rose said, 'It's horrible. I mean, it's cool to visit and the history is kind of interesting, I guess, but it's old and smelly and gross.'

'You took the words right out of my mouth,' Emma said.

Fiona gritted her teeth, shooting a look of venom at Emma before going over to Rose and saying, 'But you're not seeing the potential. Look!' She marched Rose back into the corridor and along it to a door that led into a huge space, formerly a gymnasium. Weak light entered the room through the windows high up on the walls, combining with the light from their phones to create a grey, watery gloom. She lowered her voice so Emma wouldn't overhear. 'We could have a massive indoor swimming pool here. And outside, we can build stables. Horses, Rose! Haven't you always wanted your own pony?'

'Horses?'

'And as many dogs and cats as you want. We could have our own zoo!'

'Wait,' Rose said. '*We?*'

'Yes. As soon as—'

She whirled around. Emma was approaching again, footsteps echoing through the corridor.

'I can't tell if you're winding me up, Fiona. If this is all some big elaborate joke. Even if you could somehow find the money to do this place up, it's way too big to be anyone's home, and that's before we even talk about its past.' She shuddered. 'I don't believe in ghosts but, my God, if anywhere was haunted, it would be this place. It has such . . . dark energy.'

Fiona was surprised. 'You feel it too?'

'Of course. Even before you told me it was an asylum. Think of all the suffering that happened here. The misery.' She lowered her voice so Rose wouldn't overhear. 'I bet loads of people died here too.'

'Oh yes. Hundreds. Many of them perished in a fire that swept through the upstairs rooms. A blaze set deliberately by one of the nurses, they say. That was the reason it closed down in the end. They say you can still see scorch marks on the walls, shaped like the bodies of the women who burned to death.'

'Cool,' said Rose.

Emma stared at her daughter with horror. '*Cool?*'

Fiona grinned. 'Do you want to see? Come on.'

She took Rose's hand, ignoring how the girl flinched, and led her to a staircase at the end of the corridor. They began to climb.

'Wait.' Emma was behind them, struggling to keep up. 'That doesn't look safe.'

The stairs were rickety and blackened with soot, and their creaks were like horror-movie shrieks as Fiona trod on them on her way up. 'It's fine,' she called back.

'Rose, get back here.'

Rose ignored her and, within moments, they had reached the first floor, pushing through a door that hung from its hinges and entering another corridor. Fiona heard Emma coming up the steps behind them, just as she'd known she would.

'This is where the patients lived. Can you see where the fire swept through here?' Fiona asked. Despite the rain and the gathering storm, there was still a little daylight coming in – but, as she had downstairs, she topped it up with the torch on her phone, shining it up then down. The ceiling was black and the floor was thick with a grey-white dust, like powdered bone.

She and Rose went into one of the rooms, and the heavy door swung shut behind them. There were the remains of a single bed against the wall, so rusted it was almost black, and Fiona set her phone down on it so the torch acted as a makeshift lamp. There were two windows high up on the walls, the glass broken and jagged. A chamber pot which had survived the fire was over in the corner. Fiona watched Rose examine the wall, obviously looking for the charred outline of the room's former resident. Maybe those dark patterns resembled a human figure. It was hard to tell in the near-dark, but Rose said, in a hushed and gleeful tone, 'I can see it.'

Moments later, the door opened behind them to reveal Emma, wearing a furious expression.

'What are you doing?' she demanded, coming inside, the door slamming behind her.

'Look, Mum. Can you see the shape on the wall? Someone burned to death right there, where you're standing.'

Emma looked at her daughter like she'd never seen her before, simultaneously moving away from the spot and shivering like she could feel it. The presence of the dead.

'Rose, we're leaving.' She turned to Fiona. 'You know, Fiona, I really wasn't sure about you at first, but I changed my mind, thought you were nice. I've had to defend you to Ethan several times recently.'

'Oh, doesn't Ethan like me anymore? That's a shame. But I'm sure I know the way to his heart.'

Emma stared at her. 'So there *is* something going on?'

'Oh yes. Ethan paid me a little visit last week. We've grown . . . close.'

'Oh my God. You're not right in the head.' She reached out a hand. 'Rose, come on. We're going home. Fiona can find her own way back.'

But Rose didn't move. She was staring at Fiona with horror, and Fiona realised she shouldn't have said that about herself and Ethan in front of her. It was something she needed to talk to Rose about, properly prepare her for. How, if they were going to be a family, she and Ethan were going to have to be together.

'You and my *dad*?' Rose said.

Fiona shifted around so she was standing between Emma and the door out of this room. Keeping her eye on Emma, she said, 'Rose, do you want me to answer your question now? Tell you who was third on my list?'

Rose nodded slowly while Emma stood beside her, wanting to leave but frozen to the spot by confusion and curiosity.

'I told you about the Land Rover that stopped Maisie and me from getting away, didn't I? Well, when I got out of prison—'

'*Prison?*' Emma said.

'—I found out that the Land Rover belonged to your parents. I thought at first it was probably your dad driving – making a sexist assumption – but when I looked back through his social media I saw he was away at some big record fair, had set off on the first train of the day, so it couldn't have been him. It was your mum.'

She turned to Emma. 'It was you.'

Emma stared back at her. Rose was staring too, taking all this in. After the accident that was about to happen – the mishap on this day out – Fiona would explain that she, Fiona, was going to be her mum now. Her dad would be grieving and need comforting, and Fiona would be there for him, and soon he would fall in love with her and it would be easy for her to move next door. Wouldn't it be amazing, the two of them together, all the time? *I have so much to show you*, she would say. *So much to teach you. You'll be my shield, I'll be your mentor. Together, we will be unstoppable.*

Partnerships are great, but what does society really value, Rose? I'll tell you. Family. It's the ideal way to disguise ourselves, to get away with anything we want to do. No one would ever suspect this perfect family unit. We'll be able to befriend all these rich old people, all these decrepit millionaires – you, this sweet girl who nobody would ever suspect, and your delightful stepmother. They'll be signing their estates over to us before you can say two-point-four children.

But that little speech was still a few minutes in the future. First, the accident needed to happen.

Emma emerged from the trance she'd been in and attempted to grab Rose's wrist. Rose wriggled from her grasp – and moved to stand beside Fiona.

'What the hell?' Emma clearly couldn't believe what she was seeing. 'Rose. Come. Now.'

'I'm not a dog.'

'What? I know you're not a dog. You're my daughter, and you're going to do as you're told.'

'No.'

Emma's mouth fell open and Fiona clapped her hands with glee. This was delicious. Rose's rebellion in the restaurant had been annoying, but this . . .

'She's a maniac,' Emma said. 'Rose. Come with me. We're leaving.'

'I'm sorry, Emma, but you're not.'

Fiona took the flick-knife out of her inside pocket and pressed the button which made the blade appear.

It had been a while since Fiona had seen an expression of such horror. Surprise unfolded on Rose's face too.

Fiona moved towards Emma, the knife outstretched. 'Now. You're coming with me.'

But it wasn't Emma she reached out for. It was Rose whose upper arm she gripped and pulled towards her.

She held the knife to Rose's throat.

'Come with me. Or you both die.'

39

Fiona stood with her back to the closed door, squeezing the handle of the knife, the blade held lightly against Rose's throat. Her other arm was wrapped around the girl's waist, holding her still. It was rare for her pulse to get above eighty, but right now she knew it had to be right up at ninety. Heat spread through her veins. She had reached the culmination of one plan, the end of a chapter of her life and the beginning of another.

She could sense Maisie beside her, looking as she had when they'd first met. They had both been waitressing in a little café in Freo, Fiona fifteen years old, doing the Saturday shift, and Maisie in her forties. The Englishwoman who told everyone she was travelling the world, taking an extended stay in Western Australia because it was so beautiful. Later, she would tell Fiona she had stayed because of her.

'I recognised it in you the first day we met,' she would say. 'I knew we had to be together.'

And so Maisie had stayed in Australia for several years, until her visa had long expired and immigration began to sniff around. After Maisie returned to England, Fiona had tried to get by on her own for a few years, but it was impossible. She needed her mentor. Had always needed her. So she had followed.

Here, in front of her, was the woman who had – and it didn't matter if it had been unwitting – taken Maisie away from her forever.

And between them, not moving, playing her role perfectly – even if it was unrehearsed – was the girl who was to Fiona what Fiona had been to Maisie.

Emma stood with the little window behind her. Rain hammered the glass and the wind howled with a kind of madness, shaking the nearby trees. The shock that had frozen her in place since Fiona had grabbed her daughter had now thawed a little, allowing Emma to move.

'Let her go.'

'No, Emma. I want you to leave this room. We'll be right behind you. If you do everything I say, I won't hurt her. I'll never hurt her. I promise you, after you've gone, she'll be safe with— Ow!'

She cried out and pulled her arm away, staring in disbelief at her wrist – where Rose had bitten her. Bitten her! Rose darted away from both of them into the furthest corner. Fiona stayed by the door, blocking the exit.

Emma reached out towards her daughter. 'Rose, come here.'

Rose didn't move.

'Rose!' Emma commanded. 'Come to me, now. I'll protect you.'

Still, Rose remained motionless.

Fiona, recovering from the pain and surprise of the bite, said, 'No, come to me, Rose. I wasn't going to hurt you. I was just trying to get her to do what I asked.'

'Rose,' Emma said again. 'Come here, to Mummy.'

Fiona laughed. 'She doesn't *want* to go to you, Emma. Like she keeps telling you, she's not a baby anymore. Certainly not your baby. She's something different. Something better.'

'You're insane.'

Emma tried to move towards Rose, but Fiona stepped forward, the knife held out. 'Get back. Stay where you are.'

Emma had no choice but to obey.

'Rose,' Fiona began. 'I know I should have explained everything to you before we came here, but I needed you to act natural. I promise, from now on, I'll tell you everything, okay? We'll do everything together.'

Emma sneered at her. 'You're out of your mind. Ethan's not really interested in *you*.'

'Oh, he will be. Men are easy, Emma. I'll help him mend his broken heart. And I'll make sure to remind him about you and Mike.'

'You're deluded. Also, if you think Dylan would ever accept you, you're not just deluded, you're stupid.'

'Well, a second child isn't a vital part of the plan. Perhaps he needs to have a little accident too.'

Emma took half a step towards Fiona, who pushed forward the knife, compelling her to stop.

'So that's the plan?' Emma said. 'To take my place? How do you feel about that, Rose?'

They both looked at the girl.

She shrugged, then turned towards Emma. 'I'm not like you. I'm different.'

'That isn't true, sweetheart. You're going through changes, that's all. Puberty.' Emma attempted a laugh. 'All teenage girls feel different.'

'No. It's more than that.' Rose paused, looking thoughtful. 'And I think you must have always known it, deep down.'

'What are you talking about? Rosie . . .'

'Don't call me that!'

'Sorry. I—'

'I've never felt the way I'm meant to.' Rose's voice had gone dreamy. Distant. 'The way they do in storybooks and on TV. Never felt warmth or love for anyone else. Never had a friend who didn't irritate me. Other kids . . . I look at them and either feel nothing or I want to hurt them. Like those boys across the road, Eric and Albie. When Fiona caused that accident, I was glad. I wanted him to suffer.'

Fiona saw Emma take this in. That she had caused the accident.

'But that's . . . that's kind of understandable,' she managed. 'He bullied you.'

Fiona knew she should be moving things on, but she was fascinated. Besides, it was good for Rose to articulate all this, to process it. It would make things easier afterwards.

'Haven't you ever wondered why I've never really had a best friend?'

'What about Jasmine?'

'She was an idiot. I hated her.'

Realisation dawned on Emma's face, like she finally understood something that had been niggling at her for a long time. The kind of eureka moment that doesn't make you want to leap out of the bath but jump into it and hold your head under the water. 'And what about me, and your dad and Dylan?' she asked, a pitiful, pleading tone creeping in. 'You love us.'

Rose frowned and made a noise low in her throat. 'Hmm. No, I don't. I mean, I guess I always appreciated you giving me a home. Dylan could be a lot *more* annoying, I guess. But love? I don't know what it feels like. When you're sick, I don't care. If I think about you dying, I don't care about that either – except to wonder what it would mean for me. I wouldn't want to be sent to a children's home. That would be horrible.'

Tears ran down Emma's cheeks. 'Rose, you don't mean this. You can't. What about Lola? You love her, don't you?'

'I like owning her.'

Emma wiped at her wet face. 'Rose, sweetheart. This isn't you. And if it is, we can get you help. What about that woman we met on holiday? Keira and Henry's mum. She's a child psychologist. She can help you.'

The expression on Rose's face was so full of contempt – a look that dripped poison – that Fiona wanted to clap her hands and cheer.

'I. Don't. Need. *Help.*' Rose took a step towards her mother, which also took her closer to Fiona. 'Don't you get it, *Mummy*? I like being like this.'

'Rose, please.'

Emma moved towards her, arms outstretched, trying to gather Rose into a hug. Rose backed away like a feral cat, almost hissing, and Emma shook her head and said, 'No, I'm not standing for this. You're my daughter. You're going to do as I say.'

She moved forward again, trying to take hold of Rose's arm. Rose again backed away. 'Don't touch me.'

Fiona knew she ought to do something, but she was too fascinated, dying to see how this played out. The rain was drumming against the roof, wind entering through the broken windows, and she expected to see lightning flashes, hear thunder crashing, shaking the building.

'Rose. Come with me now. We're going.'

'No!'

Emma had had enough. Fiona had seen this before, in parks and supermarkets and on beaches. The mother who tries to reason, to persuade, to threaten, and then, finally, snaps, asserting her authority, her status, her strength. Fiona's mother had done it to her all the time, dragging her out of shops, on to buses, into classrooms.

Emma reached out and tried to grab Rose by the wrist.

Rose flung herself to the side, evading her mum's grasp, and Emma shouted:

'Rose! That's *enough*.'

Rose screamed – not like a girl, but a full-grown woman. A scream of hatred and defiance and rage. And as she screamed, she darted towards Fiona, who wasn't expecting this. Before Fiona could react, Rose snatched the knife from her hand.

40

A woman screamed.

I ran towards the house.

41

Rose swung the knife in front of her, a wide arc, left to right.

The blade sliced through Emma's throat.

Emma's hands went to the wound, her knees buckling at the same time, and she slid to the ground, her back against the wall. Blood spurted. So much blood. It sprayed Rose, spattered her face and hair and clothes as she stood there, crouched and panting in front of her fallen mother. Emma was on her rear with her legs straight out in front of her, still clutching her throat, blood seeping between her fingers, eyes wide and staring in disbelief.

Fiona couldn't believe it either.

'Rose. What did you do? We were meant to make it look like an accident! A fall down the lift shaft. Bricks falling on her head. How the hell are we going to explain this?'

Rose turned to her, the knife still clutched in her fist. The girl's eyes were wide, almost bulging. She looked utterly insane. Almost inhuman.

'Oh no.' Fiona backed away.

In her life, she had rarely felt fear. Hatred, frustration, annoyance, the burning desire for revenge. All those, many times. But actual fear – that was an emotion that had hardly ever touched her. Why should it? She was an apex predator.

Rose was moving towards her – the knife, slick with Emma's blood, held out before her. She was panting, like a dog that had crawled across the desert. A starving dog, confronted by meat.

'Give it to me,' Fiona commanded, trying to make herself sound authoritative. 'Hand it over and I'll think of a way for us to get out of this.'

At the same time she heard a man's voice, coming from somewhere in the building. A man, calling.

'Emma? Rose?'

It was Ethan.

Rose heard it too, her attention drawn to the door but snapping straight back to Fiona, who dropped her voice to a whisper.

'Rose, put the knife down and I'll fix this, and then we can go ahead with the plan. A new family: me and you and your dad and Dylan. We'll be so powerful together. You and me. Think of all the things we can do.'

'No.'

Fiona blinked. She could see Emma trying to speak, but nothing was coming out except for a trickle of blood running from the corner of her mouth.

'Why would I want you as my mentor?' Rose said in a voice that was so calm, so even, that it sent a chill through Fiona's bones. 'You're terrible at this. You and Maisie allowed yourselves to get caught. Iris figured out who you were. Even that idiot across the road suspected you. You're rubbish, Fiona. I don't need you.'

'Rose . . .'

'I'm better off without you.'

Fiona took a last look at the approaching girl and made a decision.

She turned to run, to get out of there. She moved for the door.

Heard and felt the rush of movement behind her.

Then the pain.

The fall.

And the door, swinging open into the room, hitting her in the—

42

'Emma! Rose!'

The place was a labyrinth. Dark, confusing, the rain and wind drowning everything out. Where had the scream come from? I ran through what had been the reception area, almost choking on the smell of bird shit, and into a corridor. There was a shower room and what looked like it had once been a gymnasium. A vast, empty space. I went back into the corridor and listened, my ears humming in the silence.

At the end of the corridor were stairs leading down to a basement and another staircase leading up. Which way would they have gone? I was drawn to the basement. It seemed the more likely place. Switching on the torch on my phone I ventured down the steps but found a locked door at the bottom. I rattled it and pressed my ear against it, hearing nothing. Surely Fiona wouldn't have keys to lock this door behind her?

I went back up, continuing up the rickety stairs to the first floor and into another corridor which had rooms all along it on both sides. In the shaking, flattened, too-white light of my phone's torch, it was a place ripped straight from a nightmare: the former asylum, obscene graffiti scrawled on the walls, the stench of decay. Echoes of cruelty and madness and despair, the energy of human suffering imprinted in every brick and tile. I could hardly breathe as I ran down the corridor.

All the doors were open, revealing empty rooms, except one.

I pushed it, hard, and it struck and bounced back off something. I pushed again, shouldering my way into the room.

It took a moment for me to take it all in as I passed the torch over it.

The light settled on Emma, sitting with her back to the wall to my right, her legs stretched out before her, arms slumped, head fallen forward. A knife lay next to her, just beyond her lifeless fingers. Rose was crouched beside her saying, 'Mummy. Mummy.'

And lying on her front close by me in the doorway, with blood soaking the back of her T-shirt, was Fiona.

I ignored her and rushed over to Emma, throwing myself on to my knees beside her. The front of her T-shirt was drenched in blood, slick with it, and it pooled around her on the floor, soaking my jeans where I knelt. I could smell it, the sharp, meaty tang of it.

Nothing seemed real, especially when I touched Emma and she was cold, unmoving. That slumped head, her chin on her collarbone.

On the other side of her, Rose was frozen, silent now, staring at me. In the gloom, she looked like she'd sprouted hundreds of new freckles that had clustered together and also spread to her hair. It took me a moment to realise it was blood.

I put my hand on Emma's chin and, in a grotesque imitation of a romantic gesture, lifted her face towards mine. It lifted too freely. I saw the slashed throat, the gaping wound oozing blood that glistened black in the bleached light of my phone.

She was dead. Indisputably dead.

'No, Emma!'

I pulled her against me, began instantly to sob, crying out her name. 'Emma. *Emma!*' Her blood stained the front of my shirt; I could feel the cold, inert weight of her, but I couldn't believe she was dead, couldn't comprehend what was happening.

Struggling to breathe, I gently lowered her to the ground and found Rose still staring.

'What happened?' I said it quietly first, through my tears, then shouted it. '*What happened?*'

Rose sucked in a breath before she spoke. 'Fiona . . . Fiona went crazy. She and Mum started fighting because Fiona told her the two of you were in love, and then Fiona had a knife and she attacked Mum with it but Mum fought her and managed to get the knife and stabbed Fiona in the back but then *she* collapsed.'

It all came out in a rush. I couldn't take it in, not properly. The pieces refused to fit. Emma had stabbed Fiona even after her throat had been cut? I looked at Rose's hands. Like her face, they were covered with blood, except this wasn't spatter. It looked like she'd dipped her fingers in it and rubbed her palms together.

She saw me looking. Hid her hands behind her back.

Still not speaking, I went over to Fiona and nudged her with my foot. She was a heavy, motionless lump. I crouched and felt for a pulse. There was no doubt. She was dead too.

I went back towards Emma, and Rose flung herself at me, wrapping her arms around me, sobbing against my shoulder.

'Mummy's dead,' she said. 'Mummy's dead.'

I heard footsteps, then a voice calling, 'Dad?'

Dylan's voice brought me back to life. He was close by, in the corridor. I started to tell him to stay where he was, but Rose spoke first.

'We're in here.'

Before I could do anything, Dylan's head appeared around the door. He took in the scene. His mum, dead. Fiona, dead. Rose, stained with blood which was all over my clothes now too. He started to tremble, his breath quickening.

He changed in that instant. I knew, with a stab of despair, that he would never be the same happy boy he had always been.

But he didn't cry, not yet. Instead, he pointed at Rose.

'What did you *do*?' he screamed.

'It wasn't me,' Rose said, and I was thrown back to when she was a pre-schooler, caught red-handed in our living room with a box of felt-tip pens, green and red scribbles all over the freshly painted walls. She'd said 'Not me' then too, eyes wide and innocent, my little girl, so sweet, so guilty, and Emma and I had laughed, even though we knew she had done it.

'Dad, she's lying,' Dylan said, desperation making his voice crack. 'She did this. I told you, she's . . . she's dark triad. She's a psychopath.'

'How can you say that?' Rose began to cry and her tears seemed so real, her upset so genuine.

'Liar,' Dylan yelled. 'You're a liar!'

'It was Fiona!' Rose said.

'Then why is there blood all over your hands and your face?'

'Because I tried to help her.'

'Quiet!' I snapped at both of them. My ears were buzzing like they were full of flies; all I could smell was blood, and I had to get out of this room.

I ushered both my children out into the corridor, shutting the door behind me so I could no longer see the scene. Not that I would ever manage that, I knew.

My dead wife. Oh God, my *dead* wife. The knowledge hit me and I staggered, slamming against the wall, almost sliding into the same position I'd found Emma in. Somehow, I managed to stay upright. The steady drone of rain hitting the roof above my head. The light from the phone I was still holding bouncing around me, adding to the nausea. I felt like I was trapped in some nightmarish funfair attraction, a house of horrors, everything spinning and crooked and warped.

'Dad? *Dad?*'

I lifted my head to find Dylan shaking my shoulder, his face inches from mine. He looked stricken, too shocked to cry, and clearly asking for help. From me. His dad. Beside him, Rose stood motionless, except I could see she was breathing heavily, her eyes ablaze.

I looked down at the phone in my hand. There was something I needed to do. My brain wouldn't work. I don't know how many seconds passed before I figured it out.

'Did you call the police already?'

My voice was shaking so much I had to say it twice before Dylan understood.

'No. Not yet. But I couldn't wait at the car. I was scared, Dad. Scared they'd done something to you.' And that was when it really hit him, the grief taking over from his anger at Rose, and his face crumpled. He sobbed, covering his face with his hands.

I pulled him into a hug and held him for a moment. Over his shoulder, I saw Rose watching us with what looked like curiosity. Was she smiling? Whatever Dylan had said about her, it still wouldn't cut through. I still couldn't believe it of her. My little girl.

I let go of Dylan and handed him my phone. 'Can you call the police while I talk to Rose?'

He managed to get hold of himself, though his words came out strangled. 'Why do you want to talk to her?'

'Dylan, please.'

Hand shaking, he made the call while I crouched in front of Rose.

'I need you to promise me that you're telling the truth,' I said to her.

'I am.'

'What about Iris? Did Fiona kill her?'

She hesitated a moment too long before saying, 'No, we just went to say goodbye. To wish her a happy trip.'

I nodded, but that was it; my heart was shattered. Because I knew she was lying.

Standing up was like fighting against gravity. I could feel it trying to pull me down – make me lie there on the floor and give in. But then I looked at Dylan, holding the phone out to me, and I knew I couldn't do that. I had to stay strong enough to act, for him.

'You have to tell them,' Dylan said. 'Tell them it was her.'

'Dylan—' I took the phone. Disconnected the call.

'Why did you do that? She's a psychopath. She killed Mum!'

'Daddy, don't let him say those things about me.'

She never called me Daddy. Hadn't for years. I looked at her and her bloody hands, recalled the lie she'd just told me about Iris, and any final doubts I might have had were obliterated.

She was lying about all of it.

She was what Dylan said she was.

Oh God.

I didn't know what to do. It was too much. But when I blinked, all I could see was a series of images:

Emma's body slumped on the ground.

The blood on Rose's hands.

And then, absolutely as clear as the others, images of things that hadn't happened yet:

Dylan, a knife sticking out of his chest.

Rose, coming for me, eyes bright and wide, the glint of a blade as she slashed at the air between us.

Then back to Dylan, dead eyes open, staring at me, accusing, blaming: *I tried to warn you. I tried to tell you.*

My already-broken heart shattered further. I knew what I had to do.

'Go back to the car,' I said to Dylan. 'Wait for the police.'

'What?'

I shouted, 'Go. *Now!*' I could hear how close I was to the edge of sanity.

The way my son flinched, I knew he could hear me losing my mind too. But he hurried to the stairs. Rose tried to follow him. I grabbed her wrist.

'Not you,' I said.

Dylan hesitated at the top of the stairwell and I shouted at him again. '*Go.*'

He went, leaving me with Rose, who looked up at me, hurt and confused. 'Daddy? What are you doing?'

'I'm sorry, sweetheart,' I said, taking her arm. 'But I don't believe you. Maybe you didn't kill your mum, maybe that was Fiona, but I know you had something to do with Iris. I don't know what else you've done. But I can't let you come home with us. I have to put Dylan first.'

And with that, she changed.

The mask slipped away.

It was a terrifying sight. One second she was gazing at me imploringly, an upset little girl. The next – well, one word came into my head as her features twisted and she bared her teeth, and all the warmth left her eyes.

Devil.

'Let me go,' she demanded.

'No, Rose . . .'

I didn't see it coming. She scratched my face with her free hand, slashing at my eye. It hurt like hell and I let go of her. Immediately, she vanished into the room where the bodies lay. Covering the eye she'd just savaged with my palm, I followed. She stood there, holding the flick-knife that had killed Emma in her small fist.

'Rose,' I said. 'Put it down.'

'Get back!' She screamed it, jabbing at the air. 'I'll kill you too.' Her expression changed as she realised what she'd said, as though she was drawing back from the words. But then her features settled, hardened.

'I can't let you go, Rose,' I said. 'I can't let you hurt Dylan.'

She sneered. 'You always liked him best.'

'No I didn't. I've always loved you both the same.'

'Not now, though. Now I'm not your little girl anymore.'

'You'll always be my little girl,' I said, and I stepped towards her, into the range of the knife, and she slashed at me, cutting my palm, slicing my chest, withdrawing it and trying to aim it at my belly, but I hardly felt a thing. I grabbed her wrist again and squeezed as hard as I could, so she cried out, dropping the knife, which I kicked away.

I grabbed hold of her, pulling her against my bloody body and carrying her, wriggling, from the room.

'You'll have to kill me,' she shouted into my chest.

I ignored her words. Getting out of the building seemed to take forever, but then I could hear sirens, close now. I realised the rain had stopped.

Rose struggled, tried to scratch me again, but I held both her wrists. She kicked at me but I ignored the pain.

'You can't stop me,' she said as I carried her towards the fence.

She was my daughter. My flesh and blood. My little girl. I had been protecting her my whole life. I could continue to protect her, get her help. A psychologist, a professional, someone like Angela who could assess her and talk to her and maybe there was some treatment, some medication she could take. Something that would stop her turning out like Fiona and Lucy and Maisie.

But for that to happen, surely she needed to face up to what she'd done. To admit it. I was in so much pain, racked by such disorientating anguish, but I could still see it. All that she'd done. She couldn't get away with it.

'Rose, I've got evidence now. The knife wounds. They're evidence that you tried to kill me.'

She screamed, thrashed against me anew and cried out, and then all of a sudden she went very still. Stopped struggling and grew limp. My whole body throbbed with pain and I could only see out of one eye. We reached the fence and I staggered and dropped her, and then there were torches, police coming under the fence, running towards us, shouting, telling us to get down, but we were both already down.

I lay on my back and looked over at Rose with my one good eye. She was on her back in the dirt too, her head close to mine, and she was smiling. Laughing as footsteps approached and the police torches lit us up, and she turned her face towards me and whispered, 'You should have killed me, Dad.'

She laughed again as the first police officer to reach us pulled her up, two more kneeling by me, asking me if I was hurt before catching sight of my wounds. He shouted for a medic and I grabbed hold of his wrists, told him I needed him to listen.

'My daughter,' I said. 'She did this.' I pointed at her. 'She did it.'

Rose stood there, covered in Emma's blood and my blood and probably Fiona's too. She didn't try to run. She ignored the cops who were looking from me to her, trying to take it all in. The mocking smile she'd worn was gone, nothing in her eyes but darkness.

A female police officer appeared and laid her hand on Rose's shoulder. My daughter didn't flinch or try to resist.

'You should have killed me,' she said to me again, as the medic arrived and knelt beside me, partially obscuring my view as the policewoman led Rose away, out of my sight, leaving me wondering if I'd done the right thing.

I would never, ever stop wondering.

EPILOGUE

Lucy loved the prison library. Apart from the chicken enclosure – where she was guaranteed to be alone and unbothered, nobody but her and the hens – it was her favourite place at Franklin Grange. Recently she had begun to volunteer as a library orderly, helping to keep the place organised, even volunteering to assist some of the prisoners who struggled with reading. She didn't do this out of the goodness of her heart, of course. It just stopped her getting too bored, and it was always sensible to have people in your debt.

Another good thing about working in the library was that she got to put out the daily newspapers, which meant she could read them before anyone else. For the past couple of weeks she'd been avidly following the trial, which had featured prominently in both broadsheets and tabloids, of the unnamed child who stood accused of murdering two people: Fiona Woodfield and Emma Dove. She had also been charged with aiding and abetting in the murder of an old woman named Iris Green.

Children who killed were the ultimate modern folk devils – even more so than 'angels of death', the category Lucy fell into in the language the newspapers always pulled out. So the fascination with this case was so great that it would have cut through to the population here even if one of the victims hadn't spent part of her sentence in Franklin. A lot of the women remembered Fiona well.

They knew she and Lucy had been friends. Some of them also knew Fiona had visited Lucy last summer.

None of them knew, of course, that Lucy had known all about the child and that she had even spoken to Rose's father the day all of this had happened. They didn't know she'd had a visit from the police, who wanted to know about the phone Ethan Dove had found hidden in Fiona's kitchen, and the subsequent conversation she'd had with him.

And they would have gone wild if they'd known she'd offered her services as a witness for the defence, and about her plans to tell the court how Fiona had groomed Rose, that anything Rose did would have been because she was in Fiona's thrall. Lucy would have enjoyed having a day in court, not being the one on trial this time. But, in the end, the defence lawyers had decided that having a notorious serial killer as a witness wouldn't do much to help their cause.

Shame.

So this child, according to the lawyer Lucy had spoken to, was denying killing her mother and claiming that Fiona had done it; she admitted to stabbing Fiona but only in self-defence. She denied any involvement in Iris's murder. It was the kind of story a jury could easily believe, especially when faced with a cute little girl who acted like butter wouldn't melt. The problem was Ethan, who had testified that Rose had done all of it and confessed it all to him before trying to kill him too.

Lucy had passed some of these details on to the other inmates – she liked them to know she had inside information – which had led to a debate about whether Ethan had betrayed his own daughter by handing her over to the police and giving evidence against her. Most of the women here hadn't had great experiences with their own dads. Personally, Lucy couldn't blame Ethan for wanting to lock Rose up to protect himself and his son.

Because she understood. She knew exactly what Rose was capable of. And she was still so young, had so much growing to do. If Lucy were Ethan, a mere member of the lowing herd, she wouldn't want an apex predator in her house either.

But what Rose really needed was a proper mentor. One who knew what they were doing. Fiona had been such a disappointment in the end. Not keeping her promise to torment Jamie and Kirsty, blundering her way through her own revenge scheme – and then getting herself killed by a twelve-year-old!

What a letdown.

But Lucy had a strong feeling Rose would not be a disappointment. If Rose was taken under the wing of someone who had, yes, made a couple of mistakes, but who had mainly been the victim of bad luck, someone who truly understood how to go about things, the girl would go a long, long way.

All Lucy had to do was wait. The girl, who was almost certain to be convicted, would go into the juvenile system first. It would be a few years before she ended up in a women's prison. The chances were she wouldn't be sent to Franklin Grange. But that was fine. Maybe Lucy could transfer to where she was. She would find some way of getting to her. Because she had a feeling it was fated; that she had met Fiona because it was her destiny to encounter Rose and to become her teacher.

Then Lucy would show Rose how to get revenge on her dad and brother. Jamie and Kirsty too. Anyone else who had ever wronged either of them. Because Rose was only thirteen. She wouldn't be in prison forever.

She was exactly what Lucy needed.

They were going to be the perfect match.

ACKNOWLEDGEMENTS

All books are a collaborative effort, but perhaps the most important of those collaborations is the one between writer and reader. Every reader takes something different away from a novel. Everyone has a different experience while turning the pages. Books, and authors, are nothing without readers – and I thank you for reading mine . . . and hope, of course, that you enjoyed it. You can tell me what you thought by emailing mark@markedwardsauthor.com. I read every message and try to respond to all of them.

My other collaborators on this book were my editors, David Downing and Victoria Oundjian, to whom I owe a great deal, and my copy-editor, Gemma Wain, who cleaned up the many errors in the text and ensured the timeline worked. Thanks go to all of them.

I would also like to thank:

My agent, Madeleine Milburn, and everyone at the agency.

Imran Mahmood for all the advice on legal matters and prisons.

Claire Douglas for being my 'writing buddy' when I was trying to get this book finished during the school holidays (not easy!).

Ed James, Susi Holliday, Caroline Green, C. L. Taylor, Fiona Cummins, John Marrs, the QCs and Colin Scott, for keeping me sane and always being there to make me laugh. Being a writer can be a lonely business but I'm lucky to have so many great friends in the crime-writing community.

I am also extremely grateful to all the members and admins of the various Facebook groups, who do so much to encourage reading and book-buying and to celebrate this genre, including the Psychological Thriller Readers group and THE Book Club. I promise, still, that I will never a) harm a pet in one of my books and b) let out a breath I didn't know I was holding.

Finally, as always, I thank my family: Sara, Poppy, Ellie, Archie and Harry, as well as my mum, my sisters Claire and Ali, Dad and Jean, and my in-laws in Wolverhampton: Julie, Martin and the whole Baugh/Gray/Marson tribe.

This book is dedicated to the memory of my stepdad, Roy Cutting, who died while I was writing it. Roy was a big reader and loved Stephen King and James Herbert, and we shared their books when I was a teenager. He drove me to school every day, picked me and my friends up when we found ourselves stranded after gigs (a frequent occurrence), gave me a job when I was a penniless student, and was always there through my adult life, usually making very rude jokes. He was a good man and we were lucky to have him.

Finally, *The Psychopath Next Door* is part of the Magpies universe: *The Magpies*, *A Murder of Magpies* and *Last of the Magpies*. If you haven't read those yet, you can treat them as prequels to this one.

Thanks again for the collaboration.

Best wishes

Mark Edwards

FREE SHORT STORY COLLECTION

To download a free collection of Mark's 'Short Sharp Shockers' and join Mark's newsletter, to ensure you don't miss out on all the latest news and offers, go to:

www.markedwardsauthor.com/free

ABOUT THE AUTHOR

Photo © 2022 Tim Sturgess, Express and Star

Mark Edwards writes psychological thrillers in which scary things happen to ordinary people.

He has sold over 4 million books since his first novel, *The Magpies*, was published in 2013, and has topped the bestseller lists numerous times. His other novels include *Follow You Home*, *The Retreat*, *In Her Shadow*, *Because She Loves Me*, *Keep Her Secret* and *Here to Stay*. He has also co-authored six books with Louise Voss.

Originally from Hastings in East Sussex, Mark now lives in Wolverhampton with his wife, their children, two cats and a golden retriever.

Mark loves hearing from readers and can be contacted through his website, www.markedwardsauthor.com, or you can find him on Facebook (@markedwardsauthor), X (@mredwards) and Instagram (@markedwardsauthor).

Follow the Author on Amazon

If you enjoyed this book, follow Mark Edwards on Amazon to be notified when the author releases a new book!
To do this, please follow these instructions:

Desktop:

1) Search for the author's name on Amazon or in the Amazon App.
2) Click on the author's name to arrive on their Amazon page.
3) Click the 'Follow' button.

Mobile and Tablet:

1) Search for the author's name on Amazon or in the Amazon App.
2) Click on one of the author's books.
3) Click on the author's name to arrive on their Amazon page.
4) Click the 'Follow' button.

Kindle eReader and Kindle App:

If you enjoyed this book on a Kindle eReader or in the Kindle App, you will find the author 'Follow' button after the last page.